RUINS

RUINS

RAJITH
SAVANADASA
RUINS

hachette
AUSTRALIA

QUEENSLAND
WRITERS
CENTRE

Ruins has been written with the encouragement of the Queensland Writers Centre (QWC). Rajith Savanadasa participated in the 2014 QWC/Hachette Australia Manuscript Development Program.

This is a work of fiction. Characters are fictional, and any resemblance to actual persons is entirely coincidental. In order to provide the story with a context, real names of places are used as well as some significant historical events.

hachette
AUSTRALIA

Published in Australia and New Zealand in 2016
by Hachette Australia
(an imprint of Hachette Australia Pty Limited)
Level 17, 207 Kent Street, Sydney NSW 2000
www.hachette.com.au

10 9 8 7 6 5 4 3 2 1

National Library of Australia
Cataloguing-in-Publication data:

Savanadasa, Rajith, author.
Ruins / Rajith Savanadasa.

978 0 7336 3505 2 (paperback)

Families – Sri Lanka – Fiction.
Intergenerational relations – Sri Lanka – Fiction.
Sri Lanka – Fiction.

A823.4

Cover design by Christabella Designs
Author photo courtesy of Craig Peihopa
Cover photographs courtesy of Shutterstock
Cover and internal illustrations by Cheryl Orsini
Text design by Bookhouse, Sydney
Typeset in 11.9/15.6 pt Bembo by Bookhouse, Sydney
Printed and bound in Australia by Griffin Press, Adelaide, an Accredited ISO AS/NZS 14001:2009 Environmental Management System printer

For Yasa

LATHA

THIS FAMILY IS GOOD. THAT'S WHY I WORK FOR THEM. AIYA doesn't know because Aiya hasn't seen. When he came, he came when no one was home. Today was the third time. He came on his shiny motorcycle, parked in front and rang the bell. I opened the gate wide and he bent his neck to pass the low branch of the araliya tree. My brother's tall. He's not like me. He's handsome. He wears clean shirts and trousers made of good material. The slippers on his feet were the only difference between him and a mahattaya – that and the motorcycle.

'Why don't you come in your car?' I asked.

He smiled and said, 'No need to bring the car, no? It takes more petrol.'

'One day you can bring it for me to see.'

'Okay,' he said.

He stood at the front for a little while, looking at our garden, at the flowering anthuriums with their bright red petals, at the fish tank on the veranda where he tapped on the glass to try to get the goldfish to see him. But the goldfish was a fool. He only ate, swam through plants, made bubbles next to the oxygen tube and sometimes went into his little house to sleep. That's all the goldfish knew to do.

'This is nice,' said Aiya.

'The motor keeps the water clean,' I said.

Aiya walked into the saalay – the living room I had just swept. He looked at photos on the wall, photos of Lakshmi Nona and Mano Mahattaya getting married, the old picture of Niranjan Baby wearing a cardboard on his head and getting a rolled-up paper in Australia, the whole family standing on top of a rock next to the sea, another one in front of a waterfall. Aiya asked me if the person in the big picture with Mano Mahattaya was really the president. I said, 'Yes. Mano Mahattaya talked to the president one day.'

'He's good, this president,' said Aiya. 'Did you hear the army captured Kilinocchi? We'll win the war very soon.'

'They always say that.'

Aiya moved away and looked at some of the things on the shelf, the books, all of them Ingrisi, the vases with small Cheena people drawn on them, Niranjan Baby's music discs stacked high. While he looked I removed covers from the furniture. I didn't ask him to sit on the plastic stools we give servants. He wasn't a servant, so I thought it was all right. But he didn't sit. He kept going round, through the big door and into the dining room, looking down the corridor that led past the rooms and into the kitchen. He even put his head into the garage where Nona's shrine full of Buddha statues and god paintings were, before he came back to the armchair.

'Do you want a tea?' I asked.

'Okay. Just one spoon of sugar,' he said.

'Milk?'

'No.'

Because he's a guest I took one of the nice cups, the one with flowers, out of the cupboard. When I put it on the saucer, poured the tea and brought it out to him on the tray, he was wearing glasses and reading the newspaper. When I saw him like this, sitting back with his feet crossed, face covered by the paper, I wrongly said, 'Mahattaya, here's your tea.'

'I'm not your mahattaya,' he said without a smile.

'Sorry,' I said. 'Normally it's a mahattaya sitting here.'

He folded away the paper, took the cup in one hand, the saucer in the other, poured tea on the saucer and blew away steam. When he did this the little finger on the cup hand was straight like a soldier. It was like my akka. My sister drinks tea the same way.

—

He was my aiya, my older brother, but I didn't like it when he asked too many questions. He came again a week later, sat on the chair like some important person and started drinking tea the same way as my sister. Smiling, he asked me to sit. I brought a stool out, one that servants sat on.

'Latha, what do you want to do?' he asked, resting his chin on his hand.

'Today, I'm going to buy some lotterai,' I said. 'Last week a woman from Horana won a lot of money – five lakhs.'

'What will you do with the money? If you win?'

'I'll give some to Nona, some to Mahattaya and Niranjan Baby. I'll buy something for Anoushka Baby, maybe a small compitu. She likes to play them.'

'What about you?'

'I'll buy a small TV. I don't want a big one. Now there are very small televisions – have you seen? The nearby shop has one in the window. This size.' I showed him the size with my hands.

'And us?' Aiya smiled like he was telling a joke – but inside, he wasn't smiling, I could tell.

'You?'

'Me and my wife?'

'I'll give you some too. Five lakhs is a lot. Sometimes you can win more.'

'Your sister?'

I didn't say anything. I looked at my feet and saw that the nail that I dropped a coconut on had started growing a hard lump in the corner.

'I was joking,' he said, handing back the empty cup and saucer to me. 'You don't have to give us anything. I just wanted to know what you might do – with your life. You can't do this forever.'

'Anicche dhukké,' I said.

He turned my Pali prayer into Sinhala: 'Everything ends and so we suffer.' He smiled. 'You listen to pirith? You're a good Buddhist?'

'Sometimes. The monk on the TV said that.'

'Yes, yes. But have you thought about what to do after this?'

'No.' I got up to put the cup and saucer in the sink.

When I came back, Aiya sat up and scratched his head. He had been thinking. 'You like your nona and mahattaya, don't you?'

I nodded.

'Are they good to you?'

'Yes.'

'Does Mano Mahattaya pay well?'

'Yes.'

'He gets enough money writing newspapers?'

'Yes.'

'And Lakshmi Nona . . . she's Tamil?'

'Yes. But she's just like a Sinhala person.' I was already tired of Aiya. I hoped he would leave soon.

He didn't stop. He kept asking things. 'What does Niranjan Mahattaya do?'

'He plays the compitu.'

'For a big company?'

'His own company.'

'Really? But he's still young.'

'Twenty-four. He has a very good brain. Studied in Australia.'

'Anoushka Baby – is she doing the O-Level this year?'

'Yes. School just started after the holidays.'

'You're like a mother to her, no? She was born after you came to work here?'

I nodded. 'Even Niranjan Baby was born after me.'

'You're part of the family.'

'Yes,' I said, looking around for a way to get Aiya out. 'What's the time?'

Aiya looked at his watch. 'Appey! It's almost one. I have to go. Roads will be busy soon.' He got to his feet.

A few dark clouds hung in the sky. After watching the motorbike disappear, I picked up an umbrella, locked the house and went out, down the lane and to the main road. I crossed on the yellow lines and went to the bus stop. There was a beggar with a bandaged arm asking for money. I ignored him. Mano Mahattaya said all those fellows were thieves; they put food colouring on their bandages and tied up their arms to look like they were wounded. A CTB bus slowed and I got on. It was half empty so I sat and looked out the window. School hadn't ended and traffic was still moving quickly. A motorcycle went along right next to me, so close I could touch the three people on it – the woman with her sari blowing in the wind sat on the back, one hand holding on to the man who was steering, the other on the small child between them. The boy had a little helmet of his own. He saw me watching and smiled. I wanted to wave – but what if I upset the driver and they had an accident? I slowly lifted my hand. The boy waved.

They turned at the Thunmulla junction, away from us, and went towards Galle Road, towards Majestic City, the big building with the expensive shops inside. I watched them go, hoping the little boy would get home safely. I thought of Aiya. Does he take his family around on the motorcycle, his wife holding on to him, his son and daughter holding their mother from both sides? I hoped they had helmets.

Dreaming of Aiya's life, I almost missed my stop. I stepped off the bus and walked towards the school. There were many cars and vans – some parked properly and others parked in funny places, like on the pavement, in front of gates or blocking lanes, three-wheelers on footpaths. These were all fights waiting to happen, so I hoped the children would come out quickly. The drivers of private vans ate bulath and spat red against a tree or smoked on the other side of the road. I went right up near the gate and stood with nonas wearing trousers and so much flower scent it smelled like a funeral home, beside mahattayas in their ties who always looked at their watches in a hurry to get back to work. I smiled at everyone. Very few smiled back. The nonas, even the ones who knew me, like Natalie Baby's mother or the nona with the short hair and red lips, pretended not to see.

When the final bell rang and the gates opened the girls came flying out, noisy like flocks of white birds. The little ones got hugs and kisses from fathers and mothers, had their cheeks wiped with clean handkerchiefs or heads patted as they were led away to waiting cars. Older girls in groups of two or three, all laughing, got into vans, happy that school was over. Anoushka Baby's messy hair was right at the back of the crowd. Her face didn't change when she saw me and she didn't stop when I said, 'Hullo, Anoushka Baby.' She kept walking, right past as if I wasn't even there. What could I do but follow? I was almost running because she was going fast, losing breath as I asked if I could carry her bag or water bottle. It was only after we were a good distance from school that she finally spoke to me. She spoke Sinhala, not her normal Ingrisi.

'What's for lunch?'

'You won't like it today, Anoushka Baby. I made kohila.' The stringy vegetable was one of the things she swallowed without chewing. 'Your thatthi asked me to make it. It's good for you.'

'Can you fry some chicken when we get home?'

'I don't know, Baby. Thatthi won't be happy. He says you eat too much meat.'

'Just tell him I told you.'

'I don't know,' I said again, taking the bag from her. 'So heavy. What do you have in here? Rocks?'

Anoushka Baby said nothing. She crossed her hands and turned her back to the road, away from the smoke and the sound of car horns trying to blow a hole through the traffic. I knew she didn't want to be seen with me. She worried her friends would think I was her mother. Sometimes I wanted to tell her, 'When you're standing next to me, anybody can tell I'm just a servant, and you're my baby nona. Nobody will mistake it.' But I kept quiet.

I saw an empty three-wheeler and waved it over. Anoushka Baby got in and sat back, finally letting out her breath. I told the driver what Mano Mahattaya had told me to say: 'We'll only pay if you go very carefully.'

As usual the driver started slowly, moving through the busy part of Colombo 7, the rich parts where the lokkas lived and the big schools and offices were, carefully avoiding the private buses and their daily race, but as we moved out to smaller districts, past Colombo 5 and Kirulapone towards where we lived, vehicles went in different directions and more space appeared in the road. The driver forgot my message and began to play tricks. He went broooom!, increased speed, cut in front of a car and went over a pavement, nearly dropping us all through the open sides of the carriage.

'I won't pay if you drive like this,' I shouted.

'It's not me,' said the driver. 'It's that bus fellow!'

'Hold on tight, Anoushka Baby.'

She didn't listen. She pushed out her legs against the driver's seat to stop her from falling forward and looked straight ahead – didn't hold on to anything.

When we got home she ate all the food I put on the plate and didn't say a word. Then, without even changing her school clothes, she went into Mahattaya's room and closed the door. I knew from the peep-peep and tak-tak sounds she was playing with his compitu.

Sometimes I wish she was still little. She was my good friend. She used to skip out of school and call me 'Latha katha!' and hold my hand all the way home. I used to feed her rice and hodi squeezed into little balls; even when she was as old as ten, I'd give her a kiss on top of her head when she finished eating. She always wanted to play badminton in the burning sun. It was fine for her because she wore her straw hat and tennis shoes, but my bare feet were cut open by rocks on the street. We always stopped in time for cartoons, watching *Tom and Jerry* or *Scooby-Doo* as she ate a whole bowl of ice-cream . . . she's changed. My Anoushka Baby isn't my Anoushka Baby anymore.

—

They are good people. Even if my brother didn't think so. He didn't know. Aiya wanted me to leave. He wanted me to go back to the village, calling on the telephone, saying, 'Nangi, come and stay with me. There's a room with a bed, even a bathroom, just for you.'

I knew there was nothing in the village but paddy fields, and that you had to walk miles along the bund of the river to get to a kadé that doesn't even have tinned fish. That was what I wanted to buy for Akka when I visited, but it wasn't there.

Sometimes he said, 'You can help my wife look after the children.' He said this without thinking and then, when his own words went into his ears, changed them as if they were written in sand: 'But only if you want. You don't have to work.'

While he talked, the telephone made a kara-kara sound. I kept quiet, thinking it must be windy in Sinhagama. I kept looking at the spot on the wall where Lakshmi Nona's habit of leaning had left a circle of black hair dye. I didn't know what to say to Aiya.

How could I leave? Who would do the cooking here? Who would look after Anoushka Baby? Who would bring her back from school? Who would wash Niranjan Baby's shirts when the sweat under the armpits dries and becomes yellow? Who would pack Mano Mahattaya's lunch and cut the apple the way he likes and put it all in the siri-siri bag on the table before he goes to work? Who would take morning tea to Lakshmi Nona and tell her not to worry and say something to make her smile? Who? I thought of all this too late – after I'd put the phone down and wiped the speaking piece with Dettol.

—

It must have been a week after his last visit when Anoushka Baby answered the telephone and shouted at me from the corridor, 'Latha, call.'

I was in the kitchen where a pot of kiri hodi was about to boil. It needed less than a minute but Anoushka Baby called out again, louder. 'Latha! Call!'

I turned off the cooker, wiped my hands on my skirt and rushed out. Anoushka Baby had left the speaking piece of the telephone lying on the small table. I picked it up.

'Hullo?'

'Latha?'

I recognised the voice. 'Aiya?'

'How are you?'

'Okay . . .' I spoke slowly. I knew why he was calling and I didn't have an answer. He had told me to think about all the good things that would happen if I went back to the village. But that was what I didn't want to do – I didn't want to think about it. It was too much for my head to hold.

'How much did you win from your lotterai?'

'Is that why you called?' I said, surprised. 'I didn't win anything.'

'No, no!' He laughed that deep laugh that comes from somewhere in his stomach. 'Can't your brother call to see how you're doing?' He waited for an answer, and when nothing came he continued, 'I'm calling to ask what you've decided. I'm going away for a few months. To Dubai for a job. You know my work is in Dubai, no?'

'You told me.'

'I'll be working in one of the big buildings. Did you know they have one of the tallest buildings in the world?'

'No.'

'That's where I'll be working. In the tallest building. I have a contract for three months. The money's very good, so I can't say no. The problem is my wife and the children will be all by themselves.'

It was just as I had thought. He wanted me to say, 'Yes, I'll come.' If I went I wouldn't have to worry about what to cook every day. I wouldn't have to wash everyone's underwear and clean the toilets. I wouldn't have to go to the kadé at night and run away from kuddas who put drugs in their blood and dirty men who lick their lips and look at me funny. I wouldn't have to chop meat and clean gutters and walk to the post office in the heat. Maybe Aiya would make me do the same things but at least I'd be doing it for my own family. I wanted to say yes but the words that came out of my mouth were different: 'What can I do?'

Aiya breathed into the phone and then the kara-kara sound happened. It happened for a while and I wondered if the call had been cut. I was thinking of putting the speaking piece down when his voice came like a slap in the dark. 'All right. You don't have to come and help us. But think of this – do you think those people will look after you? Do you think they'll let you stay forever?'

That was when I got angry. Aiya had no right to say these things. He didn't know my mahattayas and nonas. 'They look after me better than you village people.'

'So Colombo is now bigger than us, then?'

'I don't know what's bigger or smaller,' I said, my voice becoming too loud for a servant, 'but they don't leave me alone and only call when they need help.'

I cut the call quickly, putting the speaking piece down hard. My heart was going dag-dag in my chest and my breath was getting stuck in my throat.

'You'll break the phone if you hammer it like that,' said Niranjan Baby. I hadn't noticed him standing behind me, his long shadow darkening the corridor.

'Sorry, Niranjan Baby.'

'Niranjan Mahattaya,' he corrected me.

'Sorry, Niranjan Mahattaya,' I said, turning to leave.

'Wait,' he said. I turned back to see him pointing at the piece of cloth next to the phone.

'Sorry.' I picked up the bottle, poured some Dettol onto the cloth and quickly cleaned the speaking piece so my germs wouldn't go to him.

'Who was that?' he asked.

'My brother.'

'What did he want?'

'Nothing, Niranjan Mahattaya,' I said. ' He just wants me to come to the village.'

'Are you going?'

'No.'

I went back to the kitchen.

—

The last time I'd polished the floor was to make sure the house was nice before the new year. Not even a month had gone and it was already dirty. Now there were guests coming from Emarica. They were Mano Mahattaya's relatives and very important, so I had to polish again, but I knew they'd bring in dust and trample it into the floor and it would look dirty again. What was the use in polishing? I didn't understand. 'Don't walk everywhere, stay in one place,' I said to Anoushka Baby. 'I'll bring you everything you need.' She glared at me.

Polishing the floor was not nice work. I had to mix the maroon polish with smelly kerosene oil, rub the paste into the floor in little circles and run the polishing machine over it. I did the same with wax and watched the floor shine like a mirror. I only liked the last part. I didn't like when the maroon colour got in my nails and it didn't wash off. It was worse when it got on my clothes.

I finished putting the polish on, then carefully turned on the polisher and held it steady, sweeping side to side the way Lakshmi Nona had taught me. Polishing closer to the door I thought I heard the sound of a motorcycle. I quickly turned the polisher off and opened the door but it was nothing – there was nobody outside the gate.

This happened again a few days later. I was making the garden look neat, moving the flowerpots, when a motorcycle stopped. I left the pots where they were and ran to the gate. But it was only the fishmonger. He opened the ice box on the back of his bike, showing me crabs, prawns and thilapiya, saying: 'Fresh from Meegamuwa.' That was when I remembered Nona had asked me to buy some prawns. I had forgotten all about it. I had been thinking too much.

'Don't worry,' the man said, reading my face. 'These are good prawns.'

The next few days more motorcycles went up and down the lane. Our doorbell rang a few times, but I knew Aiya was in Dubai. He wouldn't be back so soon. Would he come and see me? Would he call me again? Was he angry because I didn't do what he told? Why did he really want me to come to the village? I had so many questions.

—

On the weekend Mano Mahattaya and Anoushka Baby took the guests from Emarica all over Colombo. Lakshmi Nona stayed home, walking back and forth, thinking about faraway places, worrying and sometimes sleeping. I didn't want to bother her, but this was my chance, so, very quietly, I asked if she could help me talk to my sister.

'Now?' asked Nona.

'Yes, Nona. Is that all right?'

She walked to the telephone and I followed her.

'Your akka still doesn't have a phone?'

'I don't think so, Nona. You have the neighbour's number, no?'

Lakshmi Nona opened the blue book where all the telephone numbers were written. She found the number, picked up the telephone and pressed the buttons. She listened for a while and said, 'Hullo. There's someone who wants to talk to you,' and gave me the telephone.

'Hullo?' I said. 'I'm calling from Colombo. Can you hear? Can I talk to Seelawathie? Is she home?'

I heard Akka's neighbour put the phone down to go find her. I listened to the sounds coming from the telephone, thinking which sound is Akka, which sounds are her neighbours, which sounds are things happening to the telephone wires going from here to the village. While I waited, Lakshmi Nona walked into her room and closed the door. I was glad.

'Who is it?' said a shaky voice. Akka's voice.

'It's Latha,' I said.

'Who?'

'Latha. From Colombo.'

'Ah.'

'How . . . how are you?' I asked.

'Who?'

'You and your husband.'

'We're living.'

'How is your daughter?'

'She's there. In her house. She's having a baby soon.'

'That's good.'

'Good? She's struggling. She's not feeling good. Then there's my husband. His liver is bad. My son, Kumara, is in the jungle fighting those Tamils. The north is a real hell. The Vanni forest is swallowing all our boys. Our boys and the boys from the south – they're the ones getting killed. All the Sinhala boys from poor villages. We're the ones keeping the country from being cut into pieces.'

I looked towards Lakshmi Nona's room. She couldn't have heard. The sound was only inside the telephone. 'When did Kumara join the . . .'

'It doesn't matter.'

Akka was never happy. I should have known. I just had to ask her what I had to ask and finish the call before the bill was too much for Nona and Mahattaya.

'Aiya came to see me.'

'Who?'

'My aiya. Your malli.'

'I don't know what you're—'

'Our brother,' I said. 'I didn't know I had a brother. You didn't tell me.'

Akka's breath was going in and out of the telephone. 'There was no reason.'

'But . . . he's my brother.'

'So?'

It was useless talking to Akka.

'Is that why you called?'

'Yes.'

'I have to go,' she said and put down the phone.

—

April was already half gone and the Aluth Avurudda was almost here. Like every Sinhala and Hindu new year celebration, Lakshmi Nona wanted to do it properly. This time the new year came at 5.05 in the morning and I had to cook everything the night before. There was no time to sleep. Nona listened to the saasthara men on TV. They weren't talking about horoscopes, only saying how the sun had gone from one place in the sky to another, then come back to the first place. Nona, Mano Mahattaya, Anoushka Baby and Niranjan Baby gathered in the kitchen to watch the kalaya full of milk froth and overflow at the lucky time, just as the new year came. After that, I placed all the food – the milk rice, fish curry, seeni sambola and dhal that I had just made, and the sweetmeats like kevum, kokis and athirasa that I prepared the week before – on the dinner table. Just before six, as the television told them it was the next lucky time, Nona and Mahattaya fed Anoushka Baby and Niranjan Baby the first meal of the new year. Everyone got new clothes for presents. Even I was given a new blouse by Nona. Niranjan Baby tried to play a traditional game, a pillow fight, with Anoushka Baby but she was not interested, so he got dressed in his new clothes and said he had to go to work, even though it was a holiday. Nona and Mahattaya were surprised but they couldn't stop him. The rest of the day was just as busy.

That night I had a dream. I dreamed of a family on a motorcycle. The man was sitting in front wearing a clean white shirt and a red helmet. He had shiny shoes on his feet. The boy was in a blue suit. He had his little blue helmet the same colour as his suit. And the woman – the woman was . . . she was me. I wasn't wearing a sari, no – I was wearing a nice long skirt and a pink blouse. I was holding on to the boy and the man and we were going so fast. I don't know where we were going but I knew it was a good place. I was so happy. The wind was making my hair go everywhere – I had forgotten to bring my helmet – but it was all right. I wasn't afraid, because I knew we'd get to the place safely.

I woke up late the next morning and had to work quickly to cook breakfast and lunch in time for Nona and Mahattaya to take to work. I was tired. And I couldn't stop thinking about the motorcycle, about the three of us, just riding. I was thinking about it so much I forgot to cut apples for Mahattaya.

'What's happening to you, woman? Can't even do a simple thing anymore,' Mahattaya scolded me, pulling the lunch bag from my hands and throwing it in the car, next to Anoushka Baby.

Not long after they left, the telephone rang. It was Aiya. 'Subha aluth awuruddak,' he said, wishing me a good New Year.

He was back from Dubai. It had been difficult. He said that the Araabi people made him work very hard and didn't give him a cent more than they promised. 'And if you stole something – they cut your hand off. If you lied – your tongue.'

'You didn't do anything wrong, no?'

'No. I did my work properly. And I slept. That was all. It was a hard life, just working and sleeping.'

'What about Kusum and the children?'

'I tried to call them once a week. My cell phone wasn't working so I had to go to a telephone place. The Araabi fellows, the ones who were paying me, didn't like it. So I had to do that at night, from my hotel. It was expensive.'

'Are they all right?'

'They're fine. The children have grown. The boy will start school next year. How are your nona and mahattaya?'

'They're okay.'

'And you?'

'I'm fine . . .' I wasn't sure if I should have, but I felt like I had to tell Aiya something, so I said, 'My nona and mahattaya are not very happy. There's a lot of things happening.'

'Like what?'

'Mano Mahattaya is coming home very late.'

'Is he working too hard? The newspaper business is not so easy.'

'Yes.'

'What about your nona?'

I thought I shouldn't tell him about Nona. But Aiya was good. He would understand. 'Lakshmi Nona works hard too. She looks very tired when she comes home. So tired her mind is not working. I think it's because she's very worried.'

'About what?'

'She's worried about some people. Her friends or family in the east, where the war is happening.'

'Tamil people?'

'Yes.'

'Where's she from?'

'Nona lived in Batticaloa.'

'Batticaloa is not dangerous anymore,' said Aiya. 'The war is in the north now. In the Vanni. Where Akka's son is fighting. You know Akka's son is in the army, no?'

I didn't say anything. I didn't want to talk about Akka.

After waiting for a while Aiya said, 'How is Anoushka Baby?'

'I don't know what's happened to her. She gets upset about the smallest things.'

'Sometimes people turn small things into big things. What about Niranjan Baby? Is he doing well?'

'I don't even know Niranjan Baby anymore. He's a different person after he came back from Australia. Always running around doing his new business. He's also not so happy. Must be a bad time, rahu kaalaya for everyone . . . still, they're good people.'

'Yes,' said Aiya, letting out a big sigh. 'They're good people.'

—

I served dinner and washed the dishes. I gave Anoushka Baby her sugary tea and went to the kadé to get bread for the morning. After everyone had gone to bed, I locked the gate with the big padlock and chain, turned the key and bolted the front and back doors and turned off all the lights. Shutting the kitchen door behind me, I opened my drawer and took out the photo album. The plastic cover was coming off and I thought I should ask Nona for some sellotape so I could fix it. I turned the pages. There was a picture of my akka and her son, the boy who joined the army, and the girl who was about to become a mother. I hadn't looked at it for a long time. Today, I was looking for the picture of Akka and me. It was too small for the plastic pocket and had slipped to the bottom. I took it out. Our black and white faces had faded and turned brown, but we were both there – standing together, not knowing what was happening, wearing clothes other people had given us just for the photo. The clothes were too big but we couldn't take a photo in our dirty rags, no?

It wasn't long after the photo was taken that I was sent here. I must have been Anoushka Baby's age. I scolded myself for thinking such things and slid the photo back in the pocket, closed the album and put it away. In the bottom drawer I found the stack of lotterai tied together with a rubber band. It had grown almost as fat as my arm. I pulled it out and looked at the numbers on the newest ticket – twenty-two, five, seventy-three, forty-eight, nine. I would have to remember these weren't good numbers. Next time I won't choose them. Next time I'll win.

ANOUSHKA

I TOOK LATHA'S LITTLE TRANSISTOR RADIO FROM HER cupboard, ignoring her 'Haa haa, Anoushka Baby' and silly headshake. As if I needed her permission. (She's got too big for her boots, just because her brother visited a couple of times.) I snuck back to my room. Luckily it was a time when Ammi and Thatthi were taking their afternoon naps and Niro was off gallivanting (as usual). Latha was the only other person who might disturb me, so I shut the door and got into bed. I lay on my side to have a clear view of the door and shoved the radio under my pillow, then wound the wire of the headphones behind my neck, keeping it taut so the bare minimum could be seen. The wire going into my right ear was the problem – it was exposed, and if anyone came in – patass! – they would've seen it.

There have been times when Ammi's walked in. She never knocks, never asks, 'Anoushka, can I come in?' No, just barrels through and starts looking for something – a hairclip, a blank sheet of paper (now that she's gone and put all the stationery in my room because, as she says, 'You're the one who has to study, no?') – and then tilts her head and looks at me with a little smile, whispering, 'Are you sleeping?' And me? I quickly push the headphones from my ears but haven't had time to turn off the music, so it's at full blast, and with my luck it's usually one of the really raaa! tracks with a heap of bleeped-out fucks in the lyrics, so I pretend to sleep, one eye open less than a millimetre, watching, praying she doesn't come any closer, because she might hear the sound and ask to listen in. That would be a disaster. Imagine that – 'Anoushka, what are you listening to? It's very loud. Let's hear it . . . what's this? It's just horrible noise, no? They call this music? My god, and the things they're saying? Can they put such things on radio? What's the station? I'll call them. They can't just play this sort of thing, children could be listening, no?' – and this would go on and on and on. Luckily for me, lately she'd been like a zombie, staggering around worrying about some goday Tamils in some faraway place.

I have no privacy. I'm telling you, it's always, 'Anoushka, why is your door closed? What do you need to close it for?' or 'Anoushka, why are you in the bathroom so long?' or 'Anoushka, did you get your marks? Natalie's mother said you got them yesterday. Why do I always find out these things from other people? Why can't you tell me?' or 'Anoushka, why is Natalie not talking to you? I just spoke to her mother and she says you two have had a fight and aren't talking.'

The ads stopped and the music kicked in – stopped my mind from running a gazillion miles an hour. The station music came on (Paparapaa! TNL rocks!), and then my program started. We used to listen to this, you know.

Natalie and I. Together. I don't know if it's because the music's not good anymore or if it's me but it's just not the same.

—

Monday morning, the posh girls sashayed in and started jabbering about some party or some boy. I called them TMMs (too-much-makeups) because even though they weren't allowed to wear it to school, as soon as the afternoon bell rang the makeup went straight back on. She was with them now, Natalie Jansz, aka Natalie No-brains. I used to call her Natalie Nutcase or the Cheese Burgher (because she was from a Burgher family, descendants of the Dutch who took over Sri Lanka after the Portuguese), but that was last year, when we used to talk. Why don't we anymore? Who knows? Actually, it's because she changed. She turned into one of those ridiculous idiots with their fake accents. Somehow, as if by magic, Natalie's hair straightened and her legs became like a gazelle's, her eyebrows, all neat and symmetrical, curved above her eyes like a pair of boomerangs. And she grew boobs. Big ones. Suddenly she was beautiful.

The TMMs were talking about some party on the weekend. Natalie had been there with the rest of her kind, with boys – cricketers, ruggerites and other dudeheads with slicked-back hair and halfway-buttoned shirts. I didn't care. I didn't want to go to those parties anyway (and if I did Ammi would kill me). And that was fine. They could talk about whatever. But then they turned around and laughed at the goday girls, you know, the supremely uncool characters like Chamari and Dushanthi who've come from rural places like Mulleriyawa and Monaragala on a scholarship. The godays didn't seem to give a shit. They were just like, 'Whatever,' and buried their faces back in their books. One of the TMMs (Maneesha) flicked back her hair, gave one of those piercing laughs and said, 'I hear all the happening parties are in Mulleriyawa these days. Aiyo, it's too bad we can't go to the village, no? Wonder what sort of music they'll play?'

I snorted – because the joke was so mean and unfunny it was hilarious. But then I realised the godays would think I was laughing at them and my skin felt like it was trying to curl in on itself. I looked at the godays and one of them (Chathuri) stared at me so blankly I thought I was going to shrivel up. I didn't say anything, though, because the TMMs might set their sights on me. It's not like I've been spared. They've called me plenty of names, like 'Vampire Bada' or 'Emily the Strange and Plump' or 'Chunky'. Responses like 'I'm almost as chunky as your mother' or 'You look just like a Barbie doll – plastic and hollow' came to me, but they always came via thapal (i.e., Sri Lanka post, which is pretty much a week late), so I laughed again and pretended to be doing something. The conversation went back to dresses, boys and songs by Justin Timberlake and Rihanna that made me do vomit sounds in my head.

Natalie hasn't been that bad. She hasn't said anything to me, just echoed other TMMs and giggled, really. Then again, the stuff about my dark tastes must have come from her. Nobody else knew about the music.

—

At PT, the TMMs refused to play. They didn't want to sweat and pretended to be sick (all of them) and Gunatilleke Sir sent them to the sick room. 'Go, go,' he said, sounding tired. 'Otherwise your parents will have my head.'

As they smirked and giggled and walked off, everyone else formed a circle. For some reason Natalie had decided to stay on. She didn't make much of an effort, though, catching the basketball like it was something gross. I found myself next to her in the circle. That was the only reason I tried to talk to her. It's rude not to, no? She stood there looking bored and inspecting her nails.

'Did you get hurt?' I asked.

'No, but I think I chipped one of my nails,' she said, bringing a thumb close to her eyes. 'I can't believe I have to do this . . .'

'Do what?'

'Play silly games. Like, it's bad enough we can't wear nail polish. I have to get my nails done every weekend. Half my allowance out the window.'

'Why don't you do them yourself?'

'Do my own nails?' Natalie stared at me as if I had said something rude.

'Anoushka!' someone yelled out. The ball came flying at me. Slap! I caught it, yelled out, 'Chathuri!' and threw it hard so old butterfingers would drop it and make Natalie laugh. Too bad Chathuri clung to it with her stick-like fingers.

I decided to change the subject. 'I listened to *Spinning Unrest* yesterday.' I watched Natalie's face to see if she'd show any emotion.

Nope. She was a robot. Her focus stayed on the nails.

'You still listen to it?' she asked.

'Yeah . . .'

'Okay.'

'There was a good song by a band called Deathstars.'
I wasn't totally honest. There weren't many songs on the
countdown that made me feel like I wanted to jump out
of my skin anymore.

'Sounds heavy.'

'Yeah . . .'

Someone threw the ball at me without calling out and
it would've smashed my face if Natalie didn't say, 'Look
out!' Luckily I managed to duck out of the way. I had
to run after the ball and bring it back. Returning to my
place, I threw it back to Nilanthi, who was being scolded
by Gunatilleke Sir for not calling.

'Do you remember *Fear of the Dark*?' I said.

'Oh my god, yeah!' For a second she sounded like the
old Natalie. 'I had almost forgotten about that album.'

'Do you still have it? The CD?' I was the one who'd
discovered it. The artwork with Eddie as some sort of tree
monster, creepy branch fingers reaching out beneath a full
moon, was the most awesome thing among the hundreds
of cheap pirated CDs and DVDs in that dusty kadé in
Nugegoda. I gave up a hundred rupees, pocket money I
was supposed to spend at the tuckshop, and bought my first
Iron Maiden album. I hid it deep inside my bag because
I was sure Ammi wouldn't like it.

'It must be at home, somewhere,' said Natalie.

She'd probably never find it again in that haunted
mansion. When I used to spend the day there we ran wild
on the third floor. We could've exploded a bomb in the
living room and nobody would've said a word. Her mum

always had the cordless phone stuck to her ear, pacing up and down on the ground floor. Her dad was always abroad and the servants were never seen. It was in those days we started listening to *Spinning Unrest* (Sri Lanka's only alternative rock countdown!). We played air guitar on Natalie's dad's squash racquets and headbanged like crazy. All that was cool at Natalie's, but I couldn't do it at mine. Couldn't even listen to a simple radio show – I'd get into so much trouble. I mean, that was the only reason to take a (pretend) nap every Sunday with Latha's transistor radio under my pillow, right?

'"From Here to Eternity", that was your favourite song, no? Track number two?'

'Yeah,' said Natalie, letting the girl next to her pick up the ball that rolled near her feet. She also liked the sad-happy (I secretly called them sappy) songs by Matchbox Twenty or Third Eye Blind. And then, as if that wasn't bad enough, she went totally mainstream. Started listening to all that R&B nonsense. Still, I wanted to be able to tell her about the raaa! stuff, about Korn and Disturbed and System of a Down and how all the scream-singing was like freedom or whatever.

'My favourite's still "Fear of the Dark" . . . title track.' It was true. I loved it. That spoken word intro about a man walking alone on a dark road. The pause. The silence shattered by the most awesome guitar riff you've ever heard. 'I'd listen to it every day if I could.'

'Too bad you don't have an iPod,' said Natalie. As the bell rang and PT ended, she took something out of her pocket, showing off a perfect little silver rectangle, then pressed a button and quickly hid it again, pushed the ear buds in her ears and walked off. I would've killed to know what she was listening to.

—

When Ammi asked what I wanted for my birthday next month I said, 'Nothing,' because that was what I was supposed to say. I didn't want to seem like a greedy pig. But then Ammi went, 'Don't say that, Anoushka. There must be something you want.'

So I said, 'An iPod.' I only said it because she asked.

'What do you need an iPod for, Anoushka?' said Ammi. 'You have so much studying to do. Your O-Levels are very close. Maybe if you get good marks.'

'But—'

'Those things are expensive, no? How much is one?'

'I don't know.'

'Ask your father.'

I went into Thatthi's room.

'Thatthi – Ammi said to ask you if I could have an iPod. For my birthday.'

He put down the book he was reading, got off his broken cane chair and tied his sarong. He looked like a weirdo, scratching his balding head, the unnaturally dark hair dye contrasting with the snow-white chest hair poking through his torn undershirt. He took the cover off his computer, turned it on. 'Let me do a search on the Google,' he said. Afterwards he came out to the living room and spoke to Ammi. 'More than twenty-five thousand, Lakshmi,' he said. 'It's too much, this iPod.'

'A very expensive toy,' said Ammi. 'We can't afford. You don't even listen to music, no?'

'Can't you listen on my computer? Surely,' Thatthi said with a smile. He scratched his big bundy, belly-fat stretching like melted plastic, and waited for my response. What was I going to say? 'I can't listen with all of you around. My music's too dark and there are too many fucks in the lyrics?' No. I didn't say anything.

'These days there are other little gadgets that work just like the iPod. I'll buy you one of those.' This was typical Thatthi. Always trying to make me happy but never able to give me what I want.

'I just want an iPod.'

'She wants one because Natalie has an iPod,' said Ammi, and turned to me. 'We're not rich like Natalie's parents.'

'You wait, Anoushka. I'll see what I can find,' said Thatthi.

—

I had to help Ammi tidy up the house because Thatthi's American cousins were coming. We put a new tablecloth on the dining table and some flowers in the vase on the coffee table in the living room. Latha swept the front garden. They came in an A/C cab, not a three-wheeler. Aunty got out with one of those suitcases with the extendable handle and wheels that you could roll along, but of course you couldn't do that on gravelly Sri Lankan streets and Latha had to carry it in. They came into the house, smiling, and sat down – Ratnasiri Uncle, his wife, Padma Aunty, and their daughter Shani (their other daughter, Ruby was at university in Rhode Island, so she didn't come). Uncle was Thatthi's only cousin and childhood friend. Thatthi had stayed with them, a long time ago, when he went to

America for work and felt he had to return the favour. He kept saying, 'You should have stayed with us,' even though there was barely enough room in our house with Niro back.

Of course Ratnasiri Uncle, dressed in his slightly crumpled American shirt and pants, fanny pack hanging loose below his waist, said, 'Don't want to trouble you, Mano. We booked a hotel.'

They were rich. They had booked into the Hilton. Shani even got her own room. And Shani! I couldn't stop looking at her, sitting there all nonchalant like some rock goddess with her bright green hair and shin-high Doc Martens. I knew right then, I wanted to be like her. No. I wanted to be her! She was eighteen, just a couple of years older than me, but she was already unbelievably cool.

Padma Aunty, who looked a lot like her husband in similar shirt and pants and even shorter haircut, put the suitcase on our coffee table. She opened it and pulled out a stack of shirts. 'Ratnasiri has lost so much weight with his new diet – these shirts are too big for him. I didn't throw them out because that'll be a waste. I thought Mano would like them. Maybe even Niranjan can wear, no?'

I was like, 'Uh oh,' because I totally expected Ammi to tell Padma Aunty to go fly a kite, but she didn't. She had a weird smile plastered on her face as Aunty pulled out old blouses, her daughters' used T-shirts and jeans. I was hoping we'd get to keep some of that stuff Aunty was pulling out, you know – I kind of liked everything.

After they finished blabbing, politely declined dinner and left, I rummaged through my new (old) T-shirts. They were band T-shirts. I didn't know any of them but when

I googled the names I found out. Sonic Youth? Band. Times New Viking? Band. The Breeders? Band. Titus Andronicus? A Shakespeare play or a punk band from New Jersey. After I got home from school the next day I quietly plugged in the headphones on Thatthi's computer and listened to some of their clips on YouTube. The music was weird. It sounded like it had been recorded in a nut factory – the guitars were all crackly, the drums tin, the singing was off key and sleepy or harsh and shouty. I didn't get it. I just wasn't cool enough. But I was confident with a little help from Shani I could learn.

So, the next few weekends, when Thatthi didn't go to the cricket club 'to be a drunkard' (as Ammi said) and instead went to the Hilton to pick up Ratnasiri Uncle and his family and take them sightseeing, I went along. Ammi said she wasn't feeling well and stayed back, so I could breathe freely, breathe in as much of Shani as I could. I sat in the back seat, next to her, as Thatthi somehow got us through all the army checkpoints to the large hall surrounded by neat lawns and fountains. We were at Independence Square. I stayed alongside Shani as she walked at least ten metres behind everyone else. As the others clambered onto the rectangular platform, inspected the carvings on pillars and inscriptions on the walls, Shani rested on the steps and sipped bottled water. It was obvious she wasn't a regular tourist – she was special – but it'd be a shame to miss out on the info, so I hung between her and Thatthi to somehow connect her with all the details pouring out of him.

'This was built like the Kandyan courthouses. It's built in honour of our independence from the British,' Thatthi droned. He turned towards us. 'Did you hear, Shani?'

'Thanks,' Shani said without smiling.

Later, Thatthi tried to get her to pose like everyone else (standing at attention, saying 'cheese' like morons) in front of the lion gargoyles or the DS Senanayake statue. 'Come, Shani!' he said. 'Get in the photo!'

But she wasn't someone who ever did anything she didn't want to. 'No thanks, uncle,' she said firmly.

'But . . . but that's the father of the nation,' he stammered. 'Our first prime minister!'

Shani glanced at the statue of the man in the suit with the bushy moustache and smiled. Thatthi used that opportunity to show off some more. 'You see the two guardstones there?' He pointed at the stones either side of the steps leading to the statue.

'You mean the two tombstones?'

'Adey, they're not tombstones! They have carvings of pots. With the plant growing out of them. Those are punkalas. They stand for prosperity. You see the thing on the ground, in front of them?' He pointed at the blank, semicircular slab at the foot of the stairs.

'Mm-hmm.'

'Normally, that'll be carved also. It's a moonstone. In Sinhala we call it sandakada pahana. This one has nothing on it. There are different ones from different eras, but the proper moonstone shows the cycle of life. There are five rings, from biggest to smallest coming in from the outside. The outside ring is fire. The next one has four animals – an elephant, a horse, a lion and a bull. The next ring has a vine. After that, swans, and the last one is the lotus. Do you know what they mean?' Thatthi looked up to see if Shani was listening but she had already walked away.

The weekend after that we went to Galle Face Green (which was more brown than green because people had trampled and killed all the grass) and watched the sea slamming into the rocks, the kites tumbling all over the sky. The smell of prawn vadai from the roadside stalls made her hungry, so Shani tried to buy some. But Thatthi said, 'Don't buy that stuff. Chi! It's dirty. Don't know what these fellows put in them. I'll take you to a good vadai place.' She let the adults walk in front and as soon as they were out of sight quickly bought two vadai, one for her and one for me, both topped with onion and chilli sauce made from dirty water. We quickly gobbled them down before anyone could see. I had never had one before – never guessed it'd be so delicious! Of course when Thatthi took us to Shanti Vihar, the sweaty old South Indian restaurant with noisy ceiling fans and aluminium crockery, for 'clean vadai' we weren't hungry. We just smirked and said, 'No thanks!'

—

Every Saturday and Sunday for three weeks, we drove around in Thatthi's car, the radio set to TNL. (I had set the channel and nobody bothered changing it.) I explained to Shani that it was the best station for rock. One time, when Uncle, Aunty and Thatthi were busy looking at gemstones in a shop on Galle Road and we were standing outside in the car park, she said, 'Do you like punk?'

'Um . . . y-yeah,' I stammered.

'You should listen to the Slits or Bikini Kill.' She stared into the distance, speaking with the tone of a music expert. 'Those guys never sold out. It's not like they didn't change. They evolved, but they've always had integrity, y'know? The politics is as important as the music.'

'Yeah . . .' I nodded like a bobblehead, pretending I knew about everything.

'I'll give you some . . . if you're interested.'

I didn't know what she meant by 'give you some', but I said, 'Okay!'

The next day, in Wadduwa, while the others were walking slowly down the beach, peering into catamarans, staring out to the foaming sea and bending down to pick up shells, I followed Shani, who made straight for a rocky outcrop. When she got there, she climbed, fearlessly, right to the top. Ammi wasn't there to stop me and Thatthi was distracted, chatting to Aunty and Uncle, so I scrambled after her. We gazed out to the horizon, the sun disappearing into the sea in a haze of red. 'Oh, I almost forgot,' Shani suddenly said. 'I brought this for you.' She took something out of her jeans pocket, casually, as if it was just loose change, and gave it to me. It was an iPod.

'I uploaded my favourites. You'll find a good playlist . . . or three.'

It was beautiful. I held it on my palm as if it was the triple gem, Buddha's tooth from the Dalada Maligawa. But did she expect me to return the iPod after copying the files? 'I . . . I don't have an MP3 player for these songs.'

'Keep the iPod,' said Shani. 'It's my old one.'

It was like a dream. It was the same model as Natalie's but black. It was a little scratched but I didn't care. I had an iPod! I should have kissed her but I was too shocked and just stood there like a big fat lump, mouth open, eyes popping out of my head. Shani smiled, patted my hair and climbed off the rocks.

—

On Monday I wore my ponytail a little sideways – it wasn't very noticeable, but my rebel days had started. I took my wonderful (old) new iPod out as soon as the first period finished and plugged in. I listened to my favourite new album, *Revolution Girl Style Now!* I could see the TMMs looking, surprised about how bold I was being, listening to music inside school. It was banned. I could've got into trouble, even had the iPod confiscated if a teacher saw. And the girls sensed it, the new coolness, as if it had been transferred from Shani to me just by spending those few hours together. By the time the interval came along, the TMMs were following me around, asking questions about my American cousin. 'Wow, New York, she must be like someone from *Sex and the City*.'

I had secretly watched an episode of *Sex and the City* once. It made me want to stab my eyes out with a pencil. 'No way,' I said.

'Does she work on Broadway?'

'Does she have a chihuahua like Paris Hilton?'

'*No!* She's a punk.'

Natalie didn't ask me anything, just kept to herself while the other TMMs were being nice. One of them even offered me a sandwich. 'Cucumber and cheese?'

Then, as the final bell rang, I plugged in again. I was hanging back mainly because I knew Natalie would wait. She didn't like getting squished in the rush to get out. As she was leaving I went right in front, smiled at her and took one of my ear buds out.

'What?' she said.

'You'll never guess what I'm listening to.'

'I don't know. Something weird?'

'Bikini Kill,' I said. 'They're awesome.'

'Never heard of them. I'm not into that cult stuff.'

'You should check them out. It's about how it's cool to be a girl, to be strong and all. There's this song called "Rebel Girl" on the *Pussy Whipped* album and it goes, "Rebel—"'

Natalie let out a big sigh. 'Anoush—'

'It's like . . . like underground punk. Riot girl punk.'

'So it's rock.'

'Sort of. It's got loud guitars and all. But different. It's about the politics as much as it's about the music,' I explained as we passed through the gates.

'Really?'

'My cousin Shani says everything's political. You can't take politics out.'

Natalie sighed again. 'I don't care.'

'Shani says not caring about politics is still political. It's a conservative—'

It was too late. Natalie had run off towards her car, and Latha, the idiot golem, had found me.

—

We were sitting around after dinner watching boring TV when the lights went out. I thought it was a regular power cut – that was the Electricity Board for you, always losing power or cutting it without warning (Thatthi said the minister for power and energy had a business selling generators) – but then Latha came from the kitchen with the transistor radio crackling on her shoulder. 'LTTE prahaarayak!' she said. 'Ahasing enawalu – plane ekaking!'

'Don't be a fool,' I said. 'There's no plane attack. It's just a power cut.' I hadn't forgotten about two or three years ago, when the LTTE flew a small plane to bomb the oil refinery in Kolonnawa and they turned off all the power in Colombo so the terrorist pilot wouldn't see anything. Some of our neighbours had seen anti-aircraft fire and the glow from the explosions from the street, so I got out of my chair and went towards the window.

'Anoushka! Where do you think you're going?' That was Ammi.

'It's nothing!'

The radio crackled as if laughing at me and the newscaster announced that two LTTE planes had been seen making their way towards Colombo.

'Anoushka, come here!' Ammi ordered, getting to her feet. 'If you hear explosions, any shooting, anything that sounds like a plane, go under the table. Mano, you stay here with Anoushka.'

'Where are you going?' said Thatthi.

'I'm going to call Niranjan and see where he is.' She asked Latha to fetch a candle and went down the corridor.

I smiled because we might get to see some explosions. I knew it wasn't nice – someone was probably going to die, but it was never anyone we knew. I mean, come on! It was exciting, a bit of action, and if we were lucky school was going to be cancelled. Through the window and above the wall I could see the faint beam of a searchlight scanning the sky. Suddenly, there were streaks that looked like laser fire from *Star Wars* (except there weren't blue lasers for goodies and red for baddies – you just couldn't tell who was shooting). There was a dull pop-popping, the sound coming a split second after the sparks. Like me, Thatthi watched the spectacle until we heard Ammi put down the phone and the candlelight spread through the corridor.

'Come here, Anoushka,' said Thatthi, dragging me into the dining room, getting ready to go under the table, doing a dramatic pause for effect, as if listening for more fire – just for Ammi's benefit – but by the time she came back carrying a Milo tin with a candle stuck to the lid, everything was quiet again. All we could hear were a few neighbours who had come out to the lane, murmuring nervously.

'Niranjan's at Isuru's house,' said Ammi. 'Did you hear a noise? Was there gunfire?'

Thatthi and I looked at each other. 'No,' he said. 'Only firecrackers.' Of course he didn't tell Ammi about the anti-aircraft fire we just saw – she would've lost her marbles.

The newsreader was rattling on in tedious Sinhala about a 'Deshiya Aadayam' building. 'What's that?' I said.

'Inland Revenue,' said Thatthi. 'Buggers have bombed the Inland Revenue building.'

'Does that mean we lose money?'

'No. But maybe our taxes are gone.'

'Yay!'

'Anoushka! Is that how you behave? People are dying!' said Ammi.

'But no taxes!'

'You know what they say, Anoushka,' said Thatthi. 'Death and taxes are the two things you can't avoid.'

'Maybe this time we'll avoid both!' I cackled.

'Eyi! Stop that! Don't talk about those things. It's not good.' Ammi kept playing party pooper. 'Isn't the Inland Revenue building right near the Hilton?'

My heart stopped.

'The Hilton.' Thatthi brought a palm up to his forehead. 'Yes, yes. It's walking distance.' He grabbed the candle from Ammi and went to the phone. I followed, a sorry shadow. Was it my fault? This was retribution for thinking all those terrible things, wasn't it? What if something had happened to Shani?

Thatthi held up the light for me as I opened the Yellow Pages and found the number for the Hilton. He dialled while I stood there, my heart smashing around in my chest.

'Can't get through,' he said. 'Line is busy.'

'They didn't say anything about the Hilton on the radio – did they, Thatthi?'

He tried dialling again but had no luck. 'I'm sure they're fine,' he said. He tried a couple more times, then shook his head and went back out to the dining room, where Ammi said the planes had been shot down but not before fifty people were injured. Two were in a critical condition.

I crept away to my room, sat at my desk and reached into the drawer, feeling for my iPod. It was there, cold and sleek against my fingers. 'Lucky I got you before they died,' I whispered and gave the screen a little kiss. Slipping on the headphones, I turned it on. The distorted guitars enveloped me, the really heavy, sweet, noisy end part of 'Candy' where Kathleen Hanna goes 'ah oh, ah oh, ah oh-uh ah oh' pulling me into its cocoon, so deeply I felt completely protected. No bomb could get through to me. I closed my eyes and hit repeat and went in again. Something touched me on the shoulder. I opened my eyes. It was Thatthi.

The lights had come on in the living room. Thatthi flicked the switch on the wall and looked at me. He was like, 'What are you doing?'

'Just listening to some music.'

'What's that?'

'This is an iPod.'

'Where did you get that from?'

'Shani gave it to me.'

'Really?'

'Yeah.'

'Is it good?'

'It's an iPod,' I repeated. 'Of course it's good. It's better than good. It's awesome.'

Thatthi took another look at the beautiful thing in my hands. 'Is it new?'

'I think it's Shani's old one.'

'Anoushka,' he said, shaking his head and lowering his voice. 'You know what your ammi will say, no?'

'She didn't say anything!'

'Does she know you have Shani's iPod?'

'No. But—'

'You know the shirts and things Padma Aunty gave – I'm returning them all. You know your mother. She's a proud woman. Before she gives me hell for taking those things, I'm returning.'

'But Aunty and Uncle might be . . . dead.'

'They're not dead, Anoushka! I got an SMS message from Ratnasiri Uncle. They weren't even in the hotel. They're fine.'

I held the iPod tight, bringing it closer to my chest as if Thatthi was about to snatch it away.

'Come out,' he said, turning towards the door. 'Come and talk to your ammi.'

'Please don't tell her,' I said.

Thatthi didn't listen. He went out into the living room. I shoved the iPod deep into my drawer and followed him out. Sitting on the sofa next to Ammi, he patted the middle of the seat, in between the two of them, asking me to sit there. I crept across and plonked myself down.

'That was scary, wasn't it?' said Ammi.

'I wasn't scared,' I said.

'But you were a little worried, no?'

I shrugged.

'She was worried about her cousin,' said Thatthi. 'Anoushka, has your ammi told you the story of our wedding? About what Ratnasiri Uncle and Padma Aunty did?'

Ammi turned to me. 'Don't you know that story, Anoushka?'

'No.' I shook my head. 'What is it?'

'Before our wedding, when I married your thatthi, Padma Aunty came to the room where I was getting my makeup. Her handbag was so heavy, and with a big effort she put it on the table. Then she started taking out all this gold – chains and bangles and earrings. "Here," she said. "You can wear these." She said it belonged to her mother, who was the daughter of so-and-so Muhandiram, and that it's very valuable and that I'm so lucky to have it for my wedding. You know what I did?'

I shook my head again.

'I said no. I had only a small pair of earrings – they were my mother's – and a necklace. My father worked as a clerk for forty years. He did two jobs but still wasn't rich. He had to beg and get a bank loan to pay for the wedding and buy my necklace. This one.' She touched the simple little chain she always wore around her neck. 'That's all I had. But I said, "No. I will wear my own things."'

I thought about brides these days, how they wear so many kolang things – diamond tiaras, chandelier earrings – it's all silly. I prefer what Ammi wore. I've seen the wedding photos. Ammi was a very simple bride.

'What did she say?' Thatthi asked with a chuckle.

'Nothing. Just took all her gold and went.'

Thatthi laughed, making his bundy heave. 'They're leaving tomorrow, apparently.'

'Shani's leaving tomorrow?' I said.

'Yes. They're scared. One little bomb and they run away – bloody Yankees.'

'You're one to talk,' said Ammi. 'As if you'll wait when there's a bomb falling on you.'

'It was nothing! They must have seen a little bit of a lightshow, a bit of anti-aircraft fire . . . a couple of hours of power cuts. That's all. People complain too much.'

'You try living in the middle of a war zone,' snapped Ammi. 'Try living in the north or east.'

Here we go again, I thought. Another fight.

'Of course I know. I'm a media man.'

'We all know what kind of media man you are, Mano.'

'How long has it been since you lived in the east?' said Thatthi. 'What do you know about war?'

Ammi went white (as white as a dark person can go). She shook her head, got up and went to her room.

'I don't know what's happened to that woman,' Thatthi muttered. He turned to me. 'You saw what she's like, no? Tomorrow, give that gadget back.'

Before I went to sleep I wrote down all the names of everything in the iPod. Then I lay in the dark and listened, one last time, to all the songs, one after the other after the other. Ammi was the only interruption, walking around in the corridor like a zombie, waiting for Niro to come home. I listened and listened and listened. I went through the whole lot of them twice, only falling asleep when I'd started the third round. Then I woke up and it was morning. It was time to give up my treasure.

—

Ammi said she'd come with us to drop them off at the airport and I was like, 'We'll never fit everyone in the car.'

'You can sit on Ammi's lap on the way to the airport,' said Thatthi.

'They won't like that,' I said. 'They have safety standards. They wear seatbelts.'

'Don't you want me to come, Anoushka?' asked Ammi.

I couldn't stop her. 'Why wouldn't I?' I said.

There was extra security because of the air raid and we couldn't take Galle Road and had to go a roundabout way. Up on the tenth floor of the Hilton, Aunty and Uncle were ready. They were dressed in going-away clothes,

Ratnasiri Uncle wearing a blazer with gold buttons, Aunty in a beige pants suit. The suitcases, all matching in purple, were piled up in the living room.

'Where's Shani?' I asked.

'Still in her room,' said Aunty. 'Why don't you go and see if she's ready, darling?'

I went along the corridor and knocked on Shani's door. Nobody opened. I knocked again a little louder. Finally she opened it, just a crack, and poked her head out. 'What?' she said. Her hair was wet and she looked pissed off.

'I, um . . . your mother and father are ready, Shani.'

'Coming, coming,' she said and disappeared. She left the door open. Must have been an invitation, right? I went in. The room was messy, but not as bad as Niro's. Just a couple of towels on the ground, a few magazines open next to bottles of cream and makeup on the coffee table.

'Sorry,' said Shani, who was still in her underwear – a black bra and tiny panties that showed her flat stomach and round backside. 'I'm in a rush.' I didn't want to be seen staring so I sat on the unmade bed and watched TV. It was on a cable channel, Star Movies. There was a vampire stalking a couple of girls in a forest. I watched it as Shani rushed around, throwing things in a small suitcase and a big backpack. I put my hand in my pocket and felt the iPod. I should've taken it out and handed it over, but I didn't. I mean, Shani was only half-dressed, right? I didn't even have the guts to look at her. What would she say when I gave it back? She might get mad.

'Did you listen to the music I gave you?' she said while looking in the mirror, putting on her eyeliner.

'Yeah,' I said. 'I love it.'

'I'm really glad. I don't know how you survive.'

On the TV the vampire edged closer, its eyes red, mouth open, snarling, showing sharp teeth.

Shani put on a Screaming Females T-shirt and a denim skirt. 'There's not much here for you, is there?'

'Umm . . . no?'

'Trust me, I know what it's like. All our parents ever talk about is a culture from like a thousand years ago. They're *so* happy to claim something ancient and – and dead. They don't care about creativity, about progress, about making something new, something cutting edge. Like, where's the music? Where's the subversive writing? The boundary-pushing art? It's *so* depressing. And why's everything here such a blatant rip-off of western media? And the Indian stuff – all that Hindi shit – it's so sexist! God, it makes me so—' She snorted like a horse and rushed into the bathroom.

I wanted to say something. To defend my country. But I didn't know how. Didn't know the words, didn't know all the things she knew. On the screen the girls had seen the vampire and were running away. The vampire was doing that thing where no matter how fast the girls ran, he was always close behind. I turned off the TV. Walked over to her backpack. One of the pockets was open. I slipped the iPod in and walked out of the room. Didn't even take a final look. I'd had it for a whole week and it was good while it lasted.

—

It was like they smelled it on me. The utter lack of cool. No iPod, no American cousin, nothing to write home about. Mrs Balasuriya was absent during science period and the TMMs turned their attention to me.

'So? Who's listening to rock these days?' said Maneesha.

'I don't like rock,' said Shimi. 'Only R&B, thanks. Give me Usher anytime, any day.'

'Ooh! Usher! He's *so* hot!' One of them hummed a line from what I guessed was an Usher song.

'What about some punk?' Maneesha continued. 'I've heard there's an awesome band called Bikini Murder.'

'It's Bikini Kill,' I said, staring at Natalie.

She gave me a sweet smile, completely innocent.

'Oh my god! Sounds horrible!' That was Ruvina, the skeletal phoney. 'Sounds like some kind of – lesbian serial killer music!'

The TMMs shrieked so loud they would've been heard in Point Pedro. 'Is that what you like, Anoushka? Lesbian serial killers? Oh my *god*!' said Maneesha.

'Natalie likes it too,' I said.

'What's this, Natalie? Are you into this Bikini Killers band too?'

'Bikini Kill,' I hissed.

'Never heard of them,' said Natalie.

'You'll like it if you tried,' I mumbled.

'How do you know that?' said Ruvina.

'I just know.'

'I just know,' said Shimi, imitating me in a nasal voice. Everyone laughed again.

There was no point talking back. I decided to ignore them. I stared at my book, pretending to read while they called me names (Bikini Bada Killer, Chunky Freak, etc.). I only raised my head when a teacher came in. I didn't even go out during the interval, just stayed in class and chewed my sandwiches while the goday girls opened up their rice packets and ate with their fingers. Natalie came back before the interval ended. I looked at her, secretly, out the corner of my eye, as she crept towards me. I thought she was coming to talk to me, to say sorry for sharing our secrets with everyone else. But no. She had come for something in her bag. She dug out a small stick of lip gloss, rubbed some on her lips, smacked them together and skipped back out, leaving me all alone with the godays.

—

On the morning of my birthday Thatthi came to my room (without knocking) with a box that had the word 'Maxtra' written on the cover. He said, 'Happy birthday, Anoush!' and gave me a kiss, then sat beside me on the bed. I opened it up. Inside was a small grey square – an ugly plastic thing with one of those black and white displays like a Casio watch. 'This is a music player,' said Thatthi. 'Just like an iPod.'

'Okay,' I said. 'Thanks.'

'You're not happy?'

'No, it's good . . . thanks.'

'I asked the man in the shop. He said there's no difference.'

I picked the user guide out of the box and skimmed through, a bit of anger burning in my chest when I saw there was very little disk space and no slot for a memory card. 'Only 10MB,' I said, 'and this doesn't have a radio.'

'Radio? What do you need a radio for? This plays the . . . what do you call, NP3?'

'MP3 . . . iPods have a radio also.'

'Why do you want to listen to the radio? We have one in the living room, no? Or you can borrow Latha's.' Like I wasn't doing that already. Thatthi took the booklet from me and leafed through it. He picked up the box, squinting through his glasses as he read, looking increasingly helpless. He put it down, sighed and said, 'I don't know, Anoushka. I did my best.'

'It's fine,' I said.

MANO

I STARTED DOING IT AGAIN THE SUNDAY AFTER RATNASIRI AND his family flew back to America. Downed a couple of arracks at the cricket club, said goodbye to my friends after eating the last piece of devilled chicken the buggers were too polite to eat and gave the waiter his twenty-rupee tip. Outside I checked my car. Drivers these days were notorious for pretending they hadn't gone anywhere near when your bumper would be dented or your door scraped, so I made sure there weren't any scratches on the doors and polished the S on the grille – S for Swift. I got in, turned off my cell phone and turned on the radio. Niranjan had tuned it to the Golden Oldies station for me, and when I left the car park, nodding at the security fellow who gave me his salute, Jim Reeves sang in his wonderful, deep voice. I went past the air force flats, through Borella, which wasn't so busy because the supermarket was closed, the big red-brick building looking sad with all the half-torn posters on the walls, no people spilling out its mouth. Only a few private buses were on the road, the drivers all bloody idiots, jumping lanes and speeding. I took the lane furthest from the green cemetery fence, as far away from Thattha's headstone as possible when I turned right into Colombo 7. Why did I do this? I don't know. Did I feel guilty? No. Why should I? I've been a good chap. Careful. Sensible.

Sensible enough not to get into a tangle with some big shot's son rocketing down Bauddhaloka Mawatha in a Lamborghini – I could have taught him a thing or two about defensive driving but I took my time, even though Lakshmi was sure to ask me where the hell I'd been. I drove slowly past the Wijerama temple with the Buddhist flags flapping in the wind, past the embassies and high commissions and their clean white walls topped with spikes, and slowed at the massive metal barricade blocking the way into Buller's Road. Here, I idled a little, waited for that military police guy, Jayantha, to come up and check.

Jayantha had been a driver for a travel company before joining the army, and picked up a few sentences from tourists. Today, he tried his broken English on me. 'You are going for same story today, Herath Sir? When are you putting in newspaper?' The bugger was bold – a real pandithaya. He looked around, softened his voice and leaned in so far his beret edged through the window. 'You take photograph also?' The gun in his belt banged against the door and I jumped. 'Sorry, sir.' The fellow took a step back. I tried to laugh it off and reached for the media ID in the cubby, but as usual he said, 'It's okay, Mr Herath, you go,' and signalled to the other man with the AK-47 around his neck to open the boom gate. While he'd never been anything but polite, Jayantha was beginning to make me uncomfortable and I was still feeling a little put out when I passed the beautiful houses – the Senanayakes', the Wijewardenas', the Abubakers', the Gardiners' – all of them at least four storeys, rising above the high walls and thick iron gates.

I parked on the left, across the road from the Amarasinghe mansion, next to the massive tree that I always kept one eye on. Those trees sometimes fell in the wet season when there were breakneck winds. Weak roots, they said, and the municipal workers cut all the old ones before they could hurt any of our prominent businessmen or parliamentarians. Why bother? Those buggers are like the things Anoushka watches in her movies – what are they called? Vampires, that's right. They never die. I was only worried about me. I parked there and watched.

How long did I take? Less than ten, fifteen minutes. It was quick. I had a cigarette and listened to a lovely song by Tom Jones and waited for the light to go on in the room on the fourth floor. To be safe, I turned the volume down. I had to be careful. The security situation was sensitive. Once, someone called the police. And the police, lazy buggers, called the military police at the checkpoint and told them to see what I was doing. Luckily for me Jayantha was there. He walked up and tapped on the shutter and said, 'Mr Herath, police thinking you have bomb, sir. Maybe you go and come.' After that I kept it very quiet and moved on quickly.

Today, I spread open a file and pretended to take notes, as if I was preparing to walk into the UN office a few doors down. Only then, secretly, did I look across the road, at the east wing of the Amarasinghes' house and all the way up to the fourth floor, where I could see her silhouette through the rich teak window frames. As she walked back and forth, she combed her hair with her fingers, then twisted it around her wrist and arranged it around her head. It was my lucky day – she opened the door then and came out to the balcony, leaning against the polished metal railing. I was worried she might see me, recognise me, and tell me to leave. She didn't. She just looked around. After almost five, six months I'd been coming here, she must have known. That must be why she stayed out on that balcony looking at nothing at all, talking quietly on her cell phone and smoking. Her every movement told me something, making a connection without saying a word. When she looked away, towards Thunmulla junction, it meant she was angry because I was late. Looking past me, towards Gerald Perera's house? She was glad to see me. Looking down? She'd had a fight with her husband and wanted me to take her away.

More than any of that, it was her smoking that made me excited. Surely, she remembered our Plantation Ministry days – how I came out and lit a cigarette just to take a chance with her. Bought a packet of Gold Leaf and tried my level best to stop coughing just so I could stand outside and watch the sudu kakul she showed off in those short skirts. Budhu Ammo, I still remember! Mind you, they weren't short by today's standards. Colombo girls these days – they should just go out in their jungies. But in that time a skirt that showed a little ankle would get all the office buggers salivating and Ramani's was knee-high. Below the knee or above? Borderline case, I believe. I wanted to take a closer look – that was the whole idea when I started smoking.

Of course, she didn't even look at me. You could count the words she said to me on your fingers: 'Excuse me,' on the way back to the office. Those days, the woman didn't care that I was assistant director of public relations. She was more interested in making relations with the minister. That was a rumour, but I wouldn't be surprised if it were true – our minister was such a cad they said he had a child in every district.

But now, she was the wife of Anuruddha Amarasinghe, the third richest man in the country. She was waiting to escape, I was sure of it. One day I'd walk right into that house, grab the arm Anuruddha Amarasinghe had raised to hit her, give him a thundering whack on his head, and as the police dragged him away, Ramani would take my hand and say, 'Why don't you stay here, Mano? Stay with me. I have a nice house – I just need someone to protect me.'

That's like the Hindi bioscope pictures I watched in my younger days – where the hero meets a beautiful woman, they fall in love, another man tries to hurt the woman, the hero fights and wins and then they sing a song and dance. Not so different to what I imagined with Ramani. I was the hero. That thought alone nearly made me get out of the car. She was leaning towards me as if signalling, and my fingers wrapped around the door handle, but then a car went past. One of Ramani's neighbours opened a window and looked out. The army fellows at each end of the road paced and shouted something and it made me think. What if someone saw? They knew who I was and the word would spread, no? It'd go back to Lakshmi. She would murder me, no two words about it. And the kids? What would they think? The relatives? Nelunka? And Sumith? That bugger and my sister would be happy they could put one over me. Junius Uncle? Ratnasiri and Padma? I'd be crucified, surely. So I stayed in the car. Tried to catch my breath. I started the engine and pulled out, leaving Ramani standing there alone.

—

She went missing. Week after week, I went and waited but the light didn't come on. There was no shadow, no silhouette, nothing to be seen on the fourth floor. Nobody opened the door to the balcony to come out.

It wasn't the first time she'd disappeared. There had been two or three-week absences but I always had an idea of her whereabouts – the business pages never failed to mention that Anuruddha Amarasinghe was in Dubai or Australia, selling tea or expanding his financial services empire, and I guessed Ramani went with him. This time the bugger was in Sri Lanka for sure – his court case, the one about fraud at his credit company, was in full swing and I was enjoying the coverage. But where was Ramani? The house was dead quiet. What if Anuruddha Amarasinghe had lost his temper and killed her? The pressure of his legal issues and the discovery that his wife loved me must have driven him to murder. All the stress – these big shots had to face it, no?

I was enjoying not having to work this week, recovering from the milk-rice-and-astrology-party we called the Aluth Avurudda, relaxing in bed reading the new-year editions of the papers, full of good wishes and blessings from every man and his dog, when a notice in the obituaries section caught my eye. *Amarasinghe, Mrs Ramani. At rest with Jesus. Dearly beloved wife of Anuruddha Amarasinghe, loving mother of Harin and Shanika, now living in the UK . . .*

I was shocked. I had imagined her death, yes, but never wished it to happen. Life, after all, wasn't a Hindi film, no? For about an hour I couldn't get up. I was like a statue. Only my eyes were moving as I read the obituary again and again. Then I got out of bed and looked around but nobody was there. I was in my room. Just me and the books on my shelf, the desk full of files and magazines. The big white clock was beating like a heart. There was no one I could tell. I poured a shot of whisky – just a little Johnnie Walker – and downed it in one go. I went out into the living room and it was empty. In the kitchen the servant was falling asleep next to a half-grated coconut. Normally, I would've blaggarded the woman, but today, I couldn't. I went out to the garden. The fellows building the five-storey apartment at the top of the lane were, as usual, making an unholy racket. I barely heard it. The crow on the roof was making its ugly kaak-kaak sound. I didn't shoo it away. I didn't do a thing. I just turned around and went back in, went down the hall. As I opened Lakshmi's door it creaked. She was sleeping. I made sure my slippers didn't make any noise on the floor as I went in. I sat on the bed and watched her lying there on her back, arms on top of her stomach. She was breathing, her chest going up and down, but the way I saw her in that light – it was like she was embalmed. The only thing missing was a coffin.

—

I went to the funeral. It was on a Tuesday at the Cathedral near Anuruddha Amarasinghe's house. I parked and combed my hair, but getting out of the car took a little effort. It took more effort to walk, because my knees felt like they would fail as I went past the lawn and up the steps. You know what churches are like, frightening places with bleeding bloody Jesus hanging from his cross, the stained glass filtering the harsh afternoon sun. Somehow, I went in. Luckily I had worn my white shirt and black tie, because everyone was dressed well. Most of the men were, despite the stinking heat, wearing suits. The women were dressed in skirt and blouse, all prim and proper. The few saris were worn by grey haired acchi types keeping an eye on their grandchildren. The crowd was surprisingly small, less than a hundred, and I didn't know anybody there. I didn't see anyone from the Plantation Ministry, but it's not like I could have talked to someone, no? I only had time to go up and have a look at the body. The face didn't look much like the Ramani I remembered. It was puffy, and her skin looked grey, especially around the eyes. She had been dressed in a smart suit, with a jacket. The skirt went lower than her knees and I, very slyly, took a hora look at her legs. The first and only close-up. They looked like wax or something. 'Sorry,' I said to her softly.

I went right to the back and found a seat. When all the biblical ha-ho began I pretended to listen, getting up and sitting down when the priest said so – it was a typical Catholic affair. Ramani's brother, a stocky fellow, fair like his sister, got up, sweating profusely, and made a speech. He made the usual noises, said what a good person she was, that she loved everyone and was the ideal sister, that she had helped him through many hard times and her loss left a massive gap in his life.

Then came the husband. From behind you could see his hair was almost gone! I must have been a few years older but I had my hair, no? Still, I had to say he had height over me. He must have been what, five-eleven or six foot? He walked up to the podium looking very smart – his suit was expensive, made at Savile Row or something – and adjusted the mike so he could talk into it. I first thought, 'This man doesn't care about Ramani. Look how calm he is.' But he started badly, as if he had forgotten the words, breathing heavily and saying sorry in a woman's voice. He took a handkerchief from his pocket, wiped his eyes and started again. He said the same things as her brother – about Ramani being a good wife, a good mother and a good person, that she was irreplaceable. Then he said something that made me feel sorry for him: 'The last few years have been difficult.' When he said that his voice cracked and scattered through the speakers, went all over the hall like dust. That was it. The bugger was crying so hard he couldn't talk anymore.

—

No matter what happened, you had to carry on, no? I kept working through the week. The staff kept trying to make me join Ramani, send me to my grave early. On Friday, the intern, Yashoda, wanted my help getting hold of someone at the airport. From what I knew, some racketeer had tried to smuggle foreign currency, at least ten thousand undeclared dollars into the country. Yashoda was in my office, dialling the airport from the phone on my desk because there was a queue for the other one. I had a little chuckle, knowing those buggers at customs would give her the run-around.

'Hullo. Is this arrivals?' said Yashoda. 'Can you tell me about the man who was caught with the money? The foreign currency? Who? Me? I'm calling from— So, departures have the file? Okay, I'll call departures.' She put the phone down and looked at me.

'What's wrong?' I said, playing the idiot.

'They want me to call departures.'

'So call departures.'

She picked up the phone again. 'Hullo. I'm calling about the man who was caught with the money— But they just told me to call you. They said you still have the file . . . so was the man trying to come in or go out? I thought he was— What do you mean, you don't know? So where's the file? No, it's not at arrivals!'

I couldn't hide my laughter anymore. Yashoda frowned. She looked almost nice when she was angry. Almost. Yashoda was plump, carrying extra weight around her arms and stomach. And she was a makeup-pappa. All that colouring on her face made her look old, not young. She didn't have the sophistication of a woman like Ramani. When she was alive, Ramani knew how to make herself look a million bucks.

But Yashoda, when she got angry, did this thing with her mouth, lips pressing so hard they were pouting. It was like Lakshmi – whenever she was angry, she pressed her lips together until they nearly burst. There was a time I used to make Lakshmi angry on purpose, just to see it happen. Nowadays, of course, she was forever angry with me. Not so much angry but disappointed, the natural disappointment that comes with seeing someone every day and knowing someone too well.

'Mr Herath,' Yashoda said.

I swivelled my chair back towards her. 'Yes, child.'

'Can you help me?'

Lakshmi would never ask for help, least of all from me.

'You want help?'

'How can I find the information?'

'Why should I help?'

'These people will never tell me anything.'

'If I help how will you learn, ah? Necessity is the mother of invention. Have you heard that saying?'

'No.' She shook her head. 'Aiyo, Mr Herath. Please!' Yashoda leaned against the desk cheekily.

'Ah, okay, okay. Sit down. Listen carefully. I'll show you once.' I opened my drawer and took out my phone book. Turning to the L page, I found Sarath Liyanage's number. He was now the DC at customs and he owed me more than just one small favour. I dialled the number.

'Hullo.'

'Hull-o! Deputy Commissioner Liyanage!'

'Ah, Mano.' He recognised my voice immediately.

'Who else! How are you? How is the DC's chair? Is it comfortable? I hear you're doing an excellent job.'

'Good, good. So you got my message.' He was a good fellow. He was grateful. He remembered how I saved his skin. There was that massive ha-ho about a senior government minister who redirected a passenger flight and got a kitten flown in from Austria and straight through customs in time for his son's girlfriend's birthday. I was the one who turned a very negative story by my most senior reporter, Mihil de Soyza, into something positive and added the words: *Mr S. Liyanage of Katunayake Airport customs has confirmed that all the standard rules and procedures for animal import had been followed.* A week later, Sarath was promoted to DC.

'Can you give me some details? About this fellow who was caught today?' I added that last part for Yashoda's benefit.

'I was wondering what time you'd call. I gave you my tip-off in the morning, no?' said Sarath.

'I was busy, Mr Liyanage,' I said. 'So, tell me.' I showed the intern how it was done, writing everything in the notepad, things like how much money the fellow was trying to take, where he was going, what sort of racket it might be, whether he was Tamil or Muslim or a foreigner and how the customs found out. 'Thank you, Sarath.'

'No problem, Mano. You know, there are two bottles of Black Label, duty free, if you want. I can keep them for you.'

'I'll . . .' I looked to see if Yashoda was listening but she was miles away, looking out the window and playing with her hair. 'I'll come and get them next week,' I said to Sarath.

—

I stopped at Flower Drum on the way home and bought the chicken with cashew nuts, hot butter cuttlefish, kangkung and fried rice – all Lakshmi's favourites. I thought of getting chilli crab as well but the bill was already over five thousand rupees and I already had seafood, no? As I put it all in the back of the car, the delicious smells made spit roll into my mouth, but I didn't even open a box to have a taste.

I walked into the house with a bag in each hand like Father Christmas. The greeting I got was the same as Santa – nobody was there. I went into the kitchen where the servant was sitting on the floor with the radio in her ear. I put the food on the bench and quickly looked away as she got to her feet – didn't want to risk seeing up that woman's skirt, god no – and told her she didn't have to cook dinner. 'Ada reta kéma hadanna oné na.'

'Hondai, Mahattaya,' she said. The lazy woman was obviously happy.

After a shower I tried to read the papers, keep up with the competition, but when I turned the pages of *The Island*, the *Daily News* or even the *Hindustan Times*, I couldn't concentrate. I went out and looked for Lakshmi. Her door was closed. Out in the living room Anoushka was sitting with her legs on the settee, hypnotised by the television.

'I brought some Flower Drum, Anoush.'

'Okay,' said the girl without even turning to look at me.

'You can have it when Ammi comes out of her room.'

I went over and sat on the far end of the settee. The girl started changing channels, pata-pata, going from the news to a Sinhala talk show to an English comedy show in a split second. She stayed for a little while on the channel showing *Friends*, a comedy where a tall, thin chap spoke fast to a good-looking girl with straight hair and a short skirt. They were flirting like no tomorrow, but just as it was getting somewhere Anoushka pressed the button on the remote control.

Lakshmi finally came out of her room in a daze, with a hand raised to stop the light getting in her eyes. Her hair was all over the place and she shuffled around like one of those dead things in Anoushka's movies. Zombies? That's right, zombies. I wondered if there was something wrong with Lakshmi, an illness. 'I brought something for you,' I said. 'It's in the kitchen. Go and see.'

Her face didn't change. She didn't even look at me but slowly turned and disappeared into the kitchen, her slippers making a sandpaper noise as they slid on the concrete. She came back empty-handed. 'Anoushka, go and serve some food,' Lakshmi said.

'Is there beef with kangkung?' Anoushka asked.

'Normal kangkung. There's chicken and cuttlefish,' I said.

'But beef with kangkung is the best!'

'Your mother doesn't eat beef, no?'

'I'll have it without kangkung, then.'

'You have to eat some vegetables, Anoush,' I said.

'Go and serve. You can take what you want,' said Lakshmi, leading the girl to the dining table where the servant had piled the Flower Drum onto dishes. I got up and took a couple of steps towards the table as Lakshmi heaped Anoushka's plate. I leaned against the wall and watched.

'Don't drop it!' Lakshmi said sternly as the girl skipped back to the TV.

When she looked at me, I said, 'Take, take,' insisting she ate before me for a change.

Lakshmi served herself a handful of rice and a little cuttlefish and kangkung.

'Take more.'

Lakshmi had always been a poor eater, but even by her standards this was bad.

'Aren't you eating chicken?'

She served a piece the size of her little finger.

'Take some more, Lakshmi. Here, what about some chilli paste?' I reached out and opened the small polythene bag.

She looked at me as if I was asking her to eat poison but in the end dipped a teaspoon in the bag and took some chilli paste.

'We had some bad news at work. Sales are down,' I said, thinking I might get some sympathy.

But what did she do? She turned her back on me.

'You're not eating at the table?'

She went into the living room and sat on the end of the settee.

'That's all right. I'll come and join,' I said, quickly taking my share. I tried to sit next to Lakshmi but she told Anoushka, who was sitting at the opposite end of the settee, to move to the middle. Eyes stuck to the TV, the girl shifted. I sat in the corner and dug my fingers into the rice.

Sumith always bought Flower Drum for my sister's birthday and boasted about the chilli crab being the best in the country – the food was usually fresh and delicious so I didn't make fun of his boasts – but today it didn't taste so good. It was dry. Maybe it was because I didn't buy the classic chilli crab. How to afford? I mixed more chilli paste with the chicken and cuttlefish to improve things. I just hoped Lakshmi was enjoying.

I leaned forward to take a look at her. She was going through the motions, slowly mixing the food with her fingers and putting it in her mouth. She chewed like it was grass. On TV, the people eating noodles were loving every bite. That local pop singer, Dushantha or someone, did a song and dance because the noodles were so good. But you can't believe a minute of that. Cheap bloody ad! Bugger does a bajau, a party in a big house full of people, and all they're having is noodles. What a joke. Nobody likes noodles that much.

Anoushka changed the channel. Now it was one of those music shows where the presenter, although he was local, spoke with an American accent and said things like 'funky track' or 'groove-delicious' and played that nasty rap stuff with some black fellows dancing – it was like they were trying to have sex with their clothes on. Luckily Anoush changed the channel again.

News. There were the usual reports of how many Tigers had died, pictures of smoke blowing over palm trees, wretched bloody refugees with their children crying. The pretty newsreader, the girl with the nice smile, read a warning issued by the UN.

'Bloody NGOs can't keep their noses out of our problem,' I grumbled.

'Change the channel, Anoushka,' said Lakshmi.

The channel-changing business was getting out of hand. Even if news was what I heard all day at work I'd rather watch that than a hundred things at once, no? We settled on a Sinhala show for a minute. *Kopi Kadé*. Of course, it didn't last. Patass! It was gone from the screen in a second.

'What's wrong with you?' I said. 'You can't just watch one thing?'

'Were you watching that?' said Anoushka like a pandithaya.

'Yes. I was watching!'

'You were watching *Kopi Kadé*?'

'Yes. I was!'

'Really?' Anoushka's finger had stopped pressing but hung over the channel button. She was going to change it back.

'Look, it's finished now. Too late. Just leave it.'

'No, it's not. I'll put it back.' She knew that I wasn't really watching that cheap show but her finger came down on the button, just to annoy me, and changed back to *Kopi Kadé*.

'What are you doing? I just told you not to change it.'

'But you said you wanted it.'

'I told you no, Anoushka. I don't want it.'

'But—' Anoushka stopped talking. Lakshmi had fixed eyes on her. A mother has some real power over a daughter. Fear or respect, whatever it was, Lakshmi could make Anoushka listen with one look.

Just like that we had to watch *Kopi Kadé* where the village idiots were having rural problems and second-rate comedians made third-rate jokes – that and a whole lot of slapstick. The woman with cowcatcher teeth, Dayawathi, was biting her fingernail and twisting the edge of her sari around her finger as that lanky fellow, Gajang, talked to her. He was smiling and bending his neck and brushing his curly hair with his hand. Abiling, the joker, was making silly faces at the lovers. Dingi Mahattaya and the women drinking tea in the *Kopi Kadé* were frowning at the scandalous behaviour.

I'd had enough of that rubbish. I finished eating. 'Shall I take your plate, Lakshmi?' I said. 'Or do you want to eat some more?'

It was as if she hadn't heard. She stared through the TV at some faraway place. I thought she might eat more later, so I left her there, went to the kitchen and put my plate in the sink, washed my hands and got a glass of arrack from my room before sitting back down in front of the TV.

Anoushka had changed to an action film but I couldn't follow. Too many thoughts. Too many questions, like why doesn't Lakshmi say anything to me? I hadn't done anything wrong, no? So why was she treating me like I was nobody? All I wanted to do was talk.

These days, the only time we had together was in the car, when I dropped her at work in the mornings. Sometimes she came to the market to make sure I bought the right groceries or to the gas shop to buy a new cylinder. Other than that she took a three-wheeler to the temple and kovil to make an offering, a puja to this god and that god. Always praying to someone in the sky to make things better. They're the only ones she talks to nowadays – gods. Doesn't talk to me about anything.

I thought I'd try one last time and said, 'We have an intern, Yashoda – really useless. Lazy. Doesn't do anything. Always wants help.'

Lakshmi sat there like a brain-dead bummatta, empty plate still on her lap, bits of rice drying on her fingers.

'Did you hear, Lakshmi?' I tried a different approach. 'You ate very little, no? Why don't you take some more?'

'Shh,' Anoushka hissed. 'I can't hear anything.'

'Is the food not good? Flower Drum is not so good now, no? But there's a lot left. Do you know how much it cost? Better finish—'

'Aiyo!' said Anoushka.

'I'm trying to talk to your mother here. Maybe it's time you went to sleep.'

'It's not even nine-thirty,' Anoushka grumbled. 'I just want to watch this movie.'

'Lakshmi? Why aren't you eating? Are you not feeling well? Is it because you want to leave some for Niranjan? There's plenty. Take and eat, will you?'

'Niro's gone gallivanting,' said Anoushka. 'He won't come back till four in the morning.'

'He has work to do, no?' I said.

Suddenly Lakshmi found her voice. 'What kind of work do you think he does at this time?'

'That's how big companies are these days, Lakshmi. People work very hard, especially the chaps who are getting somewhere. He's young. He can do it. Let him do what he wants.'

'Young, ah? Will you let Anoushka do the same thing?'

'Anoushka's a girl, no?'

Anoushka jumped in. 'Why can't I do it if he can?'

'You don't get cheeky with me, now,' Lakshmi said in a loud voice. 'I'll never let you do the things he does—'

'Enough, enough, stop fighting,' I said, but Lakshmi had got started and when she starts she's a runaway train: impossible to stop.

'Don't you learn things from your brother,' she blasted Anoushka. 'Don't you take him as an example! Your father doesn't say anything to him because your father doesn't care. He should be the one to tell Niranjan the things he's doing are wrong, to stop him from doing them. Niranjan doesn't listen to us. He has to be told by a man. But there aren't any men here, no? There—'

'Stop it, Lakshmi,' I said. 'I just wanted to have a nice meal together, but we can't do that in this house. I work hard all day and spend all my money on you, but I don't even get a single thank you.'

'Who asked you to spend your money? We don't want your Flower Drum.' Lakshmi's voice trembled. 'You think we'll forgive you because you brought some food? You better think again. We know what you've been doing.'

What did she know? Had someone been spreading stories about me? I hadn't done anything wrong. I should have defended myself, but I was too tired. It was time to go back to my room to have a drink in peace. I walked off. Gunfire rattled on TV as Rambo or Commando or some other action hero killed a whole lot of terrorists. I just wanted to sleep and forget.

In my room I finished my drink and started making the bed. I was putting up the mosquito net when there was a knock on the door. 'Come in.'

Anoushka poked her head in and said, 'Thank you, Thatthi. For the food.'

'You're welcome, kella,' I said. I wondered if she had come on her own or whether Lakshmi was standing behind her, just out of sight. 'Did you enjoy?'

'Yeah. Thatthi? Next time get beef with kangkung.'

'Okay, kella. Are you going to sleep now?'

'Yeah.'

'Okay, goodnight.' Before I closed the door I peered out to see if Lakshmi was there. The lights had been turned off but I saw the hem of a skirt disappearing around the corner. She had sent Anoush to thank me. No two words about it.

I went to bed but had trouble falling asleep. All I could think was that, all along, I'd had someone to love. That's what kept tumbling through my head. I love her. She's beautiful. Kind. Intelligent. She used to be so good to me. What happened? Was it all the things people said?

'You couldn't find anybody else, no?'

'Whose side are you on?'

'It's your life, do what you want . . . but don't say we didn't tell you.'

'You're sick of us, no? That's why you married one of them . . .'

'We're not even sure if you're Buddhist anymore. What will the children be? Hindu?'

In those early days of marriage I ignored all of that, just smiled and said, 'You don't know Lakshmi,' and walked away. It was none of their business. But sometimes when you keep hearing the same thing over and over again, you begin to believe.

The worst wasn't that sort of nonsense. The worst was when they said something I was already thinking. Like the time when Nelunka, my own bloody sister, said that Lakshmi could do with some Fair & Lovely. I yelled at her. How could she suggest Lakshmi use fairness cream? But it had crossed my mind, you know. Lakshmi was a dark lady. Sometimes I told myself the colour of strong coffee was just right – that Lakshmi was beautiful. Other times I wished I had married someone a couple of shades lighter.

—

I was worried about Lakshmi. I had noticed she was like this since . . . since maybe even before the start of the year. Was it a sign of getting older or was there something wrong with her? In the mornings she shuffled out of her room like she'd lost her mind, forgetting to iron her blouses, sari pleats all over the place, strings of hair that hadn't been combed properly and plaited dropping down to her forehead. The tiny bit of makeup she used to wear, very subtle, was missing. Rings around her eyes were more prominent, lips cracked and peeled. She came and sat at the dining table and stared – not at me but some faraway ghost. Ate next to nothing, just a couple of mouthfuls, and pushed the plate away.

I kept telling the servant woman to cook better, to make an effort and add the right amount of salt and sour, to somehow make the food tastier.

Our bloody servant had the nerve to talk back: 'Lunu embul daala thiyenné, Mahattaya.' Of course she'd say she added the right amounts. I went and checked the salt bottles, the chilli and other spices to see whether she'd sold some to a shifty bugger at a kadé somewhere. I knew she didn't steal but checked anyway. Good to keep her on her toes, no?

But Lakshmi's problem wasn't food. Over the next few weeks, I brought home cakes from Green Cabin, pastries from Perera & Sons, vegetable rolls from Nippon – nothing doing. Lakshmi had none of it. We had to give her share to Anoushka. The girl was happy. She got to eat more. Niranjan polished off the rest in the morning, but Lakshmi – the most she had was one bite.

What if there was something wrong? Every night, terrible words flooded into my head. Cancer. Leukaemia. Malaria. Hepatitis. What if she was incurable? I remembered Ramani's funeral, how upset Anuruddha Amarasinghe had been. I couldn't imagine anything making me cry like that, but still, the idea of me getting up and doing a speech when I'm so sad – it was frightening! I would have preferred my funeral to happen before Lakshmi's. Some nights, I imagined the whole event – all the people who would come, all the old Wesleyites, maybe some of the current students too, and the fellows from the paper, including Mr Bamunuaracchi, maybe even the whole board. The girls from marketing and all the women I've interviewed – Belinda Joseph from the UN, that fair girl, Ruwani Pieris, who's now media secretary to the Ministry of Health. All the ladies from my old job. Tears would flow. The minister of plantations would bring a big wreath and give it to Lakshmi. Lakshmi would be devastated, crying nonstop, and so would the kids. Niranjan would make a speech about how great his father was. How I spent my life savings to put him through university in Australia. Mr Bamunuaracchi would talk about how my time as editor had helped the newspaper reach its current standard – that I fearlessly took on the Tigers, corrupt politicians and officials, but most of all, how I was good to my colleagues . . . This was better. It was better that I go first than Lakshmi going and leaving me all alone.

I made an appointment at Asiri Hospital. The doc probably hadn't seen Lakshmi in a year or so – she didn't even come with me to his daughter's wedding – so it was high time. 'I made an appointment with Dr Palihakkara tomorrow, ten-thirty,' I said to Lakshmi at the last minute, as I was dropping her at work. That way she couldn't harangue me for too long. She got out of the car, shutting the door twice because she was too weak to close it in one go, and walked off.

Saturday morning I thought she might put up a fight and refuse to come but by ten she was wearing her skirt and blouse and her hair was combed. We found parking on the street, avoided the woman who would want a tip for looking after cars in front of the hospital, and walked into Asiri. It was like hell. The smell of disinfectant mixed with sweat, and all of bloody humanity walked with a limp and crawled and rolled around on wheels. It was packed, long lines at every counter, a particularly large scrum at payments, where a forest of arms pushed cash through the bars. Some fellows were jumping the line, your typical motorcycle bugger with his helmet, some van or three-wheel driver in a sarong. They were the type who always did this while the nicely dressed ladies and gentlemen waited patiently. Pity Dr Palihakkara only worked at the hospital now. Back in the day he worked in his clinic, I was first in line because he knew me.

'You sit and wait,' I said to Lakshmi, pointing at a couple of empty chairs in the row along the wall. 'I'll go and pay. Just give me the money. I think it's seven-fifty. I can change a thousand if—'

Lakshmi fixed her gal look – that stone stare only she could do – on me and said, 'Money?'

'Yes, the money for your appointment. You have to pay before the doctor sees you.'

'You make the appointment, bring me here and ask for money?'

'The appointment is for you, Lakshmi. Because you're looking sickly, not eating and all that, so I thought . . .'

'If you're worried about me, why don't you pay?'

'I don't have enough. I didn't bring cash,' I said. I honestly hadn't thought of it. Yes, I could have paid with my credit card, but with all the fees and things, not to mention the dire state of my savings account, I didn't want to use it.

'You never have any money, no? What do you do with your salary? Do you spend it all on your firewater? On your car? On some woman?'

'Don't shout, Lakshmi – people will hear.'

'People will hear? Maybe they should. They should hear about what Mr Manoratne Herath is doing. They should hear about how you tell me you're working but go and have drinks at the cricket club or go after women.'

'Don't start your nonsense.'

'Tell me about how you bought us a new house and paid for Niranjan's education.'

'What are you talking about? Who paid for Niranjan's education if it wasn't me? I'm the one who left the Plantation Ministry so I could take my provident fund and pay those fees—'

'Right, tell us then what you did with that money,' said Lakshmi, crossing her arms.

'I'm the one who had to retire early from a very prestigious job and start working at this godforsaken newspaper—'

'Tell, tell. Tell us what you did with the money. Tell everyone how I gave my half to Niranjan and you spent your half on a car.'

'I'm the one who was sure to become the next director but instead made a massive sacrifice—'

'Tell everyone how your wife had to go and beg for money from outsiders. Tell them how your son had to beg the university—'

'I'm the one who—'

It went on like that, hell of a fracas, and I was getting properly worked up when someone tapped me on the shoulder. It was a pleasant young fellow who I didn't recognise. I wiped away the sweat with my handkerchief and tried to smile.

'Mr Herath,' said the man. 'So nice to see you. This must be your wife.' He extended a hand to Lakshmi, who sheepishly took it. 'Hullo, I'm Nath. Nath Ratnaike. I'm a member of the Wesley College Old Boys Union.'

That was when it clicked. He was the son of the old vice-principal. I met him every year at the big match and the old boys' stag nights.

'Nice to meet you,' said Lakshmi, also hiding anger behind a smile.

'Are you here to see the doctor, Mr Herath?' said Nath. 'I hope it's nothing serious.'

'Not for me – it's for Lakshmi. It's just a regular check-up.'

'I have some headaches,' said Lakshmi.

'Have you got an appointment? You know, my wife works at the hospital. I can get you one – you don't have to wait in line. Which doctor do you need to see, Mr Herath?'

'Doctor Palihakkara.'

'If you can give me a minute, I'll make the appointment.' He pulled out his mobile phone and dialled. 'That'll be seven-fifty,' he whispered, covering the microphone with one hand and extending the other.

I avoided Lakshmi's stare as she pulled money out of her purse and handed it over to Nath. The fellow then disappeared into the crowd. Lakshmi and I stood there pretending everything was hunky-dory until Nath returned with the receipt.

'Thank you very much,' said Lakshmi. 'We didn't know how we'd get to the end of that queue.'

'You're welcome, Mrs Herath. Anything I can do to help.'

'Thank you, Nath.' I shook his hand. After saying he'd look forward to seeing me at the next big match, Nath went away.

It was another awkward half an hour or so until the doctor saw us. Palihakkara checked Lakshmi's blood pressure and shone a torch in her eyes and ears and put a stethoscope on her chest. He asked us to get blood tests – full blood count, platelet and whatnot – and scribbled the details. There was a payment for that also, which Lakshmi made quietly at the outside counter. She didn't even show me the receipt, just shoved it in her purse and went and got the blood drawn while I stayed in the waiting area.

A week later the results came back. I called Palihakkara to read the reports and he said everything was normal.

Nothing to worry. He asked if we had any problems – if there was tension at home, stress, depression, etc.

'No, no, Doc, we're happily married,' I said and finished the conversation.

—

It was a month of big news. We were on the brink of winning the war, which was why Defence Ministry buggers were crawling all around the newsroom. I usually tried to keep Mihil away, send him off on some other business when the ministry men came, but my luck had run out. Today, he was standing right in front as the two fellows sweating in their army uniforms briefed the editorial team. They gave us facts, names of places, numbers – of regiments, of weapons they had recovered, of the dead. I groaned silently as Mihil jumped in.

'Is that the total number of dead? Or LTTE only?'

'LTTE only,' one of the ministry fellows said.

Mihil was always pushing, always asking difficult questions, never happy with the information that was given. I had told him many times: 'Let it go. War is chaos and they aren't reporters.' But he was relentless. 'How many soldiers died?' he said.

'We don't have that information.'

'Civilians?'

'No.'

'No civilians died or no information?'

'No civilian casualties.'

'Is it hot in the north these days?'

'It's always hot in the north.'

'Hotter than usual?'

They looked in their files. 'We don't have the information.'

'Is there enough water? Drinking water for the people?'

'Don't know.'

'What about—'

'That's enough, Mr de Soyza.' I glared at Mihil and apologised to the army chaps, saying, 'This fellow is a real joker. Thinks he's funny. Don't listen to him,' and then I guided them out of the office. 'Thank you, officers.'

After the army guys left and I closed the door, I said to Mihil, 'You always have something to prove, no?'

'I was only getting the details. How to write a good piece without details?'

'Write around it.' That's what I told all the staff. 'That's a talent only some of us have. Those are our little miracles – turning nothing into something.' Have to support the country, no?

I was going to give him the full lecture again but the phone in my office started ringing. I left Mihil to do whatever he wanted and answered the call. It was the board president himself. Mr Bamunuaracchi wanted to see me. 'Let Rozairo write this one,' I said to Mihil as I left the building.

I went through the car park, past the toilets and into the management offices. Mr Bamunuaracchi's secretary smiled and motioned towards his door. I went through and around the plant that had grown so big the leaves scratched your face if you went directly to the chair. Sitting behind his big desk in his freshly ironed shirt and tie, the gold pen gleaming in his pocket, Mr Bamunuaracchi looked every bit the respectable gentleman. He asked me to sit down and signalled to his peon to make a cup of tea. Wiji, the peon in the newsroom, had already served me first thing in the morning, so I said, 'Not for me, sir.'

Mr Bamunuaracchi put on his glasses and picked up the morning papers. Was he going to read something to me? Had we printed a mistake?

'Mr Herath, we got the latest figures. Circulation has fallen below the *Daily Mirror*. When you started we were third, no? Such a fall in five years?'

I knew why but I didn't say it: people had changed. People didn't care about the sort of news we wrote anymore. They wanted to hear about the celebrities, about the ministers' sons and daughters, about television actors, about Angelina Jolie.

Mr Bamunuaracchi knew it too. 'Our Saturday entertainment magazine is the most popular section. Then it's sports – that's if our boys win the cricket match. People tell me to my face, "That's all we read, Mr Bamunuaracchi – sports and social pages."'

'It's true,' I said. 'Things have changed.'

Mr Bamunuaracchi nodded, took out a handkerchief and wiped his big fruit-like nose. 'I know the climate is bad,' he said. He was right. There was a time when we talked about real problems, discussed politics, the security situation. Of course whenever war flared up, whenever we fought properly, the way this current government did, everything changed. Bloody Tigers forced it. None of our chaps could go out to the north or east and report – and their propaganda made all sorts of accusations, always using words like 'genocide' and 'war crimes'. All bloody lies. They were the ones who committed war crimes with their child soldiers and attacks on civilians.

'And this internet,' I said. 'The news is there and it's free and no one has to buy the papers.'

'We'll have to come up with something. Very soon,' he said.

'Yes, sir. We'll find a way. Necessity is—'

'Thank you, Mr Herath.' Mr Bamunuaracchi took his glasses off and wiped them with his handkerchief.

'Thank you, sir.' I got up and walked around the tree, out of the air-conditioned office and back into the heat.

What can we do? Can't do anything. When I stepped into the newsroom and looked around all I saw was a business in decline. The walls hadn't been painted in a decade. They were so covered in fingerprints that if the cops came and checked them against their records they were sure to solve a few cases. The partitions were old and broken, leaning this way and that. I worried one would topple and the rest would go like dominoes. There were only two telephones for ten journalists and the internet took a century for a simple document to download. Still, half the fellows wrote what they found on the Sirasa or Ada Derana news websites. Some at least took that information and added some details – others barely changed the words. They made my blood pressure rise on a daily basis. But I sometimes felt sorry for them. Their salaries were disgracefully low. Look at them, dressed in cheap clothes bought from the pavement – I mean, half the chaps wore their rubber slippers to work!

I didn't have answers. I just had to do my job, print the sort of things fed to us by the ministries – about the LTTE and their expatriate rump pulling wool over the eyes of the UN and the so-called humanitarian agencies, about the hidden imperialist agendas of the west. Stories we found on our own were things like the dengue epidemic in the south, a car accident on Baseline Road or the small-fry currency smuggling rackets and drug busts at the ports — of course, there were bigger fish behind those operations, everybody knew. But our company was already down and one kick from a big shot and we would all be out of a job — so no, we didn't get into all that muckraking. Muckrakers didn't do well. Half of them disappeared. Some reappeared, in another country or on the internet. But mostly it was a deathly silence. Lasantha, probably our last investigative journalist and editor of our most controversial newspaper, was murdered. That grave was still fresh and I wasn't keen on digging more. And I'm not Jesus. I can't give life to the dead.

Problem was, that was what Mihil thought he was — some kind of prophet. Fellow thought he could say whatever he liked and get away with it. Twelve years on the job and he still hadn't learned. Even now, I knew from the look on his face he was up to something. As he came into my office without being asked, my chest felt tight.

'What do you want now?'

'I just want to ask you something,' he said, sitting down at the desk.

'What is it?'

'Now, it's not completely . . .' He opened his hands and put them up, side by side, like he was showing me the size of his newborn baby's head. 'It's not really within our mandate, but I was hoping . . .'

'Tell me what it is without beating round the bush, you bugger.'

'I was thinking. We should do a write-up on 13 Plus.'

'What?'

'The Thirteenth Amendment, sir. This is the right time to do it.' He smiled and nodded, as if I'd agreed with him. 'Don't you think? It's the perfect opportunity to talk about devolution of power.'

'Are you mad?' I said. 'The war is almost finished. We've won. Why would we need to devolve power? All the people want, even the Tamils, is for the war to end. Not some federal system. You're a hell of a bugger, Mihil. If we publish the things you want, we won't sell a single paper. People will laugh at us. They'll call us bloody traitors, and then both you and me will be pushed into a white van, get beaten to a pulp and end up in some paddy field with bullets in our heads.'

—

I went home early for a change and found myself wandering in Niranjan's room. He wasn't there, only his clothes all over the floor. I put them in the clothes basket and looked at all his silverware. The trophies he got for water polo – little sculptures of swimmers, some without heads, others with a ball a little too big, all the bronze rusting. There were the medals he'd won at sports meets for the four hundred metres and the four-into-hundred relay, hanging from the neck of the large trophy he got for – what was it for? The essay competition! That's it! I remember all those events. I was there for most of them. I was so proud when the little fellow went up on stage and took the prize. But where was Niranjan now? Working hard, surely, and just like his old man, making a name for himself.

Then I went into Anoushka's room. She was leaning over her desk, doing homework or studying for an exam. 'Hullo, Anoushka,' I said. 'What are you doing?'

'Studying,' she said without even looking up at me. 'Why?'

'Carry on. I won't disturb you.'

I watched her write with her left hand, just like her mother, a very serious girl, very focused on what she was doing. The look on her face changed as her mind went from one thing to another like the sky on one of those raining but shining days. Her hair was growing long and kept falling onto her forehead and over her eyes and she let it fall. Why didn't she brush it away? How could she read like that? Why didn't she get it cut short like before?

'What?' she said, finally looking at me.

'Nothing, Anoushka. You go ahead.'

'Why are you looking at me?'

'Nothing, nothing. I'm going, okay?'

I went and paced around in the living room for a while. Nobody had bothered to ask me, 'How was your day, Mano?' or even offered me a cup of tea. I started noticing things, like the dust gathered on windowsills and covering the photos on the wall. The photo of me with the president was face-down on the shelf. The brass ornaments like the lamp with the cockerel on top, the three elephants holding up the bowl – they were all going green. This place was going to the dogs. Literally. Outside, the garden smelled like choo because all of the neighbourhood mongrels had started using our gate as a toilet. My car tyres sometimes trampled the balu kakka on the way out. What was the servant doing all day? Dreaming. Muttering about her brother. Shouldn't encourage that fellow to visit regularly. I still didn't believe he was really her brother. Normally, Lakshmi would have sorted it out. But Lakshmi was preoccupied. Couldn't get anything done.

I needed to have a good think so I did a couple of shots in my room. I was drinking arrack; the Old Reserve was much cheaper than the Johnnie Walker, but it was decent, and it helped clear my mind. After I had a few I realised – it'll all be fine. Maybe it was the alcohol talking, but I felt sure of it. Lakshmi had even said, 'See you later,' when she got out of the car this morning, no? She was getting better. The visit to the doctor had done her good, surely. Placebo effect or whatever it was, now she knew there was nothing wrong. Lakshmi's always reluctant to show her cards. Very tough, like the rest of her kind – not that I think of her as a Tamil. My wife was like a Sinhala woman in every way. She was waiting for me to make a move. I just had to show her how I felt. That was it!

I put the drink down and tiptoed out into the hallway, where I put my ear to her door and listened – couldn't hear a thing. The handle creaked as I twisted it. I went in. She was having a nap and it was dark in her room. I had to go very slowly to make sure I didn't fall over. When my knees hit the edge of her bed I stopped and waited for my eyes to adjust. I could finally see her, at least her outline, lying on her side, knees together, one arm underneath the pillow and the other behind her like she was handcuffed or something. I waited for her to wake up for a long time, but how long can you wait? I had an idea.

What if I got into bed so that when she woke up she'd get a good surprise? Who knows, maybe she'd even feel a little naughty. My god, I remember the days when we did a regular trip down to Galle or up country. In those places Lakshmi was more romantic. It was an unusual thing for her – must have been something to do with salt in the air, the never-ending water at the doorstep or the mountains that touched the sky that made her shower in the evening and not bother putting on a nightie when she came out of the bathroom. The lights were off but I could see her shining hips, those breasts, her hair still damp and stuck to her neck as she walked steadily towards me and got into bed. That's how I remember her when, even now, through some small miracle, I see her naked and remind myself – she's the love of my life.

Sitting down first, then leaning on my hands, I slowly lowered my body beside her and swung my legs onto the bed. Lakshmi stirred but didn't wake up. There was very little room in that single bed and if I shifted weight I would have gone over. It was a wonder I didn't fall off – even more so that I somehow fell asleep.

I woke up to a buzzing sound in my ear. I first thought it was a mosquito but the buzzing turned into words. 'Mano? What's wrong? Are you feeling sick? Did you forget where you were?' It was Lakshmi. She had her hand on my shoulder. She was whispering sweet words. 'Are you all right, Mano? What happened? How did you get here? Do you know where you are?'

I struggled to turn around and face her and Lakshmi moved to make room, even tugged on my shoulder to help. But as soon as I turned, smiling like a maniac, the spell was broken. Lakshmi made a face, as if she had seen the dirtiest rotten piece of kakka in the world.

'Get out,' she said, and pushed herself away. 'You're a dirty man.'

Was I so ugly? Was there something about that dim light that made me look so shockingly bad? 'Come on, Lakshmi,' I said. 'Sleep a little more.'

'Old drunkard. Here I was thinking you were sick. Should have known. You're stinking like arrack. Did you think I was going to baby you? If you're drunk you better go and sleep it off. In your own bed.'

'Come on, Lakshmi,' I said again. 'Come here, will you? For old time's sake.' I stayed there to see if she would change her mind.

She rolled off the bed, the springs creaking. 'Old times? This is not the old times. Times have changed.'

'How have they changed?'

She got to her feet. 'Maybe for you, nothing's changed. Maybe you were always like this. We just know who you are now.'

'What are you talking?'

'When was the last time you came home early?'

'I came today,' I joked, but she couldn't see my smile in the dark. 'You know what my work's like, Lakshmi.'

'So it's because of your work you're getting late, is it? No other reason?'

'What other reason?'

'You're not chasing women?'

'Don't be silly. You're imagining things.'

'I'm imagining?'

'Yes! Always imagining that I'm doing the wrong thing. Always trying to make trouble.'

'If it was only my imagination . . . but now, people are starting to talk.'

'What? Who's been telling you stories?'

'Doesn't matter. Question is, what were you doing at Ramani Amarasinghe's funeral?'

'What funeral?' I had to think of an excuse quickly. 'Oh, *that* funeral. That was bloody centuries ago.'

'Last month. I know you went.'

'Yes, I went! Can't I go to a funeral?'

'Who's that woman to you? How do you know Ramani Amarasinghe?'

'I used to work with her. She was at the Plantation Ministry. That was before she married Anuruddha Amarasinghe. We used to be friends . . . not friends, but friendly, you know, like you're friendly with people at your office.'

'I'm friendly but I don't get too familiar.'

'I heard she passed away so I went to . . . to pay my respects.'

'Why didn't you tell us you were going?'

'I don't have to tell you all my movements. What is this? I can't go telling you everything.'

She paused, unsure of making the big accusation. 'So you're not lying? You only went because you worked together?'

'Yes!'

'So there was nothing between you and this Ramani?'

'No! How many times do I have to say it?'

She sat back on the edge of the bed. 'I used to tell you everything, Mano. Remember? Now I'm not sure. I don't know if you'll help me or go and tell some other woman all about me.'

'Don't be ridiculous.'

'I don't know what you're doing, where you're going. I don't . . .'

'You don't trust me?'

'No. To be honest, I don't.'

I didn't know what to say. There was nothing I could tell her to win back her trust.

'There are things I want to tell you. A normal husband and wife would share these things.'

'You can trust me.'

'I don't know . . .' She thought about it for a little. 'I'll tell you, but you can't tell anyone,' she said. 'Promise.'

'I promise. If there's anything I can do . . .'

She told me all of her usual motherly worries about not being able to control Niranjan, about Anoushka not studying. I thought it was going to be the usual list of complaints, but then, just like that, she unloaded a bombshell she had been carrying all this time right onto my head. I should've stayed in my room. This is what happens when you try to be too nice.

—

I used to come and wait, holding a file, hoping to see something nice. Now I just came for some peace and quiet. I would've gone somewhere else but Buller's Road felt comfortable. Sitting here in the dark, I noticed windows I didn't know were there, the shadows of those big houses falling across the road, joining the shadows of trees and other big houses. You started to hear things happening inside the tall walls, the sound of servants moving about, cleaning, cooking and whatnot. Then the gates opened automatically, maybe with the press of a button, a switch on a remote controller, and out came the young sallalayas, the nightclub Buddhists, the alcoholic Muslims and the unrepentant Christians – boys and girls wearing shiny things, busy talking into shinier things. They didn't even notice me sitting there, smoking. I could have been a terrorist, a Tiger with a massive bomb who could blow the whole neighbourhood to kingdom come, but none of these buggers cared. Their minds were already somewhere else – who knows where.

After that it was quiet. So quiet you might think nobody in those mansions breathed. Anuruddha Amarasinghe's house was particularly dead. No light in Ramani's room. I waited and waited for her to come out, but she didn't, for obvious reasons. But I sometimes wondered, what if she had set the whole thing up and pretended to die to stop me from coming? And when she saw that I was onto her, she would've thought, 'This Mano fellow is very smart – there's no fooling him.' If she was doing that, she didn't learn quickly. She kept hiding. Then, I saw Anuruddha Amarasinghe coming home from work a little later than usual. One look at his face and I could tell Ramani was really dead. Either that or he was a really good actor. Soon, that panditha military police bugger, Jayantha, came over and leaned on the roof of my car.

'This nice car, Mr Herath.'

'My wife doesn't like it.'

'Why she not like? It's good car, no?'

'She says it's too expensive.'

Then Jayantha asked me for a cigarette. I gave him one through the open shutter and handed over the lighter. The fellow lit up and sucked it in. 'How is your work, Mr Herath?' he asked.

'I can't tell you,' I said. 'You might put me in a white van.'

Jayantha laughed quietly and said, 'That's not good thing for you to talk.' He became serious. 'Why you are doing this job, Mr Herath?'

'Why are you doing your job?'

'I am doing for my country.'

'Then I'm also doing this for the country,' I said.

'You get good money?'

'No.'

'Then why? You can get better job, no?'

'I told you, I'm doing this for my country.'

'Then you and me – same.'

He came around to the passenger side and opened the door. I didn't say anything. What right did he have to come and sit in my car? Still, I didn't want any trouble, so I let him get comfortable, let him lean the seat right back and talk his nonsense. He picked up my mobile phone that I'd left in the cup holder. He turned it on and started playing with it. Bugger must have pressed something, because it started ringing.

'What did you press?' I said.

'Nothing. It's phone call. Call for you.'

I took the phone from him and answered. 'Hullo?'

'Mr Herath?' It was Mihil. He sounded unusually excited. 'I just heard the war is about to end. The Tigers are being finished off.'

'My god! Are you in the office, Mihil?'

'I'm on the way.'

'I'll be there in ten minutes.'

LAKSHMI

NORMALLY I'M THE ONLY ONE IN THE LANE TO BE AWAKE ALL night, waiting. But the past few nights had been unusual. Everyone was up, lighting crackers, talking in excited voices, celebrating. It was like 1996 all over again, like when we won the World Cup and all of Colombo was excited.

The north and east were quiet. The war had ended, a sheet pulled over its face. I almost couldn't believe it. I stopped getting emails with pictures of the dead. No stories of devastation. There were calls, but none from the people who wanted favours. Maybe now, all those who'd tried to lay their troubles on my shoulders had finally given up. The boy was still lost, but there was nothing I could do. I had asked Mano to help the day he tried to sleep in my bed, but he was useless. All I had was a name, Khanna, and a memory of skin as dark as teak.

In the morning the party continued on the street. Acchis fed soldiers kiribath and seeyas played rabang, their fingers drumming the cowhide silly. Politicians congratulated the nation, the army and themselves. The sort of people

Niranjan called 'sarong-Johnnies' danced on the backs of trucks and waved flags. That flag – with the lion with its sword against the marrow-coloured background – it was everywhere. Lining the streets, sticking out of vehicles, flapping on top of every roof and waving from the top corner of every TV channel. The Pereras next door had put one on the aerial of their car. The Bandaras two doors up had stuck one through the metal grille covering their front windows. There was even one tied to bamboo scaffolding at the building site now owned by a Chinese businessman at the top of the lane. Only the Ludowyks didn't have one, probably because those Burghers were too old to even know what was happening.

And us. We didn't own a flag.

Latha came with the morning tea, saying, 'Nona, thé.'

I didn't open my eyes. It was a bad headache. I couldn't make things better.

'Nona,' she said a little louder. She put the teacup on the bedside table and kneeled. 'Nona,' she said quietly into my ear. 'Negitinna. Wedata yanne nedda?'

I knew it was a workday; she didn't have to tell me. 'Let me be,' I said.

'Nona, asaneepada?' She touched my head for the temperature with her turmeric-smelling hands.

'Are you a doctor?'

'Neh, mama bus condostara.' Her smile showed all her cracked teeth. It was a silly old joke my children used to make but it made me smile: 'I'm not a doctor, I'm a bus conductor.' Latha was full of that childish talk. She went over and pulled the curtains open. My eyes burned. When they got used to the brightness I saw Latha was leaning out the window.

'Nona kodiyak demmada?'

'What?'

I got out of bed gingerly and walked across to the window. There was a flag stuck between the roof tiles and gutter, fluttering lightly. It was a small one, paper and not cloth, not much longer than the length of my palm.

'Who put it there?'

The woman shrugged. 'Mang nemayi. Mahattaya-da?'

It couldn't be Mano. Mano was too busy and too selfish. Lazy. He always asked me if he wanted anything done. Couldn't even make a cup of tea himself. And Anoushka? She didn't care about such things.

I put on my housecoat and slippers and went around to the front. Reaching up, I touched the shiny print with the tips of my fingers. I could have pulled it down, but then the neighbours might have thought I didn't support the country. I support the country. I'm proud. But were the north and east proud? Were they covered in flags too? Was the poor boy wrapped in one? One with a picture of a lion or a tiger?

'Latha, did you see anyone?'

The only person tall enough to reach the gutter was Niranjan. Everyone else would have needed a stool. Latha would have needed a ladder. She looked as confused as I was.

'Who did this?' I asked her again.

'Danné na, Nona.'

'We have to find who.' I went back inside to call work. For the past twenty years I'd gone to work every day and only taken leave when the children were not well. One day of sick leave wouldn't hurt.

—

The terrible fate of a mother is that her child will one day leave. At first they seem close but boys are forever drifting away, just to trouble their parents. Ever since he got back from Australia, Niranjan's been doing things to try and upset me. Is that what Khanna was doing? Trying to scare his poor father?

Niranjan goes roung-gahanna and comes back drunk in the middle of the night, gets up late the next day, goes to work and does it all over again. On weekends he goes completely missing or returns just before the sun comes up and sleeps all day. I barely see him. I tell him, 'Niranjan, what's the meaning of this?' but he just laughs, his perfect teeth making him look mean.

A couple of days ago, I woke up when he came home. I said, 'Where did you go? Why don't you tell me anything anymore? I was very worried. And you know people will start saying things if you come back so late every night. They're already talking. That fellow who sells lottery tickets near the park asked Latha if you're doing night duty. Can you believe? What shame! We have to hear things from ordinary people. Think a little before you go and do these things.'

I kept trying, kept talking, thinking something would go into his head, but like everyone these days he didn't listen to me. Halfway through my lecture he went outside to look at his car. When he came back his hands were full of dirt and grease, and when I said, 'Niranjan, go and wash your hands before you eat,' he picked up some food with his dirty hands and put it in his mouth.

He did things to hurt me. I was the person who would be affected by the flag. He knew. I ate a banana, gathered my strength and went into Niranjan's room to see what I could find. It was like a pigsty. Like a cyclone had blown right through. He had left dirty underwear, a sarong and a couple of socks right in the middle of the floor. A shirt hung off the bedpost. A whole lot of clothes, crumpled, sat on the chair like they were trying to become a person. One sock on top of the mosquito net – how it got there, god only knows. Poor Khanna probably didn't have enough clothes. I remembered how, all those years ago there wasn't much clothing to cover his body, just wounds on his arms and legs.

Niranjan's papers and files and books and notepads were all thrown around. Not one inch of the desk could be seen. Only the computer was uncovered. Even that was filthy – the keyboard had a layer of brown dirt and the screen was black on the sides. I opened the drawers but didn't look too much – there was no point. It was full of gadgets and knick-knacks – wires, computer parts, bead necklaces, gold chains, bottles of deodorant and perfume – so many I couldn't even shut it properly. I had to move a few things around and slide it back and forth. Finally closing the drawer, I stepped back – and as soon as I did that I stepped on something. It was a packet of chewing gum. When I bent over to pick it up I noticed a bottle under the bed. I left the chewing gum where it was and got on my knees to reach for the bottle. The label said Bacardi. Rum. I opened it and took a sniff. It was strong.

Here, our fellow was drinking firewater because he had nothing better to do, but Khanna was probably struggling to find clean water to quench his thirst.

I opened the cupboard and more clothes tumbled out. Took a pair of jeans off the bookshelf and its pockets were heavy. They were full of coins, business cards, one for a Duminda Samarawickrama and one for Ramona Perera from something called CTP Associates. Who was this Ramona woman? What did she want with my son? I dug a little deeper and found a half-finished packet of cigarettes. That was something I already knew about. Niranjan learned that from his father. At least Mano did it secretly, elsewhere. Not our boy. He came home, shut his door, opened a window and smoked away. Denied everything if anybody asked. Blamed the smell on a neighbour or a passer-by. 'What are you telling me for?' he always said.

'I wasn't born yesterday,' was how I answered. 'You must be thinking I'm some kind of fool.' He made me so angry, burned all the blood in my veins. I didn't know what to do – give him a slap like he was a misbehaving teenager or hit my head against the wall. I took the bottle and the cigarettes and walked out of his room.

—

I put on a sari and asked Latha to call a trishaw. She brought that fellow called Sahan who hangs around near the repairs garage. He was a pleasant boy, but like most trishaw drivers he drove fast. No matter what I shouted, the fellow soon forgot and Latha and I always had to hold on for dear life. Today it was no different – we went all the way to Maharagama in about twenty minutes. When we got out I had to comb my hair again, make sure nothing had fallen out of my bag.

We went up to Jinadasa's office, where the secretary told us to wait until we were called. The waiting room was hot, and though the ceiling fan wheezed and stuttered, the wind just wasn't enough. Everyone in there was fanning themselves with newspapers, magazines, handkerchiefs or the tails of their saris. There were a lot of people. Not only ordinary village types but well-to-do ladies and gentlemen. Jinadasa was supposed to be good at this sort of thing. Mano's sister, Nelunka, was the first to tell me, but I had also heard from others like Mrs Bibile at work that he was more like a mathematician or scientist than an astrologer. I still had doubts – he was yet to produce a result for me.

There were no empty seats and I had to stand next to the picture of the president hanging on the wall. I couldn't bear to see his face – that's why I put away his photo at home – the one with Mano shaking his hand. I had to turn my eyes away from the man in front of me reading a newspaper. I didn't want to see the headlines. I ended up staring at a plant, an old croton with dark red leaves in a plastic pot.

My name was called and Latha followed me into the office. There was a sandalwood smell coming from the corner where the brightly coloured Lord Katharagama statue stood. He had his arms spread. Some of the weapons in his twelve hands had red on the edges. Blood. Blood everywhere. My Lord, what have you done? No sooner had the thought occurred, I apologised. Scolded myself.

There was no one else I could speak to except the gods and I didn't want to lose them as well.

I closed the door. The room was air-conditioned and the windows were closed. It was filled with smoke from the burning incense and oil lamps. There was a cobra made of brass curled on top of a stack of files on the desk, a frightening paperweight with its curved hood and forked tongue. Jinadasa was like a ghost, sitting there in a white long-sleeved shirt, his grey hair combed back neatly. He got out of his chair and put his palms together. I always expected him to greet me formally with an 'ayubowan' but he never did. Instead he said, 'Hullo, Mrs Herath. Sit, sit.'

'Thank you, Mr Jinadasa.' I sat down and put my bag on the empty seat. Latha stood behind me, her knees cracking as she shifted weight.

'How did you come? Your husband brought you?'

'No, I took a trishaw,' I said.

'Mr Herath is working today?'

'Yes.'

'Traffic was okay, no? Three-wheeler would have come here in no time.'

'Yes, it was fine.'

Jinadasa turned his chair towards me and rolled it closer to the desk. 'You brought the horoscopes, no? Let's see.'

I passed the booklets to Jinadasa. He put on his glasses and opened the first one to the middle page. I leaned in and tried to make sense of the drawings. They looked like a game of tak-tik-tuk, the only difference being the four corner squares divided into triangles. I didn't know much, only that Rahu and Senasuru were the planets to watch out for, the bad ones, and I listened out for them when Jinadasa was speaking.

'How is your husband, Mrs Herath?' said Jinadasa. 'Is he okay?'

'He's fine.'

'Hmm . . .' He looked over the top of his glasses at me, as if asking a question. Was this a general question or something particular? I wasn't sure if Jinadasa wanted me to say something more, but there was nothing to say. Mano was being Mano. He was never home, always working, out drinking and avoiding coming home. What had Jinadasa seen?

'My husband's fine. Does the horoscope say something's wrong with him?'

'Oh no, I was just asking how Mr Herath was doing.'

'What does it say? Is this a Rahu time for us?'

'Nothing like that,' said Jinadasa. He put down my horoscope and opened Niranjan's.

'That's my son's. I'm having trouble with him too . . . like you said last time.'

'I was right, no? I told you.' Jinadasa's small mouth widened into something like a smile. He took off his glasses and looked at the ceiling, then opened his diary and wrote something in it. 'Kataka lagnaya singha navaanshakaya,' he said slowly.

'That's bad? Are the planets in the wrong place?'

'No, no.'

'Don't hide anything from me, please, Mr Jinadasa. I have to know, otherwise how can I do anything?'

'I was thinking only. It's not so bad . . .'

'Is it because he's done a lot of pau in his last life? Was he a sinner?'

'Kataka lagnaya singha navaanshakaya,' he said again. 'It's a little bit like a pattern that came during Lord Buddha's birth—'

'What does it mean?'

Jinadasa didn't answer. He shook his head, lifted the brass snake, took out a file and started going through the papers. His forehead wrinkled and made his eyes narrow.

'Does that mean he's going to leave us? Please tell me.'

'No, Mrs Herath. It's only a pattern.'

'But Lord Buddha left his parents and went—'

'No, this time it's not so . . . not so big.'

'It's big, Mr Jinadasa. I can tell. I can feel it. He knows me from his previous life, no? And still he has something against me.'

'I don't think so. He's in the middle of a change. A transition happening very soon.'

'True. He's so different now. Like a different person. I can't even recognise.'

Jinadasa took off his glasses and placed them on the desk. 'That's what happens when you send our young people to those countries, no? You should have known. Anyway, I will tell you what to do.'

'Please tell me.'

'You have to do a bhaaraya. A puja every week for three weeks.'

'Another one?'

'Yes.'

I had done at least five or six puja already this year. Sometimes I felt like there was a small improvement in my situation but nothing significant. Maybe I was doing something wrong. 'Please tell me exactly what to do.'

'I'll make a list of things. You go to the kovil also, Mrs Herath?'

How did he know? Did Nelunka tell him about my background or could he tell just from looking at me? 'Yes,' I said. I thought of telling him that I believe in Lord Buddha as much as Shiva and Vishnu, but kept quiet.

'Go there. Temple is good but kovil is also good. I will give you some water. It's water that I have recited manthara over.' He got out of his seat and went across to a small black cupboard. From it he took an arrack bottle filled with clear liquid. 'Take this water and sprinkle. Use kohomba branch to sprinkle on the floor everywhere, all around your house.'

Latha reached out and took the bottle from Jinadasa.

'Come back in four weeks. There are some more things for you to do.'

'Okay, Mr Jinadasa. How much is your . . .'

'Thousand-five, Mrs Herath.'

'Your charges have increased?'

'The water is five hundred.'

Five hundred rupees for a bottle of water? I thought of getting up and walking off but I couldn't take a chance, so I gave him almost everything in my purse. Only a hundred-rupee note and a few coins were left for the trishaw back. I looked at the list. That was sure to cost me at least another five hundred, leaving about four thousand in my account for the rest of the month. I might even have to use some of the savings. I wasn't sure if all this was worth the money. 'Can you tell me one more thing?'

'What, Mrs Herath?'

'I need to find . . .'

'Yes?'

I looked at Jinadasa. What would he think if I asked him about Khanna? Would he give me answers or would he report me to the police? I remembered the photograph of the president in the waiting room – it was clear which side Jinadasa was on so I asked him something else. 'Some . . . something happened in our house yesterday. Someone hung something. From our roof. Is there any way I can find out who did it?'

'What was it?'

'A flag.'

'A national flag?'

I nodded.

'Mrs Herath, flags are everywhere this week. It's a good thing. Must have been your husband or your son because they were happy, no?'

'Yes, it's . . . it's good. I just didn't know. Is it a sign of . . . of good luck or something?'

'Freedom, Mrs Herath,' said Jinadasa, his smile glinting. 'It means freedom.'

———

It was late, almost two-thirty in the afternoon. I went into Anoushka's room to find her lying around, still in her school clothes. She was pretending to sleep, eyes closed and smiling. Headphones were plugged into her ears. It was so loud I could hear a buzzing sound like a saw cutting through wood. I said, 'Turn that off, Anoushka,' but she didn't hear me. I went and shook her and she sat up so fast it was like she got an electric shock.

'I—I was, I was just sleeping,' she said, dropping the headphones and covering them with the pillow.

'How can you sleep with that noise in your ear?'

'What noise?'

'What noise? I'm talking about the headphones.' I could tell the girl was hiding something. 'What were you listening to?'

'Nothing, Ammi. Just radio. I was just switching channels . . . and I was falling asleep and I don't know what it was playing.' She reached under the pillow and pressed a button and the sound vanished.

'Why did you turn it off?'

'I wasn't listening.'

'No? What was it, Anoushka?'

'I don't know . . . I was sleeping!' She rubbed her eyes furiously to try and show she had really been sleeping.

'Fine,' I said. 'Do you know where Niranjan was yesterday?'

'Niro? He wasn't here – obviously.'

'Where was he? He talks to you, no? Did he tell you where he went?'

'What's he gone and done now?'

'That's none of your business. Answer the question – was he here?'

'I didn't see him!' She lay back and picked up a book. 'Maybe he was at a nightclub again,' she said.

'Don't be rude, Anoushka. I'm talking to you. Put that book down.'

She put it down.

'Did he tell you he was going to a nightclub?'

'Isn't that where he goes?'

I shook my head. 'He doesn't talk to me. He's turned into a big man and doesn't need any of us.'

'He's independent. Maybe he'll move out.'

'Is that what he told you? Did he tell you he was moving out?'

'Ammi, he doesn't tell me anything!'

'Where did you hear it, then?'

'Um, I guessed . . . it was like, a deduction.'

'Deduction, ah?' The girl was bright but sometimes she got a big head and thought she could teach me. 'Deduction. Where do you learn these things? From the television? From your books? Or from that thing under the pillow? Let's see what it's telling you. Give me that radio,' I said.

'What radio?'

'That iPod.'

'I don't have an iPod. Remember I asked for one and you said—'

'That thing under your pillow, give it to me now.'

Reluctantly, she put her hand under the pillow and brought out the plastic gadget. I took the headphones and put them in my ears. 'Turn it on,' I said.

'I don't know what it'll be,' said Anoushka. 'If it's something bad, it's not my fault.' She pressed a button and a harsh sound filled my head. It was horrific – all screaming and rattling, the sound of bombs falling, destroying everything.

Even after I had scolded Anoushka and taken away the music player I could still hear it, ringing in my ears.

It echoed while I picked flowers from the jasmine vine, unbalanced me as I lit the lamps and prayed. I sat down for a little and it lessened, but something still followed like a shadow on my mind. It vibrated in my skull as I got Latha to spray the manthara water everywhere.

Anoushka didn't help with that. She sat there and laughed and asked questions when Latha and I went into her room with a bowl and a branch. 'What are you doing? Is it like, a saasthara thing? Did you pay the saasthara man a lot? Thatthi says it's all a con. Don't put any water on me, okay?'

I ignored her and told Latha where to spray the water. The servant dipped the branch in the bowl and shook it so the droplets flew everywhere. If I hadn't been there the woman would have done a half-job, missing the spaces under the beds and behind furniture, but I made sure it was done properly. Niranjan's room got an extra dose. I told Latha not to worry about the clothes on the ground. 'Just kick it all aside and spray,' I said. 'Actually, go ahead and sprinkle the clothes . . . and put some on his bed and his desk also. Be careful you don't get any on his computer – he'll get an electric shock. Open his cupboard and put some in there. Spray some over the books – his trophies as well.' We went outside and sprayed the garden too, all around the house.

When we finished I was tired. My ears were still making kunu-kunu sounds, as if an insect had gone inside. It didn't stop nagging. I went back to my room and lay on my side so that the noises would disappear.

—

Snakes. Snakes everywhere. One was curling around my neck. I pushed it away as it hissed in my ear.

'Wake up, Lakshmi.'

I opened my eyes.

'I got a call from Nelunka. She asked if we were coming to Heshan's birthday.'

My head was full of water. Mano's figure swam and shivered. Finally, my eyes focused on him, leaning over me.

'We have to go. The birthday party will start soon,' he said.

It wasn't a snake but Mano's tie tickling my neck.

'Today?' I asked.

'Yes, yes. Today.'

'It's . . . It's the nineteenth of May, no? I completely forgot.'

'Get dressed, otherwise we'll be late,' said Mano, unbuttoning his workshirt.

'What time is it?'

'Almost six-thirty. I got late because of traffic.'

'Do you have a present?' I asked, trying to sit up.

Of course he hadn't bought a birthday present. Normally I was the person who would have remembered. I would have gone and got a shirt from House of Fashions. Only I knew the size. He was Mano's nephew, but Mano didn't know a thing. If he was buying I had to tell him every time: 'Collar size sixteen for Heshan. He's half a size bigger than Niranjan.' Even then he sometimes got it wrong.

'No, I didn't remember,' he said. 'We can get something and send it to Heshan later.'

'We can't go empty-handed,' I said. 'You want to go waving your arms into Sumith's house?'

'No time. We might miss the cake cutting and that'll be much worse. Nelunka said they'll do it around seven and there's going to be traffic to Battaramulla.' Mano moved towards the door.

'No.' I shook my head and lay back down.

'What do you mean, no? There'll be traffic. At this time there's—'

'I'm not coming.'

'But . . . you have to come. How can I go alone?' He stopped in his tracks. Turned back.

'Take Anoushka.'

'But Lakshmi, it's really odd for me to go without you. What will people say?'

I didn't answer. I closed my eyes and pretended to be asleep.

'Look here.' He came back and sat on the bed. 'I'll tell you what. I'll put some money in an envelope and write *Dear Heshan*—'

'Whose money?'

'*Wishing you a very happy birthday, from*—'

'Whose money will you put in the envelope?'

'I'll put the money . . . my money. Not yours. Okay? Is that what this is about? Money?'

It wasn't only about money. It was also about a lot of other things. I didn't trust Mano. He said he was looking for Khanna, but he had nothing to show. He was irresponsible. He wasted all his money on the car. He told me it was a good investment but of course he was lying. Cars don't get more expensive when they get older – they're not wine. And that must be the other thing he spent it on. Firewater. But how much can you drink?

Maybe it was women? After my boss, Mr Muthalif, saw him looking upset at that Ramani woman's funeral, I was sure she had been one of Mano's obsessions. But he swore he only knew her a long time ago from the Plantation Ministry. I didn't know what to believe.

'Lakshmi.' He looked at me stupidly. 'Just come, will you? Otherwise I'm going to call Nelun and make some excuse, say you're sick.'

'I am.'

'But the doctor said there's nothing wrong. This will be good for you, to get out of the house, talk to some people and have a nice meal.'

'I'm tired and I don't feel good and I don't want to put up with your sister.'

'She's a very annoying woman, I know. But—'

'Okay, okay.'

'Okay what?'

'I'll get dressed.'

———

It was dark by the time we got to Battaramulla. The lane was full of vehicles. We parked among the brand-new Benzs, BMWs and Pajeros all lined up with drivers waiting. Mano started fussing over his car, rubbing a small dent on the mudguard and wiping some dust from the bonnet.

'Leave it,' I said. 'It's not going to turn into a Benz.'

It wasn't just Mano – Anoushka was also taking her time, sitting in the car and playing with her dress. 'Anoushka, what are you doing?' I said. She got out slowly. 'Go in front of us.'

She went a little way but kept turning around, looking back and fidgeting with her sleeves. I knew it was a protest about her music player. It was also because I got her to wear a nice long dress – the maroon one. She had, as usual, put on her old jeans and I told her, 'You're not wearing that.' I didn't want her looking like a boy. She was too old for it. So now she dragged her feet. When we got to the gate I had to give her a little push to go through.

The garden was all lit up with gaudy Christmas lights wrapped around the trees. People sat on the chairs spread around the lawn or stood and talked. Waiters dressed in black pants and white shirts served drinks and short-eats – things like sausages, prawns fried in batter and crackers piled with various colourful vegetables and pastes. There was a buffet table watched over by a man in a chef's hat on the front veranda.

It wasn't difficult to find Sumith. He was standing near the table with the alcohol, surrounded by all the pot-bellied big shots. He had a glass of whisky in one hand while he talked with the other. Sumith was one of those people who didn't only talk with his mouth. His left hand was moving fast, and when he saw us coming he lifted it and shouted, 'Ah, brother-in-law! Come, come! Come put a drink with us. Lakshmi! How are you? Haven't seen you in a long time. And Anoushka Baba! Please, come and have something to eat.'

'Hullo!' said Mano. 'Where's the birthday boy? We should wish him before we do anything else.'

'Bugger was here five minutes ago. Where's he gone?' Sumith shouted at the top of his voice for his wife – 'Nelun!

Where are you?' – and then grumbled, 'Mother and son are both missing in action.'

The words pricked my skin. Missing in action. When did it become such a normal thing to say? I felt uncomfortable but maintained my smile and said, 'We'll find him.' I took Anoushka's hand and left Mano with the gentlemen. We walked around the garden, Anoushka pointing out politicians and Sinhala movie stars busy drinking strong drinks and chewing cold meats: 'That's the minister who punched that priest in parliament,' or 'That's the actor who took off his pants in front of the schoolgirls.' I told her to keep her voice down but was glad Anoushka was smart enough to laugh at these idiots – and at Sumith and Nelunka for putting on this boru show.

We wandered past the pond, lit up with a spotlight so you could see the fish swimming in between the lotus leaves, and into the house, wiping our feet on the carpet, making sure we didn't bring any grass onto the marble floor. Sumith and Nelunka had many servants, who were barely seen but managed to do their job beautifully. They kept the place spotless. Pity it was all so goday – all gold fittings and flowery curtains, massive vases and shiny ceramic ornaments crowding that big house. The entry to the living room had paper cuttings hung across it, spelling out the words: *HAPPY BIRTHDAY HESH.* I wondered if they had run out of letters but soon realised it was their way of being hi-fi, their way of being, as Anoushka would say, 'cool'.

As we walked in the wives were all talking at the same time. The loudest voice was Nelunka's and she was spreading rumours, as usual. 'They're saying he's not really dead, that it was his body-double. Prabhakaran had another man, like a bodyguard, who was just like him—' She saw me and stopped. There was a panicked look on her face, but it wasn't hard for me to pretend I didn't hear anything. I was used to it.

'But they said in the news the army shot him,' someone else continued. 'They have the body, no?'

Nelunka, who was seated on the leather sofa, turned her head in a very obvious way, raised her eyebrows and smiled uncomfortably, letting the others know we were there. The room went silent.

We walked closer. It was always like this. They watched us, talked about us, but never said anything out of the ordinary when we were there. 'Hullo,' I said.

'Lakshmi, hullo!' said Nelunka. 'How are you? And Anoushka. Kohomada, darling?'

'Fine, Aunty,' said Anoushka.

'We couldn't find Heshan to wish him,' I said. 'Where is he?'

'Why don't you come and sit here?' said Nelunka, making some room on the sofa. 'Hesh won't be here for a while. He's gone for a drive. He got a new car for his birthday and he's showing it to Ravin and Rajiv . . . you've met Hesh's friends, Ravin and Rajiv, no?'

'Yes, I met them last time,' I said, moving the cushion with gold roses sewn on it out of the way. Anoushka balanced on the armrest because all the other seats were taken, and leaned against me. I put my arm around her to make sure she wouldn't fall.

'It's a beautiful car,' said Ms Boralessa, Sumith's unmarried older sister. 'A small Nissan. A sports car.

What is it called, Nelun? X or Y or something, just a letter. Funny name for a car.' She took a sip from her glass of sherry.

A waiter quickly came along and offered me wine in a crystal glass. I said no thanks and asked for soft drinks for both of us.

'Z,' said Nelunka. 'Nissan Z. It's as good as a Porsche. That's what Ravin and Rajiv said. They're Mr Kulathilaka's sons. You know, the cabinet minister?'

'That's the car all the boys are talking about,' said Mrs Fernando, a thin lady wearing a heavy gold necklace. 'My daughter's boyfriend keeps pestering his father to buy one for him. Wait till he hears that Hesh got one. He'll be so jealous.'

'Did Heshan get his licence?' I asked. 'He's not eighteen yet, no? Your driver must be driving.'

Another pause. Everyone looked at me again. The waiter came back with two ginger beers. I took a small sip from mine and hoped they would ignore what I'd said and continue.

'He's seventeen today,' said Nelunka, recovering quickly. 'And no, the driver's here. Hesh is a very good driver. And it's only for a short one. And Rajiv, Mr Kulathilaka's older son, he's there, no? He's very sensible. Did you know he studied law at Harvard?'

'Really? At Harvard! He must be a very bright boy,' said Ms Boralessa, her smile gone pink with all the lipstick on her front teeth.

'Oh, yes. He finished last year. Now he's come back to help his father. He's going to work at the Ministry of

Education. That's what good children do, no? They go abroad to study but come straight back.'

'Sometimes that's hard to do,' said a big lady dressed in a massive white kurta and pyjama-like pants. I couldn't remember her name. 'My daughter lives in London, with her husband, and she comes every year. She's settled there and it's a lovely place—'

'I'm so sorry, Yasmine – I didn't mean your daughter! Sometimes there are these fellows who go abroad and forget all about where they come from. They grow their hair and put on earrings and get tattoos – they do all these samayang things – and it looks so bad! They're the sorts of people I'm talking about. Your daughter is a lovely girl. I know her, no?'

'I know,' said Yasmine. 'That's fine, I know . . .'

'Are you worried about sending Heshan abroad?' I said, trying to be helpful. I knew it was probably in the back of Nelunka's mind, and having experienced firsthand the difficulty of sending your only son away, I thought I could share it with her.

'Hesh? There's still time for that, no? And anyway, Hesh is . . . I can trust Hesh,' said Nelunka, a little bit annoyed. 'Actually, we're thinking Princeton or Cambridge. I think Hesh will prefer Princeton. He doesn't like the weather in the UK. Last time we went there he got a terrible cold.'

It was a ridiculous thing to say. Heshan was anything but an intelligent boy. He had barely passed his O-Levels. 'Really? Princeton?' It burst out of me before I could stop myself.

I didn't mean to put her down, but Nelunka took it badly. She immediately hit back. 'What's that good one in Sydney? University of Sydney? Is that the one Niro went to?'

'No, Niranjan went somewhere else.'

'What was it called?'

'UTS.'

'I haven't heard about that one,' said Ms Boralessa. 'Is it recognised?'

'Yes,' I said. 'It's one of the top universities in Australia.'

'You know, Niro called earlier,' said Nelunka. 'He said he's coming a little late. Said he has some work to do.'

I looked at her face, at the eyelashes covered in layers upon layers of mascara, at her thin lips made bigger by fuchsia lipstick. I looked for a signal that this was also a Nelunka-way of niggling me. 'Niranjan called you?' I asked.

'Yes. He comes every now and then, to see Heshan and talk to Sumith.' Nelunka turned towards the other ladies and announced, 'Lakshmi's son, the one who studied economics in Sydney, he's a very nice boy. He comes here all the time. Really *loves* his uncle and his cousin. You should see.'

'What does he do?' asked Mrs Fernando.

'He has a start-up company,' I said.

'I have heard about this,' said Ms Boralessa. 'Start-up companies. It's a new invention.' Luckily, nobody wanted to admit they knew very little about such things and the topic of conversation changed.

—

It was with a lot of difficulty that I managed to smile and nod for almost an hour before Heshan came back with his friends. He made his way through the crowd like a hero, getting his hand shaken, getting kissed on both fat cheeks, getting gifts of all shapes and sizes, mainly from his parents' friends. Heshan didn't have many friends of his own. I had always suspected there was something wrong with him – you could see it in his squint, in the way one side of his jaw was a little shallower than the other – autism or something like that. Of course Nelunka and Sumith thought he was Lord Buddha reincarnated and gave him everything he asked. Like the time the fellow said he wanted to start a band and Sumith went and got all the musical instruments – guitars, drums, speakers, even the microphones. The boy never learned how to play anything. Now all of it is in a cupboard or the basement, getting dusty. I could have taken any bet that this car wouldn't be his favourite thing for long.

Not long after Heshan returned, all the guests were asked to come outside. A table had been cleared for the birthday cake. As everyone gathered around, I stood behind two girls who had started talking to Anoushka. One was wearing a nice collarless navy blue dress, the other an open top that showed too much of her shoulders. Mano appeared like magic and stood next to us, saying, 'Only my second,' when I looked at his drink.

The song started. I mouthed the words to 'Happy Birthday' as the candles were lit, clapped when the cake was cut. When it finished, Sumith shouted, 'Three cheers for the Hesh-man! Hip-hip!' and I moved my mouth to look like I was saying 'Hurray!'

Then Sumith raised his glass and started a speech. 'Today is a very happy day. It's a very, very special day for all of us. I don't have to tell you. You know it. It's the day when great things have happened in our country and in our family. It's the day when we have won. The war, the bloody curse that has been going on for thirty-odd years – it's finished. Those . . . those . . .' He couldn't think of a bad enough word and ended up saying 'damn'. 'Those damn Tigers are completely destroyed. And that madman, that yaka, he's been finished off – shot in the head. Same day as my son's birthday!'

I was starting to sweat. It was trickling down and wetting my blouse, even though there was a fan nearby. Something from my stomach was rising up to my chest and it was heavy like a stone. Nelunka, who had been standing next to Sumith to try and keep his speech decent, was looking at me. I tasted metal, but I smiled. Nodded. Clapped like a mother would clap when her son wins a water polo match.

Sumith carried on. 'You all know the history of my family goes back to the Polonnaruwa era.' He went back in time, which was usually a sign he was drunk, talking about how the Rupasinghes were descendants of the great king Parakramabahu, a king powerful enough to invade South India and beat the Chola hordes on their own territory. 'I have done my part, and now even this generation is doing that. This big man who is now seventeen years old – the war is ended by him!' Sumith's voice became hoarse. He coughed, cleared his throat. 'It didn't end on anyone else's birthday, no? No. It was only this fellow's. He's a real Rupasinghe. So happy birthday, Hesh-man. You are my prince. You are our champion. Happy birthday to you!' Sumith downed a whole glass of whisky in one go.

Heshan barely smiled, just took a bite of the huge piece of cake fed to him by his mother and refused to eat more. All that clapping and whistling didn't drown out my thoughts. I nodded like a bird, fixing a smile to my face, my cheeks stretched and hurting as if they were stuck with sellotape.

The crowd began to move. I said, 'Yes, it was a lovely speech,' to all the people lining up for the buffet. I told them I wasn't hungry. It was true. My stomach was cramping and I was scared that if I ate anything it would come back out. I looked for Anoushka and, seeing that she was getting along fine with her new friends, stumbled into the house. I went through the living room, down the corridor and into the bathroom. It was the one that was like a sparkling white box of light, all the shining fittings reflecting the glow from the bulbs in the ceiling. I tried to open the tap – it was one of those German taps, Grohe, and I had forgotten how. I turned and twisted and nothing happened. It opened only when my hand started shaking and I accidentally knocked the knob upwards. I took a deep breath and washed my face, then sat on that wide, comfortable commode seat. Closing my eyes for a moment, I felt safe from all the voices outside: but when I opened them again there was a stack of newspapers on the side, in a basket by my feet. My eyes caught a headline. *Nation Revels in Glory of Victory.* And in smaller letters just below: *Violent megalomaniac killed. People of the north and east liberated.* The by-line had the name *Manoratne Herath* printed right there. That was when the tears started. Everyone's happiness was my pain. Their joy was everywhere, spouting from their mouths, from the radio, television and newspapers.

Mano's work followed me, even into the toilet. I couldn't get away.

I couldn't understand. I asked the gods: What is the truth? Please tell me. I used to believe every word in the newspapers. Now I don't know what to believe. The internet? The internet was not to be trusted. Emails could be written by anyone. And I barely knew the people who sent them. Knew them so long ago. But they somehow managed to find my email address. They wrote, always starting with: *I am so-and-so's friend or relative. You must remember so-and-so who lived in the east near Batticaloa, near your parents' house. They were good friends or relatives of your parents. So-and-so told us a lot about you. Now we live in Canada, Australia or the UK.* It was always people who were overseas, people who were safe in their first-world luxuries and couldn't stay quiet. They wrote: *We are very sorry to hear your mother passed away in '84 and your father just after,* but that wasn't why they were writing. No. Not to pass on condolences years later. That was just a plan. A plan to butter me up before coming out with the real message. And the real message was: *There is a boy who didn't come back after school, from the shops or from tuition. His name is Krishnamoorthy Amurthalingam, Sanjeevan Parameshwaran, or Sunthar Suriyakumaran.* It was always the son of a neighbour, of an uncle, an aunt, a distant relative. One thing was sure. The boys were from that background, from the places I left behind.

I wanted to reply: *Why do you care?* But I didn't. I didn't respond. These were the people I had avoided ever since I married Mano. They always had excuses. Always blamed others. *It was the Sinhala-only policy of '56 that caused the problems. All the official documents are in Sinhala. All the police and army people are Sinhala. We can't get any good jobs. We have no authority.* Their heads got too big and they supported terrorism. *We'll always be second-class citizens in this country. Eelam is the solution.* They brought us all down. They always wanted help and never learned to help themselves. *Please ask your husband. He must have contacts. Could he try and find out what has happened to this boy? Could he write an article about it? The parents are sick with grief.*

Some of them tried calling but I said there was nothing to be done. That lots of people went missing and my husband couldn't write what everyone wanted. I told them not to call me in my office. I was rude. There was no other way to stop them. And they didn't stop. As the war intensified, the emails came faster. They became more graphic, more insistent. They sent pictures of children without hands and feet. Landmine victims. Multiple amputees. Infected shrapnel wounds. Blind boys and raped girls. A story of a traumatised Red Cross worker picking up all the severed hands and legs from a bombed school. A blurry video of two women, one old, one not so old – I realised they were from the north-east by the way they spoke – who, as gunfire and mortar sounds rattled outside, hurried around bundling clothes, cutlery, even useless things like plastic vases, and finally made it out the door, stopping for a moment to lay a hand on the man breathing his last on the doorstep. The house they left behind looked a lot like our old house in Batticaloa. I got used to glancing quickly at these emails and deleting them. They weren't to be trusted. Surely they were just LTTE propaganda.

I washed my hands and face again and made sure I didn't look like I'd been crying. I turned off the lights in the bathroom and slowly wandered back out. My headache was back so strong my eyes hurt. Outside, young children ran around the garden with sparklers, drawing letters in the air, making me dizzy. Everyone was eating fancy food, drinking their drinks, talking in their hi-fi accents about business and economy and property and education. I smiled. I nodded. I sat in a corner and silently prayed.

And what did I get in return? A glimpse of Niranjan. He came almost as we were about to leave, still wearing his work clothes – the shirt was a little crumpled, a bit of sweat darkening the armpits – his gelled hair pointing at the sky. He walked smartly, saying 'hi' to people, people I didn't know. He stopped to talk, very nice and polite, and when he left them they looked back and said, 'What a nice boy.' I could read it on their lips. They were wishing he were somehow a friend or relative, someone they could call their own. This was another reason Nelunka and I couldn't be friendly: she wanted Niranjan as her son, not Heshan. She would exchange them if she could, but she couldn't and she hated me for it. Hated the fact that I had been the one who carried him for nine months. I had been the one who gave birth and cared and fed and brought him up. You just had to look at him to know he was mine.

But Nelunka didn't know what Niranjan was really like. The more love you gave, the more he hurt you. The closer you tried to be, the further he walked away. Even now, as I saw him and I tried to get through, he just turned around. Didn't come and talk to me. He knew I was there, saw me across the room and pretended he hadn't. I got up and followed, despite my pain. I crawled after that boy. I avoided people who wanted to talk to me – relatives, acquaintances – it didn't matter if it was my father come back from heaven, I would have gone right past. When I finally caught him near the gate, he had his arm around Heshan's shoulders. They were laughing at something so hard it must have been the funniest joke in the world. They were laughing like crazy people and didn't stop when they saw me.

'Niranjan,' I said. 'I want to talk to you.'

He still laughed.

'Niranjan, are you listening to me?'

'Uh oh,' said Heshan, gulping. 'Someone's mad.'

'That's her usual look,' said Niranjan. He leaned in and whispered something in Heshan's ear and they laughed some more.

'Niranjan,' I said sternly and the laughing stopped. 'Let's talk.'

That wiped Heshan's smile off. He said, 'I'm going to see what Ravin's doing,' and stumbled away.

I faced Niranjan but he didn't look at me. His eyes were focused somewhere behind me, over my shoulder.

'Why didn't you tell me you were coming, Niranjan?'

'Coming where?'

'Here. Where else?'

'I don't have to tell you everything.'

'I didn't know until Nelunka told me. It was very awkward. Why do I have to hear everything about you from other people? I'm your mother. Not Nelunka, not Latha, not anyone else. Me.'

He mumbled something I couldn't make out.

'Don't mumble, Niranjan. Ever since you were a child I've taught you not to mumble, but you don't listen to a single—'

'I said, that's not my problem.' He looked straight at me, his eyes sparkling.

'We're not your problem?' I said. 'I can see that. I can see you don't care about us anymore. That's fine. You don't have to care about us. You're a big man. You can do what you want.'

'So I didn't tell you. What's the big deal?'

'Big deal? No big deal. Nothing. We're all nothing to you. Your father, your sister, me. We're all nothing. That's fine. You can do what you want. You can go and drink and go to nightclubs and do all sorts of things, and people will curse me for bringing you up to be such a bad person.'

'Same old story, no?' He rolled his eyes. 'You're never going to get it.' He turned and took a few steps past the open gate.

'Yes, we're old,' I say. 'Our ideas are old. But we do the right thing. You know what you're doing is wrong, but you're still doing it . . . you're doing it to hurt us.'

He stopped and half-turned. 'What have I done to hurt you?'

'Everything. Everything you're doing now. All this going out and coming home late business. And if that's not enough, you came and put a flag right outside my window.'

'What are you talking about?'

'You knew I was already having trouble with all the things happening. You knew I was suffering. You just wanted to hurt me some more, didn't you?' The words came scraping out of my throat, all torn up and desperate. I shouldn't have bothered. He was already gone.

—

At home, as everyone else fell asleep, I lay awake listening. As familiar as this was, as much as it was now part of my daily routine, it never got easier. As the neighbourhood became quieter my ears began to pick up all the low noises – Mano snoring away in his room, the mosquitos gathering outside my net, a dripping tap, the distant traffic. They were regular sounds playing in a rhythm that you got used to after a while. But then there was always a louder noise that broke through – a fruit on a roof, a falling brick at the building site, Anoushka sleep-talking. A phone ringing.

Phones always made me jump. Even if it wasn't our phone. When he was a teenager, when he used to listen to me, I had always told Niranjan to give me a call when he was getting late. 'Let me know where you are,' I said, 'and how you're coming back.' That was when he didn't have a car. Now there was no reason to say it. But for a while I still hoped it was him, calling to ask for help. But the more I thought about it, the less I wanted the phone to ring. What if it was the hospital calling to say he'd broken his back or was in a coma, or the police saying he'd been arrested for being over the limit or hitting someone or that the accident was so bad that . . . I couldn't even think it. There are so many accidents on our roads these days, van fellows driving drunk, private bus drivers on drugs, trishaw fellows who don't care about anything but money — anything can happen. It was in the papers, when I used to read them: *three dead, four dead, six or seven injured.*

As horrible as all that sounds, the worst would be not hearing anything. The worst would be if almost two hours before the sun came up the silence somehow wasn't broken by the rattle of Niranjan's old Benz, no thada-bada of someone who couldn't even walk straight trying to unlock the front door so the servant has to wake up and open it for him and pick up the things he drops on the way to his room. The worst would be for the night to end as quiet as can be — if he just disappeared. What if I never saw him again? Things happen these days, in this country more than in others — things I never even imagined.

I got tired of waiting in bed so I went and sat on the toilet for a while. Then I sat in the living room, in the dark. Latha heard me and came out to talk, but what could she talk to me about? About cooking, cleaning and the kids. The conversation went nowhere. She sat there patiently, quietly keeping me company. Could I tell her about my worries? My fears? About Khanna? I had told her bits and pieces but never the whole story.

It was just before Mano's relatives came for their holiday that I received the email. It was from Sandesh Subramaniam, one of our neighbours in Batticaloa, a businessman who left for Australia as soon as the trouble started in '83.

Dear Lakshmi,
I am very happy to send you this letter. I was looking all over for a Lakshmi Ramanathan but could not find you. It is from my cousin-brother, Uthayan,

that I found out you are now married to prominent journalist Manoratne Herath. My cousin-brother told me this information and my youngest son, Kokulan, put your name in the internet and found you on the website for Ceylanko Insurance. I am very happy to hear that you are working for such an established organisation.

I don't know why I kept reading, maybe because he seemed to respect and trust me. He knew I was capable.

Do you remember there was a boy who begged on our street? He used to limp everywhere. He had wounds on his body but a nice smile? His name was Khanna.

It came back to me – how people called the boy to give him the change left in their pockets or food left over in their kitchens. Others chased him away saying, 'Khanna, po!', raising arms and kicking legs. I remember feeling bad for him and disliking him, all at once.

The boy's father, Selvarasan, was a fisherman who used to find his catch in the Mullaitivu region. During the war there were many restrictions and the man lost his livelihood. He got into trouble. He got caught between the government and the LTTE and decided to leave the country. He got on a boat and came to Australia.

I could imagine how Khanna felt. Alone. I knew what it was like to watch everyone else going around being rich, fat and happy while you felt so low, so worthless. That's why I never want my children to feel the pain of an empty stomach. That was the promise I made when Niranjan was born. But Niranjan doesn't need our help. He eats oily restaurant food every day. I can't even ask him about it, let alone tell him to eat something healthy.

As you know, his mother is long dead, so the boy has nobody else. The father is looking for his son. He wants to bring the boy to Australia. Nobody knows where Khanna is. We would be extremely grateful if you could find any information. Please help reunite the boy with his father.

I trusted Latha. She had been loyal to us over the years. But I didn't tell her. It was so quiet and dark and her presence was no longer comforting.

I decided to call Niranjan. I left the servant in the living room, went into the corridor, picked up the phone and dialled Niranjan's mobile number. It rang for a little while. I had done this before and he never answered. I didn't expect him to answer now, and he didn't – but someone else did. It was a woman. There was loud music. I thought I had dialled the wrong number so I cut the call. I tried again and the same woman's voice answered. 'Wait, wait,' she shouted. 'I'll go somewhere I can hear you.'

The music got louder before it became quiet. It was a deep thumping sound. There were also a lot of noises in the background, a lot of voices, people talking, some singing along with the music. There was a sound like ripping paper, a rush of air and now I could hear her. The woman said, 'Hullo? Can you hear me now?'

'Yes,' I said. 'I want to talk to Niranjan.'

'Who's that?' said the woman.

'Sorry, I must have dialled the wrong number.'

'Wait, Aunty. This isn't my phone. A guy left his phone on our table. He must be Niranjan. I just answered when it started ringing.'

'Where are you?'

'Zanzibar.'

'In Africa?'

'No.' She laughed. 'It's a club.'

'Uh . . . what sort of club?'

'Nightclub.'

'Where is it?'

She told me the address. She said she'd return the phone to Niranjan and tell him his mother called. I said thank you and put the receiver down. I felt better. Calmer. I felt like I finally knew where to find Niranjan, had a clue about what he did all night. But knowing didn't completely satisfy me. I wanted to know more. I wanted to go there and see what was happening with my own eyes.

An image flashed in my mind – something Mr Subramaniam sent attached in another email – a young man in an ill-fitting suit. It was Khanna in one of those bizarre studio photographs that were popular in the east – where you posed in front of a painting, pretending you had visited a famous landmark or a pretty landscape. The Eiffel Tower was Khanna's backdrop. In the photo he didn't look like Niranjan but there was something in the way he stood there, hands on hips, eyes looking so far into the distance, that reminded me of my son.

But what happened to Khanna couldn't happen to Niranjan. We're not involved in politics. We have nothing to do with the militaries of either side. Niranjan's not even properly Tamil. Only half. If he suffered because of that half, the half that I passed on, I couldn't forgive myself.

I went to Mano's room and said, 'Mano, I want to go somewhere.'

He didn't wake up and I had to shake him a few times. 'Mano? Mano. I need you to take me to Colombo 3.'

'What the bloody . . .' He grunted and looked at me with half-open eyes. 'Where? What time is it? It's the middle of the bloody night!'

'You haven't done anything for me. Will you help me with this one thing?'

'Yes, but . . .'

'I want to go to a place called Zanzibar in Colombo 3. Will you take me or not?'

'Don't be silly, Lakshmi.' He turned around and closed his eyes. 'Go to sleep. We both have work tomorrow.'

NIRANJAN

'What were you saying, Niro? I didn't get you.'

'If you turn the music down you might hear me.'

'Machan, you can't just turn Eminem down like that.'

'Man, fuck Eminem. Fucking trailer trash. He's not half as good as Nas or Q-Tip but thinks he's the shit. What did you do with the mixtapes I gave you?'

'They're here somewhere.' Issa toed a pile of CDs and DVDs, the plastic sleeves of pirated media with their sticky flaps all stuck together and to the floor. He kept circling, barefoot, in the dirty little room he called an office, searching but not really looking for rolling paper. Then the weak piss that was Kanye's latest album, the one where he'd gone all emo and tried to sing with his voice completely autotuned, was blasting at full volume.

'I'd put on some real hip-hop if I didn't have to tell you about this thing,' I yelled.

'So tell.'

I reached out and flipped the switch on the old black stereo system that rose above the rubbish like a monolith from *2001: A Space Odyssey*. It made a whirring noise as it went to sleep. I sat back in the leaning chair and put my leg up on the extendable armrest. 'I said I'm going to kill him. Hit the fucker so hard he won't know what hit him. He'll come out of the club in his Armani Exchange T-shirt tight around his fat gut, his jeans falling below the crack of his arse, all wrinkled around his white clown shoes. Cocky fucker will be boasting about some chick he boned – some dirty woman with no taste, probably blind drunk or just blind if she really did go with him – but of course that'll all be made up. He'll be talking shit and I'll come up and punch his head off.'

'Righto.' Issa finally found the paper on top of a crumpled bedsheet near the window. He hitched up his shorts and lowered his flabby bottom to the concrete, propped a cushion against the wall, leaned back and settled. Kicking off his slippers, he picked up a lighter from the ground with his toes and at the same time took a pinch of weed out of a polythene bag and placed it on the rolling paper. With the lighter on his lap, Issa ripped up some cardboard and rolled it to use as a filter, then placed it on the end of the paper, which he bent into a U, carefully balancing the weed as he moved the edges up and down. He licked one side and finished the job. If there was one thing Issa was an expert at, it was rolling joints. He finally looked up and said, 'And then?'

'After I knock his lights out I'll look at his chandiya buddies and ask, "Anyone else want some?" and they'll run away like ponnayas. I'll walk over to him still lying there seeing stars and say, "What the fuck did you say? Say it again."'

'Hmm.' Issa twisted the fat front end of the spliff, putting the finishing touches on it.

'Of course he wouldn't say a word. He wouldn't dare. None of the shit-talk happens when you've been owned like that. He'll pretend he doesn't remember. And I'll remind him.'

'Remind him what?'

'Remind him what happened.'

'What happened?'

'I thought I told you?'

'Tell me again, machan.'

'Fuck! I'm not telling you again. If you didn't listen it's your loss.'

Issa didn't seem to mind. He flicked the lighter a couple of times, cupping the flame with one hand as he lit up. I tried to catch his eye so he could see how serious I was, but he was too busy sucking in fresh product grown somewhere in Piliyandala and purchased from a house on Gregory's Road.

'So, I'll grab the fucker by his cheek and tell him, "Last week, I was at Clancy's having a drink and you came. I saw you. I saw through the window, how you revved your engine and then horned so loud it made the girls near the entrance jump. Fucking show-off. So obvious you wanted everyone to see your car. Think anybody gives a shit about your Alfa Romeo? Believe me, Alfas are for fags – for ponna pakas like you."'

'You were at Clan's last week?'

'Yeah, last Tuesday.'

'With who?'

'Nobody. Just me. Thought I'd check it out.'

'How was the scene?'

'Scene was dead. No wonder that bugger showed up – it must've been goday night at Clancy's.'

'Who?'

'Angelo Arnolda! Who do you think I've been talking about? I was telling you I'm going to kill that fucker.'

'Right, right. Tell me.'

'So, when the bugger's on the ground, I'll shove my shoe in his mouth and tell him how he's fucked up. I'll say, "You got out of your piece-of-shit car. You and your friends – such a bunch of losers I've never seen – walking side by side like you're in some gay version of *Reservoir Dogs*. Do you know why sunglasses are called sunglasses? Because they're meant to protect you from the sun—"'

'They were wearing sunglasses?'

'Yep.'

'In the evening?'

'Yeah! Can you believe it?'

'What kind?'

'Ray-Bans. All three of them.'

'Nice.'

'Ray-Bans at night. What a fucking joke, right? So Angelo Arnolda walked into the bar and ordered vodka, turned around, and saw me there with my scotch. I didn't want to talk to him. Why would I? Barely knew him, no? But he was like, "I know you. You went to college with me." I just said, "Yeah, maybe," and tried to stop it there, but he wouldn't give up. He was like, "Yeah, machan. I know you. You played water polo, right?" and I was like,

"Yeah, vice-captain in '04." So he sat down and started blabbing. The whole time I was looking at my watch, going, "When's this guy going to leave me alone?" His friends were waiting but the fucker just kept talking and talking, about Pinto and Wimale and the other teachers—'

'Pinto was a funny bugger. Remember how he used to say, "Herath! Where are you going? Your grandmother died again?"' Issa said, smiling, remembering.

I chuckled. 'And every week I made up a new grandmother and jumped out of school – until Pinto caught on.'

'Nobody's ever had as many grandmothers as Niranjan Herath. It's a Guinness world record!'

I had to reach out to high-five Issa. Patass! The sound went ringing through the office, through the open door and into the bathroom, where it bounced off the mouldy tiles. 'But, you know what? Angelo Arnolda even brought up the great kakka in the Ladies' College pool controversy.'

'What, the great kakka in the pool problem that . . .'

'That you and I were falsely accused of. Yeah.'

'How did he know about that? I only remember you, me, Charith and Boosa jumping the wall and getting into the LC pool.'

'I know, right? But he knew everything. Down to how Boosa's massive boga floated on the clear blue water like Godzilla.'

'Big boga for a big guy, no?' Issa blew perfect little smoke rings that drifted up to the ceiling. We reminisced. I had always thought of Issa as the sort of guy who didn't give two shits about anything, but at the end of the day he was just like the rest of us, always talking about college.

We talked about the big match and the cycle parade, all the fights we had with the Royal College boys trying to beat us at jumping into Ladies' College, the times we joined forces with the Royalists and took on the cops – us with eggs, the kossas guarding the LC boundaries with their rubber bullets. We talked about how Charith still has the scar on his ribs where he was shot. I still had the marks from my badly scratched knees. Those were the days, man. We were close. We stood together, you know? The best bunch of guys from the best goddamn school in this country. Ever. Issa finished his joint and rolled another, going quiet as he concentrated.

'So anyway,' I continued, 'Angelo Arnolda and I were talking all that shit and it was all right, you know? I mean, he seemed okay. His friends sat down, ordered a round of beers, and it was fine – the friends didn't say much but whatever, right? We were having a decent chat and a drink – until Arnolda went and ruined it. The fucker, out of the blue, started speaking to me in Tamil.'

'Ah, yeah! He's Tamil. He was in Tamil medium, remember?'

'How the fuck should I remember Tamil medium? I wasn't there! I was in Sinhala medium – with you!'

'Right, right. Don't shout, you bugger! So tell what happened, then?'

'So Arnolda's sitting there, going, "Inga waanga ponga peenga . . ."'

Issa chuckled. 'Is that your idea of Tamil?'

'Kara kara, kuru kuru, kiri kiri . . .'

'You should know the language, bro. Your mother's Tamil, right?'

'Fuck that, man. It's hideous. I hate it. And my mum is hardly Tamil, know what I mean? She's like one of us. So anyway, Arnolda was talking and I didn't get a single word of it . . . I mean, I got the basic waanga ponga stuff, but nothing else. And you know how they speak – like a million miles per hour – so I didn't stand a chance. I was sitting there like a fucking mute, and when he finally stopped, I was like, "What the fuck?"'

'He must have thought you understood.'

'I don't know what the fuck he thought. I was like, "I don't speak Tamil, mate." Then those three fuckers laughed. "I was talking about my holiday in Singapore," Arnolda said. He said it like it was some sort of amazing achievement.'

'Singapore's a piece of shit,' Issa agreed.

'They can talk about whatever they want, in whatever language, man. Why the fuck would I want to hear about his Singapore holiday? He kept saying, "I bought ten Marks and Spencer shirts. All my business shirts are Marks." The fat fuck. All he did was shop and eat. That's all you can do in Singapore . . . I lived in Aus for five years, you know? I don't boast about that.'

'Singapore's chaarter. Boring as hell,' said Issa.

'He didn't even ask me where I'd been. He must have known I was abroad all this time.'

'Too strict. Can't have any fun.'

'Not once did that fucker ask me about my studies, about Sydney or anything.'

Issa took another puff of the joint and held it aloft like a mini Olympic torch. 'Do you know the punishment for this sort of thing in Singapore?'

'Death penalty. That's why Australia is better, Mr Isuru Panabokke. Not that Angelo Arnolda would ever know.'

'But, Mr Niranjan Herath, you didn't really like Sydney, no?'

'Granted, Sydney is overrated. Everyone's got too much padé – all up themselves, as they say in 'Straya. Especially the women – those chicks think they're too good for us. Bitches don't even look at us. Racist whores.'

'Did you try the "once you go black" line?'

'What?'

'Once you go black, you won't go back!'

'I know the line, Issa. They say, "Sorry, no Indians," as soon as you go up and try to talk to them. That's when I fucking explode and say, "I'm not Indian, you ignorant whore. I'm Sri Lankan!"'

'Stupid fucking kangaroos.' Issa shook his head disapprovingly. 'But they're hot, man.'

'Oh, for sure. Much hotter than the chicks in Singa.'

'Fuck yeah. In Singa only the expats are hot.'

'That's what I said to Arnolda! You should've seen his face. I said, "Did you like the bitches in Singapore? You like that ching-chong kinda thing, do you? Try some of your waanga ponga on them?" Fucker got real sour when I said it. He just finished his beer and gave me a gal look. I could tell his friends were getting edgy. Then, you know what Arnolda said—'

'Ha! He likes it, no? Likes a little ching-chong . . .' The weed had started hitting Issa. This stuff was a total thapal case, judging by how late the effects manifested. He started giggling crazily and repeating, 'He likes the ching-chong!'

I kept to the story. 'Arnolda was like, "Guess who I like?" I should've stopped right there. I was an idiot. I walked right into it. I knew something fucked up was coming, but I said, "Who?"'

Issa was still going haka-haka-haka, laughing madly, saying, 'He loves the Cheenas. He loves them.'

'Issa! Get a grip, man.'

Holding his stomach and rolling onto his side, Issa somehow controlled himself and we got back on track.

'I still can't believe Arnolda said it,' I said.

'What did he say?'

'You won't believe it.'

'What was it?'

'He said, "Your mum."'

Issa's laughter burst out like a punctured water main. Haka-haka-haka. He was face down on the floor, a little bit of spit dripping from his lip, hands slapping the concrete until he could barely breathe.

'I'm going to kill him,' I said.

'Your mum!' Issa rolled onto his back, wiping away tears. 'Nails the love of your life and now wants to nail your mum!'

'What the fuck? So it's true?'

'It's only a rumour, man. Bugger like that with Sonali Senanayake? I don't think so.'

'Fuck you, Issa.'

'Come on, man. She's gone. She's in the Netherlands. Married with kids. Fat, from what I hear. You were partying it up in Aussie when Angelo gave it a shot.'

'So he had a crack?'

'Rumours, bro. All lies. Chill. Here, have a puff.' He stuck out his hand and offered me the joint.

I took it from him and went over to the sofa. Swiping a few magazines off it, I lay down. 'I'm still gonna kill him.'

Issa began to cough. He cleared his throat and sat up, putting on a very serious face. 'You know who Arnolda's friends are? That Jordan guy? Najab? You know the connections, no? They're deadly buggers.' The giggles were beginning to slip through again. 'If you manage to lay a finger on him I'll give you a million bucks.'

'I know. They're gangsters.' I took a deep drag from the joint. The hit was thick and strong. 'Let's up the stakes. If I kill the fucker, you give me your tourism company. If I get my arse whipped, I'll give you my start-up.'

'Machan, that'll be as if nothing happened.'

That was around eleven in the morning, and I nearly died – died from laughter.

—

Goddamn backward Lankan investors. They just didn't get it. Didn't recognise vision if it kicked them in the head. Cash wasn't exactly flowing in, the start-up was in discovery phase and I was hungry. I didn't have the money to go to the Commons, let alone Gallery Café – but that wasn't the only reason I went home for a late lunch. I needed to use a phone, call that chick who had found my mobile at Zanzibar.

I drove into our lane and found a van parked in my spot next to our gate. I rang the bell. 'Whose tin-can dakkuwa is this?' I said to Latha when she poked her head out of the gate. I knew who owned it – one of the contractors from the building site at the top of the road. 'Who's the owner of this rusty trolley?'

'Shh, Niranjan Baby,' she said putting a finger to her lips. 'Ke-gahanna epa.'

'Whose dakku cart is this?'

Leaving the gate open, Latha went to tell the contractor to move his shitbox. She returned in a couple of minutes with the short, balding fellow with his rat-like face. 'Sorry, sorry,' he said as he scurried across.

'Sorry, thamai,' I said, frowning.

He tried to tell me he was only parking there for a few minutes, even though there were so many other places he could park down the road. Seeing I wasn't going to take his bullshit, he got in his van and drove down to the end of the lane. I parked in my spot and went inside.

Anoushka was sitting in front of the TV, staring at whatever chaarter thing was on television, picking at a few remaining grains of rice on the empty plate balanced on her knees. There was nothing good on the local broadcasts and my parents were too cheap to get cable. Anoushka didn't seem to mind – I suppose she didn't know better. There were times I thought of paying for Dialog TV or some other cable provider so I could have a movie channel – Star Movies or something that would have some quality international programming. Get a decent enough package and I could've watched the Tri-Nations, Six Nations or the French Open live, but I wasn't home enough to make any return on the investment.

Anoushka looked at me as if I had just landed from outer space. 'What're you doing here?' she said in her panditha voice.

'Why? Can't I come home?'

'Aah! You live here, no? I forgot,' she said without missing a beat.

'Do you remember now?' I said.

'Yes. I was confused. I thought you moved out to a nice apartment.' She got to her feet. 'Or maybe you got drunk and slept in a nightclub.'

'As if you know about nightclubs . . .' The words faded as I saw her pants. She strolled through the dining room, towards the kitchen, wearing the same old pair of jeans she always wore – except they were cut off at the knees, roughly, strings trailing from the edge that hadn't been hemmed. 'What the hell are you wearing? Are you trying to be like one of those idiots from Nirvana or something? Is this a grunge thing?'

'No way,' she said. 'Grunge wouldn't even be around if it wasn't for punk.' She disappeared through the corridor. I shook my head and laughed. Anoushka wasn't the fat-cheeked girl she was when I left for Sydney. She was growing up. The TV still babbled away as I sat at the table and surveyed the remains of lunch. Flower Drum again. Poor Thatthi was still trying to impress Ammi. Another failure, no doubt. Latha brought a plate from the kitchen and served me what was left of the twice-heated fried rice, a couple of chilli crab claws with a sliver of flesh in their wrists and some wilted kangkung with tiny pieces of beef mixed through. Flower Drum was past its heyday but my folks still thought it was worth shelling out premium rupee. Anoushka returned, hands wringing wet, not bothering to wipe them, and settled back on the sofa.

'You must be on a diet,' I said, turning to face her.

Anoushka didn't answer. She just pulled up her legs onto the cushion and sat there like a fat little god.

'Has to be a diet, no? Normally you would've gobbled all of this. About time, too. You're getting a real Jamaican arse. Like a black woman.'

Anoushka stared at the television, some ridiculous-sounding cartoon dubbed in Sinhala. It was hard work getting a word out of her. In between mouthfuls I tried again to have a conversation. 'So, tell us about this grunge thing you're doing.'

'It's punk. I told you.'

'I know, I know.'

'You don't know anything. Did you even know Tobi Vail dated Kurt? If it wasn't for her there wouldn't even be a "Smells Like Teen Spirit".'

'Tobi who? She fucked Kurt Cobain? Really? Before he died?'

She went quiet. Shocked. For all her punk moves, the kid was still stunned when you dropped the F-bomb.

'So what if she fucked Kurt Cobain?' I continued. 'Doesn't mean she had anything to do with his music, no? If anything, he would've influenced her.'

Anoushka glowered like someone had set off a fire inside her. I could almost see the steam rising from her head.

'What's that look, huh?'

'Niranjan Baby!' Latha, who had been watching, stepped in. 'Anoushka Baby-ta inna denna.'

'Mind your own business,' I said to Latha.

'Meka mage business thamai,' Latha said sternly. 'My business. My.' She tapped her chest with a stubby forefinger.

'She started it,' I grumbled. The women were ganging up on me, so I let it go. 'Okay, okay. Let me eat in peace.'

Anoushka got off the couch and stormed past us into her room.

'Turn the TV off!' I called after her, but she'd already slammed her door.

Latha took a few steps closer to me and said, 'Niranjan Baby?' in a quiet voice.

'Here we go again,' I said.

Latha began nagging me, saying how Ammi was stressed about trying to find someone in her home town and Thatthi wasn't around to help and Ammi lost her temper at Anoushka and Anoushka was upset because Ammi had taken away her 'sindu kaalla' and that Anoushka really missed that music player – and because of that I should be nice to Anoushka. I just ate the rest of the food. Sucked the crab bones. Swept the last bits of rice and chilli paste into my mouth. What could I do about Anoushka and her music player? It sounded like a bad influence anyway.

Then Latha began trying to figure out if I was still hungry, and said, 'Kaama madi, neda?' I didn't give her the satisfaction of a correct guess and passed her the plate. She took it but didn't go away. 'Thawa monawahari hadala dennada, Niranjan Baby?' Sure, she could make me something else, but I wasn't willing to hang around for the usual dhal or pol sambola. I needed to know if the offer was worth my while. 'What else do you have?'

'Parippu?'

I didn't want dhal so I shook my head.

'Gotu kola?'

'Chi!' I recoiled, screwing up my nose at the thought of bitter greens.

'Gotu kola hondai ne, Baby?' She tried to sell me the unsellable, realised I wasn't going to buy and changed tack. 'Haal messo?'

Sprats. If there was something Latha could do, a dish that was simple, quick and tasty, one that I missed the whole time I was away, it was her fried sprats. It wasn't a complicated thing, surely – just a few tiny fish cleaned, salted, thrown in some oil and crisped. A bit of chilli and vinegar added after they were drained and you had a winner. 'Haa,' I agreed. 'Ikmanata.' I said it twice, 'Ikmanata,' to stress that I was in a hurry.

'Five minute,' she said smiling like a child, took my plate away and disappeared into the kitchen. I stepped into the living room. My hand was still sticky from the Flower Drum food so I picked up the remote with my wrong hand. I changed through the whole range of channels and found absolutely nothing to watch.

When Latha returned with a bowl of haal messo, I looked at my watch. 'Eight minutes,' I said, getting back to the table.

She pretended to check the time on an imaginary watch on her wrist. 'Oralosuwa broken. No time. Time no.'

I almost laughed. I don't know why. Maybe it's because it was the sort of thing that I had once found funny. Before I grew up and went to school, this was the sort of thing she said to make me laugh. A bit of broken English here, a bit of self-deprecation there – that was pretty much the extent of her repertoire. And here she was, some twenty years later, still trying the same tricks. 'Haal messo goot?'

'Yes, yes, good,' I said with my mouth full. The sprats were hitting the spot.

'Goot fish?'

'Yes.'

'Fish goot?'

'Yes, I told you, no? Good.'

'Okay.' Thumbs up. But Latha wasn't done. She started asking questions. How was my work? Did I still meet my old friends, Charith Baby, Isuru Baby, Boos Baby and all the other Baby-la that Latha had got to know from coming to school to pick me up, from all the birthday parties and spend-the-days she helped organise and cater. 'Baby-la kohomada?' she asked.

'They're fine,' I told her. 'I saw Issa in the morning.'

'Isuru Baby?' She was fond of Issa and just like always, asked me to say hi to him.

'I'll tell him.'

'Thank you, Niranjan Baby.'

'Mahattaya.'

'Thank you, Niranjan Mahattaya.'

Standing up I indicated the conversation was over and to let her clear up. I went out to the car to pick up my bag as Latha cleared the table. When I entered my room I realised she'd cleaned. Latha had made the bed, moved the dirty clothes into the basket and stacked the books on my desk – all without my permission. Why the hell did she have to poke around here? I grumbled but as I stuffed the bag with gym clothes and a change I realised, she wasn't trying to pry. She was trying to help. And then, I don't know why, but I got all nostalgic, thinking about how Latha and I used to hang out, playing board games – snakes and ladders, Monopoly, which she called 'munny-poly', and checkers on the chessboard, because Latha didn't know the rules to chess. We played cricket on the street – her throwing underarm full tosses and me whacking them out of sight, only for her to run after the ball and do it all over again. I got all sentimental. What a pussy, right? I even started to worry she might leave us. Latha's brother had been calling, asking her to come back to the village, saying everything was better there. Had there been more calls, I wondered. Was she tempted to go?

I finally finished packing and went out to the dining room. She had cleared up and retired to the kitchen. I could hear her washing dishes. I went to have a word with her, but as I passed the phone I remembered I needed to get my mobile back, so I stopped and dialled my number.

'Hullo?' It was a girl's voice. She sounded hot.

'Hi, I think that's my phone you're using.'

'Yeah. I found it on a table at Zanzibar. Your mum called and said—'

'I know, I know . . .' I was totally embarrassed. This chick must've thought I was a real mama's boy.

'She said she'd come and pick it up, but—'

'No, no. I'll come and get it. Where will you be tonight?' I wondered if her looks matched her voice. 'Are you going out somewhere?'

'I'll be at Clancy's. I'll be there early, around eleven.'

'Cool.' I got her details. 'My name's Niranjan, by the way. Friends call me Niro.'

'I'll see you there.'

'Okay. Bye.'

I looked at my watch and realised it was almost four-thirty – I was in danger of being cornered by Ammi and Thatthi returning from work. I opened up Ammi's phone book, wrote down Aunty Nelunka's number on a piece of paper and headed out.

———

After my hectic gym session, I had two reasons to go see Uncle Sumith. I'd put in the hard yards, softened him up and now he was ready to be bowled over. I'd reveal my plans and his mind would be blown. I was sure of it. He had connections, a direct line right to the top. That was where my business was headed. I also needed a fresh ride, something to impress the girl at Clancy's. A brand-new Nissan Z ought to do the trick.

I borrowed a phone from one of the guys at the gym and called. Aunty Nelunka picked up. 'Niro! Hullo! How is my favourite nephew?'

'You mean your only nephew.'

'Don't say that. You're still my favourite.'

'There's no competition. I have a monopoly.'

'You and your business talk. I don't know any of that.'

'Don't you know what a monopoly is?' I was rude to her on purpose. She enjoyed being insulted, if only just a little bit. 'It's like the board game. When you have Piccadilly, Leicester Square, Mayfair, Park Lane, the whole suite of properties, no matter where you go you have to pay me. That, my dear Nelunka, is a monopoly.'

'I know what a monopoly is. What do you think I am, an illiterate from Thumpané?' She pretended to get mad at me but I knew she'd always go back to drooling. The fake annoyance lasted less than two seconds, 'Aney, you're such a joker, Niro! Don't tease your poor aunty. Sin, no?'

'Sin, sin. Anyway, I'm coming over. Is that cool?'

'Of course it's cool. Come!'

'I just want to talk to uncle. Will he be home?'

'You want to talk business? Is it about your start-up? Uncle will be home at six-thirty. Do you want to have some dinner with us? Heshan will be happy to hear you're coming. He didn't get to hang out with you at the birthday, no? Where did you run off to?'

'Too many questions. I'll see you in a sec.'

'Okay, Baba. Cheerio!'

When I got to their place she was in their cavern of a living room with the phone in her ear, so when she mouthed the words 'Hi, Niro!' and reached for me, clawing the air, I skipped away. I went to the office and opened the door to find the AC off, the windows wide open and Uncle Sumith behind his desk, leaning right back on his leather chair. His eyes were shut and his shirt was unbuttoned. Rolls of fat spilled out. It was a real Jabba the Hutt gut, on top of which he had balanced a glass of scotch. His eyes fluttered open. 'Niranjan! What are you doing here?' he said. He picked up the glass and sat up.

'Hullo, Uncle.' I closed the door quietly. 'Didn't Aunty tell you I'm coming? What—'

'Shh.' Uncle Sumith brought a finger to his lips, opened a drawer and took out another glass. 'You want a drink?' he whispered.

I thought about it as I sat on the leather chair opposite him. 'Maybe just one. I don't have much time.'

'You never have time, no? What do you do all day, you bugger? Looking at the internet? Facebook? Young people these days, they don't know where their heads are,' he grumbled as he reached into the cupboard behind him. He took a bottle of Glenlivet and poured a generous amount. 'You want some ice?'

'Yes, please.'

'Get some from that fridge, putha. There's a bucket in the freezer.'

I got up and went over to the minibar and opened it. 'You say that, but you won't believe how busy I've been.'

'Really? Adey, tell will you? Busy doing what?'

'Patience, Uncle. I'll give you all the details. It's quite complicated, but I'll make it easy for you.' I brought the ice bucket over and placed it on the tablemat Uncle Sumith pushed towards me. 'You already know this is a start-up, right? Now, think about it this way – our start-up company is like a car. No, it's like a plane. Think about it as . . . Think about this – it's a rocket, okay?'

He leaned across, grabbed the tongs and dropped a couple of ice cubes in his drink. 'A rocket?'

I followed suit, added ice, swirled the whisky in the glass and sank back down into one of his office chairs. 'A rocket. A spaceship taking astronauts to the moon. Think of all the work you have to do before take-off. Think about all the risk. You're putting people up there – and millions of dollars' worth of equipment. Billions. The Mars rover, the Hubble telescope . . . if the rocket explodes, then all of that's gone. Billions down the drain. Years of research, effort, materials – all gone.'

'Dead astronauts,' he said gravely.

'Exactly!'

'That's why we're working on making this rocket bulletproof. Fail-safe. We want to send it to outer space, out into the unknown galaxies – where no man has gone before. And it has to come back.'

Uncle Sumith guffawed, his bundy-fat rippling as the deep heh-heh-heh rolled out of his throat.

'Think of the profits. Think of what the rocket will bring back to earth – all the knowledge, all the discoveries. We'll be like . . . heroes.'

'Heroes, ah?'

'Yes! You will be the next in a long line of heroes. Another Rupasinghe hero – not that you're not one already, Uncle Sumith. But this sort of thing hasn't been done before.'

'Me?' he said sharply. There was a spark of interest in those bulging eyes, in the way he mockingly raised his palm, telling me to stop.

'Yes, you!'

'But I am not doing anything, no?' He chuckled again. 'You are the hero, Niranjan, not me.'

'Ah, that's what we need to talk about, Uncle. You've done a lot for me, and I'm a man with gratitude, unlike lots of people. As a gesture of this gratitude I'm going to bring you into the fold. You can be a part of this venture.'

'What am I going to do? You and your rocket ship business – I don't even understand.'

'It's simple. We're a financial enterprise. We just need to do the branding, get some cool design for the online presence, build a dynamic team and a loyal customer base and we'll be set. You don't worry about that. All we need from you is investment. Some capital.'

'Ah.' He nodded. He drained the glass and placed it on the desk. It looked like he understood what I'd been trying to convey. He finally *got* it. 'You want some money. Right. Okay.'

'Every venture needs some capital to begin with. And you can't expect any returns within the first few years. But as a partner you can have—'

'Five thousand? Ten? Fifteen? What do you want? I don't want any of this partner nonsense. I'll give you some money and you can give back to me when you're a rich man.'

'It's not like that, Uncle Sumith.'

'Then what?'

'It's . . . How do I put this? We need a substantial amount.'

'So tell, you bugger, how much do you need?'

'I need . . . I need at least a mill. Actually, two and a half mill. Minimum. It doesn't have to come from—'

'Two million?' Uncle Sumith's eyes almost popped out of his skull.

'It doesn't have to come from you. You have contacts, right? I can run the business and you can bring in the investment. I'll draw up a revenue share agreement—'

'That's a lot of money, putha. Where am I going to get two million from? You're a hell of a bugger, Niranjan.' He smiled to soften the blow. 'Walk in here and ask for two million, just like that.'

'I thought you could talk to your friends, people you know. Surely you know some investors.'

He laughed. 'You think I can go and tell these buggers your rocket story and they'll turn around and give me a million rupees?'

'Dollars . . . I need US dollars.'

'A million US dollars!' Now the laughter was coming hard and fast. The heh–heh–heh had become a heeee–heeee–heeee, a donkey's almost-wheeze.

'Forget it.' I got to my feet. 'You're not ready.' I stepped away and politely moved the chair back into place. 'I'll let you know when we're listed on Wall Street.'

'A million-dollar rocket.' He was still laughing. 'No thanks. I like it here on the ground, putha. You must learn to walk before you fly.'

'Thanks, Uncle Sumith. See you later.'

Even after I closed the door behind me I could hear him wheezing. I was pissed. I mean, what did he take me for? I was a graduate in economics from a prestigious university in Sydney and he was a middle-grade politician who didn't even have a university degree. I wasn't even sure he had passed his A-Levels. The only markets he knew about were the Ambalangoda fish markets. 'I'll show him, I swear to fucking god,' I promised.

Back in the cavern the TV was on and Aunty Nelunka and Heshan were watching wordlessly, Aunty stroking Heshan's head while he slouched next to her. She turned her head as I came in. 'Niro, darling! How was your business meeting? Did Uncle Sumith help you, Baba?'

I turned to Heshan. 'Nice outfit, Hesh.'

'Thanks.' The TV had Heshan's attention while his fingers absently played with the velcro pockets on his brand-new white Nike tracksuit. Milky Nike high tops squeaked on the floor as he twitched.

'What's wrong, Niro?' said Aunty. 'How was your chat with Uncle Sumith? You want me to talk to him?'

'Heshan, I haven't seen your new car properly,' I said, ignoring her. 'We should go for a ride.'

He stopped playing with his clothes and looked up to his mother. 'Ammi?'

'Not now, Heshan. You haven't even eaten dinner, no?'

'I'll buy you dinner, Hesh,' I chimed. 'We can go to Gallery Café or the buffet at Cinnamon Lakeside.'

He kept staring at Aunty.

'I don't know, Hesh.' She was beginning to crack, looking at me with pleading eyes. 'Niro, why don't you stay and have dinner with us? Heshan hasn't even done his homework.'

'Too bad, Heshan. Your ammi doesn't want you to come with me. You better stay.'

'I'll do the homework later,' Heshan said. 'I can do it when I get back. It's only a little.'

'Hesh!'

'I'll do better if I get to go.'

'Okay, okay. Go. But call me when you get to the restaurant. Otherwise I'll be worried. Niro, make sure he calls. And you better drive. This fellow nearly killed someone yesterday. He doesn't even have a licence.'

I shrugged noncommittally.

'Wait here. I've hidden the keys.' She went upstairs, leaving Heshan and I to smile conspiratorially at each other. This was going to be fun.

Aunty soon returned with the keys. 'Here, take this also.' She tried to press a roll of thousand-rupee notes into my hand.

'What's this?' I backed away.

'It's for dinner. Have something nice.'

'I can't take it.'

'Take it, Niro.'

'No. I don't want your money,' I said, but I let her slip the money in my shirt pocket.

'There. I won't tell anyone the big businessman Niranjan Herath took my money, okay?'

'Go ahead and tell. I'm only taking this for Heshan. I won't use a cent.'

'But it's for both of you!'

'Not a single cent,' I said and turned to go.

There was a flurry of activity behind me, tightening shoelaces, zipping up a running outfit, dispensing goodbye kisses and safety directions.

It was dark outside when I barrelled out the back way, past the kennels. Heshan panted as he ran to keep up with me. The German shepherds barked their heads off and Heshan snapped back, 'Shut up, Misty. Shut up, Harvey.' As I opened the creaky garage gate the driver came out of his quarters and asked if we needed help. I waved him away. Then I remembered my car was parked outside and called him back out and threw him my keys. 'Anil, bring my car into the garage when we're gone. It's parked at the front.'

I switched on the garage light. The car gleamed, its surfaces curved and symmetrical, shining like a pearl under the naked bulb. It was a nice car, even though it didn't have the romance of a classic like my old Merc. 'Not bad,' I said, 'not bad at all.' I unlocked it and got in the driver's seat, breathing in the musky new-car smell.

'Did you know it's got a V6 engine?' said Heshan. 'Seven thousand RPM!' He jumped in the passenger side as I adjusted the mirrors and the seat and started the engine.

'This is automatic. I don't like auto. Makes it feel like dodgem cars.' I turned on the air-conditioner, put it in gear and we slunk almost noiselessly past the east wing of the house.

'It can go from zero to sixty in four-point-seven seconds. I tried.'

'Really?'

'Yeah. It took me seven seconds. Hard to do better on our streets.'

'No shit.' We passed through the gate and got onto the road. The pedals were extra responsive and I raced the engine and braked intermittently to explore their range. Once I had mastered the handling, I fiddled with the radio but couldn't work it out. 'Hesh, my man, can you please get some tunes on this box?'

'It's a Bose,' he said. 'It's got a four channel amplifier and two woofers and six speakers in the doors and four speakers in the dash, and there's a subwoofer in the spare.' He hit some buttons and the music started – some loud, distorted madness. It was on TNL, the rock station, so I asked Heshan to change the channel again. He found Yes FM, which played some half-decent music. I turned up the volume, but it didn't stop Heshan talking.

'Do you know what a VEL engine is? This one has that. It means air going in and out of the engine is controlled.'

'Very nice.'

The weirdo just kept parroting the features as if he'd memorised the whole manual. That was probably what he'd done. I tried not to let it bother me, tried to respond with, 'That's great,' or 'Awesome,' or 'Fucking A,' but it didn't work.

'Hesh, I'm trying to concentrate.'

Nope. No effect. He continued robotically. 'Did you know this about the radiator and that about the exhaust and blah blah blah . . .' It got so annoying that by the time we had entered greater Colombo I thought I would go insane.

'Do you want to play a game?' I asked.

'Okay!'

'Let's play the game where we both shut the hell up for five minutes.'

He stared at me for a little while before an angry look came over his face, his jaw moving, as if he was chewing something unpleasant. 'No,' he said.

'Why not? It's a great game.'

'No. It's not.'

'Look, just try it, all right?'

'No. I won't.'

'I'm going to start. We'll see who wins.'

'I'll tell my ammi.'

'It's just a game, Jesus Christ!'

Heshan finally quietened down. I couldn't tell whether he was still angry or had decided to play along. Neon lights flashing on the shop fronts exposed the lion flags that still hung off the lampposts on Galle Road, gone grey from the smog and dust. I stayed in the right lane, speeding up to keep the private bus fuckers from cutting across, testing out the horn on idiots who decided to cross the road without warning. The bus stops were still crowded, straggling office workers heading home in the dark while the shopping centres and nightspots came to life. Majestic City or MC, home to the kabba – Colombo's great unwashed youth whose sole purpose in life was to fuck around in a shopping mall – was like an ant hill full of dung beetles. I turned left into a little laneway that looked out over the railway tracks into the pitch-black sea. The lane was hardly lit but our headlamps were powerful and I managed a half-decent park. Waves crashed in the distance and MC kabbas chirped as we got out and locked the car.

'Why are we here?' said Heshan.

'It's dinnertime, buddyboy.' I checked my watch. Barely eight. We had at least three hours to kill.

'I thought we were going to Gallery Café.'

'I'm taking you somewhere special. Somewhere you've never been.'

'I don't want to go to MC.'

'I wouldn't step into Majestic City for a million dollars. Don't worry – you're in for a treat.'

We waited until the traffic was at a standstill then threaded through the gaps across to the other side of the road. The light from the little restaurant was bright against the blue of the squat building. Heshan read the name printed on the Coca-Cola board hung above the entrance: 'Hotel De Pillows.'

'Hotel De Pilawoos,' I corrected him.

Heshan screwed up his face in disgust. It was a typical saivar kadé, with the smudged glass counter at the front where the moustachioed sarong-Johnny sat at the register selling cigarettes, bulath, beedi – even some of the special roll-ups if you felt like getting high – and taking payments from the typical clientele – i.e., other sarong-Johnnies. He never left the counter. It was left to the other waiters to go running and suck up to the rich kids who parked their cars in front and demanded the service come to them. The kata-kata of kottu roti being sliced, the smell of fried onions, sweet tea and sweat all mingled with the fresh sea breeze. 'This, good sir, is the best twenty-four/seven restaurant in Colombo,' I said with a sweep of my arm.

'You'll be sick.'

'Heshan, I've been here every night for the past . . . I don't know how many months. There hasn't even been a hint of a loose motion. I haven't had the runs in a long time.'

'Ammi will be mad.'

'Don't be a pussy. You don't have to tell your mother everything. Besides, they do the best iced Milo in town. Not to mention a killer faluda.'

'Is it made from tap water?'

'It's one hundred per cent piss. Now are you coming in or not?'

I left Heshan standing there and went in, past the counter where the man recognised me and said, 'Ah, Niranjan Mahattaya!'

I responded, 'Kohomada, boss!' and took a seat at an empty table. The waiter quickly came over and passed a wet cloth over the chipped wood surface, wiping grains of rice and spilled tea onto his open palm. I watched, chuckling a little, as Heshan crept in, his white contamination suit zipped up to his fat neck. He sat down and stared through the hole in the wall at the cooks wiping sweat off their temples with their shirtsleeves. Then he turned and looked at the fossilised fried chicken and plastic-looking godambas and kottu rotis on display in the glass cabinet.

'Boss!' I called out to the waiter. 'Ice Milo dekak genna.'

I ordered for us both because Heshan seemed petrified. In addition to the Milo, I ordered two chicken kottus, two egg rotis and a bowl of dhal. The food arrived in next to no time and I jumped straight in, not bothering to rinse in the fingerbowl. Heshan would learn. As I expected, gluttony trumped fussiness and he started slowly, asking for a fork with which he stabbed at the shredded roti drenched in curry sauce, speckled with chicken. I watched as his expression changed from apprehension to surprise to sheer, unadulterated joy.

'Good shit, no?'

The kid began stuffing his face so fast he couldn't even speak. He was sweating, from the spice of the meal, from the heat that couldn't be driven out by the ceiling fans that seemed only to blow away flies. Together, we whacked the whole meal in about ten minutes flat – it was brilliant. And the best bit was it cost less than five hundred.

—

We were soon back on the road, heading north. I turned in to 5th Lane where, after getting through the bottleneck, the traffic eased a little. My mood was excellent after that dinner but Heshan was grappling with an ethical conundrum – to tell his mother about eating from a saivar kadé or lie. I felt it was my duty to show him the grey areas, the necessity of deceit in service of the greater good. 'Think about it this way,' I said. 'If you go home and tell Aunty Nelunka that you ate from a dirty place, she's going to get upset. Not only will she be upset with you, she's going to be upset with me – she might even call my mum.'

'But I—'

'Then my mum will be upset and I'll get into trouble. And your ammi, knowing her, will want to make sure you haven't got any diseases from the food you ate. She'll take you to the doctor and the doctor will ask for a whole lot of tests – maybe even take some blood and give you an injection. Maybe even put on a glove and give you an inspection, down in your . . . know what I mean?'

'But I—'

'Your ammi, she'll get so angry she'll complain to your thatthi – and you know what he's like. He'll probably go and get Pilawoos shut down.'

'I don't want any pau.'

'Are you saying you haven't done any pau before, Heshan?'

He shrugged.

'Maybe you'll get a little pau for lying. But think of all the pau you'd get for shutting a whole restaurant down – all those people losing their jobs – they'll have no money to feed their children. That's a lot more pau.'

'You'll be born without a tongue in your next life if you lie.'

'You'll be born without a mouth if you take the food out of other people's. You know the whole reincarnation thing is just a metaphor, right? Our lives go through various cycles that . . .' I glanced at Heshan and he looked confused. 'Look, it's your choice, Hesh-man. Do what you want. Anyway, what matters is that you're all right. How are you feeling? How's your tummy?'

Another shrug. 'Okay.'

'The food hasn't killed you, no? Hell, you could've been drinking water from Beira Lake – nobody would know. Even karma might give you a free pass this time.'

He grumbled and slid forward in his seat, his arms crossed tight against his chest. 'Niro Aiya?' he said. The game was up. As soon as he called me aiya and we could play big brother, little brother, I knew I'd won.

I chuckled. 'Yes, Malli?'

'So you won't tell Ammi about Hotel Pillows?'

'What? Hotel Pillows? Never heard of it.'

'The one we just went to. Hotel De Pillows.'

'Never mind . . . no, we don't have to say anything.' Problem solved.

We got through to Reid Avenue without getting stopped at a single checkpoint. Must have been the car. The kossas had enough common sense not to stop a Nissan Z. I saluted the home of the old foe, Royal College, with its Victorian arches, the elegant orange brick with white borders. It was nice, but not nicer than S. Thomas' – it was no match for our sandstone buildings and beautiful lawns. I said goodbye to Royal and whizzed towards Torrington, sighting Independence Square I did a left onto Maitland Place. Another left and we were directly opposite the Colombo Cricket Club, where I braked smartly at the chain that stopped people from zooming straight into the Clancy's car park. The security guy took one look at the car and skipped across to drop the chain. One thing was for sure. This car got attention. All the dudes and chicks milling around just straight-out stared at us. Heshan got all self-conscious, wriggling in his seat and smiling at his sneakers, which squeaked as he rubbed them together. I didn't take notice of anyone, not even the people I knew, keeping my eyes front and my jaw set like Eastwood from *Unforgiven*. I found an empty spot near the tree next to the northern fence and parked. A security guy ran up and opened the door for me and I told him to keep an eye on the car.

'Haa, sir. Thank you, sir,' he said as I tipped him a hundred rupees. Heshan was excited, hands plunged deep into his jacket as he stared greedily at the babes strutting past in their hottest evening wear. I offered him a cigarette and was surprised when he took it without question. He was learning. Actually, it appeared he already knew a few things, because the little bugger took the lighter from me and lit up like a pro. As he chugged away I realised he had done it before. 'Who taught you to smoke, Heshan?' I asked.

'Thatthi,' he said.

'Really? Uncle Sumith lets you smoke?'

He nodded, blowing smoke out the corner of his mouth. We sat on the car and people-watched as the nicotine sharpened our nerves. Guys like Jason Jayasinghe and Aravinda Samaranayake, who usually had too much padé to look at me, now acknowledged me with a nod and smile as they went past. Jason even gave me a little wave. A group of ex-LC girls who had been part of that too-cool-for-school crowd smiled like crazy, their brightly lipsticked mouths widening like fresh gashes as they walked past wearing short, strappy numbers. After drawing maximum attention in front of the car, we threw our cigarette butts down and went inside.

The bouncers stopped us at the door to the club on the third floor. I showed them my national ID, but Heshan didn't have one. Could I have talked them into letting a seventeen-year-old inside? Probably, but when the barrel-chested man in the white shirt blocked Heshan's path, I said, 'Sorry, Hesh. I forgot you were just a kid.'

He opened and shut his mouth. 'But, I'm . . . I'm . . .' he stammered.

'No identity card, no entry, sir,' said the bouncer, smiling.

'Niro, let's go somewhere else,' said Heshan. 'This place is fucked.'

I was already past the door. 'Wait there,' I shouted. 'I'll be back in a few . . . back soon, all right?' I saw the shoulders of the white tracksuit slump – and then I lost sight of him.

Clancy's was happening. There were some amazing birds. The younger crowd was loaded with talent, proving the point I had once made to Issa: the incidence of hotness within a population of babes was directly proportional to quality of life. These chicks were definitely products of boom-time Colombo. It was evident in the fairness of their skin, the healthy hair, the gleaming eyes, the perfect teeth, the toned abs, the slim but muscular legs – and did I mention tits? Glorious, voluptuous, fresh-as-ripe-melon tits. And they had style to burn, man. All the fashions you'd see in New York or London or Sydney were right here in

Colombo – from the arse-hugging pants to belly-button-low cleavage – it was up to date for sure.

And you know what? My luck appeared to have turned. The stars that Ammi prayed to every day must have aligned, because the ladies had finally opened their eyes and seen me. I had barely walked in when a couple of girls approached, casually, saying, 'You're the guy who was downstairs, no?'

'I could be.'

'You were in the car park, smoking. With your brother?'

'Oh, he's not my brother. He's my driver.'

'Really? He looked young.'

'Yeah. I sent him home.'

'Did he go home in your nice car?'

'Oh no. He must have taken a three-wheeler. The car is mine to drive whenever I like.' Niro Herath was The Man. My time was finally here, and my options were limitless. I had a couple of drinks, starting with a gin and tonic before moving on to rum and coke. The music was killer. The DJ was playing some old soul numbers that made me move involuntarily. I got on the dance floor and pulled out the moves, and, man, they just flowed out of me – I don't know how but that night I was like Michael Jackson on speed. The girls were going crazy, dancing around me, grinding up on me, but I wasn't going to be cornered. I left them wanting more and went back to the bar and bought a round of drinks for the ladies sitting there. Of course, one or two snobbish women refused, and the men were pissed off, but plenty of girls gathered around and did shots with me. Sure, it was going to cost almost half the day's earnings (courtesy of Aunty Nelunka), but it was worthwhile. The chicks started asking questions like, 'Which school did you go to? How come you have an Aussie-sounding accent? What do you do, like, for work and stuff?'

I told them I was a Thomian, that I'd been in Sydney for around five years and was bringing all my knowledge of economics to Lanka to exploit an undiscovered market. Some of the more panditha women were like, 'What sort of business? Tell, will you?'

'If I tell you, I'd have to kill you.'

Then an absolute babe emerged through the crowd, with a mole or a beauty spot on her dimpled cheek, long hair curled and resting on her bare shoulders, turquoise dress cut off at her thighs showing off a pair of spectacular legs – I was either really drunk or she was completely amazing. She came up to me and said, 'Are you Niranjan?'

'How did you know?'

She flashed a brilliant smile. 'I just knew.' She reached into her handbag and pulled something out. 'Here's your phone.' I couldn't believe it. This was an unbelievable stroke of luck.

We talked. About work, about travel, sports, school, life ... we talked about everything. By the time I was done, she let me take her hand and lead her through the crowd, down the stairs and into the car park.

Outside, I looked around and couldn't see Heshan anywhere, but I didn't care. I'd deal with it later. Tonight was for fun. I was relieved he wasn't sitting on the hood of the car, but there was someone else standing in front admiring it. Arnolda. Pot-bellied, dark-as-goraka, clown-shoed Arnolda. Him and his two cronies – Jordan and

Najab. 'This is the new Nissan Z?' Arnolda asked without even turning to look at me. He touched the bonnet lightly, lovingly.

I kept my answers abrupt. 'Yep,' I said.

He turned to me and said, 'This is yours, Niro? Which model? Three-seventy?'

'Three hundred and something, man – why do you care?'

Arnolda wouldn't be dismissed. 'Just asking, machan. Must be the 370Z,' he said gently. He went around to inspect the rear, then came back around and looked at me as if he was looking at a completely different person – with respect and admiration and jealousy. 'It's beautiful.'

I felt vague regret. I wanted to spend more time showing off the car and the girl, basking in the feeling of finally being able to put him in his place, show him who's who, but I didn't want to be seen with his kind and was itching to get laid. 'Well, the lady and I are about to leave,' I said.

Arnolda dropped back, still gazing at the car as I opened the door for the girl. And then a strange thing happened. Arnolda's eyes narrowed and focused on her as she climbed in and sat down. She looked at him with a weird, sad look in her eyes and said, 'Hi Angelo.'

'Hi,' he said. 'Hi Amrita.' The way he whispered her name, with a sweetness, an affection, it made something break inside me, like a wall, a barrier that had for so long held back my rage – and all I could hear was the sound of blood rushing to my head.

I stopped, still holding the door open. 'Do you know him?'

'Angelo? Yeah, we used to go out,' she said. 'Long time ago.'

'Get out,' I snarled.

Her lips quivered. 'Why? What's wrong?'

'Get out of my car!'

I felt Arnolda coming closer, to see if there was something wrong, and the whore got out and rushed towards him – as if the fat fuck could protect her – and I spun around to find a whole bunch of fellows surrounding me. Arnolda's cronies had multiplied. All the leeches that hung around that place had gathered to watch the cool dude with the nice car get into trouble.

'This is the last time,' I spat at Arnolda. 'Think it's funny, do you, messing with my life?'

'Sorry? What?'

'Don't pretend you don't know, you prick!' I jabbed him in the chest. 'First Sonali, now her.' I pointed at the deceitful bitch standing next to Arnolda.

'What the fuck are you talking about, you crazy bugger? Are you mad?'

I shoved him. 'I'm going to kill you.' I pointed at the rest of them, at all the bastards standing around, watching. 'All you fuckers stay out of my way. You don't know who I am.'

'Who are you?' some smart-arse yelled out.

'I'm Niranjan Herath!' I roared. 'Remember that name.'

'Niro,' said Arnolda, reaching for me, 'calm down, bro. Don't get all—'

'I'm not your bro, you filthy Tamil.' I swung hard, my fist scything through the cool night air, straight at his jaw. He ducked too late and I hit him in the nose with a crunch. Something had snapped. My hand felt shattered. I brought it up to my chest, just as Arnolda staggered backwards, blood seeping through his fingers as he covered his face. The whore, who had been standing like a statue, opened her mouth and let out a scream. The tall bugger, Jordan, moved quickly, but before he could reach me two huge fuckers got between us. The Clancy's bouncers had arrived at the scene.

'Okay,' I said, putting my hands up. One of the bouncers grabbed me and I tried to shake him off, but his grip was solid. The other grabbed Jordan with one hand and Najab, who was frothing at the mouth, with the other. They dragged us out. The onlookers hooted like a pack of jackals. Arnolda followed, plugging his nose with the bitch's handkerchief, muffling his curse words. The bouncer took me almost to the exit but didn't go all the way out. Lazy fucker. He let me go just before the gate. The bouncer following us with Arnolda's friends did the same. I turned back towards them but the bouncer pushed me away.

'Let me get my car!' I said.

'No. Out.'

'Fine. I'm going. But you're going to see me again. Remember this face. You'll see it very soon.' I turned on my heel to stride out but tripped over the chain hanging across the exit and lost my balance. Thadaang! I went down straight on my elbow, body twisting as I landed. The side of my head thudded into the ground. A high-pitched crackle ignited in my ears and searing pain shot through my neck. My arm felt broken. The world went hazy. When the sounds and visions settled only four figures loomed over me. Arnolda, his buddies and his prostitute ex-girlfriend. Everyone else had lost interest. Five of us on the empty street, the throb of a hundred bodies in a nightclub suspended above us. 'You broke my hand, you fuckers,' I mumbled. 'Third-class dogs. You should all be shot. Fucking terrorist filth.'

'You know what's wrong with you, Herath?' It was a whisper. 'You don't know when to shut your mouth.' They kicked me in the ribs, even the girl, her heel sharp against my bones. My arm, surely broken, hurt like nothing I've ever felt before. Najab grabbed me by the leg and dragged me onto the road. I struggled and my sight blurred again, flickering between dark and light. Suddenly, all I could see was the moon between the trees, hanging in the sky like a curved piece of heaven, stars all around it. Arnolda leaned over, his face blocking my view, his broken nose crusty with blood. 'You bastard. Why did you have to go and do that?' he said.

'Fuck you,' I said, spitting in his face. 'I'm going to kill you. Then I'll kill your family.'

'Smash him,' I heard the woman say.

Arnolda's face moved away and the moon was there again, bright and dappled. Latha used to tell me about the rabbit up there. She used to show me the spots on its surface and say, 'Can you see, Niranjan Baby? Can you see the haawa?' Little snotrag that I was, I always said, 'What haawa? There's no haawa. Don't be stupid.' Why was I such a prick? Why, of all the people, did I have to be an arsehole to her?

It was Arnolda's friend, Jordan, who now blocked my view. He had one of those concrete bollards, heavy and phallic in his hands. I was like, 'I'm sorry, I'm sorry, I'm sorry,' but it wasn't to Arnolda and his friends. I was saying sorry to Latha, for being such a coward, for not caring, for not asking what she wanted to do with the rest of her life, whether she wanted to go away and live with her brother in the village or stay with us, sorry I had never thanked her for everything she'd done – but it was all too late. Jordan raised the bollard above his head like a massive dick pointed at heaven. I was paralysed, knowing it was all over, knowing he was going to bring it crashing down on my head. My skull was about to be smashed into a million pieces. But then a thing, grunting like a farm creature, white and fat, came hurtling across and slammed into Jordan's side. He lost balance and the bollard fell, crashing onto the tarmac, sending Arnolda's mob scattering as it rolled out to the middle of the road.

'Niro?' said Heshan, kneeling beside me. 'Don't die, okay?'

Somewhere in the distance I heard a siren. 'What did you do that for?' I said. 'I was going to kill those fuckers.' And then everything went black.

LATHA

IT MUST HAVE BEEN BAD KARMA. I WAS WORRIED ABOUT NIRANJAN Baby. His arm was broken, his head was aching and he had to sit down from time to time because he was feeling kalanthaya. If he didn't sit he might fall and hurt himself again.

Then I found the goldfish floating on the water that had gone green. There was too much work for me and I had forgotten to clean the tank. I had forgotten to feed the fish. I caught his dead body with my fingers, took him out to the garden where I dug a hole next to the anthurium plant. Buried him. I turned off the motor. The tank was heavy and I couldn't lift it so I used a bowl to take out the water. When it was lighter I took the tank down from the shelf and cleaned all the moss. I was finishing the job when I heard the tilling-tilling sound of the phone, so I wiped my hands on my skirt, hoping Niranjan Baby didn't see, and ran to answer.

It was my aiya. His voice sounded rough, like he had some sort of illness. 'Latha?' he said. 'Your akka's son is dead.'

'Who?' I asked, not because I didn't know, but because I was surprised. Everything was happening so fast.

'Kumara,' Aiya said, the kara-kara sound on the bad phone line making him harder to hear. 'Your sister's son. The boy who was in the army.'

I remembered Kumara from the time I visited Akka in the village. That was when he was still going to school, a long-armed boy in a yellowing uniform. He was shy like his father, said very little, just smiled and chewed his nails. 'What happened?' I whispered into the phone.

'Died on the battlefield.'

'But . . . the war is finished. They say all the Tigers are dead.'

'There are still Tigers hiding,' said Aiya. 'Kumara stepped on a landmine. The body . . . the remains will be brought to the village in two days. They said it's taking time because the doctors have to do tests and see what really happened.'

I didn't know what to say. My head was empty. I was still feeling bad for killing the goldfish.

'Are you coming to the funeral?'

I didn't know them, didn't even know my akka very well. I should have been sad about the boy, I should have said something to make Aiya feel better, but I didn't try.

'The army is paying for the coffin and cremation – for most of the funeral. But there is a lot of work. Cooking and cleaning, arranging things for the priests – a lot of things you can do to help us.'

'I . . . I have to ask Mano Mahattaya.'

'He won't let you take a day for your akka's son's funeral?'

'It's been very difficult—'

'It's always difficult for those people.' Aiya's voice changed. It became hard. 'Come if you want. If you can't – then all of you can get hit by hena.' And before I could say anything, he cut the call.

I put the phone down and stood there in the corridor. Maybe the call was cut by accident. Maybe he'd call again. Aiya was angry. The phone didn't ring anymore. I was scratching my head when Niranjan Baby walked out of his room. I quickly picked up the Dettol and started cleaning the speaking piece of the phone.

'Who was that?' he asked.

'Nobody,' I said, avoiding his eyes, looking closely at the phone, making sure I rubbed the Dettol over all the places my spit could have gone.

'Nobody?' he repeated. 'Then why did you talk for so long?'

I put the phone down. 'It was my aiya,' I said quietly.

'Is he asking you to come to the village again?'

'Yes.'

'What did you say?'

'I said I'll ask Mano Mahattaya.'

'Do you want to go?' Niranjan Baby played with the rope around his neck with his good hand. 'You should go . . . if you want.'

'It'll be good if I can go.'

'Yes,' he said, putting a finger in through the opening of the plaster cast, trying to scratch a place on his elbow he couldn't reach. He sounded less angry than he'd been in the past few weeks. 'You can do what you want in the village, no? You can be free.'

'Do what I want? No, Niranjan Baby. Not at the funeral.'

'What funeral?'

'I'm going to the funeral. My akka's son has died.'

'Ah,' he said, taking his finger out of the plaster and looking at me. His face became brighter as he smiled. 'I thought you were leaving us.' He let out a small laugh.

I laughed too. 'No, no. My aiya called to ask me to come to the funeral.' Then I felt bad and made my face normal again. 'It's not good to laugh.'

Niranjan Baby also forced himself to stop smiling. 'Right,' he said, turning away. 'When are you leaving? Tomorrow?'

'I have to go tomorrow or early the day after tomorrow to get to the village in time.'

'I'll tell Thatthi,' he said and went back to his room. 'You don't worry about it.'

—

What would the funeral be like? Would Akka be crying? Would her husband still look at me with his scary, red eyes and say nothing? Maybe I'll get to see Aiya's wife and kids. My head was full of these things as I came home with Anoushka Baby in the three-wheeler. We got home and Anoushka Baby stopped in front of the empty fish tank. 'What happened to the fish?' she said, frowning.

'The goldfish died,' I said, putting the heavy schoolbag down.

'Died? How did he die?'

'I forgot to give him food. I was busy looking after Niranjan Baby and—'

'How can you forget to feed the fish! You starved it!' Anoushka Baby's eyebrows got closer, the gap between them on her forehead almost closed. That was what happened when she was angry. 'You're useless!'

'Sorry, Anoushka Baby. I was looking after your aiya. You know what it was like, no?'

'You couldn't have done anything for Niro anyway. You can't do anything. Can't even look after a fish – how can you look after a person?'

'I'm not a doctor,' I said, trying to make her laugh. But the joke was old and I realised it won't work and the last part came out softly. 'I'm a bus conductor.'

'You're an idiot!' she said, throwing the door open and rushing into the house. 'Fish murderer!'

I followed her inside, put the bag on a chair and took out her lunch box. 'Anoushka Baby?' I called out to her as she closed the door to her room. 'Please give me your school clothes. I have to wash them.' But she wasn't talking to me. By the time she changed clothes the dirt got into the white and I had to scrub very hard to get it out.

—

When I was making indi-aappa for dinner Mano Mahattaya came into the kitchen. While I mixed the dough with my hands he asked me what had happened, why I needed to go to the village. I told him what I knew. He asked which army Kumara was in, where he was fighting.

'I don't know, Mahattaya,' I said.

'Don't know anything about your own sister's son? What do you and your brother talk about?' he asked, as he tied his sarong tighter. 'When he comes to see you, when he calls – what does he say?'

'Aiya talks about his own family. His wife and children,' I said. 'And I listen.'

'This akka, she's the one you were living with before you came here?'

'Yes, Mahattaya.'

'But you don't know her? Haven't seen her since?'

'I saw her once, Mahattaya. A long time ago – I saw the boy also.'

'This woman is your real sister? Not someone you're calling akka because she's older than you?'

'No, Mahattaya. She's my sister.' I finished kneading and put a small amount of indi-aappa dough in the metal mould.

'And this aiya?'

'He didn't live with us. He lived somewhere else . . . but he's my aiya.'

'How would you know? You don't even have a birth certificate,' said Mano Mahattaya.

I fixed the long pushing piece into the big hole where the dough went and squeezed the handles together so the flour mixture came through the small holes like worms. I moved my hands so it fell properly into a circle on the mesh tray.

'Who will do the cooking? I don't have money to buy food from outside every day.' Mano Mahattaya put his hands on his hips, making his stomach push out. 'How long did you say you needed?'

'The funeral is day after tomorrow, Mahattaya. After that there's the day-seven dhanay.'

'The alms-giving always happens after seven days, no? A week. Budhu ammo! How will I afford food from outside for seven days? I still have Niranjan's hospital bills – doctors are expensive these days. I don't get money from a tree—'

I finished the first lot of indi-aappa and put them in the steamer. Then I turned on the cooker, put the pan of water on and covered it with the steamer.

'—and Niranjan has still not recovered fully.'

I put the kiri hodi on the fire. 'I don't have to go, Mahattaya,' I said. 'I can stay.'

As Mano Mahattaya walked away shaking his head, I stirred the kiri hodi. What would happen if I didn't go? Nothing, but I didn't want to tell Aiya that. He'd shout at me if I called and said I wasn't coming. No, I'll keep quiet. The funeral and the day-seven dhanay would pass. Nobody will miss me. Aiya will be angry but at least I won't hear it. Maybe he'll stop calling me. Stop coming to see me. But even that won't make a big difference. I'll be here and he'll be there.

After serving dinner I sat on the floor taking a rest. I had been on my feet all day. I was listening to Mohideen Baig sing that song about the sansaaré on the radio, the one where he sings, 'The name doesn't die, the body dies.' He sings so well I'd never know he was Muslim if I didn't know his name. When he's singing, he makes me think about my next life and what I'd like to be if I had enough pinn. How much pinn do you need to be born a bird? I didn't want to be a crow because that would be a curse, having to eat dead animals and garbage, being so black and ugly and always chattering like a Tamil. I want to be a parrot or a mynah or one of those little vee-kurullas. I'd fly from tree to tree with other birds, eat mango and rambutan and all the tasty fruits . . .

The sound of Nona's slippers came surra-surra right up to me. I turned off the radio and jumped to my feet. 'Nona,' I said. 'Give me the plate.'

She handed the plate, looking at me in an odd way. Maybe there was something on my face, some flour or hodi that had rubbed on. I wanted to wipe my face but knew Nona wouldn't like me touching her plate afterwards.

'Latha,' she said. 'Who's the boy who died?'

'My akka's son, Nona.'

'Your akka. The one who lives in Sinhagama?'

'Yes.'

'How old was he?'

'Maybe twenty, twenty-two?'

Nona's hand came up to her mouth. 'So young! He was in the army?'

'Yes, Nona.'

'Does your akka have more children?'

'A daughter.'

'How old is she?'

'She's older, Nona. Must be more than twenty. She has a baby.'

'So your akka was the oldest? You and your brother are younger than your akka?'

'Yes, Nona.'

'This boy — what happened?'

'Stepped on a landmine.'

'And they couldn't do anything. Didn't take him to hospital?'

'I don't know, Nona. Aiya didn't tell me.'

Nona was standing close to me. She wanted to tell me that she was very sorry. I could see all this was reminding her of her people in the north. 'You want to go to the funeral, no?' she asked.

I lifted my shoulders. 'I don't have to go.'

'You should go,' she said.

Just as she said this, thada-bada, Mano Mahattaya rushed into the kitchen again. 'She doesn't want to go,' he said, with a finger pointing at me.

'Yes, she does,' said Nona.

'What? Did the woman change her tune? She told me she doesn't want to go.'

'She didn't say anything – but anybody with feelings will want to go.' Nona frowned at Mano Mahattaya.

'Why did you have to come here and ruin it?' he said to Nona. 'I told you to just let it be, no?'

They were starting to argue so I stepped away, put Nona's leftovers in the bin and went to the sink with Nona's plate. I took the coconut skin I used for a brush, scrubbed the plate with soap.

'You're a gentleman in name only,' said Nona. 'This woman's sister's only son dies – her only nephew – and you won't even let her go to the funeral.'

I opened the tap again and washed off the soap.

'She's the one doesn't want to go. She's the one who said, "I don't want to go to the funeral, Mahattaya." Don't blame me. You couldn't let her be. Came here and mollycoddled her. Of course after that she changed her mind.'

I dried the plate with a cloth and put it on the rack.

'You think she's some sort of robot who's here to cook and clean and wash your clothes without taking a rest? You think she doesn't feel anything when someone dies? You think she's—'

The shouting stopped for a little as Anoushka Baby came in and put her plate in the sink and washed her hands. She turned around and shook her fingers, sending drops of water all over the floor, and muttered, 'She killed the fish.'

I took Anoushka Baby's plate and started washing it.

'You see!' said Mano Mahattaya. 'You see what happens when you baby her? You're coddling this woman, Lakshmi. She neglected her work and now the fish is dead.'

'Anoushka, this is none of your business,' said Nona. 'How can Latha do a hundred things at once? She has to do everything around the house, and after Niranjan was hurt she had to look after him too. Any of you could have fed the fish but you didn't do it, did you? Did you?'

I wiped the water off Anoushka Baby's plate with the cloth.

Anoushka Baby went to the fridge and took out the ice-cream. 'It's her job, she's the servant.' She took a bowl from the cupboard, a spoon from the drawer and scraped two big balls of ice-cream. 'We don't get paid.'

'You and your father are the same, aren't you? Too lazy to do a thing around the house but you can complain. You don't care about anyone but yourselves.'

'Niro doesn't do anything either,' said Anoushka Baby.

Just as she said that, Niranjan Baby appeared. Anoushka Baby put a big spoonful of ice-cream in her mouth. Everyone stepped aside to let Niranjan Baby and his sideways arm into the kitchen. It was getting crowded.

He gave me his plate and turned to go, all of them again making room for Niranjan Baby to pass, but before he left, Mano Mahattaya asked him, 'What do you think, Niranjan?'

'What do I think about what?'

'Should Latha go to the village for this funeral or not?'

'It's not my decision.'

'You're the fellow who came to me and said her sister's son had died, no? What's your opinion?'

'Have you asked her?'

Everyone turned to me. I quickly scrubbed the plate with soap and washed it. I had dried it and was about to put it on the rack when Nona said, 'Do it properly. We don't want any more illnesses in this house.' They stood there and waited as I washed the plate again. I was afraid I'll make a mistake with everyone watching but I did it slowly, properly, and after I finished drying and put it away, Nona asked me again. 'Tell us, Latha. What do you want? Do you want to go to the funeral or not?'

The four faces, all almost the same but a little different, looked at me, all giving me different looks. Anoushka Baby broke the silence. 'Fish murderer,' she muttered.

'Tell them what you told me,' said Mano Mahattaya. 'Tell them. You don't want to go.'

'Shut up, Mano,' said Lakshmi Nona. 'Let her talk.'

'What do you think, Nona?' I said, hoping Nona would decide. It was becoming too difficult for me.

'Just tell us what you want,' said Niranjan Baby.

I didn't want to say it but it jumped out of my mouth. 'I . . . I want to go and see if my aiya and akka are all right.' I wanted to push the words back in. 'But I can't go because there will be no one to do work here.'

'Haiyo,' said Mano Mahattaya under his breath. 'We'll have to buy lunch and dinner for a week. Don't expect Flower Drum every day, I'll tell you now.'

'We don't want your Flower Drum,' said Nona.

'Are you going to cook, then? Ah?'

'Why should I cook?' said Nona. 'You do it.'

'Me?' Mano Mahattaya let out a little laugh. 'Now I know you're pulling my leg.'

'If you can't do it, why should I?'

'What do you think we're going to eat then?'

Nona stepped across to Anoushka Baby, who was licking the spoon, and put her arms around Baby's shoulders. 'You know, we haven't gone on a trip in a long time. What do you say, Anoushka?'

Mano Mahattaya stared at Nona. 'What do you mean? Like a holiday?'

'You're the one who's been saying, "Let's go somewhere, Lakshmi. Let's do something together, like the old days." This is your chance. We can go up to Anuradhapura.' She turned to me. 'Sinhagama is near Anuradhapura, isn't it, Latha?'

'Yes, Nona,' I said.

'But,' Mano Mahattaya stammered, 'but, I didn't . . .'

'What, you can't keep your promises?'

'That's a great idea,' said Niranjan Baby. 'You guys can go have a nice holiday while Latha checks in on her people.'

'You're not staying,' said Lakshmi Nona. 'How are you going to manage with your broken bones? You can't even walk to the shop without falling down.'

'I hate Anuradhapura,' said Anoushka Baby. 'It's hot and boring and there's cow dung everywhere.'

'Anoushka!' said Mano Mahattaya. 'It's one of our sacred cities. It's a very important place. Don't say kata-kedana things.'

'I'm not coming,' said Niranjan Baby. 'I'll manage.'

'We're all going,' said Nona. 'I don't have much, but I have a little savings. Can you contribute, Mano?'

'No,' said Mano Mahattaya, shaking his head. 'I don't have any. I can't afford.'

'Fine,' said Nona, looking around at everyone. 'I'll pay. After everything that's happened, Lord knows we need it.'

—

I got up at four in the morning and went to the bakery in the dark, bought a can of fish and a fresh loaf from the baker. The bread was still hot in my hands when I got home. I mixed onions and green chilli with the fish and sliced the bread. Butter, cheese and fish – that was how Nona had shown me how to make sandwiches. My sandwich didn't need butter because butter was expensive. I didn't toast them, knowing they'd sweat on the way, and wrapped them in polythene leaves and newspaper. Before I started cooking breakfast and lunch, I filled a big can of water and put some plastic cups in a bag. Breakfast was the green-coloured rice porridge, kola kenda. Lunch – rice, chicken, dhal, karola and sambola. I had prepared the dhal and karola the day before, knowing they wouldn't go bad overnight.

Nona woke up before six o'clock, just as the sunshine fell. She came into the kitchen and asked me if the food was ready, then woke up Mano Mahattaya and brought the car keys from his room. Everyone's clothes had been packed – Nona had made sure of it – one suitcase for Nona and Anoushka Baby, a bag each for Niranjan Baby and Mano Mahattaya. When Nona opened the dickie of the car, I carried them all out. I pushed my bag, Nona's old one with the broken zip, in the side, next to the shoes. 'Don't forget your identity card,' said Nona. 'We'll get stopped at a checkpoint or two.'

I served the kola kenda with a piece of jaggery. While everyone ate I finished the rest of the cooking and packed all the lunches, making sure I kept the hot sambola away from Anoushka Baby's meal and replaced meat with some leftover fish in Nona's. After I put the lunch in the car I went around the house to check if all the doors and windows were locked, that none of the taps were leaking and the gas cylinder was properly shut. I locked the front door. Mano Mahattaya reversed the car out and I closed the gate and padlocked it. I got into the back seat, next to Nona, and gave her the key. On Nona's other side Anoushka Baby was still half-asleep, her head on Nona's shoulder. Niranjan Baby was sitting in front, his broken arm on his lap, his seat leaning back. Mano Mahattaya said, 'Right. Let's go,' and we started.

It was still early and there wasn't much traffic, just a few buses and three-wheelers. Beggars woke up and moved their cardboard and newspaper beds from the front steps of kadés that were beginning to open. Big shops rolled up their shutters. Televisions were turned on in the windows and a few people going to work early stopped to watch them. Fruit sellers hung bananas from hooks, spraying the mangoes, apples and oranges with water. In the small kadés, men stacked newspapers, opened up the gunny sacks full of grains, sprinkled the front pavement with turmeric water to keep away flies. The lotterai men cleared their throats and started to make their announcements into loudspeakers. We passed through Colombo and the buildings became smaller and smaller, the houses less clean and looked after. Walls that had gone without paint were black with mould. Some houses were half-built – people building them must have run out of money before they could finish, their dreams going nowhere like the concrete staircases that didn't have a second floor to reach. There was green everywhere – long grass, banana trees, kos fruit fallen on the side of the narrowing road that twisted like a snake through the paddy fields and coconut plantations.

Mano Mahattaya and Lakshmi Nona argued about whether to go on the Kurunegala Road or take the Puttalama way. Nona said that although the road was being built it'd be much faster on the Puttalama Road, but Mano Mahattaya thought the Kurunegala Road was better and he was the driver and in the end he decided. 'This road has more things to see. We can see the ruins in Dambadeniya and Yapahuwa.'

Nona pointed at mountains far away that looked like elephants lying down, at temples, lime-washed and clean, standing like milk teeth against the earth and blue-green paddies. Her children didn't say anything. 'Look,' she said. 'Look at that kingfisher on the telephone poles. And those king coconuts hanging from the tree! So big!'

I saw some mee harak with curved horns, white birds on their backs, and I said, 'Look. Mee harak.'

'Why look at those buffaloes when you're right here,' Anoushka Baby mumbled.

'Don't say that, Anoushka,' said Nona. 'It's not nice . . . Look at the egrets, picking fleas on the water buffalo's back. See how they're helping each other?'

'Yes, yes,' said Anoushka Baby.

The only talk after that was when Nona asked if anyone was hungry. We stopped at a roadside stall where she bought some mango, papaw and pineapple. I took the fruits from her and put them in the car. The fruit seller was friendly. He let the family sit on one of his benches and eat sandwiches. I stood next to a culvert and ate mine.

Back on the road we passed lakes and forests with prickly bushes, little birds and insects flying in and out. A big lizard – a kabaragoya – flicked its tongue and disappeared into a stream, its tail cutting through the muddy water. After we passed a tea kadé and a hospital, Mahattaya said, 'We're coming into Athuruwela, the place they used to call Dambadeniya. You know how the ancient capital moved from Polonnaruwa to Dambadeniya, no, Anoushka?'

'Yes.'

'Who was the last king of Polonnaruwa?'

'Um . . .' Anoushka Baby said sleepily. 'Vijayabahu?'

'Vijayabahu! What are you talking? It was Kalinga Magha. Remember how the bugger came from India with his Chola armies, sacked the place and tried to take over the whole country?'

'Ah, yeah,' said Anoushka Baby.

I looked at Nona. Did she know Chola was what they called Tamil people in the old days?

'This trip is like we're going through all the kingdoms – Dambadeniya, Yapahuwa, Anuradhapura, Polonnaruwa . . .'

'We're not going to Kandy,' said Anoushka Baby. 'We should've gone to Kandy. Kandy's much better.'

'Kandy's a nice place,' said Mano Mahattaya, 'but I think the best part is here. All the big fights against the Cholas were up this way . . .' He looked back at Nona in the mirror but she kept looking out of the window. 'And the best castles and temples.'

'The Temple of the Tooth is nice,' said Anoushka Baby. 'At least it's not all broken.'

'I thought you'd like broken things,' said Niranjan Baby.

'Huh?' said Anoushka Baby. 'Why would I like broken things?'

'I thought you like the grunge stuff, ruins are pretty grungy—'

'Shut up, stupid cripple.'

'Ah yeah, you're into what – punk – not grunge, no?'

'Shut up!'

'Enough, enough,' said Mano Mahattaya. 'Look, we're coming to a checkpoint. Stop fighting or they'll arrest both of you.'

He slowed down as a soldier waved his red sign, asking the car to stop. There were two of them, young boys like Kumara, wearing army clothes. They put their hands on the guns hanging on their shoulders, looked at us closely as we stopped. I could feel Nona next to me, her body tightening as if someone was going to hit her.

The smart, straight-standing one in dark green clothes must have been the lokka. He came walking up and said, 'Identity cards, please?'

'Yes,' said Mano Mahattaya, reaching in his back pocket. 'How are you, officer?'

'Fine,' said the army lokka. 'Where are you going today?' He looked at Mano Mahattaya's ID card.

'Going to Anuradhapura,' said Mahattaya. 'We're coming from Colombo. It's a holiday,' he said.

'We're actually going to a funeral, Thatthi,' said Niranjan Baby.

The army lokka bent to look at him through the car window. 'Is it a holiday or a funeral?' he asked, handing Mano Mahattaya's ID back to him.

Niranjan Baby and Mano Mahattaya looked at each other. Mano Mahattaya spoke first. 'Our servant is going for a funeral. Her sister's son died.'

'Your servant,' said the army man. He looked at the three of us in the back seat as if he couldn't tell I was the servant. The blood was leaving Nona's face fast.

'My sister's son,' I said.

'You're the servant?' he asked me.

'Yes.'

'What happened to your sister's son?'

'He was in the army,' I said.

'Is that true? Which regiment?'

'I don't know,' I said. 'I haven't seen him since he was small.'

'Why is that?'

'I couldn't. I had to work.' That was all. I couldn't say more. How could I explain everything to him? How could I tell an outsider that I never liked my akka because when I was small she was always too tired to play with me, she never gave me toys, never lifted a finger when I was hurt, always made me do things for her like walking miles for water and filling a kalaya from the well and bringing it back on my head, sorting chillies drying on a mat in the burning sun? And all the times she got angry and hit me if I made a mistake? How could I tell him that as soon as I got the chance I left Akka with no one to help and came to Colombo because I thought Colombo was better?

'Hmm,' said the army man leaning on the car, still looking in. 'So you're going to the funeral?' As if he'd already forgotten what we told him before.

'Yes.'

'But everyone else is going for a holiday?'

At first I didn't say anything. Nona was looking down at her lap, a hand gripping the other wrist.

'Hmm?' said the army man, making the noise like a question. 'You know there's been a war, no? Do you think it's a good time for a holiday?'

'They're taking me to the funeral,' I said. 'And staying at a guesthouse in Anuradhapura because there's no room at my sister's house. It's not a holiday.'

He straightened and walked around to the other side of the car. 'Okay,' he said. 'Let's see the other identity cards.'

I took mine out of my blouse pocket. Niranjan Baby took his from the wallet in his shorts. Anoushka Baby was looking at Nona because her card was in Nona's purse, but Nona was still looking down at her hands. 'Ammi,' she whispered. 'Ammi, I need my card.'

Nona looked at her suddenly and said something in Ingrisi. The soldier bent again to look inside the car. Nona took out both cards and gave them to Anoushka Baby, who handed them to the army man.

After he looked at all the cards he handed them back and waved us through. 'Okay,' he said. 'Go.'

—

Nobody spoke. It was only after we were far from the checkpoint that Nona's breathing went back to normal and her body loosened. When the car finally stopped in a sandy place surrounded by trees, Nona let out a long sigh. We left our slippers in the car, jumped over rocks and thorns and went towards the slope covered in grass. At the top was an old doorway made of raw bricks and concrete. We went in. The buildings inside the temple looked a lot like other temples I had seen before – with the square wooden pillars and pointed roofs – all of them looking the same, different only in size. Mano Mahattaya went straight in, over the long stone step and between the posts sticking out of the sand, leaning and worn like old, bald men. He stopped in front of some steps going into a building, the moonstone near his feet, and looked back. 'Come, come,' he called out to all of us, waving his hand.

Anoushka Baby dragged her feet, making lines in the sand as Lakshmi Nona led her along. Niranjan Baby, wearing his sunglasses, came slowly behind. He walked right past everyone, over the moonstone, and sat on a step.

'You all know what this is, no?' said Mano Mahattaya, pointing at the stone carving. 'The sandakada pahana.'

'Here we go again,' said Anoushka Baby.

'You don't want to hear it?' asked Mano Mahattaya. 'That's fine. You can go. Everyone else will listen.'

'We've heard about the moonstone a billion times,' said Anoushka Baby. 'Can we just go?'

'No,' said Nona in a strong voice. 'You need to learn some respect. Listen.'

We looked down at the half-circle but it was so old and faded you couldn't properly see any of the carvings.

'This one's not a very good example,' said Mano Mahattaya. 'I'll explain it anyway.'

He kept talking, in the temple and then in the car, all the way from Dambadeniya to Yapahuwa until we finally stopped at Polonnaruwa. Mano Mahattaya kept telling us about all the kings and their wars, about queens and palaces and rock temples, about princes who ran away and paintings that were washed off, mountains with messages in them, tanks that gave water to rice fields, rice that was grown and sent over the sea, the old hospitals and water fountains and toilets – he talked a lot about the toilets and how they were very good for their time. I didn't remember the order, didn't remember which story belonged to which king. What I remembered was what Mano Mahattaya said about the sandakada pahana: 'Different people have different ways of reading the moonstone. According to Professor Paranavithana, a very famous archaeologist, the Anuradhapura stones are the originals. He says it's a representation of the sansaaré – the great wheel of life.

'The fire ring, that shows how life is difficult – we're always burning because we want things – you know how Buddha says desire is the cause of pain – that's what this means.

'The animals going round and round, one after the other – that's for four noble truths, or chathurarya sathya, the never-ending circle of being born, growing old, getting sick and dying. The elephant stands for birth, the horse means old age, the lion is illness and the bull is death. This happens over and over and over again.

'The next ring, so third one from the outside – that one is the liyavela. You know what liyavela is? It's a vine. Like the one Tarzan swings from, Anoushka. Once again, that's desire. It's keeping us tied to this life, even when we are trying to let go.

'The one after that? Swan? You know what the swan can do? Separate milk from water. So this swan means you have separated the truth from all the lies. The real meaning has been found.

'Finally, what do we have in the middle? The lotus. It's the end. Nibbana. After that there is no more suffering.'

—

In the morning I wore a grey skirt because I didn't have a white one. The white blouse with small blue flowers on the chest was good for a funeral. They weren't lotus flowers but I felt good when I wore that blouse. Doing a puja with flowers gave more pinn, I knew that, but did wearing flowers give us pinn too? But if we were trying to get to nibbana, to stop being born again, why did we need pinn? What good was collecting pinn if you didn't have another life to use it? I tried to understand, but when we left the guesthouse I felt more confused, the liyavela winding around my feet. Like the forests we passed as we got closer and closer to my village, my mind was twisted and dark. A hundred people with manna swords couldn't clear it.

I wasn't smart enough. The proper meaning of things didn't stay in my head. Why were the animals going around in a circle, all of them going the same way? Why couldn't they turn and go straight to the flower? Was it pau to think of old things this way? But I wasn't the only one to do it, no? Mano Mahattaya said it himself: 'The moonstone changed. The bull was removed because of the Hindu people. They didn't want anyone stepping on things they worshipped. The lion was removed because it was the sign of the Sinhalese people. So all the later ones changed, they went from half-circles to triangles and full circles – all kinds of shapes – and the meaning in the original moonstone was lost.' Was that happening to me? All the meanings, what's good and bad, what's true or lies, what's wrong or right, being mixed up in my head?

We stopped at a restaurant where there were no separate tables for servants. I had to sit on the same chairs as everyone else. I went to a table in the corner, as far from the family as I could, so that nobody made the mistake that I was one of them. Still, the waiters called me 'Miss', even when Nona and Mano Mahattaya did the ordering and paying. I was afraid someone from the village might see, maybe a waiter would recognise me and say, 'Latha? What are you doing here in the nice restaurant? Sitting on the nice chair, eating nice food?'

'I'm going to see my akka,' I said, finishing the conversation in my head. 'I'm going to help. And my nona, mahattaya and the baby-la are also coming. They're coming to help me. To help us.'

After breakfast, when I said I could take a bus from the restaurant and find my way to Akka's house, Niranjan Baby said, 'I want to see where you lived.'

Nona said Mano Mahattaya would drive to the house. Mahattaya didn't say anything, just shook the keys in his hand and looked at the ceiling. Anoushka Baby noisily sucked up the last drops of fruit juice through her straw.

I said very quietly, 'I can go alone, really. I'll go.' But nobody heard me, or they didn't listen. I was grateful, but also ashamed of them seeing how poor I really was. But Nona and Mahattaya had decided so I followed them and got in the car.

'Latha, you'll have to tell me where to go,' said Mano Mahattaya as he started the engine.

—

Mano Mahattaya complained about the narrow, broken road. I was getting worried. What would they think of the house? What would they think of my family? Mahattaya turned onto the dirt path that went as far as you could see, shaking his head and saying it was ruining the car. I said, 'I can walk from here, Mano Mahattaya.' I thought I had forgotten the way and got us all lost. 'I'll find it alone. Don't waste your time.'

'What's that?' said Niranjan Baby, pointing with his good arm. There was a white thing on a tree in the distance.

'Must be a bird,' I said.

It wasn't a bird. It stayed on the tree, flapping in the wind. It was a white flag, and the car rolled slowly towards it, bouncing as the wheels went into holes. On one side there was empty land where a fire was going out. Crops were burnt and smoke was coming out of the ground. More white flags appeared on lampposts and fences – all telling us the funeral was near. We went over the bund, the river almost dry because it hadn't rained in months. Naked little boys ran from mud huts, stopping at the bamboo kadullas, gates they were too afraid to cross, watching the car like it was something they had never seen before. An old man on a bicycle looked at me, his eyes made bigger by the thick glasses, nodding his head as we passed. Turning into a smaller road and up the hill, we were almost there. Two dusty green army jeeps were parked on the street. The kadulla in front of Akka's house had been made into a big doorway with a white banner hanging across. There were soldiers in the yard drinking tea. Nona looked at them nervously as we slowed.

'The pleasure of nibbana to Kumara Priyanjana,' said Niranjan Baby, reading the letters on the banner.

'This is the place,' said Mano Mahattaya, bringing the car to a stop.

'Thank you, Mahattaya,' I said, pulling the handle on the door. 'Thank you, Nona. Bye, Anoushka Baby.'

I got out, waving at Anoushka Baby and Niranjan Baby. Anoushka Baby waved back and for a moment I felt sad for leaving them, even if it was for a short time.

'When are you coming back, Latha?' Anoushka Baby asked.

'In seven or eight days,' I said. 'I'll catch the bus.'

'Here,' said Nona, putting her arm out of the window, giving me money. 'Take a trishaw. We'll be at the guesthouse.'

I took the money, saying, 'Thank you, Nona, thank you,' again and again.

'Latha?' said a voice and I turned to see Aiya. He was standing there in his clean white clothes. 'I didn't know who was getting out of the car – it's you. I didn't think you were coming.'

'Aiya,' I said happily. 'Nona told me I have to come. And Mahattaya,' I said. I showed him to everyone in the car. 'This is my aiya.' Nona and Mahattaya finally got to see my aiya. They saw I wasn't a person who had just appeared out of nowhere, that I had someone.

Aiya bent to look into the car. 'Nona,' he said, putting his palms together to say ayubowan. 'Mahattaya.'

'Hullo,' said Mano Mahattaya, taking his hands off the steering wheel to say ayubowan.

'Thank you for coming so far,' said Aiya. 'Please come inside and have something to eat. We're giving lunch very soon.'

'We had breakfast less than an hour ago,' said Nona, still looking at the army men. 'We're going to Anuradhapura today – and we didn't dress for a funeral.'

'That's no problem,' said Aiya. 'At least have a cup of tea before you go. Please. You have come such a long way – you must come inside.'

'We'll have a cup of tea,' Mahattaya said to Lakshmi Nona. 'And pay our respects. Otherwise it's not good.'

'You can park the car under the kos tree, Mahattaya,' said Aiya, pointing to the tree at the far end of the property. 'We picked all the kos yesterday so there's nothing to fall on the car.'

Aiya stood with me, watched as everyone got out of the car. A stray dog with no hair, so thin you could see its ribs, started barking. Aiya said, 'Chip, chip!' to try and chase the dog away. I felt funny leading the way in. The dog followed, still barking, and soldiers in their green clothes and families in funeral white stared at us. I knew the villagers were thinking, 'Who are these outsiders? Why is Latha walking with them?' I walked in like a lokka, very important, proud to show everyone I was part of this respectable, rich family. 'Look at my mahattaya,' I said to everyone with my eyes. 'Look at his nice shirt and cricket hat. He's very well known in Colombo. Look at Nona. Isn't she beautiful in her skirt and blouse? And Niranjan Baby, tall, handsome, wearing his sunglasses. And Anoushka Baby, so sweet in her cut-off pants, her hair combed all on one side.'

The dog didn't stop barking until Aiya yelled, kicked up dust and bent down to pick up a rock. A boy in a little white sarong came running and helped throw stones at the dog until it ran away. 'That's my son,' said Aiya as the boy ran back to a woman who must have been his mother, Aiya's wife, who was carrying her daughter. She smiled at me. She seemed like someone I had known for a long time, even though I had never seen her before.

'This is my nona, my mahattaya, my baby-la,' I said to everyone who came to talk to me. Some of the people got up from the plastic chairs and greeted, doing ayubowan. Nona, Mano Mahattaya and Anoushka Baby did it like me, all except Niranjan Baby, who couldn't bring his hands together. He bent his neck and nodded as we went up to the house.

My old house looked small. The blue paint was faded and there was a big crack going across the front wall and up to the roof. The bars in the windows were reduced to paper, eaten away by veyas. It was dark inside, all the curtains closed and the only light was from the oil lamp. The place smelled the same, like rice grains, chicken kakka and coconut oil all mixed up and blown around on the hot wind. I remembered things. I remembered climbing the veralu tree to pick the sour fruit, filling my pockets and falling, muddying my only dress. I remembered trying to wash the dress in the river before Akka saw, remembered hiding in the backyard, telling the chickens not to shout because I was so afraid Akka's husband, who always came home late smelling of kasippu and shouting filth, would hurt me.

I went through the door. In the middle of that dark living room I saw the coffin. It was shut. Must be because Kumara's body had exploded into little pieces. On one side was Akka, sitting on a wooden stool. She looked like a piece of fruit that had been in the sun too long. Her head was leaning on the coffin as if she was trying to sleep, grey hair spreading everywhere, her tears on the polished wood. Her tiny body was wrapped in a sari and a couple of women from the village patted her back, trying to stop her from shaking. Her husband was at the other end of the coffin, standing, his eyes red as jumbu. This time I didn't think it was from drinking. This time I wasn't afraid. His bottom lip shook. I felt sorry for both of them. I went close and said, 'Akka.' She turned her head, saw me and cried harder, her arms tightening around the wooden box. Akka's daughter, Sunila, came out from the back room with her child. She didn't look as upset as her parents, but the little boy on her hip was woken by all the noise. He started crying too.

I smiled a small smile at her and turned towards the coffin to give pinn. I gave a little to the dead boy but I gave most of my pinn to Nona, Mano Mahattaya, Niranjan and Anoushka Baby. They were being kind, praying for someone they didn't know. I was so grateful. They were here because of me. I must have done lots of pau in my last life to not get any parents, but I had done enough pinn in this life to earn a family.

We stared at the coffin as Akka hugged it and sobbed. Sunila's baby cried with her – it was like they were playing a game to see who could make the louder noise. The women around Akka kept petting her and wiped their own tears on handkerchiefs. I finished praying and looked around. There were two round wreaths – one with white flowers, the other white and red – standing next to the coffin. They were both from the army. I knew from the small piece of paper stuck to them with a picture of the government badge and two swords. There was another bunch of flowers on the coffin, pink and purple, made from nelum and manel – lotuses, just like in the moonstone. Could these flowers, brought here by other people, help Kumara reach nibbana? I couldn't believe it.

Lakshmi Nona, Mano Mahattaya, Anoushka Baby and Niranjan Baby finished their prayers and went outside. I spoke to Akka's daughter. Her husband, a small man with a moustache, didn't say anything, just nodded and stood next to us. Sunila talked about Kumara but her words were damp with sadness. 'I came as soon as I heard, Latha Nenda,' she said, bouncing the baby in her arms, trying to make him stop crying. 'Didn't even tell my boss. I don't know if the garment factory will take me when I go back.'

I didn't know what else I could do for them, so I passed the roll of money Nona had given me into Sunila's hand. I hoped everything would be okay. She was a good girl. She even said my nona, mahattaya and baby-la were nice. She said there was another mat they could put in one of the back rooms for me, that I could sleep there the next few days. I said, 'Thank you.'

Outside, Aiya was sitting on a plastic chair next to Lakshmi Nona and Mano Mahattaya, his little daughter on his lap. I leaned against the wall nearby, next to the baby-la. Aiya began showing his family to mine. He said, 'This is my wife, Kusum,' when she came up and served tea to everyone and smiled shyly. Nona and Mahattaya said hullo.

I drank from the same kind of cup everyone else was using – a nice porcelain cup with a silver handle. Sweet ginger tea was warm on my throat. Aiya picked up his son, who wriggled to try and get away.

Nona patted his head. 'He's very naughty.'

Aiya put him down and he ran into the house. 'Yes, he's a real dahangalé.'

It was strange. This was such an unhappy place, with people crying and pulling out hair because a boy was in pieces in a wooden box, but somehow good things were also happening. All the people I loved had met – and they liked each other. It was strange, but I would have given away the winning lotterai ticket for this.

Then Aiya said, 'I have another person you should know.' He gave his teacup back to Kusum, got up from his chair and crossed the yard to one of the old men sitting on a stool in a corner. He helped the man get up and tie his sarong, picked up his walking stick and put it in his hand. The old man fixed his glasses on his nose, leaned heavily on Aiya's arm and came limping up to us. He had a crumpled face that hadn't been shaved in a few days. Thin white hair had been combed across his spotted head and a shirt and sarong hung off his skin-and-bone body. He smiled, showing a mouth all pink without teeth.

'Nona and Mahattaya,' said Aiya, 'this is my father.'

'Ah.' Mano Mahattaya's face changed like he had tasted something bad. He stood up, put his teacup on his seat and his palms together.

The old man did ayubowan, still holding the walking stick, losing balance so Aiya had to hold him. Aiya brought a chair and helped the man sit, leaning his walking stick against the chair. I was confused. Who was this old man? Why was Aiya calling him Thattha? I was thinking and thinking and then I understood. He must be my thattha. Lakshmi Nona, Mano Mahattaya, Niranjan and Anoushka Baby had all realised this before me. They looked at me, their faces full of questions. I didn't know the answers. I had never thought about it. I thought an amma and thattha were just things I didn't have. I stared at the old man, who looked the other way, like he didn't even want to see me. Was it true? Was this ugly old man really my father? Why didn't he want to look at me?

'Latha never told us she had a father.' Mahattaya found his voice.

'No?' said Aiya with a funny smile. 'Why didn't you tell them, Latha?'

I didn't know what to say. Aiya didn't look at me when I tried to see what was in his eyes.

He looked at Nona and Mahattaya and said, 'She doesn't like our thattha.' He said it as if I had known my father all along. He lied so easily – as if he deserved gold coins in his mouth. Then he leaned towards Mahattaya to say something, a secret, but the words were loud enough for everyone to hear. 'Sometimes a man can't do everything for everyone, no? What do you say, Mahattaya? Sometimes we have to choose.'

'Ah . . . yes, yes,' said Mano Mahattaya.

I wasn't angry. I wasn't sad. I didn't feel anything. Didn't even want to ask the old man, 'Why didn't you look after me? Why didn't you come and see me?' I knew why. He chose to look after my aiya and gave me to my akka. He chose the right person – now he's old and Aiya's looking after him well.

The old man made a funny sound, like he was getting a cough. He cleared his throat, spat on the ground and tried to get up. 'I'm going home.'

'Thattha – we can't go home now,' said Aiya. 'It's Kumara's funeral. Did you forget?'

One of the things I knew as a servant was to go away when I wasn't needed. I went around the corner, to the side of the house without any windows. There was sand near the fence that divided Akka's house from the neighbours. The sun was almost in the middle of the sky and it was burning. Sweat came flooding down my face. I used to come here a lot, to play in the sand. To get away from everyone else. I broke a stick from the tree and started drawing things. This was what I used to do – draw all the things that were on my mind, all the nice things, the things that made me happy. Today I drew a moonstone.

I wasn't very good at drawing but I did my best. It may not have been what Mahattaya called 'the proper moonstone' but it was how I remembered, how I saw it in my mind and felt it in my body. All the things were there, the story of life, in the sand.

Then a little boy in a dirty sarong came running around the corner. It was Aiya's son. He stopped. I smiled at him and he turned and ran back the way he came. I heard him stop and come back, slowly. Every time I looked, he ran away, stopped around the corner of the house and put his head out to look at me. I lifted the stick and tried to give it to him. The boy came, slowly, ready to run away if I moved.

'What are you doing?' he asked.

'Drawing,' I said.

'What are you drawing?' He took the stick and waved it.

'A moonstone,' I said.

'What is this?' he said again, poking the stick all around the drawing.

'Moonstone,' I said again. 'Do you know it?'

'And this?' He poked with his stick.

'It's fire,' I said.

'No,' said the boy.

'What is it, then?'

'Lines.'

My drawing wasn't very good but it wasn't hard to see what it was. 'That's fire in a ring . . . and those are animals.'

'No.'

'You don't see the elephant? Horse? Lion?'

'No. Only lines.'

'Don't you see that? That's the elephant's trunk. This is the bull.'

'No. It's not.'

'You're not looking properly. Look.'

'No!'

I got angry. 'You're a stupid boy.'

'You're stupider. You're a mottaya,' said the boy and drew all over the face of my moonstone, completely ruining it.

'Give me that,' I said and tried to take the stick back, but the boy wouldn't let go. He held on like a crab. I pulled hard, so hard it came tearing out of the boy's hands, sending me backwards, almost into the fence. The boy looked at his hands. I had hurt him. His palms had been wounded – blood was starting to come out. His face changed, his mouth opened and tears came out of his eyes. He ran away crying. I dropped the stick. My head felt like it was going to burst.

Out in the front yard, more people had gathered. The family was still sitting in the plastic chairs, drinking tea, eating biscuits. Mahattaya was talking to Aiya, and Nona was talking to his wife, watching the army man who was talking to Niranjan Baby. Niranjan Baby didn't like it, even though the army man was being friendly. So friendly he had put an arm around Niranjan Baby's shoulder. Another army man was talking to Anoushka Baby. Everywhere, people were talking. I didn't want to talk. Didn't want to say anything to anyone. My legs were shaking. I walked towards the kadulla as quickly as possible. The hairless dog had come back and it was barking, not letting a monk in orange robes pass. The monk was trying to move the dog away with his words, and when that didn't work he called the people to come and chase it. The dog was growling, showing its teeth. I went past them as people shouted, 'That dog! That dirty dog is troubling the haamuduruwo. Chase it away.'

Nobody looked at me as I crossed the kadulla. Not the monk or the dog or any of the people getting ready to throw rocks. I could still hear the people saying, 'What a foolish, good-for-nothing dog. Thinks it owns this place. Thinks it's more important than the haamuduruwo. Thinks the haamuduruwo is coming to take its things.' I passed Akka's neighbour's house, with its newly built veranda and flower garden. The noise grew smaller but the words stayed in my head: The dog thinks it's more important than the haamuduruwo. The haamuduruwo thinks he's more important than the dog. I kept walking, the slope making it easy, right past the army trucks with muddy tyres. The army men thought they were more important than Niranjan Baby but Niranjan Baby thought he was more important. All the way at the bottom of the hill there was the bus stop with half-torn posters of the president. The president thought he was the most important person. People thought they were more important than the dog. The haamuduruwo thought he was more important than the people. There were nidikumba growing on the side of the almost-dry river, their leaves fanned open. I kicked them and the leaves closed and went to sleep. Both Niranjan Baby and Anoushka Baby loved to make nidikumba sleep. I used to tell them, 'Be careful, Baby. You'll get pricked by the thorns.' The baby-la thought they were more important than the nidikumba. The nidikumba thought they were more important than the baby-la and tried to prick them. A bullock cart went past, the bullock so tired it had a long string of spit coming out of its mouth. This man thinks he's more important than the bull. One of my slippers broke and I left them there, on the road on top of the bund. It was hot and my soles burned but my soles were used to burning. Men not bulls. Lions not Tigers. Sinhala not Tamil. Colombo not Anuradhapura not Jaffna not Batticaloa. Men not women. I had to get off this road. I turned onto a small path, the grass cool against my feet. Stems grew longer and longer. Plants were more important than weeds but the weeds had won. Bees and dragonflies flew all around. Houses were better than trees but trees were growing close together leaving no room for houses. Liyavel hung in this forest. Moss on the bark. Birds singing. Smoke from a fire in the distance. A small animal disappeared into a bush. A wild boar. Not lions not tigers not elephants not bulls not swans not horses. The story of the moonstone was everywhere and nowhere. Just lines in the sand. And there's a deer. A baby deer and its mother. Or was it its sister? Where was the father? The story of my family, the story of Nona and Mahattaya and Niranjan Baby and Anoushka Baby was everywhere. Where? Where was I?

The deer run away . . . the moonstone disappears . . . I'm climbing up this mountain and it's easy because I'm light . . . feathers in the wind . . . I'm here and I'm not listening to the stories . . . not dreaming about things that happened long, long ago or will happen tomorrow . . .

wet grass . . . stone on stone . . . not letting it build, story
after story, word after word . . . no Sinhala no Buddhist no
woman no servant no poor no small . . . no memory . . .
no me . . . I'm nothing . . . just air and body and breath.

ANOUSHKA

WHEN HER BROTHER BROUGHT LATHA BACK TO THE GUESTHOUSE I saw it was true. She had changed. She looked taller. Like she'd eaten a Super Mario mushroom and doubled in size. Maybe it was just that she stood up straight, didn't huddle in the corner of the room or slink away to the kitchen, stood front and centre as if she owned the place. There was a smile on her face, a super-calm, slightly creepy smile. She spoke slowly but clearly. It was not like a servant. And when she looked at me it was scary. Like she had X-ray vision. Like she could see my bones, my heart pumping, my food digesting, all the secrets buried in my brain. What a freak! Her brother took Thatthi to one side and spoke to him. After he left – and Latha had finally disappeared to the servants' quarters – Thatthi said the brother was a total con artist and all the hocus-pocus stories he told were lies. Thatthi said it was obvious Latha was not well. Mentally. And because she was pissu we decided to come home. It was too weird to keep holidaying with a crazy person around.

But now I needed her help. I was desperate. Confronted by a spider and a freak I chose the freak, even though I barely knew how to talk to her. I stood in the doorway without going into the kitchen. I would've normally said, 'Eyi!' but that didn't seem right. I almost felt I had to talk to her like to a monk, saying 'swamini' or 'your excellency' at the end of every sentence. I was standing there scratching my head when she turned around, looked at me and in her new calm voice said, 'Anoushka Baby?' She knew I wanted something.

'I can't find my history book,' I said. 'I think it's in the cupboard. And there's a spider there.'

She got up from her stool and glided behind me. Ammi, sitting at the dining table, gave me a look that was like, 'Are you sure about this?'

In my room, Latha gathered her skirts and knelt in front of the cupboard. She reached in and pulled out a book, saying, 'Mé thiyenné.' But that wasn't it. She may have found enlightenment but she sure hadn't figured out how to read.

'That's my commerce book,' I said. 'Put that on the desk – I'll need it.' I was standing back in case the spider fell out and ran all over me. That was what I was most afraid of. I knew they didn't bite but the idea of one running up me with its spindly legs was freaky.

'Meka.' She raised another.

'No. History book.' I translated for her. 'Ithihaasa potha. Textbook ekak.'

She pulled out book after book and piled them on the floor. None of them were my history book.

Big trouble.

All this was because my marks in the last social studies and history test were terrible. Below sixty. The social studies part was okay – I got thirty-seven out of fifty for that. It was history that let me down. Nineteen out of fifty. Ammi was furious. 'How can this happen, Anoushka? That's not even a credit. You have only five months until your O-Levels. If you don't get at least six distinctions, where will you end up?' Ammi always underestimated me. She thought Niro was a genius but he only got four distinctions. Seriously. I could do that with my eyes closed. Six? Easy – English, English lit, Sinhala, science, maths (with a little work on substitution) and commerce were sure Ds for me. Seven if I could by-heart the dates in Buddhism. I hated dates. I just couldn't remember them. BC and AD. Before Christ and After Dog's Years (or Anno Dominoes or whatever). That's the problem with history. It's all one million years here, two and a half thousand there, this king after that king after this king.

Maybe Latha could remember her past lives, everything, all the way back to the beginning of the Sinhala race, back to when Prince Vijaya got kicked out of India and landed here with his gang. Maybe Latha saw Vijaya making passes at the queen, Kuveni. She was probably one of Kuveni's tribe – I mean, she looks indigenous, like a vedda, no? Maybe she could tell me the whole thing. All the stupid details I needed to pass the test. Maybe she could transform that science book she was staring at, fill it with all her ancient knowledge. She probably could. Apparently, the man who found her had said she was floating on top of some mountain in the middle of the forest – and there was light coming out of her, like a halo. It was late, around nine, but this guy could see the way through the forest because it was so bright. Anyway, that's what Latha's brother had said to Thatthi. When Thatthi relayed the story, Niro laughed. 'Come on, there were brush-fires everywhere that day, remember? And that idiot must have been drunk.'

That was how that search had ended. Our search for my history book continued. We looked everywhere – no history. I was in trouble. Ammi expected me to keep up with the scholarship girls – but how could I? They recited things as if it were all written inside their eyeballs. Ammi didn't give up, though. Every day she had been quizzing me on all the subjects except history. She left history to Thatthi, so she had no idea I hadn't used my book all term.

Now, she was in my room to see what all the fuss was about. There was no escape. She was going to kill me. But first she asked Latha to clean out the dust and cockroach eggs that had collected at the bottom of the cupboard.

I worked through a list of excuses as Ammi kept a close eye on Latha. She was still checking if Latha's pissu had passed. Ammi had given it a good week and then tried to talk to Latha, figure out what happened, but she got nowhere. She'd been like, 'Where did you go, Latha? We thought you must have gone to visit someone, a friend in your village, a relative. Then your brother called that evening and said he couldn't find you and we got worried.'

Latha had just said, 'I was looking for something. There was nothing. That's the truth. No truth.' It was completely nuts.

Pissu Latha swept everything up onto the dustpan and Ammi turned to me. 'So where do you think you left your book, Anoushka?'

'Must be in class.'

'You better not have lost it! The one day your father's home to teach you history, you don't have the book, no?'

'I must have left it at school. It's in my desk. For sure.'

'I don't know what's happened to you, Anoushka. You better not have lost the book,' said Ammi as Latha floated back to the kitchen. Luckily Niro came home and Ammi went out to greet him. Yep. Niro. He was home. The world had been flipped upside-down.

Seriously, the weirdest thing around here wasn't Latha going mad. It was that Niro had started looking for a job. A normal job. He didn't drive his car very much. Took a taxi or a three-wheeler. Sometimes he took the bus. He came home the same day he left. At home he was doing things like sweeping the floor and washing his plate whenever he used it. He cleaned his room. Can you believe that? It was even more surprising that he'd started coming around to chat, as if he was concerned about us. It was turning into a habit, so much so I knew who it was when there was a knock on the door.

'What're you knocking for?' I said, lowering my social studies book. He opened the door and took a couple of steps in.

'Just in case,' he said.

'In case of what?'

'You know . . . if you were doing something private.'

'I have nothing to hide,' I said. 'Not like you.'

'Of course. You're an open book.'

I hated when he turned it back on me like that. 'What do you mean?'

'Nothing, Anoushka.'

'Nothing, Anoushka,' I mimicked.

I propped up a pillow as he closed the door behind him and came up near the bed, his broken arm slung across like a gun. 'What's up?' he said.

'What's up with you?'

'Not much.'

'Me too.' I gave him a look designed to show him how much of a weirdo he was being. I picked up the book again.

'That's good. So you're okay.'

'Why wouldn't I be?'

'You know . . . changes.' He lowered his voice.

'What changes?'

'Latha . . .'

'Yeah. She's gone nuts. Completely pissu. What to do?'

'Don't say that!'

'Thatthi said it.'

Niro shut his eyes, rubbed his temples and quickly sat down on the bed next to me.

'Headaches again?'

'Yeah.'

'Are you going to faint?'

'No. It'll pass.'

'So it hasn't stopped? Did you tell Thatthi or Ammi? Did you tell the doctor? Don't be a chandiya. Last time you tried to be a hero you got hammered, remember?'

'Shut up. I told you, it'll go away,' he said grumpily and stopped rubbing his head. 'So, what do Ammi and Thatthi think? About Latha.'

'How should I know? Ask them.'

He tilted his head in annoyance and stared at me. 'I'm asking you.'

'I have a theory,' I said. 'But it's only a theory.'

'And? What is it?'

'They're going to send her to Angoda.' I said it just to scare Niro. I didn't even know if Angoda was real. It was supposed to be a lunatic asylum. Everyone knew about it but nobody knew anyone who had been there.

Niro looked worried. 'You're joking, right?'

'Nope.'

'But there's nothing wrong with her. Sure, she's changed. She's not the same. But there's nothing wrong . . . She's still doing all the work. If anything she's doing a better job.'

'She's a weirdo.'

'You're a weirdo too but we're not sending you to Angoda.' He started getting angry but stopped himself. 'Look, it was a weird couple of days, I'll give you that.' Niro shook his head and stared out the window like *he* was on top of that mountain. 'Do you remember those soldiers? At the funeral?'

'Um, yeah?'

'That one guy, fair one, real friendly, remember? Like he was real happy to meet me. Did you hear what he said?'

I shook my head.

'He was asking all sorts of things. Which school I went to, what I studied in university, what sort of job I'm doing now. And when I told him he repeated everything. He elbowed his friend and was like, "Look at this malli. He studied in Australia. He's only twenty-four and he already has his own company," as if the other guys needed to be told twice.'

'So?'

'So it was weird. And then he was telling me all this stuff about his life. How he's twenty-eight, has a wife and two children in Morawaka, wherever that is. Then the bugger put his arm around me, and I'm like, "Dude, don't hurt my arm!" . . . I didn't say that, but I was worried the guy would make a sudden move. Ammi was sweating like crazy, obviously worried . . . for a moment back there it got real tense, no?'

It had been weird. One of the army guys had patted me on the head, saying, 'Look at this nangi. Isn't she sweet?' but I didn't think much about it. And then we decided to leave. We couldn't find Latha but we didn't think much of that either.

Niro took a deep breath. 'It was sort of scary.'

I chuckled. 'Scary? What were you scared about?'

'Weren't you scared? We were the odd ones out in the middle of nowhere. Those army guys could've done anything to us.'

'You're such a baby, Niro. You're like Ammi, worrying about everything.'

'Oh, shut up.'

'You shut up.'

———

Of course my history book wasn't at school. I never left anything there because it'd be stolen. I checked in the compartment in my desk anyway. Nothing there. Obviously. Maybe I didn't get a history book at the start of the term. I didn't remember getting one. I hadn't needed it in class, just listened to the teacher or shared a book with Manju or Chathuri sitting either side of me.

I looked around the classroom, on the shelves, in the cupboards, to see if there was a spare book lying around. Nope. No luck. Maybe I could ask the teacher. Make some excuse. 'Miss, the cockroaches ate my book. Can I have a new one?' I'd have to do better than that. Maybe 'Someone robbed our house and took my bag,' might work. No. Nobody was that stupid. It wouldn't fly. Ammi and Thatthi would find out.

Maybe Thatthi would forget about my book, but Ammi? Hell no. She'd swoop on me as soon as I got home, barking, 'Anoushka? Did you find your history book?' She was going to kill me. I was sure of it. And after she was done with me she'd put me in another tuition class. More torture. My only hope was to ace the O-Levels, then Ammi and Thatthi would give me everything I asked for. At least that's what they promised.

Then I had a brilliant idea. I could borrow the history book from Natalie. I hadn't been able to talk to her for like, ever. I could sneak up to her and say, 'Hi Natalie! How's it going?'

By now she'd have tired of the TMMs. She'd remember all the good times we had. She'd turn her head with a flick of her hair and go, 'Fine, thank you, Anoushka,' and smile her sweetest smile.

Then I'd say, 'Can you do something for me?'

'What is it?'

'Can I borrow your history book? I just need it for a week.'

'Sure, Noush, you can have it.'

'Thanks! I'll buy you lunch in return. We can go somewhere on the weekend. Maybe to Coffee Bean and have iced coffee.' We'd start hanging out again. And sharing music. And going to movies.

But the thing was – TMMs. They were everywhere. I couldn't talk to Natalie in class. I had to wait. I spotted her alone at the canteen and rushed up, but Maneesha cornered her. Then I saw her in the corridor, but Ruvina and Shimi were flanking her like bodyguards. There didn't seem to be a moment when Natalie was alone.

That evening after Sinhala tuition, when Ammi asked if I'd found the book, I said, 'Yeah. It's in my bag.'

Luckily Ammi seemed preoccupied and my bluff worked. She said, 'Okay. Give it to Thatthi when he gets home,' and went to the temple with Latha. I got a whole two hours of TV but there was nothing good and I spent most of the time swapping between Channel NewsAsia, to see if they'd show anything about the noise rock scene in China, like they did once, and ETV, where they were showing an episode of *Everybody Loves Raymond* for the billionth time. Thatthi was only likely to have time on Saturday and by then I could convince Natalie to give me her book.

—

On Tuesday, when the teacher wasn't there, Natalie sat on top of her desk chatting to the TMMs. Her dress, which was as short as you could wear without getting into trouble, rode up above her knees and halfway up her thighs, her long legs crossing and uncrossing as she talked without opening her mouth very much, lips pouting, like she was chewing gum while trying to put on lipstick or something. I was sitting near the front and didn't get a chance to look back at her for the rest of the day.

Then, on Wednesday, after school, as I walked out slowly because I didn't want to go to commerce tuition, she was coming out of the phone booth, transformed (like Superman), her hair undone and flowing like black lava down her shoulders, lips the colour of blood, eyeliner giving her the full panda-eyes effect. She was by herself.

I went up and said, 'Hi, Natalie.'

'Oh, hi.' She looked at me out the corner of her eye as she started walking towards the gate.

'How was your day?'

'Okay.'

'You, um, look . . . nice.'

'Thanks.' She brightened a little.

'Did you get a haircut?'

It was a good guess. 'Yeah. I went to Ramzi's on Saturday,' she said. 'Ramzi himself cut it. He's like, an artist. With hair.' She twirled a strand around her finger.

'I go to Ramzi too,' I said confidently. Thatthi always took me to that barber salon in Nugegoda where the guy still used one of those old-style razors, the ones where the blade folds into the handle, and made me think he was going to cut my throat.

'Really?' Natalie looked at my hair suspiciously. 'I've never seen you there.'

'No? When do you go?'

'Normally on a Saturday morning, so I can check out the old Dutch Hospital – you know how it's been refurbished and they have shops there? I have a coffee, drop in to Harpo's, do a bit of shopping at Odel . . .'

'I go on Sundays.'

'Does Ramzi work on Sunday?'

'Yes,' I said, completely believing myself. 'He works.'

We had reached the gates. Latha was waiting there, smiling mysteriously.

'Latha still comes, no?' said Natalie.

If it wasn't embarrassing enough, Latha said, 'Hullo, Natalie Baby,' suddenly behaving like she used to.

'Latha, kohomada?' said Natalie.

'Hondai, Baby.'

'You haven't changed,' said Natalie, smiling. I wasn't sure if she was talking to Latha or me, but then she said, 'How's your punk rock? Do you still listen to that radio program?'

'No,' I said. 'I don't have time.'

I wanted to get away before being humiliated any more. I was about to say bye when someone, a boy, came up and jumped all over Natalie.

'Kamran!' she shrieked and hugged him.

Before I could make a move, he said, 'Hi,' and held out his hand. 'I'm Kamran.' He was tall and fair in his clean blue jeans and cotton shirt, his wavy hair gelled solid. He was one of those posh Muslims with the 'I can do whatever I want' sort of confidence. I shook his hand slowly, looked at him suspiciously. Then he turned and said 'Hi' to Latha. It was outrageous.

'What's your name?' Kamran asked me.

'Anoushka.'

'Anoushka was telling me about being a punk,' said Natalie, spluttering with laughter.

'I . . . no.'

'You should meet my friend Suranga,' said Kamran. 'He's a rock guy.'

'Ah, yeah,' said Natalie, giving me a funny look, like I was some strange and interesting sea creature. 'Suranga! Anoushka should totally go out with him.'

'I'm having a party on Saturday. Why don't you come?' said Kamran. 'A house party.' I wasn't sure if he was trying to make fun of me, whether these two had plotted to humiliate me, like in *Carrie* (the Stephen King book I read secretly last year), but Kamran didn't seem like the type. He was just a dumbo.

'You should totally come, Noush,' said Natalie. I was surprised. She hadn't called me Noush in centuries.

'Our house is on Gregory's Road,' Kamran said. 'Not the side with the Australian embassy – the other side. Near the Bayleaf. Do you know Bayleaf?' The words kept rolling out of his mouth.

I had no idea what Bayleaf was, but I nodded.

'All right. We'll see you on Saturday!' With that Kamran gave Natalie a wink and said, 'Shall we go?'

'Let's,' said Natalie, playfully. 'We're going out for lunch,' she told me. 'Maybe we'll go to Cinnamon Grand.'

'Or Barefoot,' he said.

'That's a brilliant idea,' said Natalie. 'See you later.'

'Bye,' said Kamran, then waved at Latha before turning towards Viharamahadevi Park with Natalie.

I watched them go, strides synchronised, left-right-left, mouths working, talking about Lord knows what.

What were all those things she was saying? How could she have such a good conversation with him but not with me? I'd known her for ages – what did he know that I didn't?

'Goot,' said Latha. 'Goot boy.'

'He's not good,' I said. 'How do you know?'

'Hondata katha karanawa,' she said.

'Yes, he talks,' I said as we walked towards a three-wheeler. 'Talks too much.'

—

I changed my plans for Natalie. Getting the book was easy. I just asked Chathuri if I could borrow hers. Her big black eyes squinted and her curly hair shook. She seriously looked like a lamb (a black sheep – she was that dark) when she muttered, 'You want my book?'

'Yes.'

'You don't have one?'

'Obviously.'

'But all this time you didn't need a book.'

'Now I want one.'

'For how long?'

'I'll just take down the dates – and put the kings' names next to them, and a few things they did. You can have it back on Monday.'

'But . . . how to study all? All the things?'

'I'll google or something.'

Chathuri looked like she'd been told she was adopted. 'Do you need the other books also?'

'No, I have all the others, I'm pretty sure,' I said.

'So, only the history book?'

'I'll look after it. I won't dirty it or anything.' It took a bit more effort than I expected but the problem was eventually solved.

'Okay,' Chathuri sighed.

Getting permission to go to the party would be harder. Thursday was a day when I didn't have any tuition. I went home, showered, ate (the same garbage Latha always cooked) and got straight into the maths. I did a whole section, even learned a few new tricks in trigonometry. I took one short TV break, timing the back-to-my-room-for-more-work bit perfectly so when Ammi came home I was bent over the books making serious progress.

She came into my room taking the safety pins off her sari, saying, 'Good girl! You're doing your homework. Is it for school or tuition?' She gave me a kiss on the top of my head.

'Just practising,' I said.

'Do you need help?'

'I can show you what I did.'

'Let me go and change. Then we can see, okay?'

That was a good start. I carried on with the statistics, which I finished in no time. That stuff was easy. When Ammi came back wearing a housecoat on top of her nightie, I showed her my handiwork. She took my book and looked at the sums. 'Yes, yes . . . correct.' She ticked things off with a pencil as she checked my answers. Sometimes she did her own calculations in the margins, doing neat long division or writing out an equation – but most of it was done within a few seconds, like a genius, all in her head. 'What's this?' She pointed at some of the lines where she couldn't make out my handwriting.

'It's a five,' I said, where my fives had grown their tail bits too long and looked like sixes. I wasn't worried because I knew all the workings were right.

'Correct. It's all correct, Anoushka.' Ammi beamed. 'Only thing is you have to write neater. Your handwriting is terrible.'

'Okay.'

'Look.' She showed me some of my sevens, which had a habit of looking like ones because their nose bits were too short. 'You can have all the right answers, but if the teacher can't read them, what's the point?'

'I was doing them fast.'

'Why do you need to do them fast? You've never run out of time. You always finish early.'

I shrugged. 'I like to.'

'Aiyo, Baba. Don't do that. You'll waste everything. All your good work is down the drain if the examiner won't be able to read. Do it slowly.'

'Okay.'

'Take your time and write everything clearly. What's the hurry?'

I shrugged again.

'Your maths is good,' said Ammi. 'It's your history that I'm worried about.'

'Yes, yes. History the mystery.'

'Mystery thamai!' Ammi laughed. 'Won't be a good mystery if you get an F!'

'An F? You think I'll get an F?' After all the work I'd done, this was what I got from her – a list of all my faults. 'I've never got an F in my life.'

'That's what'll happen if you don't study.'

'But you just said I'm doing well!'

'In maths, you're doing well. But in history—'

'Yes, yes. I'm useless. I know.'

'I didn't say you were useless, Anoushka. I said you weren't good enough. You need to work harder. What's the point being good in one or two subjects? You have to be good at all of them. If you want to get somewhere in life, that's what you have to do – work hard. Get good marks for everything. Do you know how hard I worked? Every night, past midnight, I studied. We didn't even have electricity. Have you heard people say, "Burning the midnight oil?" That's what I did. Studied by oil lamp. You have everything at your fingertips. Your life's too easy. That's the problem with children these days. We give you too much. Do you want to end up like that servant woman?'

I didn't bother saying anything because that would've made Ammi go on for even longer. Couldn't even ask her what I was planning to ask.

Luckily, Ammi didn't forget so easily. The next morning she felt sorry for me. We were in the car, on the way to school, and she started telling Thatthi about how I was doing maths when she got home. 'She's very good,' said Ammi. 'If she can do history properly, then I think there's a good chance at the O-Levels.'

'Kella! Doing well, ah? You're working hard. Like your father?' Thatthi looked at me in the rear-view mirror.

'Yeah,' I said.

'Good, kella! Tell me, what do you want? Some nice dinner? Ice-cream?'

'No,' I said. 'It's okay.'

'Tell, Baba. Good work must be rewarded.'

'No . . . it's fine.'

'I'll bring you something,' said Thatthi. 'It'll be a surprise.'

This was my chance to ask if I could go to the party, but I didn't know how to bring it up. We rode along and I sank deeper into the seat, my chances narrowing as we got closer to school. Closer. Closer. It was almost too late when I blurted, 'Thatthi, there's a party on Saturday,' and braced for impact. 'Birthday party,' I quickly added, so Ammi and Thatthi would think it was a typical cake and candles affair, all girls in frilly frocks playing lame games like musical chairs or pillow passing. 'Can I go?'

'Whose birthday?' said Thatthi.

'Nafiza,' I said, using the name of a girl from my science tuition class.

'Who's this Nafiza?' said Ammi. 'Muslim girl? I don't know her. Is she a friend from your class?'

'From tuition,' I said.

'From your school?' Ammi was asking hard questions. I was already beginning to regret lying. There were too many ways it could go wrong.

'No.'

'Which school?'

'Bishop's.'

Luckily, Thatthi intervened. 'You go, Anoushka,' he said. 'It's good for you. Make new friends. Where's this party?'

'Gregory's Road.'

'Saturday, no? I can drop you.'

'You have to buy a present,' said Ammi.

'Nafiza said don't bring presents.'

'That's what they all say,' said Ammi. 'That means she wants a present.'

'Don't bring a present means don't bring a present,' grumbled Thatthi.

'You want her to go empty-handed? Is that what you want? Everyone else will have a present.'

Here we go again, I thought. Ammi and Thatthi couldn't talk for five minutes without fighting.

'If they live on Gregory's Road they must have a lot of money,' said Thatthi. 'They won't care about presents.'

'If they have money they're the sort of people who will want a present. They'll talk about it too.'

'Why do you have to be so negative?' Thatthi said in a tired voice. 'Always suspecting things.'

'That's because there are things to suspect.' Ammi stared at Thatthi so hard I thought a hole would appear in his face.

Ignoring her, Thatthi said, 'Anoushka, we'll get a small present and go to the party, okay?'

'Okay,' I squeaked. He brought the car to a halt in front of the school gates. I said my goodbyes and got out, a burst of happiness spreading through me. It looked like I'd really get to go to that party. At the same time I was a little worried, because I knew Ammi and Thatthi would argue about money, about Niranjan, about that Tamil boy in Batticaloa I sometimes heard them talk about, till Ammi was let out at her office.

—

On Saturday after lunch, Thatthi sat with me and went through some of the history stuff using Chathuri's book.

(I managed to take off the brown paper cover so Thatthi wouldn't see her name on the front – he didn't bother asking why there was no cover.) The thing with Thatthi was that he couldn't help rambling – he'd ask me a question, but instead of just correcting, he tried to turn it into a story and then, instead of telling one story, he told about ten, putting in his own life experiences or examples and explaining how he remembered things and trying to make it clearer, instead confusing me even more.

'. . . now when it comes to this bugger, Sri Wickrama Rajasinghe, you have to remember his real name was Kannasamy. He was Tamil – our last king. You've seen his throne in the museum, no? The one in the glass box? The gold one? That's his. Because Rajasinghe was Tamil and not properly Sinhala, bugger was always suspicious of the Radalas. He thought the high-caste families were plotting against him. Ehelepola was Radala. What Rajasinghe did was he used the sort of divide-and-rule tactics used by the British—'

'I know the story,' I said.

But that didn't stop Thatthi. 'When there were riots in Sabaragamuwa the king sent Ehelepola to stop them. When he didn't come back, the king got nervous. He thought, "This bugger has surely run away and joined the British." He panicked and sent his soldiers to capture Ehelepola's family. The next day everyone was . . .' He did the throat-cutting signal with his fingers. Thatthi carried on like that, assuming I was getting it all, and by the end seemed really satisfied. 'You understood, no?'

'Yes.'

'Everything?'

'Yes.'

He went out to the living room and told Ammi, 'Anoushka will be fine. I taught her everything.'

'Okay,' said Ammi. 'Let's see after the exams.'

'You'll see,' said Thatthi.

Ammi wasn't convinced, but at least she was willing to let me go to the party. She wrapped a pencil case I got for my birthday two years ago that had been banked in her almirah for just such an occasion. I felt bad because I was probably going to have to waste it, throw it away or give it to a beggar rather than suffer the shame of going to a house party with a present. After she put the finishing touches, neatly taping down the edge of the sky-blue wrapping paper with sellotape, she asked me if any other friends were coming to the party.

'Natalie's coming,' I said.

'Ah,' said Ammi. 'Your old friend.' She didn't like Natalie anymore.

'You can get a lift home, no?' said Thatthi. 'Natalie and them still have the driver?'

'Yes,' I said, happy with Thatthi's suggestion. 'I can come with her.'

'Give her a call and make sure,' said Ammi. 'Otherwise she'll leave you there. She's not very reliable, that girl.'

'And get the correct address,' said Thatthi. 'When you say Gregory's Road, you have to tell me which side.'

So I went into the corridor and picked up the phone. I hadn't called Natalie in a long time. She had a mobile but I didn't have the number. I only had her home number from years ago. I dialled. Of course Natalie wouldn't be there. I wanted to surprise her at the party, give her the

CD I made yesterday. Maybe she'll hand it over to the DJ and he'll crank up 'Rebel Girl' and everyone will look around going, 'What is this?' because none of them have heard it before, and then she'll see me in the middle of the dance floor, cleared of TMMs – the power of Bikini Kill sending them running for cover – and she'll be drawn by its magnetic force . . .

'Hullo.' One of Natalie's servants answered.

'Natalie Baby innawada?'

The servant didn't say Natalie wasn't there. She said, 'Poddak inna, Baby,' and went away. In a couple of seconds Natalie had picked up the phone and said, 'Hi? Who is it? Why didn't you call on my mobile? Hullo?'

'Natalie,' I said when I finally found my voice. 'It's Anoushka.'

'Oh, hi. What's up?'

'I . . . I just called.'

'Um, yeah?'

'I'm . . . I'm coming. To Kamran's party.'

'Oh-kay?'

'Can you give me his address, please?'

She read it out in a monotone.

'I'll . . . I'll see you there,' I said. As soon as I'd hung up I realised – I forgot to ask her if she could drop me home. But that was fine. I'd figure something out.

I put on my school shoes because they were the closest I had to Doc Martens. My jeans were a bit baggy and I had to fold the legs. The short-sleeved top, the dark red one, was smaller on me now and my shoulders were almost showing. Ammi saw me in it and was like, 'You can't wear that, Anoushka. It's too small. Why don't you put on a dress? You're going to a Muslim house, no? They won't like it.'

I changed into the long-sleeved black one. Ammi said, 'Why are you dressed in all black? It's very gloomy.'

I changed into white with dark blue stripes. 'That one's transparent, Anoushka. Don't you have any good clothes to wear?' She herded me into my room and started pulling out blouses – ones she had bought for me, pinks, purples, bright greens – all the popsicle colours that I hated. 'What about this one?' she said, finally handing me a blouse that used to be hers, collarless, with thick, rust-coloured cotton. 'It's your sort of thing, no?' She was right. I kind of liked it, if only it didn't have those flowers sewn into the pocket.

'Okay,' I said. I put it on and looked in the mirror. It was a bit big but kinda cool.

Ammi had also rescued an old handbag from her almirah – it was a simple black one with a silver buckle and a long strap to hang off my shoulder. I tried it on and it looked good. Ammi handed me the present and her mobile phone, which I shoved into the handbag.

'If Natalie can't drop you, if you don't have a way of coming back or anything else, give us a call,' said Ammi.

'Okay, Ammi.' I was looking for a way to put the CD in my bag without being noticed. I fiddled with my shoes and ran a comb through my hair, waiting for Ammi to leave the room. I had spent hours putting all the songs I had hidden in a secret folder on Thatthi's computer onto the CD in the right order, making sure they began with high-energy rockers, slowed a little, got psychedelic in the middle (without getting boring) and ended with a bang.

I even did a cool cover by writing the titles in my neatest hand, drawing a little dragon in the corner.

Thatthi was pacing outside my room. 'Let's go, Anoushka,' he called.

'Come, that's enough,' said Ammi, putting a hand on my back. 'You look nice.'

She led me out to the front door, kissed me on both cheeks and said, 'Bye, Anoushka. Be careful.'

I had to act now. 'Forgot something,' I said and rushed back to my room. I reached up to the top of the bookshelf and took out the old encyclopaedia – that was where I stashed CDs – and slipped the one I made for Natalie in my handbag and ran back out.

'What did you forget?' said Ammi.

'Nothing. It was a mistake.' I jumped in the car.

—

Gregory's Road was already busy. There were a lot of cars parked nearby. The house at the address Natalie gave me seemed quiet. It was a nice house, two storeys with a balcony that looked over the white wall, the only blemishes being a couple of ACs jutting out above sealed windows. Thatthi stopped the car in front of the gate, which was half-open, and strained against his seatbelt to see if there was anything going on inside. 'Are you sure this is the right address?' he said.

'Yeah.'

'I don't see any balloons. Where are the balloons?'

'Thatthi, even I didn't have balloons for my birthday.'

'Didn't you?' Thatthi looked confused as he tried to remember.

'No,' I said, opening the car door.

'Are you sure? I can come and see. Only problem is I'll have to find parking. Bloody difficult around here.'

'No, no. I'm sure.' I quickly jumped out of the car. 'This is the place.'

'You have your ammi's cell phone, no? Give a call if there's anything.'

'I'm fine, Thatthi.'

I closed the car door and waved, but Thatthi didn't drive away. He was waiting for me to go inside the house, so I walked through the gates. A pair of servants ignored me as they carried furniture through the front door. They moved a heavy-looking table and set it under an awning. From the shed they brought out some metal chairs and put them in rows on the lawn. One of them opened the French windows. I stepped into the hall. It was big. Empty. A disco ball hung from the ceiling, and two guys, one in a New York Knicks cap and shorts and the other dressed in proper pants and a shiny shirt, were fixing laser lights, their voices echoing off the granite floor. They noticed me, looked up from their work to say a quick 'Hi' and got back to it.

I wasn't sure if I should stand somewhere, go up the staircase at the far end or go outside and sit on the chairs. I decided to sit and went outside. Parking myself on a cold seat in the furthest row, I watched the gate for a while. When I realised not even a stray dog was wandering in, I pulled out Ammi's phone from the handbag. It was one of those old Nokias, which was good for one thing – Snake! I played for a while, beating the highest score twice. (The top scores were already mine – nobody else played Snake on Ammi's phone.) When I looked up the servants had put some food on the table. I had hoped for some short-eats – cutlets, patties, maybe some Chinese rolls – but there were only Pringles, Tipi Tip and some nuts. I filled a paper cup with some Fanta, took a handful of chips and went back to my seat. Ammi and Thatthi expected me to have had dinner, so I had to stuff myself with what was available.

It must have been eight when the first guests – a couple of girls in sequinned dresses and a guy in a tight T-shirt and pointy shoes – arrived. They glanced at me and one of the girls whispered something. They giggled and went inside. They must've gone up the stairs because I couldn't hear them anymore. Should I follow? What would I say to everyone? Would they laugh at me?

I didn't go. In the hall, New York Knicks guy got behind the DJ deck, put on a pair of massive headphones and started playing music. It was the sort of deep, thumping bass that was purpose-built for idiots who liked to 'shake booty'. It was going to be a long night. I grabbed another handful of chips and settled down to watch the lasers zooming about making shapes on the walls. Sometimes light struck the disco ball and the beam scattered like broken glass. As more people filed in I looked out for Natalie. I didn't know anyone, except maybe this one girl Natalie sometimes hung out with, but she looked really different out of school clothes and I wasn't even sure it was her. Everyone else seemed to know each other – all those girls with their glossy hair and white teeth, perfectly flat stomachs shown off in crop tops and dresses with missing middle parts, a few saris worn with bikini tops instead of blouses and the boys all flash, with their gold chains and silver watches, shoes shining when the light suddenly illuminated them. They were all so happy, the fools, chattering away, drinking drinks, laughing at servants who appeared to clean up a spill or top up a bowl, screaming 'whoo!' and throwing their arms up when they recognised a song. Were they all part of a club? Some not-so-secret society? How did you become a member? Who cares, I told myself. I don't want to be part of this.

From the middle of that vortex came Kamran, hugging girls, slapping the boys' backs. He saw me sitting on the far side of the garden and threaded through the crowd, stopping at arm's length. I didn't know if I was supposed to hug him like all the other girls and ended up doing an awkward little wave.

'Hi, Anoushka,' he said. 'Thanks for coming to my party.'

'You're welcome.'

'How are you?'

'Fine.'

'You're probably not loving this music.'

'It's fine.'

'I can ask the DJ to play some rock, but it's still a bit early for that, no? Suranga, the guy I told you about, would have definitely got them to. It's a shame, he couldn't make it. You would have liked him.'

That was a relief. I didn't want to be stuck with some loser who didn't know the difference between punk and pop-metal. 'Okay. Where's Natalie?'

'She'll come. You know what she's like. Fashionably late.'

'What time do you think?' I looked at my watch. It was almost eight-thirty.

'Why? Do you have a curfew?' said Kamran.

'Um . . .' I quickly figured out what he meant by curfew. It sounded like a normal thing that happened to these people. 'Yep,' I said.

'What time?'

I added an hour to the time Ammi would want me home. 'Eleven-thirty.'

'So early!' said Kamran.

'Yeah.'

'Are your parents strict?'

I didn't reply. Whether my parents were strict was none of his business. Luckily, some guy came and put a hand around Kamran's shoulders and whispered in his ear. He said, 'Excuse me,' and the two of them slipped away.

I sat and watched the crowd. Some girl, tall and shimmering in a little gold skirt, squealed and ran into the arms of a guy. It was like she hadn't seen him for years. Idiots. A group of boys gathered around the drinks table, one of them pouring some clear alcohol from a bottle and passing out paper cups. Troglodytes. They sat together on the far side, slowly sipping their drinks and ogling girls. The crowd on the dance floor had transformed into a sweaty, multi-limbed organism, like the Blob if it had become colourful and started throbbing when crap music was played. The air was charged, like there was static that I felt in my hair and on my skin.

I felt tired. I was hungry, and Pringles and Fanta did nothing to fill my belly. I was thinking of going looking for the kitchen when Natalie strode through the gate.

She was dressed casually, like she was going shopping or something, but it made her look all the more beautiful. She was wearing a white tank top, the fluorescent yellow lines of her bra running parallel to the thin straps across her shoulders. Everyone was looking at her, saying, 'Hi Natalie!' and giving her hugs and kisses on her cheek or the air just in front of her flawlessly made-up face. Her hair swished back and forth, polishing her bony shoulders as she turned her head to talk to each person. She was surrounded and I lost sight of her. I did another round pretending I hadn't seen her, then got myself another soft drink and peered at the dance floor. When I circled back, I found myself conveniently right next to her.

'Hi Natalie,' I said. 'When did you get here?'

'Just now,' she said and turned back to another girl. What were they talking about? Who were these people? I took a good look at my competition – she was a total TMM, dressed to the nines in a halter top, face caked with makeup. It was time to bring Natalie back from the dark side. Or was it *to* the dark side? Yeah, I was dark. 'Natalie,' I announced. 'I brought something for you.'

'What?' She made it seem like an unwelcome surprise.

'It's a CD. A mix of my favourite songs.' I took the CD out of my bag and presented it to her.

'Oh . . . um . . .' She didn't take it immediately, surveying it from a distance, as if it was dangerous, before reaching out and carefully picking it out of my hand.

'Thanks.' She winced.

'No problem.'

I was going to tell her all about the CD, how I'd put it together painstakingly, when Kamran appeared and grabbed her, putting his hands all over her back. What the hell? She let him do that? He dragged her away and she went with him. I didn't get it. Why? Sure, he had money. He was tall. But he had an ugly mouth and didn't know anything about . . . well, anything. All I could do was watch them glide out towards the gate. He led the way, finding gaps and clearing the path for her until they disappeared. Should I go and try to find her? Squeeze through, track them down and challenge Kamran to a fight to the death? But I couldn't. I was afraid of what Natalie would say if I confronted them. ('I don't love you, Anoushka. I love Kamran.')

I went back to my chair and took the phone out of my pocket to play Snake. Instead I found I had missed three calls, all from Ammi. I was checking to see what time the calls had come in when it rang again. I couldn't answer right there, so I went outside. Past the gates, the high walls blocked out some of the sound. I looked around, but Natalie and Kamran were nowhere to be seen. I pressed the green button and answered.

'Anoushka?'

'Yeah?'

'What's that noise?'

'What noise?'

'That sound?'

'What?'

'Never mind. Why aren't you answering the phone?'

'I . . . didn't hear.'

'Are you going deaf?'

'No . . . there was music. Someone's playing music here.'

'That's what I said, it's loud. I can hear the music. Are you on your way home?'

'No . . . um, Natalie's still here.'

'It's almost ten o'clock. Tell Natalie you have to come home now.'

'Ammi—'

'Be firm. Say your mother wants you to come.'

'Okay.'

'Okay, bye.'

I looked at the phone, wondering what to do. There was no chance of getting a lift from anyone. People were still coming to this party. Nobody was leaving. Who knew what time they'd leave. I looked around to see if there were any three-wheelers about. It was dark and I was a bit scared of getting into one by myself. I didn't have any money anyway. I went back inside to see if I could find Natalie. I poured myself another Fanta. My stomach was groaning. The phone started ringing again and I went outside.

'Anoushka, don't go anywhere.'

'Ammi, Natalie will—'

'No. We're coming. We'll be there in ten, fifteen minutes. Stay there.'

Ammi knew. I heard it in her voice. I was in trouble, for sure. I didn't want to risk Ammi coming in here and seeing everything. I took one last look at this party. The DJ had started playing a sappy love song. The guys and girls on the dance floor had paired up, their bodies so close they were touching, arms grabbing each other as they swayed. Some were kissing. I saw it. It was just like in movies or on TV when they forgot to censor the bad scenes and make the picture blocky – lips touched, going mmm-mmm, tongues slipping between teeth. This was what they called 'making out', and it really happened, even in our country. I turned away and headed out.

There were two boys and a girl on the roadside, smoking. One of them, a fatty in a T-shirt with the letters *G-Unit* stretched across his bundiya, sang the sappy song completely out of tune. 'All my life, I wanted someone like yoou!' There were cars parked all around, most of them with drivers standing outside, talking. Even they knew each other. There was a garbage barrel near the three-wheelers parked on the sidewalk. I went over and took the pencil case out of my bag. Destroy the evidence. I'd tell Ammi that Nafiza got her gift. As I dropped it in, I saw a CD in the barrel – a CD with a paper cover that had handwriting a lot like mine. Reaching in, I grabbed it and brought it out to the light. Natalie's CD. The one I made for her. She was a fool for throwing it away but I was so stupid for thinking she would like it – that she would love me. I was garbage to her.

'Missy, three-wheel ekak oneda?' I got a shock and dropped the CD back in the barrel. It was a fellow in the three-wheeler nearby. He finished chewing and spat a mouthful of red bulath on the pavement and repeated, 'Three-wheel – you want?'

'Neh,' I said, moving away from him.

'I'll reduce money,' he said. 'Where you want to go?'

'No,' I said again. 'I don't need a three-wheeler.'

He seemed confused. 'Eyi missy, bayada?'

I looked at the puny fellow with his veiny hands and stick-thin neck. I wasn't scared of him. I could've whacked him silly. 'My ammi and thatthi are coming.'

The man cackled as I went back towards Kamran's gate. There were more smokers gathered around, drivers of the partygoers, and I felt safer.

Then I saw Thatthi's little car with its fish-eye headlights in the distance. As it came closer, I saw Ammi sitting in front. She looked angry, her lips tight and her eyes frowning. They stopped near the pavement on the other side of the road, the motor running as I quickly crossed and got in. Ammi turned to look at me. 'So, this is your party,' she said as we drove past Kamran's house looking for a place to turn. The music shuddered in the background as voices spilled out onto the street. I kept quiet.

'Very loud music. Is it a disco?'

We turned into a dark lane, the headlights cutting through the night, revealing hedges and another row of cars. A guy and girl who were leaning against a wall, kissing, suddenly broke away when they realised they were spotted. They shielded their eyes and ran off, laughing.

Ammi was horrified. 'My god. The things that are going on here! Do you know those two, Anoushka?'

'No,' I lied, clamping my eyes shut. It was Natalie and Kamran.

Thatthi reversed the car and we went past the house again, a beam of laser light streaking over the wall and through the night sky.

'So,' said Ammi again. 'Quite a party you came to.'

'Let her be,' said Thatthi. 'She didn't know what sort of party it was going to be. Did you, Anoushka?'

'No,' I said.

'Very innocent, aren't you? Both father and daughter – such innocent little children. Don't know anything. Even Natalie's mother, when I called her, didn't know what time Natalie was coming home. "I'll see her in the morning." That's what she told me – can you believe? What kind of mother is that?'

'That's none of your business, Lakshmi,' said Thatthi.

'Not my business? I was worried. She didn't even answer the phone when I called.'

'But I answered, Ammi!'

'Who did you say you'd come home with?'

My chest tightened. 'With Natalie,' I said.

'Imagine if we hadn't come. You'd still be there. At that disco party. Who knows what time Natalie's going home – do you even know how she's going home? Is she going with her boyfriend?'

'He's not her boyfriend,' I said angrily.

'Ah, so you know about him, then?'

'No,' I said.

'Don't lie. Latha told me everything.'

So that was how she knew. The all-knowing oracle had spilled the beans. 'What did she tell you?' I asked, carefully.

'Everything. I had to get it out of her, but she told me. About the boyfriend, how this fellow, Imran or Kamran or someone, Muslim fellow, was coming to meet Natalie after school. How the fellow invited you to this party. Is he related to this Nafiza woman?'

'Latha doesn't know anything. She's an idiot.'

Thatthi tried again. 'You shouldn't listen to the servant woman, Lakshmi.'

'Your company is not good, Anoushka. This is a very bad crowd. You saw the things happening there, no?'

'Latha doesn't know!' I yelled.

'Don't you dare raise your voice, Anoushka,' Ammi threatened. 'I'll give you a hammering.'

'She doesn't!'

Patass! Ammi reached back and slapped me, her fingers grazing my cheek. It didn't hurt but I was stunned.

'What is this!' Thatthi roared. 'Stop this nonsense or I'll leave you both on the road. I can't drive like this.'

At home I went straight to bed but couldn't sleep. I felt bruised. My ears were still pounding from the music, my brain throbbing, still trying to make sense of everything. I tossed and turned all night, the lights still flashing, images of Natalie and Kamran clutching at each other, my CD in the garbage barrel, all spinning round and round in my head until the sun came up and forced me to bury my head in the pillow.

—

Thatthi came into the room. 'Still sleeping, kella?'

'I don't feel good,' I said. I didn't want to go to school again. Not tomorrow, not ever. I wanted to die. Wanted the world to end, wiping out every memory of my whole wretched life in an instant.

'Do you have a temperature?' He came back with a thermometer and asked me to lie on my back and say aah.

AIDS. Ebola. Spontaneous human combustion. I prayed for a quick death as Thatthi placed the cold bulb of the thermometer in my cheek. He watched the clock. Latha was lurking just outside, her shadow slipping under my door like a ghost. Was she waiting to say more things about me? She had already ruined my life — was she trying to finish me off? He took the thermometer and went out. Latha stopped him. I could hear the kunu-kunu of her lies, Thatthi's stronger, deeper voice sometimes making her repeat things. Latha could read my mind and was telling him all about my feelings, about my dreams of Natalie. I was sure of it. Everyone would find out my secret, know that I'm a freak and stone me to death. The whispering stopped and I went back under, drowned in the dark ocean.

Thatthi woke me up for breakfast. He had a plate of steaming pittu, fried chicken, parippu and pol sambola balanced in one hand. 'Get up, Baba,' he said in a soft voice. 'Let's sit at your desk so I can feed you.' Thatthi moved the chair back for me. Still standing, he put the plate on the table and mixed up the food with his fingers.

I sat hunched, feeling like my body would go to dust any moment, spreading ash all over the furniture. Thatthi made little globes with the right amount of rice and hodi all mixed in, and said, 'Say aah.' He tipped the food into my mouth. 'It's tasty, no? Latha has made your favourites.'

I hated Latha. Hated her. But the food was good, so I kept my hate boiling inside.

'Eat a good meal and you'll feel much better. It's been a difficult few days for you, hasn't it? But it's all for the best. Eat, be strong and study. If you study hard and get somewhere, become someone, all those people will come behind you.'

He fed me another warm, tasty mouthful. 'One day you'll be someone important and you'll look back and think, "My thatthi was right." It's hard sometimes, when your friends are misbehaving, going roung-gahanna with boys, and you feel like doing it too. But this is not the time.'

I nodded and wiped my mouth with my sleeve.

'Was that boy nice to you? That Kamran or Imran? Latha said he spoke to you. But you see what happened, no? He's chosen Natalie. In a few days he might come back and try his luck with you. That's what boys are like these days. Can't make up their minds. You have to forget him. You're only sixteen. There's time for you. You'll find a nice Sinhala boy, not some wayward Muslim. But first you have to study. Become a doctor or a lawyer. After that everything else will come.'

Thatthi kept talking in his soothing voice long after I'd finished eating. The gravy was drying on his hands. I wasn't even listening to the things he was saying – the sound took me back to another time. I felt like I was five. Like I had hurt myself, falling off the bike or off some steps, and he was comforting me.

'If there's anything I can do for you, just tell me.'

'Thatthi,' I said. 'I . . . I lost something.'

'What?' He looked at me, his face so close I could smell toothpaste.

'I lost my history book.'

'Aiyo, that's not a problem, kella. I'll get you a new one.'

MANO

KEEPING EVERYONE HAPPY WAS IMPOSSIBLE. SOMETHING GOES wrong, always. But this was one of those times, rare bloody days, when I thought 'now everything will be all right'. The servant seemed to be recovering from her mental breakdown and finally doing some things around the house. I was relieved. Imagine if I had to pay for her treatment? It would have been better to pack her up and send her back to her brother. Niranjan had finally got himself a job in a respectable firm, private sector, of course, and was earning his keep – the fellow even slipped a thousand-rupee note into the envelope before I went to pay the electricity bill. It was what Lakshmi always wanted – to have the kids home and behaving. Her mood had improved. She hadn't come to me asking about beggar boys. There were more important things to do, no? She had to make sure Anoushka was studying, with O-Levels only a couple of months away. I wasn't worried about the results – Anoushka was bright. But she did seem a little down. I had noticed the girl had been very quiet and thoughtful. Must be exam pressure, no?

Even at work, I thought everything would be fine – it would be peaceful. We'd be writing happy stories about people returning to their homes, rebuilding the villages in the north and east, and forgetting that this bloody war even happened. I thought the newspapers would finally have a bit more freedom – no Defence Ministry buggers dictating every word, no restrictions on where we could go and what we could report, no fear of being swallowed by a white van. But things never happen the way you imagine, do they? Peacetime editorial wasn't something I had experienced. I was a little, what do you say, unsettled? Disoriented? Sure, we were writing about progress, about hope. But it didn't feel right. We were going the way of the government papers, following the *Daily News* and showing how our wonderful leaders were improving every facet of life – from the jungles in the east to the hill country and coast, everything was hunky-dory.

Why not? I was ready to believe it. But if there was nothing to be afraid of, why the gloomy feeling? Was it the weather? Was it the monsoons that had started, rain pouring every day? We were lucky our house was on higher ground so our lane never flooded. Twenty minutes of heavy rain and everywhere else went under water.

But the problem wasn't even that. I didn't know what it was until the problem waltzed into my office, sat on the chair before I could say anything and started talking about white flags. It was Mihil.

'Slow down, slow down,' I said. 'You're saying our soldiers killed LTTE fellows who had surrendered?'

'That's the rumour, Mr Herath. They came waving white flags but the army guys shot them. Apparently the orders came from high up – "If they're LTTE leaders, shoot."'

'How high?'

'Right from the top.'

'How do you know this?'

'I have a source, Mr Herath.'

'Who?'

Mihil smiled. He wasn't going to tell me.

'How do you know if your source is telling the truth?'

He shrugged. 'There are things you hear, details that seem . . . reliable. True. Prabhakaran was shot. Nobody even saw his body. There are only photos – why?'

'Prabhakaran was a monster. He should have been shot!'

'But there are rules, even in war, Mr Herath. This could be considered a war crime.'

'What did you say? War crime! You're sounding like that TamilNet or the BBC! This is LTTE propaganda! Have you turned into an LTTE supporter?'

'Mr Herath,' he said gravely, 'you know I'm not . . . I don't take sides.'

'But if you go and write something like this, you're automatically on their side. Don't you see?'

He got up from the chair, knowing what my verdict would be. 'I'm doing my job, Mr Herath. Our job is to tell the truth. I don't know if you've forgotten.'

'Truth! Nobody knows what the truth is anymore. I'm saving our skin! That's what I'm doing.'

Mihil walked out of the office, closing the door with a loud thadaang.

I got to my feet. Just when you think the trouble is over, something always comes, no? I looked out my window and for some reason the new girl from marketing, Charika, was in the newsroom. She gave me a smile as she went past. She was a nice lady, trim, always wearing high heels, her hair tied in a ponytail. She used to be married to an Indian diplomat, apparently. Lord knows what that bugger was thinking, to divorce a woman like that. She was already the talk of our office. Every time she came to talk to the typesetters or the graphics fellows, the other buggers decided they also needed to talk to the typesetters or someone in that area. Maybe I should have put a stop to it, but then again, that's all these chaps had for morale, no? I let them have it. Otherwise even they could become like Mihil.

—

I battled the traffic, taking a different route to avoid the flooding, only getting sprayed by the motorcycle and three-wheel fellows hammering past a couple of times before I got home. After I gave the car a quick wash, I took a peek inside Anoushka's room. Lakshmi was sitting beside her, making sure the work was being done properly. Anoush had her head down, sighing as she worked.

'Lakshmi,' I said quietly, trying not to disturb the work.

Lakshmi turned around and raised her chin inquiringly.

'Come and talk to me after.'

A few minutes later she came into my room with a cup of tea and I lowered the newspaper as she looked for somewhere to put the mug down. The only place was on the stool near the bed. There were a couple of books there, and the glass I used for a quick drink at night. 'Give it here,' I said before Lakshmi could get too close and start inspecting the glass, which had a few arrack stains I could see even from my spot on the chair.

'I'll put it here.' She moved towards the stool.

'Give, give.' I folded the paper quickly and put it aside but Lakshmi ignored me. She took the glass in her hand and looked at it. I thought, right, I'm in for a haranguing, as she sat on the bed. I prepared my defence, but no, she didn't yell. Lakshmi was fidgeting, pulling the housecoat across her chest, covering her legs, looking all round as if she had never been in my room.

I opened my mouth the same time as she did – our voices crashed. Then we both waited for the other person to speak, the clock going tak-tak-tak, reminding us that time was passing. Finally, I said, 'Niranjan is late today, no?' I put the paper on the floor, got up, retied my sarong and picked up the tea.

'Yes,' said Lakshmi. 'There's a meeting, it seems.'

'He called you?'

'Yes.'

'Good, good. The fellow is finally using his head. Everything settled after he got a job. Keells is a very good company.'

'Hmm . . .' Lakshmi nodded.

'It's one of the biggest firms in the country, no? He'll do well. I told you.'

'Yes.'

'I wanted to ask you – why is Anoushka so upset?'

'You noticed her bad mood?'

'Yes. Is there something wrong?' I said.

'No, she's lazy. Doesn't want to work. Always wants to watch television or listen to that music player.'

'Did you give it back to her?'

'No. She can have it back after the exams.'

'Let the girl have it, Lakshmi. She has to have some fun, no?'

'Fun? That's all you want, no? You have your fun but you don't think about anything else.'

'What do you want me to do?'

'I asked you for a favour. Have you forgotten?'

'What favour?' I knew what it was but hoped it'd be something else.

'You want me to remind you?' She lowered her voice. 'That boy. Khanna. What have you found? I keep getting emails from the father and I tell him my husband is looking. Looking, looking, still nothing.'

I should have known. Lakshmi never forgets. The bomb was already tied to my body, and now she set the clock for the countdown.

'I told you, it's a very sensitive situation. I can't go rushing in asking questions.'

'When do you think you can do something?'

'I don't know. We'll have to wait and see.'

'Mano, I've been waiting all this time. You haven't found a single thing.'

'That's how it is. I'm not a miracle worker.'

'So you'll start looking as soon as you can?'

'Yes, yes. As soon as possible.'

—

It turned into a habit for Lakshmi. Bringing tea. Even though I said there was nothing I could do she appeared like clockwork, came and sat on my bed. She started talking about regular things, about the children, about something that needed to be done around the house, like painting the walls or repairing the gate. Then she started asking questions: 'What's going to happen to the people who lost their homes? Will they be given new ones? And the children? The ones who have been orphaned? Injured? What about the psychological problems? The men – are they still suspected? What if they were forced to fight? Brainwashed? What do you think is going to happen?'

I wasn't a soothsayer, no? Still, I gave her some answers. 'It's all being dealt with. There's a resettlement program, Lakshmi. This time it's organised.'

I didn't mention the aid agencies because all of them had been told to get out. Even the Red Cross had been asked to pack up and leave.

Lakshmi didn't seem satisfied. She kept going back to the things she was being told by various people – about killings and disappearances and whatnot.

She kept nagging and I lost my temper. I said, 'Those are all lies, woman. How many times do I have to tell you? It's a foreign conspiracy. That Channel 4 video – you remember how all the experts said it wasn't real, no? The western buggers want to keep us under their thumbs – those Norwegians and the British. They're using whatever they can to upset our little country.'

When I explained it like that Lakshmi accepted, at least for a little while. Of course in a day or two she was going to forget and go back to the start, asking the same questions over and over again.

'Where's Anoushka today?' I tried to change the subject.

'Tuition class.'

'Where's today's one? Bambalapitiya?'

'Maharagama. It's the maths tute.'

'I should go and get her,' I said, getting off the chair and moving towards my cupboard. 'Can't let her get wet in the rain, no?'

'But the class only finishes at six-thirty,' Lakshmi said. 'There'll be less traffic in about ten minutes.' I was already in the bathroom, changing clothes.

The rain had almost cleared when I drove slowly past the Nugegoda intersection, where the shops were closing and the pavement hawkers were packing up cheap plastic goods under their polythene roofs. People were starting to move from under shop awnings where they were sheltering, closing their umbrellas, jumping over puddles and joining the crowd gathering at the train station. As expected, traffic was bad. But I wasn't bothered. If anything, it was the most relaxed I'd been all day, sitting there in my car, stuck between buses and vans and three-wheelers. I turned off the AC, opened a shutter and smelled the fresh water in the sky. After crawling along High Level Road all the way, past the blue Arpico Supercentre buildings in Maharagama, the traffic eased. The sun disappeared and it was dark near the Bo Tree junction, only the lights of my car and other vehicles' to navigate. Not a single streetlight was working. I turned left into Pamunuwa Road and right to the small lane. It was empty. There, the streetlights were bad, only shining in a dim yellow that reflected off the massive puddles in that road. I parked and turned on the radio. A Jim Reeves song I had heard a thousand times was being played. I turned it off. I'd rather listen to the sound of the drizzle on the hood of my car. Why was I was tired of Jim Reeves? He was an excellent singer, no? The best. But sometimes you listen to a song hoping it'll give you the same feeling it did when you first heard it – but it's never as good. That was life.

At least it wasn't like Anoushka's music. Lakshmi had listened to her music player and got a real shock. Some band playing loud, nasty rock and roll stuff, screaming filth, screaming their heads off. The girl had got it from the internet – where else would she have found such a thing?

Since then we made sure one of us was there when Anoushka used my computer. It was very easy for a young girl to be led astray these days. Lakshmi had also caught Anoushka trying to shave her legs and given her a blaggarding. 'I'm not going to let you become like your friends! You know that hair will get thicker every time you shave? You'll look ugly.' I thought of telling her, 'Let the girl be, Lakshmi. She wants to be like her friends,' but then thought better of it. It was never a good idea to interfere with women's business. Naturally, the girl must be feeling left out. I had to do more for her. Show her some support. At least I had come to pick her up. That was something.

The voices of youngsters spilling out of the class broke the silence. I checked my watch – it was barely six-fifteen. I got out of the car and tried to recognise faces in the low light. I saw Anoushka's short hair knotted into two stubby plaits. She was walking alone with exercise books pressed against her chest, behind the boys and girls still in their white school uniforms, some splattered with mud. She didn't give me her usual smile as she walked around to the passenger side of the car, tiptoeing on the edge of the overflowing drain to open the door.

'Hullo, kella. How was your class?' I said.

'Okay.' She put her bag on the back seat and clicked on the seatbelt.

'You finished early?'

'Yeah.'

'We're paying for what, two hours, no?' I said, starting the engine.

She shrugged.

'Does this happen all the time?'

'Sometimes.'

'Don't mention that to your ammi,' I said, turning onto the road. 'She'll tell you to ask for the money back.'

'It's okay, Thatthi,' said Anoushka with a big sigh. 'Some parents have already complained.'

'But you don't mind leaving early, do you? Ah?' I tried to get her to laugh. 'You can tell me. I won't say anything to Ammi.'

'No,' she said. 'I want to learn.'

I got onto the main road where there were a few cars, buses and skeleton-like vans rattling along. 'I thought you were like me – always looking to jump out and enjoy. Have some fun.'

Anoushka was gloomy, just said, 'No,' and looked straight ahead.

By now there was enough space in the road to avoid water-filled potholes and keep away from the 138 buses splashing everyone on the way to Fort. We went quickly through Navinna and past Udahamulla. It was only approaching the Jambugasmulla junction that we had to slow down. Must have been an accident or flooding – whatever it was, soon it was chocker-block. We waited and waited, no movement. It was getting late and I pulled out my cell phone and gave it to Anoushka.

'Baba, call your ammi and tell her there's traffic. Otherwise . . .'

'She'll hit the roof,' said Anoushka.

'Yes,' I said, laughing at how she had picked up my words.

The girl dialled the number and spoke to Lakshmi. 'Hullo,' she said in that childish voice she uses for her mother. 'Ammi, we're going to be late. There's a traffic jam . . . Okay, okay, I'll tell Thatthi.' She lowered the phone and pressed the off button. 'Ammi says don't drive fast, even if you're getting late.'

'I can't even drive slowly in this traffic. Ah, your ammi! Everyone has to do what she tells, no?'

'Yeah,' the girl said in a downcast voice.

'What's wrong, kella? You sound sad.'

'Nothing.'

'Is it something Ammi said? Did she scold you?'

'No.'

'Then did Niranjan do something?'

'No.'

'What then?'

'Nothing.'

I stared at her for a little but she gave nothing away – real poker face she had, just like her mother.

It was when I looked back out to the road that she said something. 'Thatthi . . .'

'Yes?'

'Remember when those people came to propose to Niro, just after he came back from Sydney?'

'You mean those buggers who wanted to arrange their daughter?'

'Yes. Why did you say they were not a good match?'

'They were low caste.'

'Why?'

'Apo! They're Karaava people. Descendants of fishermen.'

'So?'

'Do you want to marry a fisherman?'

'No . . . but . . . what kind of name is Jansz? Is it good or bad?'

'Like your friend Natalie? That's Burgher. Burghers are well-known professionals but there aren't many left. Why, are you proposing Natalie to Niranjan?' I chuckled.

'Niranjan? That idiot's got no chance. She's way out of his league,' Anoushka said in an angry voice.

'No! Niro could marry any girl he likes. Still, people are happiest with their own kind,' I said.

'But you married a Tamil.'

'Did you know your mother is a high-caste Tamil? She's Vellalar Tamil. Same level as us. You know we're Govigama, no? The farming and landowning caste.'

'At least we won.'

'What do you mean?'

'Sinhala people – we won, no? The Tamils lost.'

'That's not true, Anoushka. It's the Tigers who lost. The war was against terrorists, not Tamils.'

'I put a lion flag outside Ammi's window one day. She was mad. Don't tell her.'

Rain started falling so hard I could barely see out of the window. The fellow driving the van behind me was getting impatient, horning and racing his engine. I was stunned. Even Anoushka thought the war was a Sinhala–Tamil thing. If my own children believed that, what would others think? What is wrong with our people? Why can't anyone understand? The horning didn't stop. Peep-peep! Peeep-peeep-peeep! The van bugger was driving me insane. Anoushka crossed her arms and went quiet.

—

Mihil had been grumpy since our last disagreement. He took his time when I asked him to come and see me, pretended he was on the phone with someone, did something on his computer, loitered outside speaking to Cader and Sumathipala, and gave his teacup back to Wiji. Only then did he come into the office. He stood there and said, 'What is it, Mr Herath?' quickly, as if he had somewhere to go.

'Take a seat, Mihil.'

Reluctantly, he pulled back a chair.

'I know you've been angry about some of the things we have and haven't written.'

'I wasn't angry, Mr Herath.'

'Annoyed, then. Whatever it is, you haven't been completely happy, no?'

'It's okay. I understand, Mr Herath.'

'I didn't forget what you said, Mihil. I've been thinking about it.' I was telling the truth. I had thought about it.

Mostly, I had thought about Anoushka and Lakshmi and how there was an invisible wall between them. All of these things we were dealing with, it was all connected – I wasn't sure how, but I knew it was. 'You should go ahead.'

'Sorry, sir?'

'You should write your article, Mihil. Don't worry about the board. I'll look after that. We'll do it and see what happens.'

'Are you serious?' Mihil suddenly got up from his seat.

'Yes,' I said, extending a hand. 'Yes. You have my full confidence. Go and do it, putha.'

'Thank you, sir,' he said, grabbing my hand with both of his. His face was shining. 'Thank you.'

It was exciting, you know. Watching the fellow go and do his job the way he was supposed to. He didn't need any help. Not from me. I wasn't fooling anyone. I wasn't a proper journalist like him. I was only brought in from the Plantation Ministry because I was organised and followed orders – and because my brother-in-law was Sumith Rupasinghe. I had muddled around for years watching things go from bad to worse, not knowing what to do. I hadn't suddenly found answers – there was no chance of that. But at least this was a good parting shot, a last firecracker before retiring next year.

When it was time to go home Mihil was still working, soaked in the light of his computer screen, going tak-tak-tak on the keyboard. I was going to leave without disturbing the fellow, but as I walked past he said, 'Goodnight, Mr Herath. I'll put this on your desk. You can read in the morning.'

That night when Lakshmi brought my tea I wanted to say something, to let her know I was doing my best. But it was as if she knew. She sat there and smiled at me, talked only about the household and nothing else.

—

There was heavy rain again in the morning. The servant gave me my lunch bag and said something about a difficult road ahead. I thought she was ill again but when I started driving her words came true. The roads were wet. Some had flooded. Buses were packed and I knew everyone would be late. When I got to work only Wiji and Shantha Rozairo were there. Shantha was sitting and talking to Wiji, who was stupidly mopping the floor that was about to be muddied. Thunder rattled through the whole building and I wondered if the trip switch would go off. It happened often at our house. I opened the door to my office and Mihil's article was there, printed, stapled and placed neatly on my desk.

I hoped the power would fail and we wouldn't be able to work for the rest of the day. I was having misgivings about the whole thing. Who knew which sleeping giant it would wake up? What was the worst-case scenario? Losing our jobs, or getting the same treatment as one Mr Lasantha Wickrematunga – brains sprayed across the windscreen by some unknown shooter? Getting shoved into a white van, never to be seen again? Whatever happened, it wasn't going to be good for me. I didn't know why I'd agreed. Muttering to myself, I stepped inside. I put my bag down and glanced at the headline. *Summary Executions of Tigers with White Flags: The Final Miscommunication?*

I put it aside for a while, started my computer and tried to be busy with other things – going over the morning edition of the *Daily News* and *Daily Mirror*, a quick read of things happening around the world on the internet. Eight British soldiers had been killed in Afghanistan. One man had died during the running of the bulls in Spain. I looked at Mihil's article again, then looked away. I got up and went to my window to see who else had come in. It was ten minutes past nine and only a third of the newsroom was full. I took that book I bought from the Sarasavi Bookshop on the weekend, *The Da Vinci Code*, and started reading. I got through a good fifteen pages, wondering how Dan Brown came up with these things. He was a genius – imagine all the research, and that Robert Langdon character, sha! Bugger was fantastic.

That was when I noticed there was some sort of fracas in the newsroom. Most of the fellows were standing up to look at something. It was a group of people, at least four huge fellows who looked like thugs, brushing water off their shoulders, waving their umbrellas around like batons. They were dressed in their white collarless shirts and black pants, the uniform of the ministerial bodyguard. Leading them was a tall, moustachioed man in a white Nehru-collar shirt hanging loose over a white sarong. He was of course completely dry. This was none other than the honourable deputy minister of internal affairs, Hector Pushpakumara, and he was looking for something. Or someone.

I realised the cat was out of the bag. How did that happen? I thought only Mihil and I knew about it. The trouble was going to start even before we had published. I quickly turned back to my desk and hid Mihil's article in one of my drawers. Then I put my Dan Brown book in my bag, opened the door and walked out.

'Where is he?' The honourable deputy minister started to raise his voice.

None of the staff said a word.

The bodyguards started going up to the nearby people to ask questions. The clean-shaven one was getting very close to Cader, his nose almost touching the sports reporter's. Another stood stroking his beard and said in a calm, too-friendly voice: 'Mihil kiyana eka kawuda?' as two more guards stood like boulders next to the deputy minister. My suspicions were confirmed – they were looking for Mihil.

I had to do something before things got out of hand. I walked up to the deputy minister and said, 'Sir, can I help you?'

'Who are you?' said the tall man.

'I'm the editor, sir.'

'You're the man in charge?'

'I'm in charge of the English paper.'

'Who is this Mihil de Soyza?'

News of the deputy minister's visit must have spread to the other departments because people from accounts, marketing, publicity – they were all gathered outside, looking in through the windows or the glass door. This wasn't the first media organisation the honourable Hector Pushpakumara had visited. He'd assaulted reporters at Swarnavahini, had his men break some ITN cameras at a press conference, even walked into Radio Ceylon and harangued a newsreader. There were stories about him tying the principal who dared discipline his son to the school gates and giving the poor man an almighty flogging. It was also said he'd destroyed wine stores and bars in his constituency because it was against Buddhist tradition, while at the same time his brother opened the most exclusive chain of nightclubs in the country.

'Sir, shall we go to my office and discuss?' I tried to be polite, tried to keep his famous temper from boiling over.

'Fine. Let's go.' He followed me, bodyguards close behind. I held the door open as they all went in. Some of the staff – Sumathipala, Cader and the peon – took hesitant steps towards my office, stopping just out of sight. The rest of them were stunned. I wondered which one of them might be the traitor. Who else had Mihil spoken to when he was writing his article? Maybe we could figure it out, give all the staff a good scolding and see who came back, hat in hand, to apologise. But first I had to survive. I took a deep breath and closed the door behind me.

The minister was sitting in my chair. He picked up the framed photo from my desk. 'You have a nice family,' he said. It was the only photo I had at the office. It had been taken at home, in the living room, five or six years ago, before Niranjan had gone to Australia. Anoushka was still a child and Niranjan still growing, his body too long for his young features, a look that was half-cocky, half-doubtful on his face. Behind the two of them were Lakshmi and me – smiling. We looked happy.

'Thank you, sir,' I said, still standing.

One of the bodyguards, the clean-shaven man, was standing right next to me, tossing my paperweight, the glass one with flowers trapped in the middle, and catching it one-handed. The bearded one walked, back and forth, back and forth, right behind me, sometimes nudging my shoulder as he went past, the water from his umbrella dripping on the floor. A third fellow stood guard outside, staring at the gathering crowd.

'Who is this Mihil de Soyza?' asked the deputy minister.

'He . . . he's one of the reporters.' I took out my handkerchief to wipe some sweat off my forehead.

'Where is the fellow?' Pushpakumara still had the picture frame in his hand. I was wishing he would stop looking at my family, praying he wouldn't remember any of their faces.

'He was working till late, sir. And the rain must have delayed. He'll come soon.'

'Do you know what sort of things he has written?'

'Sir? What do you mean?'

'Don't tell lies!'

'Sir, Mr de Soyza writes a lot of articles . . .' I was sweating so much, my handkerchief was soaked.

'Do you read your own papers before they're printed?'

'Yes, sir.'

'And do you correct things if you find something wrong?'

'Yes, sir. Of course, sir.'

'But you published something wrong! You didn't correct it!'

'I . . . sorry, sir?'

'Don't play the fool with me!' the deputy minister roared. 'You know very well I was there yesterday, at the party organiser's meeting. But you and this, this Mihil fucker – together you decided to leave my name out. Did you think I wouldn't notice?'

'Sorry, sir? Come again?'

'In your article yesterday! Where was my name?'

'The article about the party meeting?'

'Yes, you fucker!'

'Sir, we—'

'Fucking pig.'

That was when I breathed again. This wasn't about Mihil's white flag article. 'We'll print a correction, sir.' Nobody had tipped off the deputy minister. Still, with his murderous thugs breathing down my neck, I didn't feel safe.

'Today. I want it today.'

'Of course. Yes, sir. We'll do it right away.'

'No! Not today!' He changed his mind.

'Not today, sir?'

'No! Tomorrow. I want it in the morning paper. The one everyone reads.'

'Yes, sir. Of course, sir.'

The honourable Hector Pushpakumara got out of my chair. He still had the photo frame in his hand. 'Fucking journalist pig,' he spat. The bodyguard who was pacing opened the door for the deputy minister. The clean-shaven one put the paperweight down. Thadaang! I must have jumped a metre off the floor. Then the deputy minister, as he was walking off, tossed the photo frame. Maybe he was aiming for the desk or one of the chairs, but it missed and fell to the ground. Shattered. I went over and looked at the photo – my family was smiling through the broken glass. Outside the thugs had formed a protective ring around their boss. The staff moved out of the way as they opened up their umbrellas and led the deputy minister out.

'What were they saying, sir? Are you hurt, Mr Herath?' The staff piled into my office. 'Shall we call the police?

We have told Mr Bamunuaracchi and the rest of the board. Do you want some water?'

As Wiji cleaned up the broken glass, I sat down and had a drink of water. I told one of the reporters to write a correction for yesterday's article. 'No police,' I said. 'Don't call them. Forget this happened.'

Cops would probably throw all of us in jail. Of course I wanted to hurt them – the deputy minister, his thugs – I wanted to show them that they couldn't just walk in here and treat me like a dog. I wanted to show the world that these were the sort of buggers who ran our country. But I couldn't. I couldn't do that because to them I was nothing but a dog. A pariah. A pig. That's what he kept calling me. I was a pig he could come in and kill anytime. He could kill me and my family and nobody would say a word.

What to do? I chased everyone out of the office. 'Back to work!' I shouted. I sat there and stared at the empty desk for a few minutes, feeling sick. I opened the drawer and took Mihil's article and a pen and got started. It must have been well past ten when Mihil knocked on my door and came into the office. I must have looked like a ghost because he shook his head and said, 'Are you all right, Mr Herath?'

'Fine.' I didn't look up. I kept cutting out whole paragraphs of Mihil's article with the red pen. Anything about executions or war crimes, anything related to the armed forces and their misdemeanours, I cut. I went through the whole thing again, Mihil sitting there, watching. Finally, I handed it over.

He took it, a resigned look on his face, and said, 'What to do?'

'Nothing. There's nothing you can do.'

Almost every word of his article was struck out.

—

I didn't feel like going home. I might lead the thugs right to my family, no? It would have been fine if my Lakshmi saw me take on one of those bastards and knock him off his feet. But it was more likely to go the other way. Who would want that? To have your wife, son and daughter watch as you're beaten mercilessly? Nobody. I certainly didn't. I thought of going to see Sumith. He was the most powerful man I knew. But the bugger was all talk – it was a miracle he even got me this job. No, I didn't want to listen to my brother-in-law's empty boasts. Didn't want to put up with Nelunka's pettiness. In the end I decided to get in the car and indulge in an old habit.

I went down to Buller's Road. There was still a checkpoint but it wasn't as intimidating as before. The big, spiky barricade had been taken away. Only the boom gate was there. The military police guy, Jayantha, was still around, smiling under a big black umbrella. 'Long long time, Mr Herath,' he said as I rolled down the shutter.

'I've been busy.'

He waved me through and I drove in, parked in the same place as before. The tree had been cut down, so there was nothing there to fall on my Swift and damage the hood. Only the rain fell, making a whole lot of noise. The Amarasinghe house looked dark and empty. The windows were streaked and moss was starting to grow on the walls. It must have been sold, because the words *To Let* and a phone number were written in big letters across the parapet. A crow, completely soaked, had settled on one of the pipes, under cover of the balcony I used to see Ramani on. Was it her, reincarnated?

There was a knock on the passenger-side window, almost making my heart stop. It was Jayantha. 'You nearly gave me a heart attack,' I said.

The fellow laughed. 'Nice to see you, Mr Herath.'

I didn't care about the fellow being too familiar anymore. I unlocked the door and he folded his umbrella and got into the passenger seat. His boots were muddy but what to do? I rolled the shutters down, lit a cigarette and offered another one to Jayantha. He took off his army cap and put it on the dashboard, leaned the seat right back and started puffing. 'What happened to the Amarasinghes?' I had to say it louder than normal to be heard over the rain.

'Gone, sir. After missus die, they sell house. Abroad – mister, children – everyone.'

'Everything's changed.' I looked up to the floor where Ramani used to be.

'Anicche dhukke,' said Jayantha.

'Impermanence and suffering. Life is suffering . . . but why is it only us, the small buggers, who are suffering?'

'Only you?'

'We're the ones who suffer for everyone else's mistakes, Jayantha.'

'Why, sir? Why you are suffering?'

'That's life. That's what you just said in Pali, no?'

'That is just Buddhist saying, Mr Herath. Why you are suffering?'

I took a long suck of the cigarette. He was looking at me with eyebrows up. 'Your wife giving you problems? Or your children?'

'Yes, my wife is one of the people putting me in a spot.'

'She is taking your money?'

'No, no . . . it's not like that.'

'Then what?'

How much could I trust Jayantha? He was a military police guy and it was dangerous – I could be putting everyone at risk. But I knew him now, no? And look at the fellow's face – it was innocent. Surely, he couldn't hurt a fly. I decided to tell him about one of my many problems. I left out details like Lakshmi being Tamil and the boy being from Batticaloa and gave him a heavily edited report. 'My wife has a friend living abroad. This friend knows I'm a newspaperman, so he thinks I can find some boy who was lost. The friend keeps calling and pestering Lakshmi.'

'You can't find the boy, sir?'

'Jayantha, I don't want to go and start digging around the war—'

'Apo, sir! LTTE boy?'

'No, no, not one of their child cadres. He's just a beggar who was living where Lakshmi used to . . .'

'No, sir. You right. You don't do anything.' He brought a finger to his lips. 'Hmm kiyanna epa.'

'That's what I told my wife. "Not a word." Just keep quiet. But she's stubborn. I should just tell her he's dead.'

'Yes. Yes, that is good idea.'

'No. Lakshmi will find out. I'll land in hot water. She's a very perceptive woman.'

Jayantha finished his cigarette, tossed out the filter, took another from the pack on the dashboard and lit up. A gust of wind blew rain onto me and I raised the shutter a little. Jayantha blew out smoke, filling the cabin. 'I tell you what you can do, sir.'

'What?'

'You can give your wife good shock. Then she stop everything. I tell you how.'

I listened to his plan. 'No, Jayantha,' I said. 'I can't do that to my wife.'

—

Almost a week had passed since the fracas with the deputy minister but I was still shaken. I was at home sitting in my chair having a quiet drink when a knock on my door made me jump. 'Let me be, Lakshmi,' I said. Every time there was a knock on my door I felt my throat tighten.

'Thatthi, it's me.' It was Niranjan. 'Can I come in?'

'Ah, wait a minute.' I downed the glass of arrack and hid the bottle behind a shelf. 'Come in.'

Niranjan came in wearing his shorts and T-shirt. The plaster cast had been removed from his arm. The right arm was smaller than the left, which was strong and muscled, making the poor fellow look like a bird with a broken wing.

'How is your arm? Better?'

'Much better.' He opened and closed his fist.

'Doesn't hurt?'

'No.'

'But you have to do some rehabilitation?'

'Yeah, I spoke to a physio at my gym. He'll give me some exercises. Should be fine in a couple of months.' Niranjan straightened his elbow and bent it again to show me.

'Excellent. And your work? Busy?'

'Yes, Thatthi.' He looked around, decided my bed was the best place to settle and lowered his body. He looked uncomfortable as he sat there, leaning forward, his long legs bent to keep his feet from touching mine.

I tried to make conversation, make Niro feel comfortable. 'Do you know a fellow called Janaka Pothupitiya? He works at Keells.'

'Which department?'

'He was, let me think . . . he was in shipping. Or travel. One of the two.'

'I only know the financial services people. I know a few property guys as well, but not many others.'

'It's a big company, no?'

'Yeah.'

'Largest list of stocks in Sri Lanka.'

'Yup.'

We looked at each other. Smiled.

I moved on to cricket. 'When is the next match?'

'I think it's Sri Lanka–India. It's in December.'

'First one since our boys were attacked in Pakistan, no?' Niranjan nodded.

'Samaraweera was injured, badly. Sanga as well.'

'Yeah.'

'Hope they're fully recovered.'

'Yup.'

Another pause. What else could we talk about? I was going to try and say something about the weather, how the monsoon season should end soon, when Niranjan cut in.

'Thatthi, I've been thinking . . . for a while, now.' This was not going to be good news. I could tell. 'I've been thinking. Life is short.'

'Don't say that. You still have a long time left, no?'

'Things can happen. Accidents, diseases . . .'

'You're still a young chap. Why do you have to think these things?' I tried to make an educated guess. 'Are you still getting those headaches?'

'No, I'm fine.' Niro was still manoeuvring his arm, stretching each finger, all without looking at me.

'Are you telling the truth?'

'It's fine. Just a little headache sometimes.'

'And feeling faint?'

'Rarely.' He gave me a quick look. 'Don't tell Ammi.'

'No. She'll cause a massive stir. What did the doctor say?'

'He gave me some medicine. Said it'll go away in a few days. But he'll keep monitoring.'

'You have to be very careful, putha!' I wanted to look at Niro closely, inspect him to make sure everything was all right.

'Yeah. But that's not what I wanted to tell you.'

'What is it, kolla?'

'I need to live my life. Otherwise I'll regret it.'

'Of course. You must do what you like.'

'That's why I'm moving out.'

'Out?'

'Yeah, I've found a place – not far from here. Pamankada.'

'When?'

'In two weeks.'

'Really?' I had always known Niranjan would go and live somewhere else, by himself, but when it happened I felt like I was going to lose an arm or a leg. 'Don't go, kolla. Your ammi will—'

'Sorry, Thatthi. I have to.'

—

Niranjan went. What could I do? He didn't take many things but the house felt empty when he packed up. Anoushka asked me if it was because she fought with him all the time. I told the kella it wasn't her fault. It wasn't anyone's fault, but Lakshmi, as usual, took it all on her shoulders. She didn't say a word but her lips were trembling when Niro said his goodbyes. She overdid it, pretending not to notice, and stayed home when we went to Niro's new house. I had to drive his car there because the fellow was still unsure about getting behind the wheel. We helped him set up the place. His arm was still weak, so Latha and I moved the bed into place. The servant folded his clothes and put them in the cupboard, dusted the books and put them on a rack. Even that woman was affected, telling Niranjan that he could come home whenever he was hungry.

It was a nice house, designed by Bawa, apparently – with the wide windows and open living area that old Bawa was known for. When I saw his housemate I was glad Lakshmi wasn't there. She wouldn't have liked it one bit. Why? Because the housemate was a girl. Quite a nice girl with a posh accent. But Niro didn't seem interested in her. Maybe he was pretending because I was there. Anyway, it was his life, no? I didn't want to interfere. It would be good for the fellow, he'll learn a few things and that'll hold him in good stead.

Of course, Lakshmi didn't think like me. Too sensitive. The next few days her eyes were red when she came out of her room. I tried to tell her that Niranjan was fine, that he was doing what he wanted and it was good for him. But she ignored all of that. All she wanted to talk about was that bloody Khanna fellow. Morning, noon and night. She started calling me at work almost every day and hassling me if I didn't have answers. She had moved her obsession from one boy to another.

I was trying to get the final copy of our front-page story finalised, trying to get Shantha Rozairo to stop writing half-baked headlines. It was always, *Highest Number of Deaths in Dengue Epidemic* or *Ties Depend on Welfare*, and I had to call the bugger into the office and say, 'Ayise, Rozairo, what is this? Highest number of deaths in dengue epidemic since when? How is anyone supposed to know what you're saying? And we don't say deaths – it's too strong. You'll scare the whole bloody readership. We say casualties or victims.' I wasn't going to let him off lightly. 'Every bloody day! This sort of thing happens every day. What's wrong with you, Rozairo?'

My cell phone rang. I took it out of my pocket. Lakshmi again. I rejected the call and kept blaggarding Rozairo. 'How can I run a newsroom when my most experienced reporters are so shoddy?'

Another call. I held down the power button, turned off the cell phone and carried on. 'If you keep going like this, Rozairo, I'm going to have to do something . . .'

The old telephone on my desk started shouting. Tilling-tilling-tilling. We both stared at it. The bloody thing just wouldn't stop, so I told Rozairo it was my wife and he politely went out of the office. I picked up the phone.

'Hullo.'

'Hullo, Mano.' Lakshmi sounded out of breath. 'Why aren't you answering your phone?'

'Lakshmi, I was in a meeting. I have work to do.'

'Did you find anything?'

'You can't keep doing this. I'll get into trouble with—'

'So there was nothing on the list?'

'What list?'

She paused, probably to make sure no one in her office was listening, and whispered, 'The Red Cross list. Missing persons.'

I had to think quickly. I had made up a few stories to keep Lakshmi off my back. The problem was that she remembered everything. 'Aah, yes. I'll try. I'll get someone to go and check.'

'No, no! Don't tell anyone.'

'Don't worry. I can trust Mihil.'

'Please, Mano. Do it yourself.'

'Why are you so worried? You know Mihil, no? He's a trustworthy fellow.'

Her voice wavered. 'I . . . I got a call.'

'What do you mean?' I thought it was another one of those international calls, from the people who were asking favours. 'Who called you?'

'I don't know. He didn't say anything. Just a breathing sound.'

'A nuisance call? How do you know it was a man?'

'Must be. Seemed like a man.'

'But why?'

'Maybe someone's . . .'

'Yes?'

'Must be nothing, Mano,' she sighed. 'Are you coming home soon?'

'Yes. I can come and get you from your office.'

'No, don't waste petrol. But come home before you go for Anoushka. You have time to get changed and have a cup of tea.'

'Right. Don't get upset if I'm five minutes late. You know what the traffic's like.'

'I won't . . . but answer your phone.'

'Again with the bloody phone.'

'Don't be late.'

'Okay, fine.'

'Bye.'

After a ten-minute conversation with Lakshmi I was exhausted. She was panicked. It was becoming too much for me. I felt like talking to someone, getting advice. Who knows – people may have dealt with this sort of thing. But it wasn't our way. 'Gedara gini pitata nodenu' – that was the proverb. The fire in your home must stay within. Those were the rules, and rules were things Lakshmi obeyed like someone was watching from above. There was no choice but to keep quiet.

I got back to work. There was an article the new fellow, Indika, was working on. He was probably the best we had. His spelling and grammar were fine, only a couple of mistakes here and there, a few punctuation marks missing. The main thing was that he could tell a story. And he was thorough. Got all the details from all the right people. I walked over to his desk and read through quickly. *Mother of Stolen Baby Elephant at Risk.* I didn't feel like reading past the headline, so I left Mihil to sort it out. I was walking back to the office when I saw Sumathipala, the old bugger who had all the Health Department contacts, waiting for something to come up, line by line, on his computer. I was about to say, 'Sumathi, you can go and have a cup of tea – by the time you get back your page will still be loading.' But I stopped myself when I noticed what he was looking at. The bottom halves of the pictures were not yet completed but I knew what to expect. I had seen Sumathipala do this before. I was going to put a stop to it.

He didn't know I was standing behind him, waiting for the whole thing to finish. The pictures completed. The women weren't even good-looking, a few goday locals looking bored, showing their deflated breasts and hairy lower parts. I clapped a hand on Sumathipala's shoulder.

'What is this?'

The fellow was lost for words. 'Sir, sir . . . I . . .'

'Pornography. Is this what you come here and do? You come here to look at these dirty pictures?' I had raised my voice and a few fellows got to their feet and looked over the partitions. I didn't want to cause a big scene, so I said, 'Take that off the screen and come and see me in my office.'

A few minutes later Sumathipala walked into the office, scratching behind his ear like a schoolboy who had been caught cutting class. 'Take a seat,' I said.

He sat down, hunched, and looked at the desk.

'You're a family man, no?'

He nodded.

'You have children?'

Another nod.

'How old?'

'One is eighteen, sir. The older boy – twenty-five.'

'We have to remember, Sumathipala, that family is the most important thing. I know it's hard. Even if you have a lovely wife and beautiful children. Sometimes we get a little lonely, no?'

Sumathipala wasn't looking at me. His attention was on the desk. His hands were in the pockets of his polyester pants. The rubber slippers on his feet scraped the floor nervously.

'Mr Sumathipala, I'm going to let you off with a warning. This is the first strike. Don't let me catch you doing it again.'

'Thank you, sir. Sorry, sir,' said the bugger, almost worshipping me, then stood up and crept away.

I got up and walked up to the glass that looked out into the newsroom. We were in a special kind of hell. But then I saw something that cheered me up. It was Charika. She walked past, wearing a pair of tight pants, her bottom going up and down as she walked. She was looking at me, smiling. She even gave me a wave and then looked away as if she was embarrassed. My cell phone rang. I didn't have to read the number displayed on the screen to know who it was. It could only be Lakshmi.

LAKSHMI

THE PHONE RANG. I ANSWERED BUT COULDN'T HEAR ANYTHING. The telephones had gone mad. Sometimes the wires were crossed and I could hear a conversation far away, like there were tiny people stuck in a tin. Sometimes the caller breathed but didn't speak. This time it was silent, just the kara-kara sound. I put it down and went to the kitchen, where I picked up the tea Latha had made and went to see Mano in his room. The arrack glass had already been hidden behind the chair. I wasn't there to criticise. I had long since given up trying to improve him. I went to his bed and sat down. As he folded the paper and put it on his lap I covered myself, pulling the housecoat down over my legs. 'Did Niranjan call today?'

'No. Not me. He didn't call you?'

'No.'

Mano seemed tired. Must have had a busy day at work. His computer had a tiny red light on. 'You haven't turned the computer off,' I said.

'It's off,' said Mano.

'What's that light, then?'

'That's the power.'

'So it's on. You should turn it off if you're not using. You know how much the electricity bill was last time, no?'

Grumbling to himself, Mano got up, his feet searching for slippers.

'You don't need to put on your slippers,' I said. 'You're not going for a walk.'

'Lakshmi, just let me do it, all right? That's the problem with you. Just can't let anything be.' Mano shuffled to the desk, got on his knees and reached under. 'That's why Niranjan didn't want to stay here.'

Normally when he said that sort of thing I shouted and left. This time I only hissed, 'You're blaming me? What happened to Niranjan wasn't my fault. That boy was ruined in Australia. I did my level best to bring him up to be a good man. What did you do? Nothing. I couldn't do it all on my own. All the pau from a previous life has come back . . .'

Mano turned off the switch, crawled out and stood up, sliding his feet back into the leather slippers.

'People will blame me for Niranjan. One day they'll say, "Niranjan became that way because his mother didn't bring him up properly." They don't know how hard I tried.'

Mano went back to the chair and sat heavily on top of the newspaper. 'Niranjan's only keeping with the times,' he said.

'I didn't bring him up to be like that, Mano. I always taught him the right way. You know what he says? "Ammi, your ideas are from the stone age." Imagine! I used to have a son who didn't dream of talking back to me. Now he's living in a house with a divorced woman.'

'It's like a hostel.' Mano, as usual, tried to push it away and hide. 'Even I lived in a hostel for a short time, in my younger years.'

'Don't defend him, Mano. You're always defending Niranjan. Why does he have to go somewhere else when he has a perfectly good house here? When I went there, that woman, wearing a tiny pair of shorts, put her feet up and started eating noodles. Didn't even ask me if I wanted anything. Is that how you treat a guest? It was like I wasn't even there.'

'Who? Niranjan's housemate?'

'Who else?'

'So she's a bit of a samayang woman. Doesn't mean Niranjan will get involved, no?'

'Our fellow? Not get involved? I don't trust our fellow. Not now. If he can go against his mother he can do anything.'

'You're making a fuss about nothing. Just let it be. The fellow will get married to a nice girl and everything will be okay.'

'You know how many proposals I sent him? He didn't look at one. Not one. I must have emailed him at least a hundred – photos and all. No reply.'

'It'll happen when the time is right. Don't worry.'

'Don't worry? How can I not worry? How can a marriage happen now? He's gone and started living with a divorced woman! What respectable girl will want him?'

Mano didn't always care about behaving decently, like a respectable man. I felt like bringing up his behaviour but decided to leave it, at least for now. He pulled the papers out from underneath him. 'These modern girls will understand. They know what it's like. Just give it some time, will you?'

'You want Niranjan to marry that sort of woman? Chi, Mano! What kind of man are you?'

'Look here,' Mano growled. 'I was reading the papers before you came and started this nonsense. There's nothing we can do. We can't force Niranjan, no? So if you don't mind, I'm going to read.'

'Fine. I'll go. But before that . . .'

He lowered the newspaper. 'What is it now?'

'The boy. Any news?'

'No,' he said and hid behind the papers again.

—

I thought of calling someone in Batticaloa, a neighbour, an old teacher or schoolmate. But I didn't have any numbers – didn't remember any names. I thought of calling a police station but the police were Sinhala. I couldn't risk it. What I could do was look at the telephone book and choose a house from my old neighbourhood on Kalmunai Road, give them a call and quietly ask if anyone had sighted the boy. I didn't want to do it from home. Our phone was tapped – why else would there be those frightening phone calls?

I decided to do it at work. Mano was busy and wasn't going to pick me up. I told the trishaw driver to only come at six. I waited for everyone to leave. Hetti, Rohan and Upuli left early as usual. Mr Muthalif locked his office room right after five and everyone in his claims department vanished soon after. The cleaning women were walking around, carrying their buckets and brooms, and when they finally disappeared I realised this was a bad idea. It was too quiet after work. If, by chance, someone was still there, a woman cleaning the windows, a peon stacking files, old Mr Premadasa trying to balance the accounts around the corner, any of them could hear everything. Our open-plan office was nicely designed, clean and spacious, lots of desks, wide windows with good views, but it wasn't good for a private conversation. Couldn't do anything when I was there alone – too conspicuous.

But on Wednesday, midmorning, I looked around and the salesmen were all on the phone making their deals, at least three phones were ringing, people were going in and out of the lunch room and there was a meeting in Mr Muthalif's office. This was the right time. I already had a couple of numbers. I had copied them down at home, using the telephone book to find an address near the corner where Khanna used to wait. I found the piece of paper in my bag and dialled. I imagined a phone ringing in a dingy, dark house with a dusty living room full of broken rattan furniture, a sooty kitchen, an overgrown garden and a well full of weeds. Someone picked up the phone. 'Hullo?' I said.

'Yar?' It was a man's voice. Was the street still unpaved? Were the fences still rickety, made of tree stumps strung together with wire?

'Is this Mr Bhuvanesvaran? My name is Lakshmi. Lakshmi Herath. I'm calling from Colombo.'

'Illé. Sorry. Ingrisi theriya illé.' The man spoke only Tamil.

Did anyone notice? In front of me, Hetti was jabbering about Ceylanko Pawul Rakshanaya, an insurance plan for the whole family. Behind me Punsala was having her usual conversation with her husband about buying a house and Mahen was doing the hard sell on VIP – the private car insurance. Nuwan was, as usual, talking to some girl. They were all speaking English or Sinhala.

'Sorry,' I said. I couldn't speak Tamil in front of everyone. They'd know exactly what sort of place I came from. 'Sorry. I dialled a wrong number.'

—

I had so much to do. Had to think about Anoushka. Her O-Levels were only a couple of weeks away and I had to make sure she was studying. She was getting better at concentrating, sitting in one place and reading for longer. Still, she wasn't happy when I asked questions and tried to see if she was doing things right. She was very irritable when I asked her to take out her Buddhism book. I had to insist she read the Dhammapada out loud.

'Appamado amatapadam, pamado macchuno padam, appamattaana miyanthi, ye pamattha yatha matha.' She read so softly I almost couldn't hear what she was saying.

'Okay. Now tell me the meaning, Anoushka?'

'Appamado amatapadam – don't be late to do pinn. If you do pinn on time, you won't die. If you don't do pinn, you'll die.'

'Is that what you were taught?'

'Yes.'

'That's wrong! Did the teacher really say that was the meaning? The meaning is more like, "You have to be mindful without delay. If you're mindful, it's like you're not dead." But it's not really about death . . . The poem is more about becoming enlightened. You understand?'

'Same thing.'

'It's not the same thing. You said if you do pinn you don't die – that's not correct.'

'How would you know?'

'How do I know?' I raised my voice. 'Because I've read the Dhammapada!' I glared at Anoushka.

'But you're not . . .' The girl looked away.

I knew what she meant. 'I'm Buddhist too, you know.'

Anoushka rolled her eyes and gave me a look.

'What does that look mean?'

The girl didn't answer. My anger rose. 'Did someone tell you a Tamil can't be Buddhist? That's what you think, is it? Listen here, anybody can become Buddhist. Where are you getting these ideas?'

I heard Mano scratching around near the front door. He had come home from work. 'Mano! Come and hear what your daughter has to say.'

He came into Anoushka's room with his briefcase in hand. 'What is it now?'

'Ask your daughter.'

'What's wrong, kella? Are you fighting with your ammi again?'

Anoushka pulled a face but kept her mouth shut.

'Don't fight, okay?' He turned towards me. 'Why is it always such a fuss, Lakshmi? Here I am, trying my best to keep everyone happy and you're always—'

'Trying your best?'

'Yes!'

'Don't get me started.'

'Don't jump the gun, Lakshmi. You don't know what I've been doing. I told Sumathipala to go to the ICRC, the Red Cross office, you know, the one near Dickman's Road, and the bugger came back saying he found—'

'Mano!' I hissed at him. 'Not here.'

Anoushka raised her head. 'What?' she said, showing interest in the wrong thing again.

'None of your business. Do your studies. I'll come and check on you later.'

I followed Mano into his room. He put down his briefcase and took off his tie. I closed the door, making sure nobody could hear. 'I told you not to discuss with others, Mano.'

'It's only Anoushka.'

'You want to bring Anoushka into this? Put her in danger?'

'Don't be silly. Anoushka doesn't care. She's not going to tell anyone.'

'It's not about her telling anyone. It's about involving her. You think she should be part of this?'

'Stop being hysterical, Lakshmi.'

'Please leave her out of it. And why did you tell this Sumathipala fellow? Who is he? Is he suddenly your best friend? I thought Mihil was the only person helping you – now you're involving someone else.'

'Don't tell me how to do my job. Do you want to hear what happened or not?'

I let it go, released my frustration with a sigh. 'Okay. What happened?'

'Sumathipala went to the ICRC and came back saying he found a K. Selvaratnam on a list from Kilinocchi.'

'But it's Selvarasan. That's the name.'

That seemed to catch Mano by surprise. 'Ah . . . but . . . so that's what I told him. Useless bugger. I told him to go back and look for a Selvarasan from Batticaloa.'

'Don't lie, Mano.'

'Why would I lie?'

'Are you saying it's true? You really asked Sumathipala to look at those lists?'

'Yes!' Mano undid his shirt buttons. 'Lakshmi, I don't know what I can do to make you happy. Everything I do is wrong.' He dropped into the chair in his slacks and torn undershirt and removed his shoes. He looked worn out. I felt sorry he had to wear torn clothes. He used to be such a smartly dressed man, always wearing clean white shirts with long sleeves. His shoes were always polished and his black hair parted neatly to the left. Now he didn't have enough hair for a side part. The shirts were still white but the material had become rough from being washed so many times. His shoes were old and even though he polished them carefully every night they had lost their shape, heels worn almost all the way through. It was his fault for being bad with money but I still felt sorry.

'I just want you to be safe,' I said. 'Don't do anything that will get you in danger. Think about the children.'

'I don't know if we'll find anything. You know the situation, no? Do you still want me to keep looking?'

'Do it. But be careful. Why can't you do it on your own?'

'No time, Lakshmi. But for you I'll try.' He sighed, telling me to leave without saying it in so many words.

'Did Niranjan call you?' I asked.

'No. Why?'

'I haven't heard from him.'

'In how many days?'

'Three.' Just as I said that the phone rang. I rushed into the corridor to answer, but it wasn't Niranjan. It was another jumbled-sounding call.

—

When the weekend came I said, 'Get ready, we're going shopping,' to Anoushka. At first she said she didn't want to go.

'I'll buy you some new clothes,' I said. 'You need a dress or two.'

'Can we go to Odel?'

'Odel's too expensive. House of Fashions is just as good but cheaper.'

She made a face. 'House of Fashions is goday.'

'You're not coming? I'll go alone.'

I went and got dressed. She delayed for as long as possible and finally came out wearing the shorts she wore every day.

'You're getting too old for shorts. I'll get you new pants.'

We got to House of Fashions in a trishaw. We squeezed through the crowds lining up at the returns counter and made our way past people fondling porcelain and glass ornaments, smelling unheard-of brands of tea and feeling the new towels and bedsheets on the ground floor. We looked at some table mats and a nice wall hanging that looked like a George Keyt painting and then walked up the winding stairs to the women's section. I asked Anoushka to try on dresses. There were some pretty colours – purple, pink and maroon – but Anoushka didn't want to try them. She went off to find something on her own. All around me ladies put their bags down on the floor to try on a new dress on top of what they were wearing, or turned round to see if the skirts made their backsides look big in front of a mirror. I unwrapped a couple of saris and placed the cloth across my chest. They looked nice but were expensive, so I settled on a nice blouse, a silky green one with big buttons on the front.

Anoushka came back with some clothes – all of them black. I held up the jeans she had chosen. They had been scratched on purpose, making the material look old. 'When did the fashion become looking like a beggar?' I asked. The T-shirt Anoushka had picked was also black but there was a pattern of small flowers embroidered in silver thread. I first thought it looked nice but later on noticed the flowers were arranged into the shape of a skull. 'This is a skull!' I said to Anoushka. 'Didn't you see it?'

'No,' she said in a flat voice. 'I'll put it back.'

'There are lots of nice T-shirts, Anoush. So many colours. Why don't you choose something bright?'

'Okay.'

I told Anoushka I'd meet her downstairs at the cashiers and went up to the men's section. After I selected a nice shirt and tie for Niranjan, I bought two new undershirts for Mano. I also bought him a new white Van Heusen shirt. He would like that. He preferred those to the local brand, the Emerald shirts he normally bought. He would be happy to wear expensive clothes and go and talk to his friends, show off what his wife bought for him. Anoushka came back empty-handed.

'Why didn't you get a T-shirt at least, Anoushka?' I asked her.

'I don't want anything.'

'Aiyo, why, Baba? Quickly go and get something. We have to go home soon. You have to study.'

She shook her head. I couldn't say anything to convince her. In the trishaw home Anoushka didn't speak to me. She looked very upset. 'What's wrong, kella? Couldn't you find any nice clothes? We can come back another time.' I put an arm around her and kissed her head but Anoushka stayed stiff. 'I know it's a difficult time for you. It's hard for everyone. But don't worry. You'll get good results. And Niranjan will come back. He won't last much longer on his own. Just concentrate on your studies and do well at your O-Levels. After that everything will be fine.'

At home, I went straight to Mano's room and gave him the bag with his new things. He smiled like a child and said, 'Adey, my birthday is not for two months! Did you forget?'

'No,' I said. 'I know when your birthday is.'

'Then why all the presents?' He took the new shirt out of the bag, his face glowing.

'I got a bonus at work . . . and Niranjan sent some money.'

'You took his money?' said Mano with a little laugh. He admired the shirt, reading the tag on the collar, and said, 'The black crow has turned white.'

'He sent the money through Latha. I was going to tell her to take it back but I remembered all your shirts were old and your undershirts were torn, so . . .'

'That's nothing,' said Mano, taking his new shirt out of the plastic wrapping. 'My shirts are still good. The undershirts are a little torn but nobody can see those.'

'I can see them,' I said. It made me happy, watching Mano try on the new shirt, buttoning it all the way up to the top.

'Perfect fit. You never forget a size, no?'

The collar was sticking up at the back so I reached out to turn it down. At the same time Mano moved his hands up and his fingers touched mine. I got a shock, like he had an electric current in his body. It made me take my hands away quickly and step back.

'Thank you, Lakshmi,' he said, staring at me.

'Don't thank me.'

'Then who do I thank? Niranjan?'

'No. He doesn't deserve it,' I said.

—

I met Mano in Peradeniya University. Some of his schoolfriends were on our campus and Mano was forever in their dorm rooms or in the mess halls, talking loudly, playing tricks, walking around with that group of boys in their flared pants and half-buttoned shirts like film stars. Mano was one of the louder ones. In the beginning I didn't want to think about him. I thought he was trouble, someone who'd distract me from my studies. But when I met him on the bus one day, he got up and gave me his seat. He behaved like a gentleman. Asked me if I wanted to go see the Peradeniya gardens. I said no. He asked if he could take me to see a film. Again, I said no. Then he said, 'There is a place near the campus where they make a nice ice coffee. I can show you.'

Ice coffee was one of my favourite drinks so I said, 'Okay, but only after I finish my exams.'

It was a few years later, after we became close, that I realised how difficult our friendship was for him. His father was dead but his mother hated me. She told him that I would condemn his whole family. But Mano's sister was already married, and he had a good job and knew he could look after everyone, so he had said, 'Amma, I'm not a gambling man. But this time I'll take a risk.'

Most of his family didn't come to our wedding. Only Sumith, Nelunka, Ratnasiri, Padma and Junius Uncle. That was all. Mano had sacrificed for me. It was a long time ago but I shouldn't forget. I had to remind myself sometimes. Years went so fast and things changed so quickly it was hard to believe this was the same man I married twenty-seven years ago. But when I went into his room today, after dinner, and he sat down next to me on his bed and explained how he was looking for that poor boy lost in that devastated town, I saw something of the young gentleman who gave me his seat. The smile was still there – it hadn't changed. The kindness, the fun, even the love that I had thought was long gone – they were there in some shape.

When did we start moving apart? Was it when he began to come home late? Was it when I found out he didn't tell me that the business trip he took to Kandy was with that woman, Sunethra or Sulekha, I can't even remember her name anymore, the one from the Plantation Ministry? Was it when he began criticising Latha for no reason? That was something that never stopped. Even now he was grumbling, saying, 'That woman is out of her head. There's dog kakka in front of the gate and she hasn't removed it.'

I was in his room, trying to have our usual conversation. I wondered if it was a tactic, a distraction. 'She's perfectly normal,' I said. 'If there's a problem, it's her attitude. No matter what unpleasant task we give, no matter how we scold her, she's happy.'

'Normal people don't behave like that, no? Always smiling and carrying on?'

'Maybe we should all be like that. I can admire it.'

'You admire that woman? Chi!'

I smiled. 'Maybe admire is not the right word. Anyway, I have told her. She'll do better now.'

'I don't know about better. She wasn't very good in the first place.'

'If you think you can find someone else, go ahead.' I challenged Mano, knowing he wouldn't push any further. He didn't.

We continued making our plans. We ignored the always-ringing phone and talked about the things we could do to find Khanna, like getting in touch with various NGOs and humanitarian organisations. Everyone knew they had ulterior motives – after all, most of them had Christian missionary roots – but they also had information that might help us. Mano said he could call the grama sevakas, the newly appointed officials in charge of the area. We could call churches, kovils, any of the holy places where people would shelter, maybe even try and get a look into the camps that had been set up for the IDPs, which he explained stood for internally displaced people. It was hard. 'You never know what you'll find. These are places you should never dream of setting your eyes,' said Mano. He lowered his voice and told me what happened to the journalists, the ones who had trespassed and poked their noses where they didn't belong. They were tied to trees and whipped or bundled into white vans and beaten to within an inch of their lives. 'I heard some of these buggers who support the LTTE, they get an S-Lon pipe . . .' He made a rude gesture, closing his fist and pushing it upwards.

'A what?'

'You know the S-Lon pipe? The water pipes? They put one of those up their backsides and push ice into the hole. That's how the police interrogate terrorists.'

'Please don't tell me things like that.'

Some people disappeared – Mano hoped they had fled to another country, but worried they might not have. 'I'm not saying it's this government, but you won't hear anybody say they're sorry. You'll never find out who did it. If anyone says a word against any of the bigwigs – finished.'

Even though I said I didn't want to hear it, Mano didn't hide the facts. He reminded me that we were taking a huge risk with almost no chance of finding anything. 'What if this Khanna fellow's already dead, Lakshmi?' he said. 'What then?'

The weight of it was all too heavy for me. I hadn't seen Niranjan in a week. I gripped my head with both hands, thinking I was going to fall to pieces, but Mano put his arm around my shoulder and kept me steady. He promised to stop involving outsiders, and from now on only the two of us would know what he was doing. He said, 'Come for a walk. Forget these terrible things for a little.'

I changed out of my nightclothes, made sure Anoushka was studying and joined him. We walked to the main street where the streetlights were dim and the traffic went flying past, screeching and horning. The two of us kept to the pavement, as far from the road as possible in case someone lost control of a vehicle. We walked under the new flyover that had been built to bypass the junction. There were beggars gathered under it, so we crossed to the other side, onto the pavement near the school that was, unlike during daytime, completely silent. We passed the mechanic's garage where rusty cars stood, their windscreens dusty and their insides emptied, through Kirulapone, where the Cargills supermarket was still open to those who could afford to buy what it sold, past the small park, which was rectangular and meant for football but used for cricket by the slum kids. We walked all the way past the market where Latha did the weekly grocery shopping, a couple of sad corridors that hemmed in a courtyard where cats and crows searched for food among the fish blood and fruit peels.

We stopped on the bridge, avoiding the shaky concrete sleepers that dropped dust into the slow-flowing water as you stepped on them, and stood there for a minute or two, watching the water flow. Mano told me stories about colonial times, when sailboats had swept up and down the canal. 'This was once a beautiful place. But that was a long time ago, Lakshmi. The slums came up and all these dirty buggers started doing all their kakka and choo in the water.' He made a face at all the shacks built either side of the canal. Together, we imagined the olden days, how beautiful it would all have been. As we started walking back, Mano tried to hold my hand and I let him, his thick fingers wrapping around mine until I sweated and had to shake them off.

When we got home, I helped Mano put on his mosquito net, tucking it under the mattress to keep the insects out. He held up one end to get into bed, turned back to me with a cheeky smile and said, 'You want to get in with me?'

I felt like getting in and sleeping next to him. It would've been okay if sleep was all Mano wanted to do. I knew the man too well. He wanted to do other things. Dirty things. He must've thought that because Niranjan was gone, he could start again. He was wrong. I said, 'Mano, stop being silly,' and walked away. Before I shut the door I asked him, 'Do you think Niranjan will come back?'

Mano turned off his light. 'Lord only knows,' he said.

'Do you think he's ashamed of us?'

'Ashamed? Why would he be ashamed?'

'Since he went to Australia he's been very offhand. We're not up to his standards.'

The bed creaked as Mano climbed in. 'Must have learned from you. You're ashamed of everything, no? No surprise if some of that shame has gone to your son.'

—

For two weeks I had kept my promise, going to the temple or kovil and praying to the statues of the Lords Buddha, Vishnu, Saraswathi, Ganesh and Katharagama, asking for forgiveness. I lit lamps, burnt incense, presented flowers, bathed trees and idols, paced and recited. Please Lords forgive me for my selfishness. I hoped they would understand. I'd had to think of my own children, my husband. I'd had to fully commit to my family. I was a Herath — and if the other Heraths found my background shameful, it was no surprise I became ashamed of myself. Maybe the gods heard and gave me one more chance to be proud of who I am — the sort of opportunity that was also a huge weight. I got another email from Mr Subramaniam about Khanna.

He wrote that one Mrs Paramanathan had some information. Mr Subramaniam didn't say how he knew her or found out about her. He only mentioned that she had lived on Lake Road, Batticaloa, and I managed to find her number in the telephone directory — there was only one Mrs K. P. Paramanathan there. During my lunchbreak, I went out of the office to one of those small kadés and bought an SLT phone card. There was a payphone nearby. I looked around to see if anyone had followed me, made sure nobody was watching or eavesdropping and called.

Mrs Paramanathan sounded like a panditha woman, speaking quickly, asking lots of questions about my job and saying she was an English teacher at a school in Colombo. Then she finally told me what she knew. 'My brother used to be a bus operator during the war, Mrs Herath. All the buses that went from the east coast to the north, they belonged to my brother. Only he had a bus service. Everyone came to him. One day, this Khanna boy asked my brother to put him on a bus to Mullaitivu. He didn't have any money, so my brother didn't. But the boy kept coming back, saying, "My father's fishing boat is in Mullaitivu — please take me there. I'll give you money when I get there." Eventually my brother felt sorry and put him on a bus.'

'So the boy went to Mullaitivu? Are you sure?' My chest suddenly felt constricted.

'Yes. Just before . . . the end.'

'My god.' There was a rumour the war had ended on an empty stretch of beach on the coast of Mullaitivu. The army had declared it a no-fire zone and all the people from the nearby villages crowded there. The remaining Tigers, thinking the army wouldn't target the no-fire zone, had used it as a hide-out. When the army closed in, the Tigers started using civilians as human shields. In the end the no-fire zone had been bombed mercilessly. The story was that thousands upon thousands had died.

'It's not very good news, Mrs Herath. I'm sorry.'

I put the phone down and recited the Dhammapada. Studying with Anoushka had refreshed my memory. *Manopubbangama dhamma, mano settha manomaya. Everything is in the mind, all feelings, all consciousness.* I had to stay steady. Be strong for the sake of the children. We still didn't know what was true. Niranjan hadn't completely abandoned me and Khanna's death wasn't a certainty.

—

When I reached home the phone was haunted again. The ghostly breathing and murmuring happened twice. I left it and went to the temple. I was picking flowers at the jasmine tree when a van appeared – a white HiAce with tinted glass. It parked in the temple grounds, near the devalaya. Two men got out. Two regular-looking fellows, one in a sarong, the other in black polyester pants and a striped shirt. They picked flowers. When I went to the chaithya, placed the flowers and prayed, they prayed too. They were right behind me wherever I went. Surely, it was because they were praying in order, like me, watering the Bodhi tree, lighting lamps and burning handun kooru. But why two men? How many men come to the temple without women? Mano didn't even know all the prayers. I was the one who knew Buddhism properly. Men don't need religion the way women do, do they? I wanted to pray at the devalaya but the van was blocking my path. I should have brought Latha. I would have felt safer with her. The woman had said, 'I'll stay home and cook. Mahattaya will be angry if the food is late.'

I couldn't leave the temple without praying to my gods – not when I needed them the most – so I went around the van in a wide circle. I arranged flowers in front of the statues, lit lamps and incense sticks and prayed hard: 'Please bless Mano and my children with all my pinn. I don't want my pinn – give it all to them. Please help me find the lost boy.'

Maybe I should have kept some pinn for myself because when I opened my eyes the two men were there. Right beside me. They were putting their hands together to pray, smiling like jackals. I quickly gathered my things, dropping the oil bottle, the wicks and the handun kooru in the polythene bag and walked out. When I was out of their sight I increased pace, until I was almost running. I was nearly home when I realised I had left the box of matches at the temple.

Latha was outside with the neighbour's servant, talking to someone in a car. As I got closer the car started moving and rolled past, another ordinary-looking pair inside it, both men, staring at me.

'Who was that?' I asked Latha when I reached her.

She took the bag from me, saying the men had asked for directions to the kovil.

'Kovil?' Why were they asking where the kovil was? What were they doing here? The Hindu kovil that I sometimes visited was all the way on Havelock Road – why did those men want to know that?

When we went inside, I scolded Latha. 'Why do you have to talk to everyone? You're always talking to the neighbours, the people at the shops, the men who sell lotterai. Why? What do you have to tell them? Are you telling them about us?'

'No, Nona,' Latha said. She went into the kitchen and brought out dinner.

'Why didn't you come to the temple with me?'

'I had to cook, Nona.' She wasn't upset by any of my questions. She calmly finished putting the plates on the table and disappeared.

I called Anoushka out of her room, saying, 'Anoushka, you can eat. Your father's late again.'

The girl served herself some miris fish, gotu kola and parippu and started eating. I watched her for a little while and decided to try and call Mano. I tried his mobile and it was off. He was always turning it off – just to annoy me. Then I tried the office. No answer. I called the number of the security hut at the newspaper and the guard told me Mano had left around five. I asked if he had mentioned where he was going – no luck. I put the phone down and went back to the dining table, where Anoushka had finished eating.

'I can't reach your father. Do you know where he's gone?'

'No.' The girl barely looked at me. She took away her plate into the kitchen. It was seven-forty-five and I went outside. The street was quiet, a few lights on in the almost-finished building at the bottom of the lane. Cats fought on a rooftop, mewling and crying like angry babies. I went back inside. The food was going cold, my stomach was rumbling, but I wasn't going to change my ways. I told Latha to put the food in the fridge before it went bad and went into Anoushka's room and watched her study. I translated a few more Dhammapada verses. *The body is fragile, it can break like a clay pot. But the mind is a fortress. Fight Mara with the sword of wisdom, keep him out by staying unattached.* Nine-thirty came and went. Mano still wasn't home. I called Niranjan and he didn't pick up his phone. I left a message saying, 'Hullo, Niranjan. It's Ammi. Your thatthi hasn't come home . . . I don't know what to do.'

I tried Mihil, Mano's friend at work, and he said, 'I don't know, Mrs Herath. He must be stuck in traffic.'

'For so long? The security man said he left at five, no?'

I wanted to ask Mihil whether they had an emergency plan, like some journalists did. They had organised with foreign embassies to immediately contact certain people high up in the government in case they were picked up by a van or went missing. At least two or three lives had been saved that way.

'There must be a good explanation,' said Mihil. 'I'm sure Mano's fine,' and he hung up.

I thought of calling Sumith and Nelunka. Sumith had the contacts to help Mano if he had been kidnapped. But since Niranjan's incident with Heshan, they had been distant. Not knowing what else to do, I went beyond our gate again, looked out towards the main road. A stray dog moved in the shadows, sniffing at some garbage at the bottom of the lane. It found something and started eating, right there in the dirt. It lay down in the middle of the road, but soon it was disturbed by strong headlights. A van came in and parked in front of the building at the bottom of the lane, turned its lights off and just sat there. Nobody got out.

'Latha!' I called.

The people in the van were watching. I could feel it. They saw I was weak and alone. The servant came out, wiping her hands on her skirt.

'Who are those people?' I asked Latha, motioning towards the van.

'Kawuda?'

'Those men in the van.'

She said it was the mason baas – the builders working overtime.

'The builders? Do you know them? Do you talk to them? How do you know all these people?'

She shrugged.

I was afraid but I didn't want to show it. I was tired of being intimidated. 'Come with me,' I said to Latha as I took off towards the van. 'Go in front.' I pushed her in front of me. She walked calmly. It was just another walk down the street to her. She probably knew the white-van fellows. It could be her brother giving them information.

Her family was linked to the army – we saw that, firsthand, at the funeral. From what I had heard, it was a special army squad that ran the white-van operations. We walked slowly, avoiding the rocky parts of the lane. The people in the van didn't move, watching as we got closer, step by step, until we were right in front of the driver's window.

'Ask them what they're doing here,' I whispered to Latha.

She knocked on the shutter and the man in the driver's seat rolled it down.

They claimed to be builders, just as Latha had said.

'Then what are you doing in the van?' I said.

Another vehicle turned into the lane, the lights blinding me for a second. I shielded my eyes with my hand and looked at the car. It was small and had an S on the grille. It was Mano's beloved Swift, the man himself behind the wheel, looking sheepish.

Latha rushed back to open the gate and I watched, hands on hips. He drove past, puzzled, and I followed.

'Where have you been?' I said as Mano got out of the car. 'We were worried sick!'

He opened his mouth to talk but I put a finger to my lips and looked back and forth to see if there was anyone watching. I lowered my voice. 'We'll talk inside.'

Anoushka came out to greet her father but I chased her back in.

'Anoushka, go inside! Tell Niranjan your father's back. He doesn't have to call the police.' I shut the door and looked out the window.

'What's happening?' said Mano.

'What's happening? How can you stand there and say that? Do you know the time?'

He checked his watch. 'Adey, it's past ten! I didn't even notice.'

'Didn't even notice!'

'So, what's the fuss?'

'Fuss? You don't know fuss,' I yelled. 'We didn't know what to do. We thought something terrible had happened. I called your office and they said you left at five.'

'I—I had to . . . to go for a meeting,' he stammered and sat down. 'The bloody meeting went for hours and I had to drop that woman home. Can't let her take a bus in the night.'

'What woman?'

'Charika. New girl at the office. You don't know her.'

'Oh, now I can see. Here we are worried out of our minds and you go roung-gahanna with some woman.'

He put his hand up to make me stop. 'I did it for you.'

'You go joy-riding with office women and have the nerve to tell me it was for me!'

He sat heavily on the settee and leaned forward. He was thinking very hard. There was something going on in his head. I didn't know what it could be.

'Tell us what you did, Mano.'

'I went to find that Khanna fellow.' He started taking off his shoes.

'Ah, you did, did you? And you found something?'

He peeled off his socks. 'Now don't get upset. I warned you this could happen.'

'What happened?'

'He's dead.'

'Who? Who's dead?' My hand flew up to my mouth.

'Who do you think?'

'Khanna? He's dead?'

Mano didn't look at me, just kept his eyes on his bare feet.

'Can't be.' I shook my head furiously. 'No. Where did you see it?'

'It was at the . . .' He trailed off and suddenly started again. 'At the UN office. I looked at the list.'

'The UN? Why the UN? Isn't it the Red Cross that normally takes the bodies?'

'UN also does. That's where I went for the meeting.'

'What was the name written there?'

'The boy's name – the one you told me. Who else? If you can't trust me then you can go to hell.' Mano got to his feet, shoes and socks in hand.

'Where did they find his body?'

'That information is not on the list. Anyway, that's all. I'm not helping you anymore. After everything I've done . . .' He had raised his voice but didn't sound convincing.

'Take me there,' I said.

'What?'

'I want to read this list myself.'

'You can't just go waltzing into the UN office like that. You need permission.'

'So get me that permission.'

He frowned at me. 'Is that what you want?'

'Yes.'

'Fine.' He went thundering into his room and slammed the door.

—

I felt lifeless when we got in the car. How could a boy like that, after suffering all his life, have it all end this way? It wasn't fair. Where were the gods when all of this injustice was happening? I was angry. But I also had some hope. Mano could be careless. He might have read the wrong name or made up the story to boast to me. Like when he said he called in a favour from his very big list of contacts, called someone at the very top and got me permission to enter the UN. He knew people in the Department of Information. He had friends in the Plantation Ministry, friends he made when he was working there. He said the management at the UN office in Colombo were on a first-name basis with him, always saying, 'Hi, Mano, how are you? How are the kids?' He was telling me all this as he drove. He was boasting but he wasn't doing his usual lazy one-handed driving. He seemed nervous, both hands gripping the steering wheel. After a while he stopped talking and looked straight ahead. I told him we could get to the UN office through Jawatta Road instead of getting blocked at Thunmulla, but he didn't hear what I said, just kept going.

'Mano, are you all right?' I asked.

He didn't say anything.

'Mano?'

He looked startled. 'Yes, yes. I told one of the secretaries that we're coming. They'll tell the military police fellows to let you in.'

'Okay.'

I wanted to show him some support. Some trust. 'Do you know I got some information about Khanna?' At least he was taking me where I wanted to go, he was helping me, so I told him about the news I got from Mrs Paramanathan.

'See, I told you, no? If he was in Mullaitivu, then no chance.'

'So all the stories about the no-fire zone are true?'

'You can't win a war without losing a few lives.' Mano sighed. 'Why can't you just let this go, Lakshmi? If we turn around and go home we can continue like normal. This is reckless. We're playing with fire.'

'We can't turn back now. I can't go on with a guilty conscience.'

'Guilt and shame,' said Mano as he drove past the Thimbirigasyaya junction. 'That's all you have.'

'If only you had a little of it.'

We went round the roundabout, taking the exit that led to the tree-lined Buller's Road, right behind the Laksala souvenir shop, and stopped at the boom gate. I looked at the army men with their big guns out of the corner of my eye and looked away – it happened automatically, a reaction, the habit of not meeting the eyes of the army or police. Instead, I looked at my lap, listening, waiting for a disaster. Someone tapped on the window, making me flinch. It was a man in dark green clothes. His cap was red-rimmed and there was a band with the letters MP around his arm – military police. He looked into the car. There was something about the way he looked at Mano, like he recognised him. Maybe they knew each other. But when Mano wound the shutter down, the army man didn't say hullo. He just asked for the identity card – he was almost rude. I started looking in my bag for my ID, praying I had brought it. It wasn't in the pocket where I usually kept it. I went through all the pockets, looked in my purse, taking out money and spreading notes to see if I had accidentally folded them around my card. Then I thought I shouldn't let these men see I had money in my bag – what if they decided to point their guns at us and say, 'Give us all your money?' I pushed the money back, deep inside.

I heard the military policeman ask Mano why he wanted to go there. Mano replied in Sinhala, saying we're journalists going to the UN office for some work. He reached into the cubby for his media identity card. I kept digging into my bag. I was certain I had checked that my ID was there before leaving the house. The soldier wasn't satisfied with Mano's answer. He asked more questions: Why do you want to go there? What business do you have? Which paper do you write for? I looked underneath the receipts, removed notepads and pens from one pocket to the next. The ID card was nowhere. Where could it have gone? Did it fall out? I started looking in the folds of my sari, near my feet on the floor of the car.

'Mahattaya, poddak eliyata bahinna.'

I was looking underfoot when I heard those words. They never did that. Never asked people to get out of their vehicles. Something was wrong. I didn't know whether to look or not. Mano opened the door and got out. The policeman came close to him, his shadow falling through the open door and into the car. A story Latha told me a lifetime ago came rushing into my head. It was in '83, during the riots, when I was hiding at home and sent Latha out to do the shopping. She came back and said she saw a truck full of thugs chasing a man in a car – a Tamil man. Seeing a policeman on the street the man stopped the car and ran towards the cop, falling at his feet for help.

Close behind, the truck also stopped. The thugs weren't afraid of police. They got off the truck, weapons in hand. What did the policeman do? He asked the man to prove he was not Tamil. Asked him to say the Sinhala word for bucket – 'baaldiya'. But the man couldn't pronounce it, his tongue wasn't practised, and he said, 'Baaliya.' The cop lifted his baton and brought it down on the man's head. Latha had felt faint. She didn't like seeing blood and there was more blood than she had ever seen.

Thank god I never saw anything like that. But I dreamed it. Sometimes I dreamed it was Mano, getting beaten by a policeman. 'Baaldiya, baaldiya, baaldiya, baaldiya,' I had practised the word endlessly. Now, the military policeman was getting Mano to turn around and put his hands on the hood, to spread his legs. Mano did as he was told, staring at me accusingly. I didn't know what to do. I told myself to keep calm. Think of what could really happen. What if they took Mano away? I started making plans – I'd first call Nelunka and tell her what happened. I might have to confess, tell her that I got Mano into this mess. She'd have to tell her husband. Sumith had connections. She'd save her brother. I took my phone out and got ready. Ready to dial the number, to fight and scream if anything bad happened. The policeman finished giving the body inspection, whispered something in Mano's ear, grabbed Mano's arm with one hand, opened the car door with the other and pushed Mano in. Mano quickly started the car. He didn't try to argue or lose his temper, just put the car in reverse and looked back at the traffic, making sure there was nothing behind us. My head was spinning. My heart was beating so fast I thought it was going to burst. Mano was calm, he turned the car around and drove home, coolly, as if this sort of danger was something he faced all the time. When we got home I followed him into his room, closed the door behind us and said, 'Mano, I can't do this. I'm going to email Mr Subramaniam and say we can't do anything.'

'You're shaking,' said Mano. He took my hand to try and stop it, but I was in a fever, sweating and shivering, teeth chattering. 'It's okay,' he said. 'We'll be okay. We'll stop doing this and everything will be fine.' He put his arms around me. He smelled like Old Spice aftershave mixed with sweat. I rested my head on his chest and listened to his heart, the regular dag-dag-dag sound, until I could breathe again.

The phone rang. 'Don't answer it,' I said.

'It's fine,' said Mano, trying to push away from me.

'Don't go,' I said, holding tightly.

Mano pushed a little harder. 'Let me go and see who it is.'

'Please.'

He was too strong. He broke free from me and went to pick up the phone. My head was pounding. My heart felt too big for my chest, like it was going to break against my ribs.

'It's Niranjan,' Mano called out.

'Niranjan?' Air returned to my lungs. My heart slowed, the pressure reduced. 'He wants to talk to me?'

'Yes. Come and talk to him.'

NIRANJAN

LAST TIME I WAS HERE I'D PROMISED MYSELF I WOULDN'T COME back. Not for a while. But I drove right down to the end of the lane and parked next to the abandoned container. Went through the rusty gate and up the stairs. There was no sign of Issa. The lights were on and the music was pumping. He was playing that Linkin Park nonsense so I turned the stereo off.

The bathroom door flew open. 'Jesus Christ,' I said, holding my nose as he stomped out, a grin that could only be described as 'shit-eating' on his face. 'What the hell did you do in there, man? I need a fucking gas mask.'

'That's a what-do-you-call? An Issa special!' said Issa, slapping me on the shoulder. 'I had a hell of a lunch. Got lamprais from the Dutch Burgher Union. Pukka meal.'

'It had egg, didn't it? Rotten egg? The kunu smell is so bad.'

'There was nothing wrong with the egg, machan. It's been through my system, that's all.' He thumped his belly, lunatic smile on his face.

'You're a disgusting bugger, Issa.'

'But you still came to see me, no?'

'I'm beginning to regret it.' I stepped through the room, kicking aside a pack of playing cards, avoiding a pair of shorts wrinkled on the carpet and set a cushion on the windowsill.

Issa collapsed onto the sofa, squirming until all the junk on it shifted, some of it falling off the seat and onto the ground. 'Where have you been, you bugger? Haven't seen you for ages.'

'I've been busy,' I said.

'I heard, I heard,' said Issa. 'New job and all. Charith told me.'

'Yeah. It's been a couple of months.'

'What happened to the start-up?'

'Couldn't get it off the ground.'

Issa felt for something on the sofa, something underneath his arse. He unearthed a lighter and pulled out a spliff from the pocket in his cargo shorts. 'Things will pick up, machan. For me this is the best time. Now the war is finished and tourists are coming in by the planeload. You can help me if you like. There's free accom and meals, if you want it.'

'No thanks. I've got my hands full,' I said.

'Me too,' said Issa, being literal, as he struggled to sit up without using his arms. Realising it wouldn't work, he dropped the lighter and used his free hand to grab the seat back and haul himself upright. He picked up the lighter, lit the joint and sucked greedily. 'But I know you won't say no to this.' He got to his feet and walked across to me, presenting the joint like a peace-offering.

'Um . . . no thanks,' I said.

'What?' His eyes widened in disbelief.

I put one leg up on the windowsill and balanced. Issa flopped down to a cushion on the floor right beside me and puffed on his toke. 'Some real serious shit must have gone down.' He shook his head gravely. 'Niranjan Herath was not someone who said no to getting high. Never.'

'No, I wasn't.'

'You need a chill pill. Here.' He raised the joint again, almost burning my pants with it.

'No thanks,' I said, pushing it away.

'Fine,' said Issa. 'More for me.' He sent a jet of smoke at me and it curled in the air, thick and reddish like candyfloss, and disappeared out the window. 'You've changed, machan. What happened to you? Tell me all about it.'

'Sorry, Issa. I can't stay long. I have to go.'

'Where do you have to be, you bugger? You barely got here.'

'Have to chat to my parents . . . do you know I moved out?'

'Adey, really? You didn't even have a party. You know I would've brought the weed.'

'No party, machan. I've been too busy.'

'Too busy? Too busy to party? Who are you?'

I shrugged.

'So where are you now?'

'Pamankada.'

He cackled. 'You moved out from your parents' house and went up the road to Pamankada?'

'It's about a fifteen-minute drive. With the traffic.'

'You're a hell of a bugger. Move out of home but only up the road . . .' Issa started laughing.

I wondered if this was going to be a waste of my time. I made up my mind – if he was going to chuckle after every sentence I was leaving. 'It's not far from here. I can always go home.'

'So, where do you have to go tonight? Is it some bird?'

'It's not a bird, Issa.'

'Don't be shy, Niro. You have a bird, no? Where are you meeting her?'

'No, it's nothing like that. I have some business to attend to. I have to talk to Ammi. And Anoushka. They're both having a rough time, from what I hear.'

Issa threw the butt out of the window and looked around for his stash. Spotting the little bag on the TV stand he crawled over and started rolling another joint. He lit it and crawled back to the cushion. 'How old is Anoushka now?'

'Sixteen.'

'Sweet sixteen!'

I kicked him in the shoulder. 'You're a sick fuck, Isuru.'

'Ow! Chill, man. I was joking . . .'

'I'm not.'

'All right, all right,' he said. 'You and your threats – we know how it ends up.'

I got to my feet to leave but Issa grabbed my ankle with his free hand. 'Sit down, man. What a temper. Jesus Christ.'

I sat back on the sill.

He went safe with the next question. 'How are your parents?'

'They're okay,' I said, looking down at him. He seemed sincere enough so I continued. 'You know, the funny thing is when I was living at home I really didn't want to talk to my parents. I didn't want to deal with shit. Especially my mum's shit. It was such a burden. I couldn't carry it.'

'Amen, brother. Don't carry any shit with you. Let it out.'

'But it was easier after I moved out. Like it's somehow easier to talk when I'm away. Perspective, I guess. I actually talk to them a lot more than I did when I was living at home.'

'Let it out like I did before. Egg smell and all.'

I ignored Issa's vulgarity. 'But I couldn't change anything and that environment just became . . . I don't know . . . toxic.'

'Like the dump I took.'

I shook my head at him. 'Yes. Like your dump . . . you know what, forget it, Issa. I have to go.'

He grabbed my leg. 'Sorry, machan. Sorry. Please. Accept my humblest, sincerest apologies . . . please stay till I finish this joint.'

I rolled my eyes at him. 'How are your parents?' I tried to maintain some sense of decorum.

'Who knows,' said Issa, shrugging. 'They're actually looking for a servant. Someone to do the cleaning. Last one was a bloody thief.'

'She must have been desperate.'

'Took an ornamental spoon and disappeared. That's how these village buggers are. They should be left in the village to live simple lives. They're happy like that. When they come to Colombo they see shiny things and get greedy.'

I looked back out to the street, where the dull orange lights had just come on, the glow reflecting off the scuffed hood of my car, making it look golden. 'You know what the hardest thing is, Issa?'

'What?'

'When you tell someone how you're feeling and that person says, "No. That's not it. You're feeling something else." Or they say, "You'll get over it." Or, "You're feeling like that because you did this and this . . ." And I'm like, "Man, I'm trying to tell you how I'm feeling. It's mine! Don't deny me that right!"'

Issa took a long drag of his joint and said, 'Getting whacked in the nuts with a cricket ball.'

'What?'

'Getting whacked in the nuts with a cricket ball's worse than what you said. Whatever that was. I didn't even get you.'

'I really have to go. Bye.'

—

'Yes, Ammi, I'm being careful.'

'I won't forgive myself if something happens.'

'Do you want me to explain it again? I used a virtual private network to make it look like I'm using a server in Czechoslovakia and created a new email account with fake personal details.' I said that because Ammi was such a worrier. In actual fact I just used my regular email for this bit of detective work.

'I don't know about all these computer things, but you're sure you're safe, no?'

'Positive.'

'So, what did they say?'

'There's no Khanna Selvarasan in Darwin. There are a few other detention centres I haven't checked. But if we exhaust those options, I don't know how we can check in Malaysia or Indonesia . . . there are a lot of asylum seekers there.'

'Why Malaysia?'

'Some people fly there and then get on the boats.'

She lowered her voice. 'But he got on a boat from here, Niranjan. From the east coast. That's what Mrs Paramanathan had found out.'

'Ammi, I can barely hear you. Speak louder. No one's listening. The phone isn't tapped.'

'How do you know?'

'It's not happening anymore after the telecom guys did their repairs, is it?'

'Okay.' She raised her voice, if only just a little. 'I said he got on a boat from the east. That's what Mrs—'

'Does she know for sure? Otherwise all of this could be a waste of time. For one, it would have cost a lot of money just to get on a boat, right? How did a beggar boy find that kind of money?'

'She says the boat was leaving and there was one absentee who had already paid for a place . . .'

'So they let Khanna board? Too bad it's a criminal enterprise. It's not like they'll keep a record of it.'

'Criminal but run by someone in the navy, according to Mrs Paramanathan.'

'Yeah, I heard that too.'

'She says the man who got on the boat matches Khanna's description.'

'But there could be hundreds of young guys from that area who look like him . . . and how come Mrs P has all these connections? And why doesn't Mr Subramaniam talk to her directly?'

'That's what I was thinking, Niranjan. I'm very scared – but I have to do it, no?'

'It's okay. We'll do what we can. I have some friends who were in uni with me who work in—'

'Niranjan! You promised. You're not telling anyone else.'

'All right. Fine. But—'

'Your father is here,' Ammi said sharply, bringing her voice back up to normal volume. 'How is your arm? Is it still hurting?'

'It's completely normal.'

'Do you have any headaches?'

'No, Ammi. I don't have headaches.'

I could hear shuffling, Thatthi's voice drifting in. 'Is it Niranjan?'

'You talk to him,' said Ammi. 'Niranjan, I have to go to the temple to make a bhaaraya. Anoushka's results are coming tomorrow. Here, talk to your father.'

The phone changed hands.

'Hullo, Niranjan,' said Thatthi. 'How are you?'

'Good.'

'Good, good . . .' Thatthi repeated slowly, as if waiting for the words to materialise in front of him. 'Your mother's gone . . . now.' He took a moment, probably looking down the corridor to make sure Ammi had left. 'Yes. Gone. So, what were you talking about?'

'Nothing special. Just regular stuff.'

'Regular stuff, ah? She didn't tell you any stories about me?'

'What stories?'

'She's a very suspicious woman, your mother. Dreams up all kinds of things.'

'She hasn't said anything about you, Thatthi.' It was technically not a lie.

'How's your head problem? What did the doctor say?'

'They're not sure what it was but it seems to be fine now.'

'The scans didn't show anything, no?'

'No, Thatthi. All normal.'

'That's good. It's a good thing we kept it from your mother. She would have caused a massive ha-ho.'

'Yeah, I'm feeling much better. Started driving again.'

'Excellent. What else? How is your work?'

'Work's going well.' I wondered if it was a good time to tell him about my weekend activity. I hadn't told Ammi because Ammi would be weird about it. Not that Thatthi wouldn't be weird, but I thought I'd test it out on him first. 'Oh, and I started doing language classes.'

'Language? What are you learning? French? German?'

'Tamil.'

He took a little while to respond. 'Really? Why do you want to learn Tamil?'

'Why not? I know your language but not Ammi's, no?'

'So you two can talk secrets in front of me?'

'You can learn it too.'

'I don't want to learn Tamil.'

'Why not?'

The response didn't come immediately. Thatthi made me wait for a while and when he broke the uneasy silence he did it by changing the subject. 'So Anoushka's results are coming tomorrow.'

'How's she feeling about it?'

'Very nervous but she's trying not to show it. She studied very hard, the kella. I'm sure it'll be fine.'

'Is she home?'

'No. Went to the temple with your mother and Latha to try and increase her chances,' said Thatthi with a laugh.

'Okay. I'll talk to her tomorrow. How's Latha?'

'She's still here. What else is there to say about that woman?'

—

After the results came out they acted quickly and within a couple of days organised a little get-together. I swung by Crescat Boulevard after work to get a gift for Anoushka. Knowing exactly what I was looking for, the whole thing took me less than fifteen minutes, and most of that was when I stopped in front of the barber salon where some Majestic City kabbas were getting their inverted-hopper cuts touched up – must've drifted north of their usual haunts and found another mall to hang out in. I was going to have to stop coming here. I chuckled at the fuckers as I made my way out.

When I got to my parents' the guests had already arrived. I could tell from the vehicles outside – the little Daihatsu parked near the araliya tree was Mihil de Soyza's and the Pajero was, of course, Uncle Sumith's. The rest of the cars in the lane were regulars. I opened the gate and went in.

'Look who's here,' said Thatthi, opening the door and clapping a hand on my shoulder. Ammi came up and hugged me.

I stepped inside and said 'Hi' to the group. It was small. Where were Anoushka's friends?

The Rupasinghes were taking up all the space on the sofa. 'Hi, Niro,' exclaimed Heshan, but Aunty Nelunka stared at him and he quietened. Heshan may have forgiven me our little escapade but Aunty clearly hadn't.

'Heshan,' I said, smiling.

'Hi, Niranjan.' Aunty's greetings were muted.

'Aunty. Uncle. Kohomada?'

'Hullo,' said Uncle Sumith, raising his glass of whisky but failing to crack a smile.

I resisted the urge to pretend to be all chummy with Uncle, to make him and Aunty uncomfortable. Instead I went and reintroduced myself to Mihil de Soyza and his wife, who were standing in between the dining room and the living room, eating short-eats. 'How's your baby?' I asked. 'Is it a boy or girl?'

'Girl. She's fine. Crying and crawling and doing kakka. Living the life of a baby,' said Mihil.

'I wish I could go back to that,' I said.

He laughed. 'We left her with the servant, so we can't stay long. I heard about your new job, Niranjan. Keells, no? Your father told me.'

'Of course he did.'

'He's very proud of you.'

'He really shouldn't be. I didn't have to do much to get it.'

They laughed as if I was joking.

'I'm not kidding. Anoushka's the one to be proud of. Not me.'

The de Soyzas seemed lost for words. Mihil bit into a cutlet as his wife deposited the crusty end of a Chinese roll in her mouth. They smiled with their mouths full as they reassessed my value.

Thatthi came over with two glasses of whisky, one for himself and one for Mihil. He quietly whispered in my ear, 'I didn't bring you one because your mother won't like it.'

'That's fine,' I said. 'I'm driving.'

'So what's this fellow been telling you?' said Thatthi. 'Has he told you about his new job?'

'I didn't have to because you've already done that for me,' I retorted.

'I was just saying that both your children are doing very well,' said Mihil. 'Niranjan was always a star, and now Anoushka is performing.'

'Speaking of Anoushka, have you seen her?' I asked.

'No,' said Mrs de Soyza. 'Not yet. Must be getting ready.'

'I'll go and see.' I excused myself and slipped through the corridor into the kitchen, where Latha was preparing short-eats – fishing cutlets and Chinese rolls out of boiling oil and placing them neatly on a tray. She saw me, paused to smile and said, 'Hullo, Niranjan Mahattaya.'

'Latha, kohomada?'

'Hondai, Baby.'

'Where's Anoushka?'

'Anoushka Baby-ge room eké.'

'What's going on?'

Latha raised her shoulders, pushed her lower lip out to say, 'I don't know.' Anoushka was never one to spend much time on appearance. I wondered what she was doing in her room. I picked up a cutlet from the tray as Latha mock-slapped my hand away. I popped it in my mouth. It was too hot and I had to spit it out. She chuckled and I joined in for a bit of a laugh.

'I'll talk to you again before I go,' I said and wandered out of the kitchen. I knocked on Anoushka's door.

'Come in, Niro,' she said. I went in and found her sitting on her bed, looking decidedly uncomfortable in a dark purple dress, her hair grown past her shoulders and plaited neatly.

'How did you know it was me?'

'Who else would bother knocking?' She tugged at her sleeves.

'What're you doing in here? Your party's happening outside.'

She gave me a withering look.

'What?'

'It's a really happening party,' she said dryly.

'But everyone's here. To celebrate your win.'

'Yeah. *Everyone's* here.'

'Your friends aren't coming? Is that why you're moping around?'

'No.'

'You're doing something else to celebrate? Are you going out or something?'

'What do you mean, going out?' She looked at me piercingly.

'I don't know, out. Somewhere.'

'Like to a nightclub?'

'I didn't think that was your sort of thing, but yeah, sure.'

'I'm only sixteen, you fool.'

'Well, that doesn't stop some. Like your friend Natalie. I bumped into her a few weeks ago at Sugar. I was only there because a couple of guys from my work—'

'She was there? With who?'

'I don't know. She was with a group.'

Anoushka scratched at the base of her thumbnail with her forefinger. She seemed desolate. Being a teenager was weird enough, but not being able to do what everyone else was doing would be hard. Ammi was never going to let Anoushka run around like Natalie – no way – but surely some sort of compromise was possible.

'Look, Noush. If you want to do something, like go somewhere, let me know.'

She didn't say anything, just kept scratching. Skin began peeling off her thumb.

'Anoushka? Did you hear me? If you want to do something, go out—'

She exploded. 'What kind of person do you think I am?' she yelled.

'I was just saying.'

'I'm not like your kind, going roung-gahanna, getting drunk and getting into fights. You can go and get your head smashed. I don't care.'

'Fine,' I said. 'You do what you want.' I turned around and walked out of her room. There was something seriously wrong with that girl. I was only trying to help and she damn near bit my head off. I went over to the dining table where Ammi was fussing over the placement of a plate of fried prawns. 'I need to talk to you,' I said. 'Afterwards.'

Ammi raised her eyebrows. She thought this was about that Khanna guy.

'It's not what you're thinking,' I said.

I took a prawn and walked back out to the living room and tried to join the conversation that Mihil was having with Uncle Sumith. My attention wavered. Maybe I could take Anoushka to see some live music. There was TNL Onstage, a band competition that happened annually. And I had heard of weird metal bands playing various old halls and broken-down stages, which she'd definitely enjoy. I could take her to a movie or two, maybe a play at the Lionel Wendt, make it a regular thing, catch up once a week, just the two of us.

'Here's the genius!' Uncle Sumith announced. Everyone turned around to see Anoushka had finally emerged, smiling weakly. Uncle Sumith waddled across and gave her a kiss on the cheek. 'Congratulations, Anoushka Baba!'

Aunty Nelunka pressed an envelope with cash in Anoushka's hand and left half her lipstick on her face. 'Aney, you look so sweet. Such a nice dress. Where did you get it?'

'Ammi bought it,' mumbled Anoushka.

Prodded by his mother, Heshan said a dull 'congratulations' and walked back to the sofa to continue watching television.

The de Soyzas bobbed in, shook her hand and politely touched cheeks with Anoushka. 'Such bright kids,' Mihil repeated. 'Well done, Anoushka.'

'It takes talent,' said Uncle Sumith. 'Real talent and dedication.'

'Eight Ds,' said Aunty Nelun. 'Such an achievement!'

'Oh, yes!'

'We're all very proud.'

'Very bright future. Very bright.'

'Now you just have to do well at the A-Levels. I'm sure you will.'

'Very bright. Very hardworking.'

The praise slowly dried up and they went back to talking about the weather, the traffic and the UN's war crimes probe. Anoushka sat on the couch in her new dress next to Heshan, a plate of short-eats in her lap, and watched TV.

I remembered the gift. 'Anoush,' I said. 'I have something for you.'

She turned to me blankly, if only for a second, and went back to staring at the TV.

I went out to the car and got it. I hadn't had time to wrap it and it was in a white plastic bag. I took out the bill, crumpled it into my pocket and handed the rest over to Anoushka. She broke her eyes away from the TV and looked inside the bag. 'What is it?' She pulled it out and stared at it. It was a CD. The Ramones. The self-titled debut. I had done my research. AllMusic.com called it *brilliantly fresh and intoxicatingly fun. Everything good that's happened to music since 1976 can be directly traced to the Ramones,* exclaimed *Spin* magazine. It was seminal punk rock and I had tried listening to some of it on the internet. I hated it. But when Anoushka took it in her hands like it was something so very precious and looked up at me, tears welling in her eyes, I knew I'd done well. 'You're welcome,' I said.

She was lost for words.

'It's fine. You don't have to say anything.'

Ammi sidled up. 'What is it, Anoushka? What did Niro give you?'

She looked at Ammi, tears suspended on her lower lids, about to fall.

'Is it a CD?' asked Ammi. 'Music? What kind?'

The first tear rolled down. A big fat globule. It streaked across Anoushka's cheek and fell onto her dress. 'I don't want it,' she said. She pushed the CD into my hands and ran into the toilet, slamming the door.

'What did you do, Niranjan?' Ammi hissed.

'I don't know. I just bought her a gift.'

'You must have said something.'

'I didn't say anything.'

'Go and see what's wrong.'

'Me?'

'Yeah, go, before everyone sees.'

I started to say, 'They've already seen,' but Ammi looked at me sternly and I broke away. 'Anoushka!' I knocked on the door. I could hear sobbing. 'Anoushka, stop being such a drama queen.' I caught myself. I wasn't helping – there was something going on that I didn't really know about. 'Anoushka? Come out when you're ready, okay?'

Everyone pretended they hadn't seen Anoushka's tantrum. They kept their conversations going, rattled on about politics and cricket and their bloody vehicles. I sat next to Heshan and waited for Anoushka to come out. Mr and Mrs de Soyza said they had to get back to their baby, completed their goodbyes and left. Aunty Nelunka didn't want to stay either. 'Heshan's getting restless,' was her excuse even though the guy was as calm as a zen master in front of the TV. Uncle Sumith backed up his wife, saying, 'Yes, look at the fellow. We better take him home,' and downed his drink. In a couple of minutes they were gone too. Thatthi was sitting on the armchair finishing his whisky. Ammi came and sat next to me, saying, 'That was nice.'

'Yeah, nice for you.'

'It was good for Anoushka too. She needed that.'

'Good? Is that why she's crying in the toilet?'

'She gets upset for the slightest thing. And that was something you did, Niranjan. What's that present you tried to give her? Show me.'

'No.' I closed the bag tight. 'It's not for you.'

'What's in there? Why can't you show me? Are you trying to ruin Anoushka? She's all I have. Don't you ruin her!'

I heard Latha in the hall. 'Anoushka Baby? Dora arinna,' she said. She started banging on the toilet door. 'Anoushka Baby? Anoushka Baby!' Bang-bang-bang! Her banging became more frantic.

'What's that woman trying to do?' grumbled Thatthi.

I got off the sofa and went over. 'What's wrong, Latha?'

She screamed unintelligibly, hammering the door with her fists.

'Move aside,' I said. 'Move.' I couldn't go in with my shoulder because I might hurt my arm again. I kicked. The first kick was badly aimed, too close to the hinges, but the latch was loosened, and with the next kick the door flew open. Anoushka was a heap on the floor, next to the toilet, her dress rumpled around her thighs. A bottle of Pynol lay next to her hand, the last drops dripping to the floor. 'Anoushka!' I rushed in and propped her up, put her head on my knee. 'Anoushka! What have you done!'

—

I called work and told them I wouldn't make it today. I drove home, picked up some clothes and my toothbrush. Nobody had had any breakfast and we were all starving, so I bought some food from Perera & Sons – the seeni sambol buns that Ammi liked, beef rolls for Thatthi, a mini pizza for me, and the cream puffs for Anoushka, just in case she was allowed to eat. After two nights in the hospital, all the tests were completed. There had been no internal damage. They were still holding her for a psychological assessment. We had to figure out why this had happened, how to stop it from repeating.

After getting snacks, I drove to Ammi and Thatthi's. The front door was locked. Latha must have gone to the hospital. The key was in the flowerpot hanging off a branch on the mango tree where Latha usually hid it. I let myself in. It was a surprise the house didn't look like a disaster zone. Latha had cleaned everything. The floors were swept and the shelves dusted. The TV had been turned off at the wall. The kitchen was spotless, dishes sparkling in the rack, benchtops cleared and the cooker shiny. I took a big plastic bag and went into Anoushka's room. Her bed was made, books stacked and clothes neatly folded into her cupboard. I took a few of her clothes and a couple of books and put them in the bag. I went into the bathroom to get the toothbrushes. It was clean, the floors mopped and drying. There was no Pynol in sight. No cleaning products at all. Latha must have thrown it all away.

From Ammi's room, I took a couple of blouses and skirts, handling her bra and underskirt with care. Thatthi's room smelled vaguely of disinfectant as I added a pair of pants, a couple of shirts and a pair of his cotton briefs into the bag. Back outside, I locked the door behind me, glad to leave because the house felt haunted. Why was it so sterile? I was hazy. I hadn't got much sleep in the last couple of days so I wasn't thinking straight.

Anoushka was asleep in her room. Ammi was sitting beside the bed, holding her hand. Thatthi, looking bleary-eyed and tired, took the clothes from me, whispering, 'Thank you, Niranjan. That's a big help.'

'I brought some food,' I said, handing him the Perera & Sons bag.

'Thank you, putha.'

'No problem . . . the beef rolls are for you. And I got some cream puffs for Anoushka. Can she eat?'

'I'll ask the doctor.'

'I didn't buy any for Latha. I got these before I went home . . . where is she?'

Thatthi didn't look me in the eye.

'She wasn't at home.'

'Shh,' he said. 'You'll wake up Anoushka.' He opened up the bag of food and looked at its contents. 'We'll manage.'

'What do you mean? Isn't she coming?'

He shot me a look, his eyes piercing, his jaw jutting out. 'This morning I told that woman to leave.' He took a roll and dropped into one of the armchairs in the corner.

'You did what?'

'One of the main things she had to do was look after you kids. That's why I brought her to our house.' He took a bite of the roll and chewed. 'I gave her a job. She didn't do it. So I told her to go.'

'Where's she going to go, Thatthi?' I spluttered.

Ammi gave me a look of anger, brought a finger to her lips.

Thatthi kept eating his roll, chewing slowly. 'I don't care. She can go to hell.'

I turned and walked towards the door.

'Where are you going, Niranjan?'

I walked down the corridor.

'Niranjan?' Thatthi's voice rang out behind me. Where could she have gone? Back to the village? Back to her brother? I hoped that was what she'd done. But I couldn't be sure. I knew there was something about that man Latha didn't like. I started the car, checking quickly if there was enough petrol for what could be a long ride, and drove out to Fort like a race car driver, taking corners at speed, leaving the private buses in my smoke as they slammed brakes and blared horns. I rounded the Lake House building, slipped between two three-wheelers that were trying to narrow the gap and block my way, got to the end of the metal rail that divided the road, did a U and then parked on the roadside before running into the railway station. At eight-thirty in the morning it was already busy. I squeezed past hundreds of people going in or getting out, people carrying bags in their arms or on their heads, past schoolkids in clean white uniforms, past the kadala sellers and the lottery men shouting sales pitches at all the poor buggers gathered there, waiting, waiting for a train out of cluttered Colombo. There she was! I rushed up to a small woman in a billowing blouse only to realise she had a baby in her arms. I looked on the concourses and on the platforms, around the counters and the offices, in the toilets that reeked of choo and under shady awnings. I asked people – officials, cashew sellers, beggars – asked them if they had seen a woman, short, with long greying hair, probably wearing a skirt and blouse and carrying a bag. They said that could be anyone.

I went back out. The people at the bus stop were women in their saris waiting to go to work, dudes in gaudy shirts and ill-fitting pants, their hair greasy with coconut oil. I ran across the road and skimmed through the market, where old vegetable women raised mangoes towards me, hoarse-voiced stall buggers offered cheap coir welcome mats or brushes. I was fooled into thinking I'd spotted Latha's smile on a woman trying out a comb on her thick hair, but the smile had a couple of teeth missing.

I got back in the car and started making my way back, slowly, towards Ammi and Thatthi's, slowing down at every bus stop, hitting the brakes every time I saw someone that looked like Latha. I stopped a lot. There were a lot of people like her. I'd never seen so many, never looked out for them, but they were there, quietly going about their lives. I went past our house and further east, holding panic at bay, refusing to set limits for this search. I passed Navinna and Maharagama and edged towards Pannipitiya where buildings grew squat and cropped up further apart from each other, where roads were dusty and brambles grew everywhere. Overtaking a truck, I noticed a woman on my side of the road – short, with long greying hair, bag in hand, wearing a long, black skirt and an oversize blouse – another Latha look-alike. I still slowed, ignoring honking trucks and observed her gait, the stubby limbs making slow progress, trudging away to Lord knows where.

What was I doing? I was happier after leaving home. Maybe Latha should be allowed to leave too. I hit the brakes. The truck screeched on the asphalt but the momentum kept it moving until the big front fender gently nudged the rear of my car. I shouldn't have come looking. I should've just let her go. The truck driver was getting out of his vehicle and coming round to berate me. My head began to ache. I felt dizzy, the consequences of past indiscretions returning. On the other side I saw her gazing at the car and at me — a familiar face listing sideways for a better view, weak eyes widening in recognition. The truck driver was knocking on my hood, yelling obscenities and making threatening gestures. She walked up right in front of the truckie, who fell silent, and I heard her voice. 'Niranjan Baby?' The tightness I'd felt in my stomach all day moved up to my throat and into my head. A torrent of tears and snot burst from me and I put my head on the steering wheel and cried like a fucking baby.

LATHA

MICHELLE NONA AND RAVI MAHATTAYA HAD GONE TO PLAY golf. The cook, Monis, was in the second kitchen, falling asleep on a bench. Made of bare concrete, it was where he did all the cutting and chopping, washing dirt off vegetables, draining blood from meat, all the steaming and frying. Now, he was sitting on a low stool, snoring so loud I could hear him through the open window. In the main kitchen where Michelle Nona sometimes cooked like she was on one of those TV shows, I polished all the shiny things – the fridge, the dishwasher, the oven, the little TV in the corner. I rubbed the smudges off the microwave and mixer and kettle that Michelle Nona wanted kept on the bench like ornaments. These were very expensive things, things Ravi Mahattaya brought from another country or from the airport, so I did it carefully. I worried about pressing the wrong button and breaking something, so I turned the current off from everything except the fridge and the microwave at the wall. Switching off the fridge would make the food go bad, and turning off the microwave would make Nona angry. 'I have to set the clock again,' she said last time. 'Who told you to turn it off?'

I tried to explain but she said, 'Clean it without pressing any of the buttons. It's not hard.'

I used the spray that smelled like lemon and the small cloth that Nona told me to use. After I finished that, I polished the black and white tiles on the wall.

Monis snorted, waking up quickly, saying, 'Who is it?'

It was Niranjan Baby's voice that answered. 'It's me, Monis. It's Niranjan.'

It was the voice I was waiting to hear. Banda, the watcher, must have let him in the gate, and instead of coming through the front door he would have crossed the lawn – knowing Niranjan Baby he would have stepped on the grass instead of the square concrete blocks you were supposed to walk on to come around the back – past the servant rooms, through the outside kitchen and into the inside kitchen.

He came in and said, 'Latha.'

I put the spray and the cloth away and said, 'Hullo, Niranjan Baby.'

'I have a surprise for you,' he said, smiling.

'I told you not to bring me any pastries. I don't eat those things. I give them to Banda or Monis.'

'That's not what I brought,' he said.

'Did you bring lotterai? Don't waste your money, Niranjan Baby. I know you're a lucky person. I've won two hundred rupees with the lotterai you brought, but still—'

He stepped aside and there she was – my Anoushka Baby. I hadn't seen her since she was taken to hospital on that terrible night. I wanted to hold her in my arms. I wanted to check her all over, make sure she was all right. I wanted to stroke her hair that had grown long and thick, and say, 'My poor Anoushka Baby.' But I couldn't. She was a nona now, standing there, wearing a nona's long dress, her eyes sad and tired like she had lived a hundred years. I can't touch a nona. It's not right. All I could do was say, 'Come in, Anoushka Baby,' in a shaky voice. She walked inside. Her step was light because she was so thin.

'Is Issa at home?' Niranjan Baby asked.

'He hasn't come out of his room. Must be still sleeping,' I said. 'He normally gets up after two o'clock.'

'I'll go and wake him,' said Niranjan Baby and left the kitchen before I could offer him a cup of tea.

I turned back to Anoushka Baby. She was standing, looking lost in that big kitchen. 'Do you want a chair? I can get one from the living room or Ravi Mahattaya's office.'

'No,' she said.

'What about this stool? Nona sits here when she's cooking.'

Anoushka Baby went slowly to the high stool near the bench. She got on and put her hands in her lap.

'Do you want some tea, Anoushka Baby?'

'No.'

'I can make it like I used to. With lots of sugar.'

'No.'

'A cool drink? Coca-Cola? Sprite?'

Anoushka Baby looked around at the shiny benches and tiles that I just polished. 'A coke?'

I went to the fridge and took out a bottle. 'How is your school, Baby?'

'Good.'

I poured the coke into a glass. 'What class are you in now?' I knew what it would be but I asked her anyway.

'12D.'

'Is it a good class?'

She nodded.

'Do you have lots of friends?' As soon as the words came out of my mouth I knew it wasn't a good question to ask. I changed the subject. 'You'll get good results for the A-Level, Anoushka Baby. I know you will. And then you'll be a lokka!' I put the glass of coke on a tray and served it to her. As she took the glass in her hands, I noticed there were wounds on her fingers, as if she had scratched them. She saw me looking, put the glass on the table and put her hands in the pockets of her dress. I stood there looking at Anoushka Baby, seeing in her face that she was scared and lonely, wondering if there was any way I could make things better for her. 'Sorry, Baby,' I said.

'What for?'

'I didn't look after you properly. I didn't know what to do.'

'But you knew.'

'No, Baby. I didn't.'

She looked straight at me, her big eyes brown and serious. 'Tell me the secret,' she said.

'Secret?'

'The secret you found. In your village.'

'I didn't find anything secret, Baby.'

'What did you find, then?'

'I didn't . . . all I found was my father.'

'You didn't know him before?'

'No. I knew my mother died when I was small but I didn't know about a father. I just thought . . . I didn't think about him.'

'And then?'

'Then I thought he didn't even lift a finger for me and I got very angry.'

'But where did you go?'

'I went for a walk. It was good to make my mind clear. I walked and walked. I didn't care where I was going – wherever my head turned, I went.'

Anoushka Baby picked up the glass and took a sip of the coke. 'After that?'

'My head got clearer. I was thinking, "If I didn't have a father, I won't be so angry. I won't be sad." Then I thought, "He's not my father. Why should I think that man is my father?"'

'But he is your father. Like your brother is your brother and your sister is your sister.'

'People can think all kinds of things, Anoushka Baby. They can say anything they want. But to me – who is he?'

She was biting her lip and frowning, thinking very hard.

'Why should I think about those things and worry my mind? Why should I think about mothers and fathers and brothers and sisters? About who's big and who's small, about lokkas and poddas, about everything that's happened so long ago, before I was born?' I looked at her face to see if she was still listening. 'That's what I learned. It's not a secret. To let go of everything and just be.'

Anoushka Baby, who had been very serious, laughed suddenly.

'I'm not good at talking about it. I don't know the right words. I shouldn't be saying these things to you.'

'You're funny, Latha.' She finished her glass of coke and held it out for me.

I smiled a silly smile, pretended I had done it all to make her laugh. 'Do you want some more?'

'No thanks.'

I took the glass and washed it in the sink.

Anoushka Baby hunched a little, leaning on the bench. 'Is your nona good?'

'Who, Michelle Nona?'

She nodded.

'Yes. They're good people.'

'Isuru is a bit pissu.'

'No. He's nice. Comes and talks to me. He asks about all of you.'

'Niranjan says he's crazy . . . Thatthi doesn't know I'm coming here.'

'You didn't tell him?'

'No. Niro said we were going to Galle Face for some fresh air.'

'You shouldn't lie.'

'But Ammi knows. She said to say "hi".'

'How is Nona?'

'Fine. Still trying to help people she can't help. She has to do a lot of work because our new servant is terrible.' Anoushka Baby started scratching the broken skin on her thumb with her nails. 'Her cooking is bad. And she's lazy. Ammi says she's more trouble than she's worth.'

'Maybe she's still getting used to it,' I said.

'I don't know. It's been two months. Thatthi says he can't look for another servant.'

'You're not friends with her?'

She shrugged. 'No.'

'Why don't you make friends? Like you did with me.'

Anoushka Baby did another little laugh, as if I was making a joke, and began scratching her other thumb.

I didn't know what to say. After all these years looking after her, doing everything for her, she didn't even think of me as a friend. I walked away, took the floor polish and a rag out of the cupboard and got onto my knees. Anoushka Baby sat there and watched as I polished the floor.

Niranjan Baby finally came back into the kitchen and said, 'We better get going, Anoushka.'

'Okay.' She got off the stool.

'We'll come again, Latha,' he said.

'Bye, Latha,' said Anoushka Baby. 'See you.'

—

I hadn't felt good for a long time. There was a storm in my head, like a kunaatuwa that blew through villages, breaking houses and trees and ruining paddy fields. Niranjan Baby had kept telling me everything was okay, that Anoushka Baby was fine now, that Nona and Mahattaya were also okay and that all were getting back to normal, but I couldn't let it go. I was thinking about it so much I couldn't do my work. Once, I got floor polish on the bottom of one of the brass lamps and Nona said, 'Can't you see? Do you need glasses?'

Anoushka Baby had laughed about how I cleared my head but I knew that was what I needed to do. I thought some more about her as I finished rubbing the polish in, how there was something deep inside her that made her unhappy. I ran the machine until the floor was so shiny it was a mirror. All the time I was thinking about Niranjan Baby and how he was much happier after moving out of Lakshmi Nona and Mano Mahattaya's house. I thought of my old nona and mahattaya as I put everything away and stepped out through the back door, thought about how they gave me my first job as I went through the lawn, careful not to kill any grass. I missed them. I would do better work if they took me back. I'd be careful. I'd be quiet and clean and do everything right. I knew that wouldn't happen. I asked Banda to open the gate for me. 'Where are you going?' asked the old watcher, throwing away the beedi he was smoking and tying his dirty sarong.

'Walking,' I said.

'Walking?'

'Yes. I'll come back soon.'

'Haa haa,' he said and slid the latch and opened the big gate, the shuddering metal making the sound of thunder as it opened. The servant next door watched me through the gap in her gate. I thought she was wondering about me but knew I shouldn't try to guess. I went out onto the street, my mind still turning, impossible to stop, going forward and back, from things that had happened twenty years ago to things that could happen to me in another ten or twenty, and I know these are just thoughts and I watch them go round and round until they slow down and finally disappear. People pass by, some looking, others pretending not to see. And then it's only me and I'm here, walking. My feet are on the hot tar, the sand pricking my soles. The sun is shining. Feel its heat on my skin. Smell the araliya flowers on the tree, the gas from a passing car. Breathe the air, in and out, in and out, my chest moving. I'm here.

AUTHOR'S NOTE

THE STRUCTURE OF *RUINS* IS LOOSELY BASED ON THE ANCIENT stone artefact known in Sinhala as the *Sandakada Pahana*. While this translates to 'moon-lamp', the commonly used term is 'moonstone'.

A semicircular stone found at the base of a staircase at the entrance to a temple or a palace, the first moonstones date back to the time of the Anuradhapura kingdom, established in 377 BC. The original moonstone contains the carved image of a half lotus encircled by several concentric bands. The band circumscribing the lotus shows a procession of swans, the next an elaborate pattern of vines, then a sequence of animals, and the outermost a ring of flames.

The widely accepted interpretation comes from Senarath Paranavitana, Sri Lanka's pre-eminent archaeologist, who suggests the moonstone symbolises the Buddhist notion of *Samsara* or the cycle of life. By his reading, the flames indicate suffering and the vines are entanglement in worldly desires. Each animal stands for a stage of life: the elephant being birth; the bull: decay; the lion: disease; and the horse: death. Swans can supposedly separate milk from water – the moment one develops the ability to distinguish good from evil, truth from lies. The lotus is the final stage: nirvana.

Over centuries, as kingdoms and ideologies shifted, so did the moonstone. Animals were removed, demarcations were altered and shapes changed, their meanings becoming increasingly confused. The moonstone was no longer a simple analogy that mapped to myth, experience or history but a space to project one's own meaning.

ACKNOWLEDGEMENTS

THANK YOU TO THE QUEENSLAND WRITERS' CENTRE AND Hachette Australia's QWC/Hachette Manuscript Development Program for showing me how to sustain a writing career, and for opening the door to publication.

Thanks to Kate Stevens for picking my manuscript out of that pile of entries, reading it closely, thinking deeply about the best way to tell this story, and shepherding it through the publishing process.

Thanks to Karen Ward and Elizabeth Cowell, the extraordinary editing team that sifted through all the slang and Sinhalese, sometimes in combination, and turned out a readable but distinct book. Thanks also to Jordan Weaver-Keeney, Daniel Pilkington, Nicky Luckie, Robert Ashby and everyone else at Hachette Australia, for the support they've shown me and *Ruins*.

Chandani Lokuge assisted with checking historical and socio-political facts on Sri Lanka in addition to advice on the proper usage and spelling of Sinhalese. Thank you.

The difficult middle chapters were written at the Wheeler Centre where I was afforded a hotdesk. This invaluable program is made possible by the Readings Foundation.

Thanks to all my writing groups and readers, past and present, especially Alexandra Roginski, Naomi Bailey and Shehan Karunatilaka for their continued support, honesty and fantastic taste in arts and literature.

Thanks to Toni Jordan for her unwavering belief and persistence.

My parents, despite their misgivings about my chosen path, have always supported and encouraged me, and for that I'm thankful.

And finally, to Melanie, my partner, advisor, co-conspirator and conscience – thank you.

Rajith Savanadasa was born in Sri Lanka and now lives in Melbourne. He was shortlisted for the Asia–Europe Foundation short story prize in 2013, the Fish Publishing short story prize in 2013 and received a Wheeler Centre Hotdesk Fellowship in 2014. Rajith also runs Open City Stories, a website documenting the lives of a group of asylum seekers. *Ruins* is his first novel.

@RajithSHS